A Lady's MAID

OTHER COVENANT BOOKS AND AUDIOBOOKS
BY JEN GEIGLE JOHNSON:

The Nobleman's Daughter

Scarlet

"Mistletoe Memories" in *A Christmas Courting*

A Lady's MAID

A HISTORICAL ROMANCE

Jen Geigle Johnson

JEN GEIGLE JOHNSON

Covenant Communications, Inc.

Published by Covenant Communications, Inc.
American Fork, Utah

Printed in the United States of America
First Printing: August 2019

26 25 24 23 22 21 20 19   10 9 8 7 6 5 4 3 2 1

ISBN 978-1-52440-845-9

To women

Imagine if the history of the world were told from your perspective. Then you might realize how it turned in your palms.

And to my sons, who step humbly and with power in their father's wake.

ACKNOWLEDGMENTS

I THINK, IN ADDITION TO the wonderful critique team and beta readers who helped with this story, I must also acknowledge the women who fought for a thousand years for the right to vote. Most associate them with the early 1900s, but if you search, women were there over the ages, working to have a voice. I thank my amazing beta readers: Amy Wilson, Heidi Kimball, and John and Adrienne Burger; my genius of a friend, Annette Lyon, for her edits; Kami Hancock, for all her work; and the whole team at Covenant. My covers are stunning. And I thank my critique group; Lisa Fenley, Jennifer Looft, Stacy Wells, Nuha Said, David Christiansen, Jessica Bell, Michelle Pennington, Mindy Strunk, and Sara Cardon; for awesome nudges and insight. Dustin is forever my biggest everything.

CHAPTER ONE

London, England, 1831

MOLLY O'MALLEY'S COAL-POWDER DISGUISE HID her creamy skin and blended with her black-clad form in the shadows of the early morning. She pressed the tip of a finger against her itchy forehead, careful not to reveal the skin beneath.

With Molly's careless shrug, the satchel fell from her shoulder to the ground. Grateful for the loss of its weight, she rotated her arms to release the ache. The home of the prime minister, Lord Grey, loomed above her, blocking light from any of the remaining night stars. She paused in its shadow, listening. It seemed every cricket had stopped its song.

The sudden stillness unnerved her. She turned in a circle. The area just outside the glow of the street lamp tormented her imagination with possibility. But there was no movement; no eyes watched from the shadows. Swallowing, she placed a hand on her heart and took a few breaths, studied the contents of the bag at her feet, and listened. She chided herself, but then a bat swooped down and brushed the top of her hair, bringing out her sharpest yelp, which sent an answering echo down the street. Fearful she had drawn attention too soon, Molly backed up with one hand over her mouth and stilled her breathing, listening.

The unwelcome memory of her father's words threatened her resolve. *Always do that which will bring honor to your family.*

Her parents were proud of her now, proud she was a lady's maid in a duke's house. Molly served Lady Amanda, who lived with her husband, Lord Nathaniel Halloway, and their children in one of his father's estates.

The Duke of Somerset owned property all over England, and Molly's parents were honored by the notoriety the great house of Somerset brought, just as they were honored by Molly's service in her lady's childhood home; Lady Amanda's own father was the Duke of Devonshire.

Would Molly's parents feel honored by what she was about to do? She hugged herself. Rocking from side to side, she closed her eyes. But she didn't imagine home. Charlie's face entered her mind, alight with passion, his words filling her heart. The memory of his voice stayed with her as though she had heard it yesterday.

Times are changing, Molly, and we can be part of that change. Our children will bless our names.

She'd hoped he meant *their* children, together. At the time, her heart had filled with anticipation.

Her eyes squeezed tight, tamping out the terror that was soon to follow in her memory—because everything had fallen apart at Peterloo—but the memories rushed back anyway. Ten years in her past but haunting her still, her hope and all the light in her life had shattered the day Charlie's body slumped to the earth. Lord Nathaniel Halloway had carried his lifeless form home, and his house, as well as Lady Amanda's, had honored Charlie in death.

She filled her lungs with one slow breath, holding on for a moment, and then let her uncertainty trickle out with the air that left her lips.

I act now for him, for Lady Amanda's daughter, for my future daughters, for every person who deserves their vote to be counted.

She would bring honor to them.

Decision made, she hefted the biggest of the rocks from her satchel, wound her arm and hurtled the stone as hard as she could toward the prime minister's home. The sound of glass breaking both satisfied and terrified her. She lifted a heavy chain from her bag and ran to the nearest lamppost. Breath coming hard, throat dry, she resisted the urge to run and hide. The chain dragged behind her, gathering sand and silt from between the stones. Never a criminal in all her twenty-eight years, she stopped under the streetlamp, trembling.

Feet pounded the cobblestone several streets over. Molly's hands fumbled in her haste at the deep shouts—of a constable, she imagined. She wrapped the chain around the back of the pillar and across herself then lifted the lock and squeezed it shut through two links, effectively binding herself to the lamppost in full view of the evidence of her crime. The more dramatic her actions the bigger the story and the more influence it would have, she hoped. She had seen the value of good press, of her lady's fliers and the *Manchester Guardian* and the campaign it had run in support of suffrage for all. Well, here was a story worth telling in that noble paper, an example worth sharing: women must be heard, no matter the cost to her personal freedom.

Molly leaned her head back against the pillar and counted heartbeats she felt in each breath she drew. As the tension began to dissipate, her lips curled up in a slow smile.

Victory. With chin held high and eyes blazing, she waited to be discovered. Minutes passed. A quarter of an hour passed. The nearby constable had long departed. Molly strained to look down the street. Should she shout? Lowering her head, she counted pebbles in the cobblestone.

Surely someone would cart her off to prison before the sun rose. She could wake the neighborhood with her shouts—scream, rage, whatever it took to draw attention and demand women have a vote as well as men. And after her arrest she'd talk about suffrage every day in her cell at mealtimes, to every guard. She'd write letters to the papers. She'd record her experience and try to publish it later. She sent things off to the papers now, but even though she and John, the founder of *The Manchester Guardian*, were close, he'd never been interested in her written words. But if she were in prison, that was a story he'd feel was worth telling, she would wager. Her arms strained against the chain when she attempted to raise a fist into the air.

She craned her neck again to catch a farther-reaching view down the street. She strained her ears for some sound of an approaching night watchman.

Instead she heard someone clear their throat. "The prime minister and his family are touring the continent."

Molly gasped. *He isn't even home?* Then she frowned. "Thomas, go away."

"Did you hear me? They aren't here, and they are low on staff. It is likely no one even knows you broke something."

Her face heated in embarrassment in front of her friend in the shadows—of all of the people to see her thus. "I said go away."

Towering, broad Thomas ignored her and moved into the light of the flickering streetlamp. Faster than she'd tied the chain around herself, he had it lying on the ground at her feet, unwound but still padlocked together.

She opened her mouth to protest. Whatever she'd planned to say was swallowed by the back of his jacket, because he picked her up, threw her over his shoulder, and began walking in the direction of their employer's home. She kicked, she yelled, she punched his back—all to no avail.

When she quieted for a moment, she noticed he was whistling.

At length, she surrendered and lay limply over his shoulder. "You didn't need to rescue me."

He grunted in response and continued his tuneless whistling.

"Thomas."

Bouncing against him with the rhythm of his steps, her eyes began to feel heavy from the blood that rushed to her brain.

With one arm, she pushed against his back so she could raise her head. "I *wanted* to be arrested."

Thomas walked as though he hadn't heard.

"Ugh! Thomas!" In defeated frustration, she pounded his back two more times with her fists.

Deep beneath many layers of feeling, a tiny emotion flickered inside her, warming her. Dear, loyal Thomas. How had he even known where to find her? More and more, he'd become a constant, solid force in her life that kept her rooted.

"Thomas, really. Put me down so we can discuss this."

"I will, once we are inside."

They approached the servants' entrance of the home of Lord Halloway, future Duke of Somerset, and Lady Amanda.

Thomas pushed open the door with his foot. Several of the kitchen staff stopped mid-stride on their way to complete their early-morning breakfast tasks.

Just inside the door, without even a grunt, Thomas lowered Molly to the floor carefully, as if she might break, and steadied her until she found her footing and the blood had drained from her face.

Hands on her hips, she tried to scowl at him, but his eyebrow was raised in such a mocking fashion as he eyed her disguise and attire that she couldn't help but giggle instead. "It would have been effective—a real newsworthy event for *The Manchester Guardian.*" They moved aside to allow other servants to pass.

Thomas chuckled. "I'll not argue that it would have drawn attention . . . were the prime minister in town." He turned away, attempting to hide another chuckle, but he soon turned back to her, eyes watering. "And you lugged rocks and that chain all the way there?"

"Well, yes." She stood taller, grinning.

He nudged her with his shoulder. "What, Molly, did you hope to accomplish? Sit in prison while we did all your work for you here? Is that it?"

This time her scowl came full force. "Not at all. You know very well what I am trying to do, and there is nothing amusing about it that I can see." She stepped away from him. "Securing the women's vote is everything to me right now."

Thomas's eyes showed a hint of sadness. "I know, Molly. And I support you—all women. You know that." He paused, and Molly was reminded just how much she appreciated him. "Seems there's other important things, too, though. Life, a family of your own . . . friends."

"Of course." She looked down, clinging to the horrible tragedy of Peterloo as though it were a lifeline, still shaken by the death of her first love, Charlie. Ten years gone and still the thought of him—his chestnut hair, his ready grin—brought such a piercing sharpness to her throat that she found it difficult to swallow. She could not raise her eyes back to Thomas's questioning expression.

The housekeeper rushed forward, her face red, her cap askew on her head, and her hair falling out of the cap and settling around her cheeks. Molly had never seen her in anything but neat and pressed uniforms and with her hair wound into tight buns at the back of her head.

"Oh! You've caused such a to-do! Do you think of no one besides yourself, child?" Mrs. Benning called everyone *child.* She motioned to the nearest chambermaid. "Tell Paul to rush upstairs and inform the master that Molly is home." She turned to Molly. "They've had half the staff out looking for you. Don't know why they keep you on, I don't. I'll be recommending otherwise. Already have, mind you." She began to mumble to herself. "Disappearing in the middle of the night. Not telling anyone where you were headed. Strange notes of warning." She held up a bony and menacing finger. "And there's Lady Amanda, awoken from the noise of searching for you, worried sick—and in her condition."

Molly's stomach tightened as the selfishness of her actions settled on her like the heavy chain from earlier. Afraid the servants would try to stop her, afraid Lord Halloway would disapprove, she'd been as vague as possible in her note. No one in the suffrage movement had ever taken things as far as she almost had. They talked on and on about peaceful demonstrations but never dared do what Molly thought they should.

Thomas rested a hand on her shoulder. "Now, let's move out of the hallway and head upstairs. The lord and lady of the house wish to have a word with you."

Molly brought a hand to her soot-covered cheek. "I must wash up first."

Thomas shook his head. "They expressly requested you come up *before* you erase any evidence of your activities from this morning."

Molly tried to take the stairs with confidence, walking with brisk, purposeful steps, but instead she found her feet slowing. Perhaps this time she'd abused the abundant kindness of her employers beyond recovery. With each step, the enormity of her crime fell more heavily upon her. If the prime minister discovered who had thrown the rock, her connection to the house of Somerset, would Lord Halloway's name be tarnished? Would he and dear Lady Amanda suffer repercussions of her actions? She groaned. "Are they in the family sitting room?"

"Aye." Thomas followed. His loyal, heavy plodding sounded behind her.

She approached the double doors. Breathing in and then out again, she reached for the door handle. The moment Molly entered the room, Lady Amanda and Lord Halloway burst into laughter.

"Now she's a chimney sweep!" Lady Amanda's eyes twinkled, but they were puffy and lined with red.

Heart clenching but relieved, Molly stepped farther in and curtsied. "My lord. My lady."

Lady Amanda beckoned to them. "Come in, Molly. Thomas, you come in, too, though I don't think I'll ask either of you to sit, if you don't mind."

Molly snorted. As if she *ever* sat in their presence.

Their laughter deepened, and Lady Amanda wiped her tears. At least she wasn't angry, not yet.

Thomas choked, trying to stave off his laughter, but his grin could not have grown any wider. He moved beside Molly in a towering breadth of support. They related to their employers Molly's early-morning activities.

Dear Lady Amanda placed both hands on Molly's shoulders. "I am glad you are safe. We were worried."

Tears welled in Molly's eyes. "I'm so sorry," she whispered. She had shared so much with Lady Amanda—their own terrors and causes and trials. Her lady was her dearest friend, and yet Molly hadn't considered anyone else before rushing headlong into her plans. The cause had taken priority over everything, and she'd naively thought Lady Amanda would approve. "I have something I must say to you and Lord Halloway."

Lady Amanda worked with Molly on the committees for reform, and she'd been a partner on several dangerous escapades, but she remained Molly's employer all the same—particularly in moments like this one.

Molly swallowed and cleared her throat. "Having given my actions further thought, I recognize that I may have harmed you and my lord, as well as your great house and name. For that, I am deeply sorry. I understand if you see fit to dismiss me from your service." She sought the eyes of her friend, seeking understanding. She did not know where else she could find better work, and she didn't want to end her efforts on the suffrage committee. "But if I may, I'd like to continue our work for suffrage, even if I am no longer needed in the house."

Reaching for her hand, Lady Amanda asked, "My dear, what did you hope to accomplish?"

"Forgive me. Might I speak frankly?"

Lady Amanda shared a glance with her husband, her mouth curling upward in a small smile. "We expect nothing less from you. Please do, and do not be concerned if you show a little bit of your personality."

"Yes, quite." Lord Halloway coughed into his hand.

"As I've said before"—Molly spared a glance at Thomas—"we must do more. Standing around with banners in our hands, writing essays, even sharing your fliers, my lady . . . forgive me. We aren't doing enough."

Lord Halloway leaned forward in his chair. "We are almost there, Molly, truly. Patience and consistent effort for even a few months more, and we will have a proposal up before the House of Lords that they will approve. The pressure for the lords to make a change is strong. The rallies have been serving their purpose. The king has ousted Wellington, and Lord Grey is committed to change. You can't see all of this from where you are, but I can. Whether or not you can sense it, the suffrage committee is making a difference. These things just take time."

"But what of women? Are we certain the proposal will include us? Will they grant suffrage to *all*, including *women*?"

Halloway nodded. "William Lovett, who will be the author of our document, has already included women in drafts." He cleared his throat. "It's a simple enough thing, really, when the current laws don't specify man or woman."

Molly shared a look with Thomas. "I hope that is the case. Because my blood is tingling, and I sense a sabotage."

Lady Amanda's expression changed, and she studied Molly intently. "We *can* increase our efforts for women, of course—explore all options and work ever harder. It seems the most natural thing in the world that the next law would continue to leave gender unspecified since that's what we've had. But we want more than this—even, dare we hope, specific language that's inclusionary for women. While many are in support of broadening suffrage, I don't want to miss the opportunity to include us. Especially now, while the people are already excited about suffrage."

Molly's heart warmed to her friend. They had begun this bold journey together, and she was grateful, yet again, that Lady Amanda had sought to include her in the movement in the first place, years ago. Indeed, Lady Amanda had needed her help as they worked in secret for increased freedom and a better life for the working classes of England. "Thank you, my lady. Shall we meet with our committee? Draft new plans?"

Lady Amanda nodded, and Molly exhaled in relief.

"But I will not countenance any destructive attention-seeking antics. They will not be part of the plan." The room grew quiet with a great, thick stillness.

Molly's mouth opened, and she forgot to close it as Lady Amanda continued.

"I will not see you arrested for breaking laws of any kind, particularly those of a violent nature. As amusing as the whole situation may seem at first glance, think on it a minute more and you will realize the gravity of what you have done."

Molly closed her mouth, and her eyes found the floor, which was not yet dusted for the day.

Lord Halloway continued where his wife left off, his great voice soft, as if in an effort to be gentle. "Of course we would like you to stay. You will always be like family to us. But consider: you damaged property. The *prime minister's* property. If they were to link your actions to our movement, do you imagine he would feel kindly toward broader suffrage? Would the other lords? Lord Grey is one of our biggest supporters of working-class representation. He is not like Wellington. The king has called back Lord Grey to help bring about reform."

Molly felt all the more foolish. She didn't know and had no interest in the personalities at work.

"If we lose credibility with the House of Lords, all is lost. As soon as they view the suffrage movement as a risk to England's peace, run by irrational violence, we lose footing with the lords. Everything we do now must be about improving opinions of us among members of the *ton*. Amanda's fliers, your banners and work with the orphans, all of it, is aimed at garnering their support. If we can maintain their goodwill and sympathy, our goals for greater representation will fly through parliament and soon become law."

Molly stood chastened, humbled, mortified. "I'm sorry. I did not think . . ." But her stubborn thoughts still broke free. "I just don't know if I want to wait, hanging my hopes on obtaining their goodwill. Parliament has not claimed women in their efforts. It is only the Liberty Seekers and the many women's groups who even seem to care. Courting the *ton*'s generosity could go awry in an instant. What if the lords change their minds? They have no reason to help but to offer a kindness."

"What other choice do we have?" Lord Halloway reasoned. "One cannot force an opinion, and goodwill must be earned."

Molly nodded. He was right, of course. But so was she.

Lord Halloway cleared his throat. "We care for you, and we would hate to lose you. But we need to know you will not continue in these more radical ways. Your position as a lady's maid depends on it." His eyes spoke kindness, and she knew the implication pained him.

A deep knot entangled Molly's insides. She could only nod in return.

Lord Halloway stood, facing Thomas. "You, my good man, have done another good service this night. I commend you." He reached for Thomas's hand.

"Thank you, my lord."

Somewhat defeated, Molly felt her mind spin with possibilities. She wanted to be ready with ideas for moving forward when the suffrage ladies met to strategize. The group of them were much too passive. They met in secret, not one of them willing to be labelled a bluestocking for fear of being shunned by the *ton*. And Molly understood their worries. Most noblewomen depended upon a good marriage to a wealthy nobleman as a matter of livelihood. Even Lady Amanda acted the part of a frivolous lady of leisure when in public, though she was much more outspoken than she'd ever been of late and was growing more so.

Molly and Thomas hurried to begin work for the day. Perhaps she had pushed too far, but she could not regret her early-morning vigil, not fully. A small smile curled her lips.

Lord and Lady Halloway did not know it, but she'd tied a message to that rock, and the staff would deliver it into the prime minister's hands as soon as he returned.

CHAPTER TWO

MOLLY RUSHED UPSTAIRS, WASHED UP as quickly as time allowed, and then hurried to Lady Amanda's room, where all the work as her lady's maid awaited Molly. She hadn't prepared a single dress last night. Her lady expected callers this morning—the duchess, if Molly remembered correctly.

Lord Halloway's stepmother made everyone nervous. His father, the duke, had remarried just two months past, and everyone lived in trepidation of talking with the new duchess. The house all did precisely what they wished when she wasn't around, but when interacting with her, no one had yet determined quite how to cross her without producing the dreaded raise of her eyebrows and the look of displeasure pinching her lips together in a tight purse.

After Her Grace's call, Lady Amanda planned a walk through the park, an early tea, and a dinner in the evening. Nothing had been set out, nothing pressed or mended. Molly moved her feet as quickly as household rules allowed.

She grimaced. She had assumed she'd be in a jail cell this morning. She felt her cheeks flame. Where had she come up with the idea anyway? Who tried to get thrown into prison? She shook her head. What good would it have done? She longed to write in her diary, to work through everything, but too much work awaited before she would have that luxury.

She hurried into Lady Amanda's room, hoping to prepare just a few things before the lady herself arrived, but was startled and nearly tripped over her skirts to stop from rushing past the young Lady Annabelle,

Lady Amanda's ten-year-old daughter. She sat at her mother's table in front of the mirror, with a brush in hand.

"Why, my lady." Molly curtsied. "Your mother will be up shortly, I'm certain."

The young lady's eyebrow lifted, and Molly knew before Lady Annabelle asked what the young girl was about. "*You've* been doing suffrage work, haven't you?" she said.

Molly wasn't sure how much Lady Amanda would want her to know. "You can be sure of that, my lady. Any time I'm not being a lady's maid." Lady Annabelle was often on her own, with her brothers now at Eton, and Molly knew Lady Amanda wanted to bring her to the committee meetings once she grew older.

Lady Annabelle grinned. "And you've been getting in trouble, haven't you?" Her eyes sparkled with energy. Lady Amanda would have her hands full with this one, and Molly was not the one to tell her, either. But the girl had best be about her mother's work sooner or later. Molly shrugged. "Ask your mum. Ask her why Molly chained herself to a lamppost in the early-morning hours." At the girl's wide eyes Molly giggled. "But you didn't hear anything from me." Molly's heart nearly burst with pride at her actions. Trouble or no, she'd actually done something, and suddenly, telling this wide-eyed miniature of Lady Amanda, that felt important.

The more she thought about it, she suspected if all the women behaved in like manner, they'd get further in their efforts. Attention— that's what the women's suffrage groups needed.

She curtsied to young Lady Annabelle and rushed into the closet. Thank the stars Molly had washed the week's chemises two days past, when Lady Amanda had had few other appointments. She pulled out a fresh chemise and began to gather the different pieces belonging to the first outfit for her dear lady.

Why had Lady Amanda chastised her, warned her against future destructive behavior? After everything Lady Amanda mixed herself up in, couldn't she find a bit of sympathy for Molly's brazen acts? Surely her work ten years ago to stop the Cato Street Conspiracy, a plot by a group that had tried to kill the prime minister and his entire cabinet, was far more brash a move than Molly had participated in . . .

A small voice reminded Molly that the two events were different: last night Molly had, in fact, *performed* an act of violence by throwing the rock. Lady Amanda's Cato Street efforts had been to *stop* an act of violence. A significant difference.

Footsteps in the hall urged her to move ever faster. She found the short corset, which tightened the lady's upper chest area only, still giving her a pleasant, rounded appearance at her neckline without unduly squeezing the unborn child. Lady Amanda wished to stay out in society for as long as possible. She had work to do. Molly smirked. It was so like her. Molly pulled out the deep-emerald-green morning dress, Lady Amanda's favorite, and after laying it out on the bed, crawled back into the corner of the closet to pull out the matching shoes. Her breath came quicker. *Dust.* Somehow she must get this dust out of Lady Amanda's slippers. The door opened, creaking subtly on its hinges. Molly hurried forward from the closet to the bedroom. Lady Annabelle had left, but Lady Amanda was still in her nightdress and robe, and Molly cringed inside at her own lack of preparation.

"My lady." She curtsied. "I am just gathering your things. Will you be wanting to dress now or after your chocolate?"

Every morning, Lady Amanda had a sip or two of chocolate in a teacup at her bedside. Grateful Molly was for the habit because Cook often saved a sip or two for Molly. Of course, this morning, nothing had been prepared—not her clothing, not her chocolate. Molly avoided Lady Amanda's eyes.

"I think I shall read in the light by my window for a spell this morning. If you could have the chocolate and my morning meal brought up, that would be lovely."

Molly searched Lady Amanda's face. Had she disappointed her friend? The kindest of women, Lady Amanda was still in her night things, with a robe tied about her person; she was making morning preparations easy on Molly.

"Very good, my lady. And thank you."

"This will be just right. My robe is far more comfortable than any other thing you are about to strap around my person." She grinned. "I may spend some time drawing and picking which fliers to send to the newspaper. The duchess comes at eleven, I believe."

"I was told eleven, yes. I'll fetch your tray at once."

"Oh, ring for it. No need to fetch it personally, not today."

Molly faltered. A small twinge hurt at the thought that her duties had been so easily passed to another. Then again, all things considered, allowing someone else to carry the tray made this morning much more convenient. Molly herself would answer the door. She curtsied.

"Thank you, my lady. I will do that right away."

After ringing the bell and giving instructions to the surprised maid who answered it, Molly rushed back into the closet, remembering that last Lady Amanda wore that gown, the hem had looked a little ragged in one spot. Molly pulled out thread and needle from her basket in the corner and began mending the hem straightaway.

Lady Amanda peeked in through the doorway. "I wanted you to see this."

Molly started, avoiding stabbing herself with a needle by a hair. "What is it?"

"Come out here, sweet."

She collected her things and followed her lady into the bedroom.

"See, I've been working on some new fliers. We need to get them to *The Manchester Guardian* today, if possible."

Molly went to the table where the fliers were spread out. Her breath caught. "They are beautiful, my lady."

The fliers showed images of women, all dressed in white, each different. Several depicted images with children teaching each other or playing. Others at orphanages. Some governesses and nurses. One had the likeness of Princess Charlotte herself; Molly assumed that picture of the little girl with the crown was the princess who passed away years ago.

Other drawings caught her eye—darker, more disturbing pictures— and her breath sped up. She swallowed, reaching for the nearest paper. Women from the Peterloo Massacre they had both witnessed, stared at her. She had never seen their likenesses, and looking at them again now brought the scene back as if it had happened yesterday.

"Oh."

Lady Amanda rested a hand on her shoulder. "They haunt me, those women."

Molly nodded. She ran a finger over one of the figures on the page in her hand. "I saw this. This woman. I saw her fall."

Amanda wiped a tear off her cheek. "I did too."

Everything about the image was dark. Boots, trousers, mud, stone. Even the sky was dark, save for the brilliant white of the dress, or what you could see of it under the feet of a trampling, stampeding crowd. Folds of white wrapped about ankles peered out from swirls of dust. The woman's face remained hidden, with just the white of her dress visible. Her hand gripped the pole of a torn and tattered banner declaring, *Votes for women*.

Molly shuddered, the lump in her throat winning. "How could you draw it? How did you not wet this with your tears?" She turned to her lady.

Amanda's cheeks were wet. Her voice caught. "All these years, I haven't dared. But now I must, or they will fester inside me, calling me and forever disturbing my peace." She searched Molly's face. "There's one more."

A great fear tore at Molly's insides. She knew what the final picture would portray. She shook her head. "I can't."

"Please. I need to share it with someone. And I think talking together about . . . him . . . might help us both. We've never spoken about . . . that day."

Molly couldn't say the words, but she shouted them in her mind: *He's dead!*

She set the flier on the table. "Forgive me, my lady, but I—"

Lady Amanda reached for an overturned flier on her table. "This image most plagues me, night and day, if I allow it."

Everything inside Molly screamed for her to run, to hide from the truth on that flier, but she couldn't. She had to obey her lady. Her hand shook as she reached for the slip of paper she knew depicted her worst dreams. As much as she wanted to run, another part of her felt equally drawn to it, wanting to witness the tragedy and sorrow, welcoming it inside to add to the great swirls of dark thought that plagued her. She fought the forgetting of it every day.

Molly took one more breath and turned it over. She raised a hand to her mouth as the image before her blurred through a great well of tears. "Charlie."

She'd never seen a likeness of him, didn't think one had ever been made before.

Lady Amanda wrapped an arm around Molly's shoulder, squeezing. She used a handkerchief to wipe her own face and offered Molly a new one.

Molly paid the cloth no heed. She gazed at her beloved, who lay on the earth, one hand raised to the sky, his face full of light, as if heaven had sent down its welcoming rays. The caption read, *For freedom*. His last words. The lines around his eyes and mouth were smooth, and serenity filled his expression. Lady Amanda had captured a great peace within chaos.

Images all around him showed blurred, fallen bodies, but the detail in his face and expression were nearly perfect with their clarity. This was the moment of his ultimate sacrifice, and in it Molly saw what she'd known all along: Charlie had willingly fallen, had given his life protecting those he loved in the very act of calling for freedom. He'd wanted this.

She remembered so often his words to her. *This work is the tribute of my life. If I do nothing else, I will die a happy man.*

The guilt of the past ten years filled her heart. What had she done of even remotely comparable importance? No matter how hard she worked, she could not yet say his death had accomplished his great aims.

The working class was yet without a vote, and so were women.

She thought of Thomas, another source of guilt. She enjoyed his attention—sought it, even. Looking at Charlie's image now, that closeness to another felt like a betrayal.

"We are doing what he wanted of us." Lady Amanda rested a hand on Molly's shoulder again. "Lord Halloway and I are pushing forward our cause."

They were indeed. Molly swallowed, speech still impossible. They educated their staff—all were learning to read—ran orphanages for children, created and published fliers, and argued in the House of Lords. Lord Halloway's organization, the Liberty Seekers, stretched all throughout England. Lady Amanda's secret work as the Sparrow, a renowned cartoonist, educated much of the *ton* on all manner of issues. And they did those things so well that a vote was scheduled, a vote that was expected to grant the right to vote to the great masses of the working classes.

What had Molly done? What was her contribution to the cause, besides running deliveries of fliers for Lady Amanda? Besides her small input on the suffrage committee?

Lady Amanda smiled at the image of Charlie, her expression hopeful. "Do you think he'd be pleased with our efforts?"

Molly nodded again. She wanted nothing more than to be dismissed so she could sob out her anguish in private.

"I could not do any of this without you, Molly. You know that, don't you?"

Molly accepted the lie because she couldn't contradict her lady and she couldn't speak anyway.

A soft knock sounded at the door. Molly excused herself, rushed to the door, and received the breakfast tray from the curious maid. Then she set up the plates, cup, and all the food on a second table by the window overlooking the beautiful green grounds. Molly hardly noticed her surroundings but worked quickly and efficiently. When the table was ready, she curtsied and returned to the closet.

As soon as the door closed behind her, silent sobs racked her body, shuddering through her like a great storm that blew trees in bending arcs, pushing away all that was not firmly rooted in the earth.

And just like the calm after a storm, when the sobs subsided, a great emptiness remained. She welcomed the quiet, though it was not quite peace—she hadn't felt genuine peace since Charlie's death. But this feeling was quiet, soft, and gentle. A feeling through which she could work. Picking up her needle again, she hurried to patch up the ragged edge of the green gown.

Lord Halloway entered the bedchamber; Molly recognized the fall of his feet. His voice carried to her. "The duchess has arrived."

Molly scrambled, collecting all the items needed to dress Lady Amanda for the day. In the doorway, she paused for another moment, allowing them as much privacy as possible. Then she stepped into the room.

Lord Halloway held his wife, whose body also shook with sorrow.

Molly stopped moving. She stepped back slowly, hoping to not be noticed.

Lady Amanda's voice was soft, muffled into her husband's shirt. "I don't know how to help Molly. She can't continue like this."

Can't continue what? Her employment? Molly remained frozen in the doorway. A future duke should not have to worry about his staff like these two did for her. Great tendrils of fear crept through Molly. Where would she go if she could not keep her position with Lady Amanda?

Others coveted her skills as a lady's maid. She could find work, but none as satisfying as what she had here.

Any other position would likely mean abandoning the cause. Who could deliver Lady Amanda's fliers and talk with John Taylor at *The Manchester Guardian*? Molly knew the editor and owner so well their exchanges were seamless. He was getting older. They would need to train a new person; perhaps she herself would be replaced as Lady Amanda's messenger. Would she be able to continue the legacy Charlie had left her? How could she ensure his death wasn't for naught?

"Molly, what's wrong?" Lady Amanda rushed to her, lines of concern across her face, Lord Halloway's kind expression behind her showing equal amounts of worry.

She cleared her throat. "Nothing. I'm sorry. My mind was just wandering through a bit of sadness, that's all."

"I'm sorry I showed you the fliers. I did not mean to distress you. I thought seeing them might help."

"I was grateful to see them, my lady," Molly said honestly. "They're some of your best."

Lady Amanda smiled. "Thank you. You would know. I think you've seen every one. What would I ever do without you?"

Fear heightened in Molly's mind at the thought.

Lady Amanda's face lined with concern. "Are you well, my dear?"

"I believe so. I'm just ashamed of my actions earlier."

Lord Halloway nodded. "But we have all learned from your mistakes."

"Not to worry, Molly. Plenty of the inane ahead to occupy us and distract our thoughts." Lady Amanda lifted her hand in the air with a flourish. "The duchess has come." She leaned closer to Molly. "And then we shall have a good talk, you and I."

Lord Halloway reached for Lady Amanda's hand and gave it another squeeze. "I'll greet my imperious stepmother." He bowed in mock seriousness and left the room, closing the door behind him.

Molly and Lady Amanda moved to warm by the fire while dressing. Molly wrapped a long piece of silken fabric under Lady Amanda's belly, around the small of her back and across the front, where she tied it so her stomach would be securely pulled in and supported. They made quick work of the corset and clothing, and then Molly worked a low knot in her lady's hair, pulling sweet tendrils around her face. She applied a new cream on her mistress's cheeks.

"You are so beautiful, my lady, and the blush of being with child adds even more beauty to your complexion."

"I don't know how you do it, keeping up with all the latest methods to present me in the best way while also working on my committees, delivering fliers, and planning your own bit of rebellion." One of her eyebrows rose, a teasing light in her eyes sparkling.

Molly couldn't help but grin. "Someone has to ensure you present yourself as a future duchess should. What with your trying to make appearances in all manner of disarray without me."

"I have never stepped foot anywhere without looking impeccable, elegant, and beautiful because of you, best of maids."

Molly secured Lady Amanda's hair in place with the last pins. "As I've said, friends though we are, workers for suffrage and the like, I am a member of your staff first, and right proud of that I am." She paused to share a look with Lady Amanda through the mirror. "You are the best of women."

"And now we must both stop, or the red puffiness will never leave our faces and Lord Halloway will begin to wonder at our sanity."

Molly stepped back. "You are ready, my lady."

Lady Amanda took in a fortifying breath, which settled her shoulders lower. Her chin rose, and the determination Molly knew so well took hold. The duchess waiting downstairs was a force, but Lady Amanda was much more.

Alone in Lady Amanda's room at last, Molly rushed to complete all her tasks, preparing for the next activity, the wash, and working a quick tidy of her space. After organizing the closet, Molly prepared the rest of the changes of clothing for the day. She removed some small stains in the fabric of a day dress then made her way belowstairs to grab a bite of tea. In the hallway Thomas pulled her aside and drew her close, his face almost touching hers so he could whisper in her ear. Every part of her that touched him warmed her through her clothing with an increased awareness. She glanced up the hallway, hoping no one witnessed them.

"You would be right proud of our lady in there with the duchess," Thomas whispered. "She is a tower, to be sure."

Creating space between them, Molly asked, "Who, the duchess or Lady Amanda?"

"Lady Amanda, of course," Thomas grunted, eyeing her in disbelief. "That duchess is nothing but tight disapproval, while our lady is all graciousness and strength. You must see them." He placed his hand on her elbow, gently tugging in the direction of the drawing room.

"What, eavesdrop? I couldn't."

"No, not that. I am merely come to tell you that someone must carry the tea tray." His eyebrows raised a couple of times in challenge.

Molly considered for a moment and then grinned. "The look on Lady Amanda's face will be worth the frown on Mrs. Benning's."

"Our venerable housekeeper." Thomas chuckled. "Hurry now. I am sent to request the tea tray straightaway."

Together they ran to the kitchen, where Molly grabbed the tray from where Cook had set it out before anyone could say otherwise.

Molly giggled. "What is it, precisely, that I need to see?" Her melancholy almost forgotten, she eyed her friend with gratitude.

Thomas, standing tall as befitted a footman, watched her from the corner of his eye. "Nothing in particular. I also wanted to give our lady a bit of support and something to laugh at." He opened the double doors leading into the front parlor as Molly entered.

Lady Amanda stopped mid-sentence. Her eyebrows raised when she saw Molly, but with a small smile and a shake of her head, she continued. "And women too. We are hoping to add them to this law."

Molly wanted to cheer. Would Lady Amanda drop her frivolous façade in front of the duchess, then?

The duchess froze. "You cannot be serious." Her forehead filled with wrinkles from the furrowing of her eyebrows. The white curls under her cap could not soften the severity of her expression and her tight, thin lips frowning disapproval as they did most of the time.

Lady Amanda lifted the teapot from the tray, pouring the first cup. "Of course I'm serious. Including women is the most natural thing in the world."

Lord Halloway took his cup. "Father and I agree with Lady Halloway."

The duchess gripped the arm of her chair, the whites of her knuckles visible from Molly's place at the side of the room. "It simply isn't done. Surely you know that."

"Forgive me, but just because it *hasn't* been done doesn't mean it shouldn't be." Lady Amanda held up a teacup. "Two sugars and a bit of cream, if I remember correctly?" She smiled sweetly.

"Yes, thank you." The duchess's lips had started to purse anew, but the tea provided a bit of distraction.

Molly stood against the wall, hoping to be ignored. She could leave, but she wanted to stay. From across the room, Thomas winked at her even as he kept his back stiff against the door. Lord Halloway tipped his head to the side, his eyebrow raised, looking from Thomas to Molly in silent question. Molly swallowed and made to leave, but Lord Halloway shook his head slightly, telling her to stay. She smiled.

"I remember well the bluestockings of my day," the duchess said. "Studying political works, quoting essays, and some even wanting to participate in the vulgarities of men, including their deliberations in the House of Lords." Her tone left no doubt about the extreme distaste with which she viewed such activities.

What would Lady Amanda do? To protect herself—including her work with the fliers—she often pretended to care little about matters of great importance. She presented a flirty and frivolous persona, hoping to deflect any suspicion. The ruse had been incredibly effective in the past and had likely saved her and Lord Halloway from accusations of treason.

But over the years, she and Lord Halloway had gradually eased into letting others know about their support for broader suffrage, and Lord Halloway openly supported it in all his efforts in the House of Lords.

But before Lady Amanda could react the duchess continued. "I myself don't completely understand why the uneducated and unkempt poor should feel the necessity to declare themselves with the vote, but I can see that it will happen." She turned her superior gaze on Lord Halloway. "Your father tells me it is inevitable." Her upper lip curled at the statement, and she straightened her dress with only two fingers, as though it were a muddy rag. "But *women*? You sully our gender with causes that are beneath us. Surely our husbands' votes are enough for one household."

Molly's hands clenched behind her, nails digging into her palms in hopes of keeping her face void of expression. Lady Amanda's eyes flickered to her own. Lord Halloway coughed. Lady Amanda took great efforts to pause before speaking. Hope rose inside Molly at the expression on her lady's face, and she held back a grin. Hopefully the duchess would hear precisely what was brewing inside the lady's mind, though the whole of it wouldn't be spoken until later that evening. They often reviewed their days together. Molly looked forward to it at the close of each day.

"As a newer and close member of the household," Lady Amanda began, "you may notice that, from time to time, I disagree with certain sentiments. For instance, I do hope women gain a greater voice, that the law will include women in suffrage, and that women will be able to educate themselves more fully. I also hope the derogatory use of the term *bluestocking* will be struck from our vocabulary." She finished off her statement by lifting her dress with two fingers precisely as the duchess had a moment before.

Molly had to bite her cheek to not draw attention to herself.

"What are you grinning about, girl?"

Molly caught her breath. Her mouth fell open. *The duchess addressed me?*

She curtsied. "I'm sorry, Your Grace. A bit of something has caught in my teeth, to be sure." Her eyes quickly found the floor. Hopefully she'd be forgiven for the lie.

The duchess was not finished. "I am displeased with the lack of proficiency with our staff, Lord Halloway. The maid is still standing there instead of removing the tea tray. And she's grinning, as if she understands the conversation."

Molly felt Thomas's gaze on her but didn't dare look in his direction. Just his presence brought her comfort.

"They did not bring enough cakes for my liking," the duchess went on. "And I didn't want to say it, but that hair, Lady Amanda; your lady's maid could do so much more with you."

Lady Amanda swallowed and lowered the teacup in her hand. She opened her mouth to speak, but the Duchess continued. "Even for morning callers, we must always look our best. I would have thought my visit could bring out a more creative style. And your cheeks. Has she not heard of the new pomade? It colors, gently, while tightening the skin. No need to sag this early on in your life. And I didn't want to say anything earlier, but it bears mentioning: your hemline is torn, in desperate need of a mend, and your slippers are covered in dust. Can your maid not perform the simplest of tasks? Perhaps I should go through the staff lists here as I have on the main estate."

Lady Amanda's face flushed, whether from embarrassment or some other emotion Molly could not tell. But as quickly as her feet could move, Molly picked up the tray and left the room, rushing past Thomas with just enough of a glance to catch another wink. His support warmed her, but under the judgmental eye of the duchess, it was not enough.

Great feelings of failure washed over Molly as she reached the kitchen and placed the tray on the table. The regular tea maid exclaimed her disapproval while Molly made her way up the back stairs to the closet in Lady Amanda's room, where Molly slept. Should she begin packing her things? She had failed her lady and her friend. She had one task uniquely hers, and she could not be successful at it. She didn't expect Lady Amanda to keep her much longer after such a censure.

CHAPTER THREE

THE CLOP OF HORSES' HOOVES echoed down the street as Chloe Wetherton's carriage stopped in front of Lady Amanda's home. She didn't care much about suffrage; rather, she didn't know much about suffrage. She would go to the meeting today because Lady Amanda had asked her to.

So she'd best be about it. Swallowing, she took the stairs one at a time, reaching the top sooner than she hoped. The Halloways' butler opened the door before Chloe could lift a hand to the knocker. Uncanny how he always knew. Of course, on this day, when the household expected many visitors, he would be ready. She hoped to one day best him and arrive early enough to actually rap the ancient lion head on the door.

"Good day to you, Lady Chloe," the butler said.

She smiled. "And to you, Mr. Harrison."

"You are the first to arrive, my lady. They are expecting you in the dining room."

"I'm so early?" That was not her intent.

Lady Amanda stepped into the hall. "We wouldn't have it any other way. Come in, my dear, and do take a bite with us."

"I didn't want to arrive late." Chloe grinned. "So many people looking at me all at once." They moved down the hall arm in arm. Warmth filled her. Lady Amanda had been a source of strength and friendship for almost her entire life.

When the footman opened the doors into the dining room, Chloe couldn't help but smile at the room, so cheery and inviting. Light filtered in through the windows on one wall, and the sweet aroma of breakfast drifted in her direction from the other wall.

Lord Halloway rose and took her hand, bowing over it. "So good to see you this morning."

"And you as well, my lord." These were the people she felt most at home with. If she could but limit her interactions at this suffrage meeting to a select few, she would be happy indeed.

"Come, take your preferred repast." Lady Amanda indicated the many offerings of food. "We are still about the work of clearing our plates. We expect Lord Annesley at any moment."

Chloe's smile started slow and grew. Lord Wutherford Annesley. Of her other childhood friends, she felt closest to those who were coming today. Annesley. She smiled at the thought. "It is as if we came straight from the fields as children around our houses."

Chuckles followed, Lord Halloway's the loudest before he added, "But please, no more of your and Annesley's tricks. I don't think I can bear those types of jokes here in my own home."

She choked and opened her mouth but was unsure how to respond.

Lady Amanda rested a hand on her friend's arm. "Nathaniel, you shouldn't tease her so."

"Shouldn't tease her!" His face lit with amusement. He pointed a finger in Chloe's direction. "As if she hasn't spent many an hour doing the very same to me, with all manner of weapons—mud pies, sticks, rope swings, and a great many leaves, if I remember correctly."

Before Lady Amanda could further chide him, Chloe held up her hand. "Fair enough. I did enjoy concocting pretend meals for you all to taste."

Annesley cleared his throat in the doorway.

Chloe's heart jumped at the sound.

He joined their laughter. "And I've never had a finer pretend meal in all my years." His grin was as wide as his cheeks as he entered and bowed before them all. "And how are we this morning? Preparing for your guests, ladies?"

Chloe's breath came quicker. She cleared her throat. "Actually, *I* am a guest this morning. Lady Amanda talked me into observing her work. I confess to being full of curiosity on the matter of suffrage, as I am incredibly ill-informed."

Lord Annesley raised an eyebrow. "A new member of the women's suffrage movement, eh?"

Lady Amanda guided Chloe to the sideboard. "She is nothing of the sort—merely a friend offering support. Whether she will join us is entirely up to her."

The others laughed. Annesley stepped beside Chloe, and at his nearness, her arms broke out in happy gooseflesh.

He filled a plate for himself. "Oh, she'll join." He tipped his head as if speaking only to her. "Lady Amanda is quite persuasive, you know."

"Oh, do I ever remember." Chloe grinned. "But I am perfectly content to observe. I have no need or desire for more than that."

Her friends gave one another knowing looks over Chloe's head, but they weren't well hidden; she sensed them all. No matter. They loved her and understood her avoidance of most social interactions.

After a lovely meal full of laughter and camaraderie, the callers started to arrive. They filed into the hallway and were directed to the main receiving room, where more chairs had been brought in. Lady Amanda bustled about, and Chloe found a quiet seat in the back of the room, ready to be amused and entertained and, hopefully, enlightened.

Lady Amanda introduced a woman to the group, one unknown to Chloe. "And now I am pleased to introduce a prime example of all that is brave on this earth. I witnessed a profound act of courage by this very person on that fated day in St. Peter's Square."

Several gasps followed that announcement. Chloe knew Lady Amanda had been present at Peterloo with Lord Halloway, had witnessed a great massacre of the working classes, but the knowledge of their participation had been kept secret. Lady Amanda continued speaking to a captive audience. "Though injured, though threatened since then, her tireless work as the founder of the Manchester Female Reform Society can be an inspiration to us all. It is through her efforts and the efforts of women like her that suffrage will one day be broadened to include all humans on this earth. All men, no matter their status or ownership of property, and all women. I give you Mary Fildes."

Polite gentle clapping followed.

Mrs. Fildes stepped forward, and after her first five words, Chloe forgot everything around her, aware only of the message the speaker so expertly weaved.

"You matter. You are more than your hairstyle, whom you marry, and even more than your title. You, as a woman, matter."

A hole Chloe hadn't known existed within her began to be filled.

"Yes, you do matter," the woman went on. "But who speaks for your needs?"

As Chloe paused to internally respond, she recognized that, besides her father, no one did. And what if her father were unkind? She had many reasons to praise the heavens he was the best of men, but if he weren't, or if she was to marry and her husband was cruel . . .

"Consider for a moment. Who speaks for you in matters of a marriage contract?" Mrs. Fildes paused, eyeing the room.

Her gaze bore into Chloe as if reaching a part of her soul, the lonely part of Chloe's heart that recognized truth.

"Who would speak for you if you were to ever need a divorce?"

A gasp followed. Divorce happened but in the quietest corners. Chloe knew it to be legal but difficult and nearly impossible for a woman to obtain.

"Divorce, indeed!" The Duchess of Somerset raised both eyebrows. "I should think not."

Lady Amanda moved to sit beside her mother-in-law.

With a brief glance at the duchess, the speaker continued as if she hadn't been interrupted. "Who takes on your cause in a hurtful marriage? We have many with us today of the upper or even noble classes. What rights do you have? If your husband were to forbid you to see your children, what recourse could you take? And those of you who are unmarried—is your only hope of happiness the endowment of a good and magnanimous husband who will increase your pin money as needed?"

Rumbling followed her statement, and Chloe felt a little nervous. People didn't speak of such things, not ever.

"But there are those of us present who are in the working classes. Who speaks for you at all?"

Molly, Lady Amanda's maid, clapped from the side where she stood. Others around joined in her support.

"You governesses—when you are too old to care for children, who will take care of you?"

Chloe sat back in shock, thinking of dear Miss Gracely. Where was she now? The family had kept her until after Chloe's second Season in

London. Then Chloe had ached to be out from under the watchful eye of a governess, so she'd felt a moment of victory when Miss Gracely was dismissed. Chloe had cried on Miss Gracely's shoulder before she left, as she loved her governess dearly, but she'd felt a glorious freedom without one.

Miss Gracely had been elderly at the time, and unmarried. She might have long-since outlived any of her own family. Chloe had written her letters for a time, but after five or six months, her efforts had become less frequent, something she now felt ashamed of. It must have been nigh unto a year since she'd heard anything from the woman who had practically raised her.

The speaker continued, listing many issues faced by women and pointing out how no one spoke for women or took care of them, not really. For the first time in her life, Chloe began to see that a real serious and treacherous plight faced all women.

Blessed, she was grateful her father planned to allow her some choice in a husband. So many fathers did not. But what would she do if her future husband were ever cruel or hurtful to her or their children?

Annesley's smiling face entered her mind, and a great peace filled her. Someone like him would be a blessing to any woman. She'd known him since they were children, knew him as well as a sister might. His future wife would never have cause to worry or seek divorce. Chloe had never before thought of him with a wife; he'd always been her friend, and she had naively assumed he would always be so. But now she thought of him as a husband. Her husband. Her whole body warmed in a silent embarrassment at her now-heated face and the direction of her thoughts.

Their speaker nodded her head while the ladies clapped in gratitude. Chloe would be thinking about Mrs. Fildes's words for many weeks.

Lady Amanda stood back up in front. "And this, women, is why we must be able to cast our votes—so that the feminine half of the population is represented, so that our issues might be dealt with fairly, so that when unfair laws are passed, ones that inflict ill will on our gender, we have recourse."

Lady Amanda was so well-spoken. Chloe wished she were half as elegant.

The women clapped, and then the room buzzed, increasing in volume as each person conversed with those seated on either side of them.

Lady Amanda returned to the group, and her lady's maid, Molly, stood at her side. The two conversed in hushed tones. *So interesting to see them interact here.*

Chloe considered the uniqueness of their situation. The two women were never precisely on equal ground, though Molly served on the committee. They each had a role and a part, and while working for women's suffrage, the strict rules of behavior between servant and employer blurred into a fuzzy distinction rarely understood. Yet they seemed to know when to act as lady and maid and when to behave as committee members and friends. She considered her own lady's maid, Becky, and wondered if such a thing would ever be possible between the two of them.

⁓

That evening, after a full afternoon pondering the thoughts sparked by her first suffrage meeting, Chloe found her father in the candlelight of his study. "Father?"

He looked up from his desk. "Come in, Chloe, my dear. Come in." He dipped his pen into his ink and wrote another line in his correspondence. "They've just brought in some tea."

"Thank you." She sat in her favorite chair and laid a blanket across her lap. She sipped her tea and then blew the surface, warming her face as the steam returned to her. She cleared her throat. When her father did not look up, she spoke anyway. "Father, whatever happened to Miss Gracely?"

He paused in his writing, frowned, and looked up at her. "Did you stop corresponding? I thought you wrote each other every Tuesday."

"We did for a bit, but one week she didn't answer, and then another week I didn't answer, and well, now we don't write much anymore. I'll send a letter tomorrow."

"I don't know how she is doing. We sent her off with a good sum. I wasn't quite sure of her plans, but I do believe she has a sister she had planned to live with."

"Does her sister have a home? Is she married?" Chloe set down her teacup on the nearby table.

"Come to think of it, I don't know. For that matter, it might not even be a sister, but some other relation."

"I have become concerned for her of a sudden and would love to locate her, to see her again if I may."

"Your concern does you credit." His eyes warmed, but worried lines formed at his mouth. "With your mother so often unwell." He reached out his hand, which she moved forward to squeeze between her own. "I'm sorry to say I didn't ask many questions about how we handled Miss Gracely's departure from us."

Chloe recognized it wasn't likely her mother had asked many questions of Miss Gracely either. And if her parents—who were kind, good people—had neglected to ensure the care of Miss Gracely, how many other nobles had likely done the same or worse? In truth, Chloe's peers spent very little time thinking about or even noticing those who served them—something she hadn't realized until that very day.

"I do hope she replies to my next letter," Chloe said. "I've become worried about her, and I hope she is taken care of."

"Let me know what you learn from her. We will, of course, do anything we can to care for her. Thank you, Chloe, for your good heart."

She loved Miss Gracely. The governess had spent more time with Chloe than either of her parents, had taught her nearly everything she knew. She hoped all would be well and felt a sharp guilt that she'd let their correspondence end the way it had.

Strange how her thoughts had taken a totally different turn from the usual today, as if the meeting that morning had cast a different light on everything around her.

There was so much more to women's suffrage than she'd previously thought.

CHAPTER FOUR

THE PARK ACROSS THE STREET seemed cold and wet this morning. It was not quite raining, but the weather was not exactly welcome for an outing. Annesley groaned in frustration. Tapping the calling card against his palm, he looked at his father. "He wants to see me right away? Why the urgency?"

The previous night he'd spent an entire dinner seated to the prime minister's left. They'd discussed all manner of issues, most benign and bland. Truth be told, Annesley had been quite bored throughout the evening.

And now, early the next day, an urgent summons.

"I don't know what he wants with you, but you had best be on your way." His father's face seemed pinched, and the lines across his forehead ran deeper than usual. He pulled out his timepiece, checked it again, as though self-conscious, and placed it back into his pocket.

"Father, you've checked your timepiece five times in as many minutes."

"I don't know what's come over me. Your espionage days may be over, but I can't help worrying about what the prime minister might ask of you." He wiped sweat from his brow with a handkerchief. "What will you say?"

"If he asks me into service?" Annesley brushed a hair from his jacket. "He cannot. We have an agreement, and he signed my release papers himself. Whatever it is he wishes to discuss, it will be unofficial business, I am certain." Checking his own timepiece, he said, "The clouds have cleared for a moment. I do believe I should be going."

His father let out such a long breath of relief Annesley eyed him with suspicion. "Are you certain there isn't something else bothering you?" He followed his father's gaze, which had been diverted to the entry drive. "Are you expecting someone?"

"What? No." His voice rose in pitch. Then he cleared his throat. "As I said, you should be on your way. Don't want to keep someone as important as Lord Grey waiting."

Every old spy instinct jarred into high alert. His father was hiding something. Shaking his head, Annesley took his hat and cloak from the butler then stepped down the front stairs toward the awaiting carriage. As the carriage pulled away, another, with a large crest on its side, entered the front drive. Curious, Annesley tried to peer inside. One passenger, a man in a top hat whose hand rested on the window with three fingers lazily dangling in the breeze, watched him as they passed. The clouds cleared, and the sun glinted off gold rings on each finger—an excessive amount of jewelry. Annesley almost stopped the driver; his father was obviously involved in something he wasn't telling his son. But the urgency of his own summons gave him pause.

Better to visit the prime minister now and ask his father about the mysterious visitor when he returned.

Annesley's carriage pulled up to the front of Lord Charles Grey's lovely home on one of the busier streets in London. A lamppost stood out in front, unlit this morning, though the sky was again cloudy, dark, and menacing despite the hour. After Annesley alighted from the carriage and approached the front door, movement in an upstairs window distracted him. Someone seemed to be carefully placing a new piece of glass in an open window and then pulling it out again, as if measuring the fit.

The front door opened, and after he handed the butler his card, Annesley was ushered into a comfortable parlor, shown a seat, and offered tea or brandy. He accepted the tea.

A few minutes later the prime minister joined him and sat opposite in a straight-backed chair as stiff and tall as its occupant.

Annesley sipped his tea and waited for Lord Grey to speak, keeping his own expression purposely open and bland.

Lord Grey leaned forward. "Let's skip the pleasantries, shall we?"

With raised eyebrows Annesley returned the teacup to its saucer on the table at his side. "Of course. What can I do for you this morning?"

"I need your services." A line of perspiration dotted the prime minister's hairline.

"I am here, as requested. Naturally I will advise you in any way I can." Annesley placed the slightest emphasis on the word *advise*. How had his father known this would be the direction of their conversation?

"I do not speak of advisement only. I am in need of your other talents also."

Suspicion rose inside Annesley. "Regrettably, I no longer offer those services. You signed the release yourself, if you recall." After five years of a quiet, safe life, his stomach twisted at the thought of a mission to France or even Spain.

Lord Grey leaned so far forward he almost left his chair. "I'm a desperate man." As he gripped his armrests, his knuckles turned white.

"What is the matter?" Annesley asked. "What has happened?" Perhaps Lord Grey's reaction spoke of more than trifling matters. Annesley could think of no foreign issues for which he could be a unique benefit presently. Surely the government had other men spying outside of England. For now, matters inside the country seemed steady, progressing toward peace. Intrigued, he waited.

Lord Grey shifted in his seat, reached for his own tea, and made to take a sip but replaced the cup on the table after merely wetting his lips. "I have been threatened." He leaned forward in his seat again.

Annesley's interest piqued despite himself. He leaned forward too. "What kind of threat? By whom?"

"I don't know. That is part of why I asked you to come." He rang a bell. When a footman responded, he said, "Bring me the items."

The footman bowed. "Yes, m'lord." He soon returned with a rock the size of his hand, a parchment wrapped around it and tied with string. He placed them on the table between the men and left the room.

Lord Grey gestured at the items. "These were thrown through my upper window while I was touring the continent with my family."

Annesley frowned, trying to understand this strange and unforeseen turn of events. Reaching for the parchment, he asked, "May I?"

"Please." The prime minister nodded. "I'd like for you to unravel this mystery, for until we discover who did this and why, I will remain uneasy over the threat to my life and over such an unconscionable interference with the rule of law."

Ever more curious, Annesley untied the string and unrolled the wrinkled and torn parchment. Written in large, bold letters were the words, *Freedom for all or none. If women will not be granted suffrage by you, then you can expect us to take it ourselves and oust you from your position straightaway.*

Bold move, but a ridiculous one. Annesley hid his reaction with the blank expression of a practiced spy. "What has been done so far to discover the author of so forceful a note?" He allowed himself a soft smile to diffuse the prime minister's angst.

"You find the situation amusing? Have you considered that my life could well be in danger? The lives of my children? Lady Grey?" The prime minister shifted in his seat again. "You know of the dissatisfaction among the working classes. You have heard, no doubt, what they threatened to do to Wellington."

"But they admire you. You are their champion." Annesley tilted his head. "There is a small chance of danger, I grant you that, but I suspect you are more concerned with the threat made to your position."

Lord Grey nodded curtly, staring into Annesley's face. "I am. I believe that's the intended message. Give women the right to vote, or they will blooming oust me from my seat." His hands shook, and the veins on his neck stood out.

"But how viable a threat is that? Women have no voice in either the House of Commons or the House of Lords, and they have no voice at all in the choice of their representatives. How could they possibly place another in your stead?"

"We must squelch these demonstrative acts. Who knows what women are capable of?" Lord Grey fidgeted in his chair, the frame barely holding his girth. "They could gain suffrage—even without my support. Very soon they could. At this moment William Lovett is drafting a bill that would give landowners the right to vote. And in his bill"— he leaned forward in is chair again—"he has included women. He proposes to give women—wives of landowners, widows, mothers of landowners, all of them—the ability to cast a vote in future elections. Do you know how many blooming women there are in this country?"

Annesley could not understand the prime minister's angst. What did he fear from women and their votes?

"We could lose our seat of power! All of us. What if they run for office? How would you like that—to be unseated in the House of Lords by some slip of a thing, some other man's wife?" Lord Grey sat back in his chair, breathing heavily.

"So what if they did? They would compete with a contender just like anyone else. And the House of Lords is secure; appointments and lineage choose our seats." Though Annesley had wished on a number of occasions some of the lords could be voted out.

"You never know with the new king. He could appoint a woman. Just watch. It's indecent."

Annesley studied him, unsure what to say. Personally, he'd rejoice in women's ability to participate in suffrage. "I am sorry, my lord. I still cannot understand your angst."

"We must appease the general populous. Our hands are tied. Greater suffrage is necessary across England. I can't risk that the addition of women would squelch that bill." He cleared his throat, his eyes darting around the room. "There's more. Powers at work. People who would keep women silent."

Annesley sharpened his gaze. *And here lies the real issue.*

Lord Grey did not look well; he was pale and perspiring. He wiped his brow with a handkerchief in shaky hands, swallowed again, and tried to wet his dry lips.

"Who would try to silence the women?" Annesley asked. "Who are these powers and for what purpose?"

The prime minister shook his head and waved his hands around. "Who is no matter. I cannot reveal much, but powerful, dangerous people do not want women to vote. They are using their methods"—he brought a finger to his cravat to loosen it—"to persuade me."

"Methods?" Annesley repeated. "You mean threats such as this one?" He indicated the rock. "Would you like me to investigate these threats?" Now, here was something he could stand behind, a task he would be willing to complete.

Lord Grey took a gulp of brandy, wincing as it went down. "No. I have come to an agreement with them—a profitable but risky agreement. I must do my part. And for that"—he pointed a bony finger toward Annesley's chest—"I need your help."

The more Annesley heard the unhappier he became. The prime minister was being blackmailed or had been threatened in some way to make a deal, and now Annesley was being pulled into the dark business. Every instinct inside him fired off at once, urging him to leave, to run from the house without turning back. Instead he held his ground with a force of steel garnered from his training and waited for the trap to fall around him. What choice did he have? One did not cross the prime minister.

Lord Grey cleared his throat. "I have an assignment for you. I will temporarily reinstate your service and detail you right away."

"No reinstatement is necessary," Annesley said. "I don't wish to allow a window for further assignments. We had an agreement." Five years ago Annesley had agreed to one last mission in exchange for permanent retirement. The assignment had been long and difficult and dangerous. That Lord Grey would call him back in to even discuss this at all was an extreme breach of trust.

"I know, Annesley, I know, and I don't plan to put you in harm's way. This assignment is domestic and nonviolent. I need only your powers of observation. Possibly a task now and then, but nothing more. The whole of my assignment will be over with the vote in one month's time."

"And if I refuse?"

He cleared his throat. "I neglected to mention the matter of payment."

"I am not concerned with money."

The prime minister continued as if Annesley hadn't spoken. "In exchange for your services, I will extend my protection—and rewards— to include your father and his rather large estate, which I understand will eventually be yours."

Small tendrils of fear began to work their way into Annesley's reactions. "Why would my father or his estate need your protection?" He searched the man's face but could find no clues as to his intentions.

"We have been offered an investment opportunity. More specifically, I have been offered this opportunity. Your father's similar offer is contingent upon your agreement. And it could save the Annesley estate—repair the damage from your father's poor choices."

Save my estate? What damage? His father's nervous checking of the front drive, the appearance of the strange gold-ringed man, gave credibility to Lord Grey's claims. Was the estate at risk? At once Annesley wanted to end this conversation and hear his father's explanation.

Lord Grey smirked. "But it hinges, in part, on the vote for women not even appearing before parliament. I have made some deals; let us hope your father will also benefit." He shook his head, gulping another half cup of brandy. "Creditors can be nasty wardens."

Creditors? Had his father fallen into debt? "How long has my father's estate been at risk?" If what Lord Grey said was true, Annesley's father had not reached out to his own son for help. The news felt almost like a betrayal. Great disappointment weighed on Annesley.

"You will need to discuss those details with him. I do know that he has taken to betting on horses. Also, a few of his investments in the mills, the Manchester mills, have proved less than profitable. But the tide could turn on those, depending."

"And you would capitalize on his misfortune by forcing me into service?" Annesley tried to hold back his anger. "You haven't bothered to make a proper request. What if I refuse?"

Lord Grey's expression hardened. "We both know you have no choice. If the possible assistance to your father is not enough to persuade you, consider the consequences of defying me. They would be most grave. You and your father could expect complete ruin; all of your financial ventures would be blocked. We, those involved in this investment opportunity, will buy your debt and force your hand until your family has no option but to seek asylum from the church." His pause carried the weight of his sincerity. "Now, let us move forward and leave such unpleasantness behind us. I will make it as painless as possible."

Annesley stood abruptly in his chair, trying to give himself time before he responded too harshly. Anger, quick and sharp, caused him to fist his hands. But as he breathed, considering all this new information, a thick gloom descended over Annesley. He paced the room, the prime minister watching like a cat watched its prey.

Annesley could think of nothing he wanted less than to spy around for Lord Grey, but he had no choice. Hundreds of people looked to the Annesley estate for their livelihood. He would work himself before he saw his mother in a church poorhouse. Blast his father. What had he done?

"What is it you want me to do?"

Lord Grey stood with great effort, grunting. "Capital, man. I knew you'd come around." He approached, ready to congratulate Annesley further, but Annesley stepped aside so that when the prime minister tried to pat him on the back, he missed and swatted air, nearly toppling forward. He righted himself, steadied both feet, and wiped his brow again. "Yes, well, down to business. Let us sit again."

Annesley resumed his seat, leaned back in his chair, and folded his arms across his chest, nodding for Lord Grey to continue.

"As I said, I am disturbed by the message that came with this dratted rock, and I am concerned about the entire suffrage movement. Our nation would be ill-served by granting suffrage to women." Lord Grey eyed him, perhaps trying to gauge a reaction, but Annesley masked his face. "I need to understand the suffrage movement's supporters. I suspect the most powerful group garners significant support from members of the *ton*. I want to know their plans, their dreams and desires."

Annesley suspected he was situated perfectly to discover nearly anything Lord Grey could possibly want to learn. The idea of using his best friends in such a way made him ill. "And how do you propose I obtain this information?"

"Oh, come now, man. They're *women*. You are single, very eligible, and noble. Do whatever it takes to gain their trust. Become a member of their group."

"That would work only if the women involved are of the noble class. And if they are and I learn whatever it is they have to share, what do I do with that information? Report what a bunch of women discuss over tea at their soirees?"

"Yes," the prime minister said. "You will report to me. And go deeper." The man's breath came faster, the red of his skin deepening. "I want to know their plans, where they will meet. Tell me all about any rallies they organize, their very hopes for the future . . . so that I may crush them." He pounded his fist on the table at his side so hard the motion rattled his cup, upsetting the spoon from the saucer.

Further disgusted with Lord Grey and his hold over Annesley's family estate, Annesley considered his options. But, finding none that appeared promising, he tried to give himself time to plan. "I would like to consider your offer—"

"There is nothing to consider. Of course you'll aid me, what with your father and your estate hanging by a thread as they are. There is paltry more to discuss, really." Lord Grey hefted a stack of papers from the table. "Here is a packet with your point of contact, some suspected suffrage leaders to investigate, and your first dinner party assignment. As usual, you will be sent the needed invitations. You will be expected to report to me every week here in my home, or if at another location, you will be informed of my whereabouts in advance."

Lord Grey offered the papers with an unsteady hand.

This was a dangerous game Annesley was about to play. Gritting his teeth, he reached forward, took the packet, and tucked it under one arm. Standing once more, he eyed the leader of parliament with barely concealed disgust. "I'll show myself out."

Annesley rushed home, tossed his things to the butler, and hurried to his father's study. As soon as the door closed behind him, the words tumbled out. "Father, why didn't you tell me how bad things have become?"

The Earl of Westchester turned to his son. "I wished to spare you in your youth. A profitable match would solve all our problems. If we can keep the matter quiet, there is no reason you cannot marry one of the eligible ladies with a handsome dowry."

Lady Chloe's pink cheeks and soft smile came to mind. But debasing his friendship with her by placing a monetary gain on it shamed him.

How fair would that be to the lady? Annesley clenched his fists. "Must we discuss my future family in this manner? When I marry, I'd rather it didn't feel like a business arrangement." Until today, he'd thought himself free to marry for love.

Usually so calm, his father began pacing nervously, stopping and starting again in an agitated manner. "I understand the romantic notions of young people, but you could at least take into consideration a girl's dowry when asking for a dance or to take her on a ride in that curricle of yours. Woo ladies that are delightful *as well as* wealthy." He raised his eyebrows, watching his son.

Annesley grunted. "How bad is our financial situation? Your debt?" He was ashamed of his father. The gaming tables, betting on horses. Gambling had always felt weak to Annesley. And he had never, before now, viewed his father as weak.

The earl sat, gesturing for Annesley to do the same. "Much better, actually. Today I worked out a situation that could save us all."

Annesley narrowed his eyes with suspicion. "That man arriving when I left. Who is he?"

His father's face blanched. Then he cleared his throat and waved a hand in the air. "Merely someone who has offered a ladder out of my pit. If all goes well, he will be our very salvation."

"And if it does not go well? What is riding on this new gamble you have taken?"

His father's face lit with a crazed excitement. "It cannot fail. With his patronage, we are bound for success. He works in the mercantile businesses in Manchester."

Annesley's concern for the situation grew. Under whose power were they really? Annesley did not want his father to know the depth of his new assignment. He needed to first understand better all the players involved. And this bizarre request of the prime minister. "And what does women's suffrage have to do with any of this, do you suppose?" He watched his father closely.

The earl's blank stare told Annesley that he knew nothing of the particulars of his conversation with Lord Grey. "Women's suffrage? I don't know. I hear there's a bit of a group chattering about it, to be sure. But it has nothing to do with us."

Annesley hadn't thought so either, but he felt certain that a connection between his father's dealings, the prime minister's extortion, and this business in Manchester, would help him solve this great puzzle and somehow save his father's estate.

Until then, would he be forced to sabotage Lady Amanda's efforts? Lady Chloe's possible new interest? Her large blue eyes stared at him in his mind, hopeful. She'd listened to his own words of encouragement on the very topic he was supposed to spy on and ruin. He shook his head. Could he possibly rescue the estate by keeping the prime minister happy without ruining Lady Chloe's efforts on the suffrage committee?

"What's the matter, son? This is great news! Our estate is about to be saved."

Annesley reached for his father's hand as he stood to leave. "I hope you are correct, my lord."

CHAPTER FIVE

MOLLY WHISTLED SOFTLY THROUGH HER teeth. After their long journey, she tapped her feet in happy expectation. A few more blocks of Manchester city streets, and she and her friend and fellow maid Becky would arrive at the orphanage. Happy to get away from the house for a time, especially with the duchess visiting, Molly also looked forward to the children. And time with Thomas. He had ridden with them inside the carriage for most of the journey instead of up on top with the driver and other footmen. Molly pulled open the curtains of the carriage, smiling just thinking about him. He made everything better, easier, more fun. And standing near him gave her gooseflesh. Theirs was a friendship, she reminded herself. Friendship could not be a betrayal to Charlie's memory. But there was no harm in a little gooseflesh now and then. She giggled.

"What?" Becky leaned forward to see what might be funny out the window.

"Oh, nothing. I am just happy to finally be arriving, that is all."

"I think she was remembering something." Thomas winked at her.

Does he know he was the subject of my thoughts? Molly's face heated, and she cleared her throat. "If you must know, I was laughing to myself about the duchess."

"Ugh." Becky wrinkled her nose. "Not much to laugh at in her."

Thomas leaned back. "Oh, but this is worthy of repeating. Our Lady Amanda gave that woman a talking to, the likes of which I have never seen."

He continued in a mock voice meant to represent Lady Amanda, Molly assumed. "'How can you say such things in front of my maid?

That girl is so much more than a lady's maid to us. She is the best of women. Many in London are clamoring for her services. I will not have my servants defamed in such a way.'

"The duchess sniffed. You know how she does, and pinches her lips just so."

Molly and Becky laughed at his expression, which was remarkably similar to the duchess's.

Thomas switched voices to a nasally, snivelly, high-pitched sort of sound. "'She didn't seem all that talented to me,' she said, which really rubbed wrong on my insides, but of course, I had to stand there silent.

"And then Lady Amanda answered, and I wanted to cheer her on. 'You will see her shine when my presentation matters. This morning, among family, I chose a more comfortable attire, as, surely, there is no need to overly impress.'"

Becky's mouth opened. "She said that? To the duchess?"

Thomas nodded. "She did, and I was right proud of her for it."

Molly's heart warmed again, thinking of it. "*She* is the best of women." She voiced a worry she'd had since. "You don't think she will regret standing up for me like that, do you? The duchess won't shun her or anything?"

Thomas shook his head. "No, I don't. Not with the duke so enamored with Lady Amanda like he is."

Molly nodded. "I've been so much trouble for the Halloways lately. I'm hoping to be more helpful than anything. Perhaps things will be calmer around here."

Thomas scoffed. "With Lady Amanda in the house? I hardly think calm is how things will be. But not to worry. I continually tell you they love you like family."

She did not answer. One could grow tired of one's family when they became overly bothersome.

Becky sighed. "I wish we had a bit more adventure around our house. Lady Chloe is all that is goodness and kindness, but she just doesn't *do* much of anything."

"Count yourself blessed to work for such a woman." Molly had known Lady Chloe since she was younger and played on the Cumberland estate with Lady Amanda. "Many ladies are not nearly so reasonable."

"Or so kind." Thomas nodded.

The wheels slowed, and the front of the townhome that served as an orphanage came into view. Thomas exited and stretched his neck, arms, and legs. His towering frame suffered the most in long carriage rides.

He helped Becky climb out of the carriage then hurried to alert the orphanage of their arrival. Her cheeks were a soft pink as she tilted her neck back so she could smile up at him.

Irritation rose up in Molly's throat, but she swallowed it down. "Becky, hurry now. I am anxious to get inside." Becky was always a little too friendly with Thomas; Molly suspected she'd like something to happen between them.

"I'm a hurryin', I am." Becky chuckled in a deep belly-laugh kind of way. "I'm just glad Mrs. Bellamy let me leave. I had to trade my day off, you know, but it worked out just fine, I should think. Lady Chloe was most excited about the orphanage, what the children do here, how they learn, what they need, so she was happy to let me come." Becky smiled. "I'm looking forward to seeing the children myself."

Molly and Becky stood in front of the carriage, not yet to the front door. "Yes, yes." Molly motioned, and she and Becky began walking up the steps. "You'll see for yourself all Lady Amanda and Lord Halloway are doing to benefit these dear children."

Becky's face shone. "I'm just so proud of all you are doing, Molly. When we were young and running through the backwoods, who'd have thought that one day we'd be saving children and trying to get a vote and the like?"

"Surely not I," Molly said. "If it weren't for Lady Amanda, I might never have been involved in any of this. She's a regular windstorm, that one." She could not stop her proud grin.

Molly instructed Thomas and the footman from the house to help unload the packages of food and supplies and to deliver them inside through the front door. Then she reached to grab a crate herself.

Thomas grinned as they passed one another, each with a crate of shoes, the anticipation of helping the children contagious. They both loved the orphanage and had been a part of its planning from the beginning. When Thomas's eyes met hers, Molly did not look away but stared back, her heart picking up a bit. Thomas's warm green eyes responded kindly, and after a moment, he winked and then turned to walk inside, giving further orders to the other footman and the driver who had accompanied them.

As soon as her feet touched the threshold, two small bodies pummeled into her, their faces pressing into her skirts.

"Ah, my lovelies! It is good to see you!" The tops of the heads of her dearest little friends were a happy welcome as the twin brother and sister hugged her legs.

Thomas laughed and grabbed the crate from her, the twinkle in his eye sending shots of energy through her.

Molly squatted down so she could be at eye level, her chestnut curls coming loose from their pins and falling forward around her face.

Jonathon and Sally moved about excitedly in from of her, grinning. Jonathon piped up first. "We're so glad you came today!"

Sally turned to her brother. "We are happy any day she comes."

He looked a bit abashed. "Of course we are, but today 'specially 'cause Miss Tipton is going to make us wash up, she is, but if you're here, Miss Molly, maybe she'll hold off until tomorrow."

Sally lifted her nose into the air the tiniest bit. "I don't mind a wash, Jonny. I prefer to smell lovely. Sometimes they even put a bit of lavender in the water." She looked to Molly for approval.

"Yes, good girl, Sally." Molly grinned. "You'll both find much greater success in life if you smell nice and look clean."

Jonathon frowned.

Laughing, Molly tousled his hair. "Come now, Jonny, it's not as bad as all that. Now, let me search my pockets, because I brought something just for the two of you."

The siblings jumped up and down, Sally squealing in excitement.

When Molly brought out two wrapped parcels from her satchel, the children's eyes gleamed.

"Some of Cook's fresh tarts, filled with jam. I told her I was coming to see you, and she made them for you especially."

Both children threw their arms around Molly and thanked her as though she'd brought them a new pony. They ran off together, laughing.

When Thomas had come across the twins on the street last year, they'd stared despondently at nothing, too tired to cry. Their large, swollen bellies, too-small clothing, and bare and cracked feet broke his heart. Wind had whipped through the streets, chilling the children, so Thomas had picked them up straightaway and carried them back to the orphanage in his arms.

As Molly watched them run, now thriving, she held back tears.

Thomas came forward to shuffle through the many boxes on the floor in the entry. She knelt to help him, and his hands covered hers. Warmth tingled from her fingertips to her shoulders. She stilled and lifted her eyes to his. He searched her features, lingering on her lips. Then he winked. Her smile broadened, and she laughed. Everything felt lighter and more fun with Thomas. He squeezed her hands, and they stood.

The housekeeper, Mrs. Featherstone, greeted them and began directing the unloading and organizing.

For the first time, guilty memories of Charlie had not interrupted Molly's moment with Thomas. And she pondered a small hope that brewed inside while they worked to organize the supplies.

Turning to Becky, she said, "Let's see how the children are doing in the schoolroom, shall we?"

Lady Amanda had asked for a detailed report on how well the school functioned and how much the children were learning.

Holding Becky's hand, Molly entered the schoolroom lined with chairs, each with a child sitting at attention. "I'm so happy to share all this with you." Molly gave Becky's hand a squeeze. "All these children would be at work in the factories if not for Lady Amanda."

"Look at all the dears," Becky said. "Wearing the ladies' last season's clothes, they are."

"Yet they are still dressed better than we are, to be sure," Molly said. "Last visit we delivered crates and crates of clothing, most of it hardly worn at all. You'd think we were running a finishing school for the nobility by the looks of it all." Molly's contentment rose inside, and a new light filled her mind.

Their conversation earned a good-natured but firm headshake from the teacher at the front of the room.

Apologizing, the maids stepped back into the hallway.

Molly pulled Becky closer so their conversation would not disturb the lesson. "I'm so proud of all the work that goes on here."

"I want to help. Lady Chloe will want to hear all about it, and I'm sure she'll want to do something to help support the children too."

The hinges of a door creaked as it swayed back and forth by inches on a breeze through the house. A nurse hurried down the hall away from them. Molly shivered at the draft. Then the sounds of the quiet sobbing of a child reached them. Her heart ached, and she moved with Becky toward the open door, sharing a concerned expression. Molly prepared herself. The pain and sadness in these orphans could be caused by anything from a skinned knee to the twitching shakes of opium withdrawal.

Becky gently bumped the door open a bit more and peered into the room beyond. There they found a boy of about ten on his bed, arms at his side, head forward. His white sheet was wet from tears that had dripped off his cheeks. His shoulders shook, and he made little sound, save for great gulps of air and shaking breaths between sobs.

Molly and Becky stepped slowly, entering and crossing the room lined with empty beds except for that one. Molly sat on the side of the boy's bed and smiled. The nurse who had rushed from the room earlier entered again, saw Molly and Becky, and withdrew to give them a moment with the boy.

"Now," Molly said. "What's wrong here, lad?"

His eyes lifted to hers, and their pools of worry tugged at her heart.

"It's me legs. They won't work." He poked them with his fingers. "Can't feel nothin'." His head sagged forward again, and his shoulders drooped.

"That's a rough way to begin a day, if I've ever seen one." Molly gently rested a hand on his head. Though she thought her heart might break, she forced cheerfulness. "But it's not the only thing happening in this great day of ours, now, is it?"

He looked up at her, confusion flitting across his face.

"Not at all," Molly declared, answering herself. "From what I can see, you have a wonderful head that still works, now, don't you?"

He looked down at his legs again, shrugging. "But I ain't got no one to talk to."

Molly tilted her head to the side. "That is an easy problem to fix around here." She tapped the tip of his nose. "And you have a nose that works, though sometimes I've been hoping for a nose that is not so healthy, if you can imagine."

His cheeks lifted in a small smile. From the doorway, Thomas laughed, his eyes twinkling. "Just so. I wish never to have smelled my pa's burned eggs, for one."

Molly winked at Thomas, but when she continued, she spoke to the boy. "And your hands. Let me see those fingers."

The young boy held out his hands for examination.

She bent each finger, testing its mobility. "Yes, you have perfectly working hands."

He grinned. But after a moment, his lips curved downward and quivered. "Me mum—she didn't want me because of me legs." His tears began to fall anew.

Molly leaned forward and pulled him into her arms, holding him close and enveloping him the best she could with her love. "Sometimes a mum doesn't know what to do."

His body shook with the sobs of the broken.

Thomas stepped into the room, his face drawn, as the nurse returned and stood at the back of the room.

Molly spoke quietly to the nurse. "Would you please ask Jonathan and Sally to come here?"

"Of course." The nurse nodded and left the room again.

Thomas rested a hand on the boy's shoulder. "What's your name, lad?"

He lifted his head. "Peter."

"Well, now, Peter, we are going to introduce you to some new friends." Thomas indicated the door. "They'll bring fun in here sometimes when the others leave for their lessons. Would you like that?"

Peter sniffed and wiped his nose. "Yes."

"Now, as soon as you get well, I'm going to need some help around here." Thomas stood tall, tapping his chin.

His head dropped again. "I don't know what good I can do."

Thomas ruffled his hair. "I can think of a few things that need doing that require healthy arms and a good mind. You have those, don't you?"

His smile started small. "I do."

"Then you are just the person. So get well as soon as you can." He placed a hand on the lad's shoulder.

Peter nodded and wiped the last of his tears with his sleeve.

Jonathon and Sally came running into the room. They scrambled onto the bed and started talking straightaway with young Peter.

Molly reached for Thomas and squeezed his hand. "Thank you."

⌒

After a full morning and a brief lunch at the orphanage, Molly sat in a small office, used mostly by Mrs. Featherstone. The home needed a director. But the housekeeper served in both positions until they could find the right person.

Sometimes the home felt full of hope, but at other times, the problems facing the orphanage itself and the children inside it were so great Molly didn't know what more could be done to help. And that reality drained her energy.

The doctor who stopped in once a week had just finished explaining Peter's medical condition. A festering illness from earlier wounds had left him immobile, a condition that would last the rest of his days. No one had told the boy yet, and for now, Molly couldn't bring herself to insist he be told or to tell him herself. The doctor had left to see to the others, and she was alone with her thoughts. She let out a deep breath slowly then stood. She wanted to get outside. A brief walk was definitely needed before any other problem presented itself.

Molly was wrapping a shawl about herself when Becky noticed her. "Wherever you're going, I'm coming. I need a bit of air."

"Be quick and quiet about it," Molly said. "If Thomas notices, he'll want to come with us, but I just need a moment without him."

"Let him come," Becky said. "I do like looking at him. His arms and shoulders are as broad as pillars."

The frown came to Molly's face before she could stop it. "Broad as pillars. Is that all you care about? Seems to me that boys—or men, rather—possess other features, I mean *qualities* to notice."

Becky's laugh rang loud in the hallway until Molly shushed her. "Oh, stop. I don't see what's so funny."

"If you can't see it, I'm not the one to tell you." Becky grabbed her bonnet. "Now, let's get some air."

They hurried out onto the street, the cobblestones smooth from years of wear; the young women's boots skimmed the surfaces as they shuffled along. Molly planned to stay within four blocks, walking up and down the neighboring street, and nowhere else. Much of Manchester had become full of industry, and towering factories darkened the skyline, their smoke filling the air.

Other areas were just not safe for a young lady. Although a better part of town had been chosen for the children's home, a short distance in any direction brought higher levels of crime, impossibly poor living conditions, and desperate people.

Shortly after the pair exited the orphanage, the yelp of a young girl grabbed Molly's attention. A man hurried along the opposite side of the street, his hand tightly pulling a stumbling child along after him, much faster than her small legs could manage. Molly nudged Becky, but her eyes were already narrowed at the scene. Three other children followed behind the man, obeying his barking orders as they tried to keep up, their clothing shredded, their faces smudged with dirt, their skin pale, and their arms overly thin.

Becky and Molly shared a look and immediately moved to follow the group from their side of the street. Their brightly colored dresses stood out against the gray of the buildings and would draw attention to the maids, but they made no sound and stayed as close to the shadows as possible, allowing the group of five to gain some distance. Thomas would be sick with worry to know they followed the group without an escort, without anyone even knowing they had left.

"They can be up to no good," Becky whispered, a deep frown marring her creamy complexion. "I doubt that man is their father."

"Surely not," Molly agreed. "What with them all the same age, or nearly."

Minutes passed, and they continued to follow. The children tired, but the man pressed on, jerking them at times and cajoling at others. Molly's heart pinched tighter the farther they walked from the orphanage. The late-afternoon sun would soon fall behind the buildings.

The streets gradually became dirtier, the air dank and heavy. The sky darkened as the road narrowed, and buildings towered overhead.

Ducking into an alley, Molly whispered, "We're coming to a seedy and dangerous place. Let's watch from here."

"But what about the children?" Becky protested.

"We'll try and determine their path, and then we'll go for help."

"But—"

"I know," Molly interjected. "But we won't last a moment if we continue. We'll be plucked off the street in an instant. Already I am afraid to be this far."

Becky swallowed, nodding in reluctant agreement.

A towering black cloud belched from the factory and further darkened the air around them. They both stuck their heads out from the alley corner, peering around the grime-caked stone walls. Several blocks ahead a carriage pulled up, and the man ushered the children inside.

Molly's foreboding deepened. "And now we won't know where they've gone."

The stranger gave a loud whistle, searched the street all around him, and then checked his pocket watch. Shortly after, another group of six children were led to the carriage, and he ordered them inside.

Gasping, the maids nearly left their hiding place.

"We'll lose them for sure." Molly gripped Becky's arm. "What do we do?" She looked up and down the street, desperately, for anyone or anything that could help.

"We have to do something. Us." Becky took a step onto the street; Molly grabbed her arm, jerking her back into the alley, but she'd already been noticed.

The men gave a shout, and footsteps pounded in quick pursuit.

Molly grabbed Becky's hand tightly. "Run!"

The maids turned and raced down the alley behind them as fast as they could, but they were no match for the men behind them. One man soon overtook them and grabbed both about the arm in a tight grip of steel. Molly twisted to wrench free; his grip tightened, and she yelped in pain, the skin pinching and bruising under his fingers. She kicked and scratched him, shouting as loudly as she could. Becky soon followed suit, and the three created such a commotion a crowd from the alleys farther in gathered.

"Let go! Let go!" Molly snaked and contorted in such a way that the man was forced to release her. She ducked behind him and yanked a handful of his hair, trying to get him to loosen his grip on Becky. She was almost successful when a loud voice stopped their struggle altogether.

"What is the meaning of this? Let these fine women go."

A tall, overweight man stepped forward with four burly men accompanying him, two at his right and two at his left. His swollen hands were covered in gold, with multiple rings on each finger except his smallest. On it he wore a purple signet ring, which stood out from the amber gold of the others on his right hand.

"Run!" Molly again shouted.

Becky obeyed, and the two sped down the alley behind them, only to hit the solid chest of another man, who must have approached without their knowledge. Three others stood at his side, all of them large in girth, all of them frowning. They wore black working-class clothing—nothing fine about them. The girls were trapped, hemmed in.

"Now, now, lamb," the gold-clad man in front of them said. "Running won't be necessary. I know exactly what to do with you." His voice slid over them like the grease from Cook's lard sizzling in her pan. Molly's legs began to shake, and she struggled to stand straight and face him. But when she did, cold pits of darkness stared back, and she knew they were in trouble. She had seen the likes of him before.

CHAPTER SIX

Near Manchester, England
The Waterford Estate House Party

CHLOE SAT AT A LOVELY table, fresh flowers cascading out of the vessel in front of her. The weather had cooperated, gifting them a gloriously sunny, cool day. But she could not enjoy the light breeze, so nervous was she that someone might approach her. She held a cup at her lips but did not sip as she searched for Lady Amanda over the rim. She tapped her foot discretely under her skirts. Every moment Lady Amanda delayed increased the odds of Chloe having to converse with someone she hardly knew.

The tables set up outside encircled a pond and an arbor full of roses, offering plenty to distract Chloe while she waited for her friend. People stood together in small groups, laughing and smiling.

Avoiding people at social events was exhausting and seemed contrary to the purpose of having them, but Chloe preferred avoiding others to speaking with them. No matter the training and hours of practice she'd had with Miss Gracely; Chloe's palms grew damp at the thought of having to dream up something witty to say. Whenever her heart started racing, she panicked, and the most awkward things had a way of exiting her lips. If only someone would feel comfortable talking to her downturned face. A master of one-sided conversations—that would be the perfect social companion.

"There you are!" Lady Amanda called out while still several feet away.

Chloe nearly melted in relief and stood to meet her.

Lady Amanda's face lit when she talked, shining her love and friendship for Chloe so obviously that the latter couldn't help but return the smile. Lady Amanda leaned in and gave a quick hug. "How are you, my dear?" she whispered in her ear. "I got here as quickly as I could."

A friend before Chloe's shyness had begun, Lady Amanda could always be counted on to ease things for her.

"I'm doing well. No one has spoken with me yet. Well, except for Lady Wentley, who talked for many minutes of her bout with lung disease and subsequently the illnesses of all of her brothers and sisters."

"No conversation was necessary from you, I'd gather."

"For which I am most grateful." She linked her arm in Lady Amanda's. "Must everything be so formal all the time? I much prefer our days playing croquet on the lawn."

With one side of her mouth Amanda smirked. "Those glorious days were killed off by endless hours of needlepoint. I can trace most miseries in life to the day I had to learn needlepoint." She smiled into Chloe's face. "But I have you to thank for making those tedious hours less so."

Chloe's eyebrow rose in mockery. "I did grasp ability with a needle much quicker than you, I'm afraid." She bit her lower lip and eyed Amanda with a small smile. "You just never seemed to master the tinier designs." Then she burst into laughter. "Remember Aunt Polly's wedding? All those dreaded green flowers on the cream-colored gowns."

Amanda laughed loudly and suddenly then closed her mouth and turned to see who had heard.

Chloe's hand lifted to her own mouth to cover her snicker, and she leaned closer to her friend. "Your gown was so terrible; I am sorry."

Amanda waved her hand about. "I know! We had to hide it!"

Chloe wiped her tears. "Poor Aunt Polly."

"I don't think she ever figured out why she had to order a new gown. Thought she had miscounted. The poor dear."

Amanda moaned. "Stop. Remember the handkerchiefs? Yours was no better than mine. The first time Lord Annesley used one he stopped mid-sneeze to stare at it like this." She drew her eyebrows together so closely they almost touched. "He couldn't help but ask—in great confusion, mind you—'Have you stitched a wild boar? Ah—choo!'"

"A wild boar, indeed." Chloe rested a hand on her friend's arm in appreciation and tried to quiet her own laughter, which instead resulted in several unladylike and mortifying snorts. Chloe put her head on Amanda's shoulder and covered her mouth with both hands. Her body shook, her face turning red in an effort to control her mirth.

Amanda nudged her with the very shoulder she rested upon, grabbing Chloe's attention. Chloe glanced up to see her friend's eyes widen, her gaze lifting to somewhere above Chloe's head. Swallowing, no longer laughing at all now, Chloe turned, a small gasp escaping her lips before she dipped a quick curtsy. "Lord Annesley. Good to see you."

"Oh, don't stop the merriment on my account. The best kind of laughter comes with a snort or two." Then he laughed, too, as if he couldn't control himself, smiling largely with a wink at Lady Amanda.

Chloe frowned, her eyes still down as if searching the ground for her shoes. *Why must I always appear at a disadvantage?*

"Oh, come now, Lady Chloe, don't punish me so."

She dared a brief glance up and offered a small smile in response to his open kindness and searching eyes. Their color matched her own, a brilliant sky blue, only his shifted in shade depending on what he wore. They looked almost turquoise at the moment, and her breath caught at their brilliance. Her gaze found her shoes again, her toes poking out from underneath her wide, flowing skirts.

Lord Halloway arrived then, and Chloe's heart warmed to see the open love shared between him and Lady Amanda.

Chloe secretly wished to be so happily situated. The two teased and cajoled each other, sometimes mercilessly, but Chloe witnessed such solidarity between them, such love—devotion, even—that she had to swallow the lump in her throat. Call her sentimental, call her emotional, but she found it moving and beautiful.

Lord Halloway pounded his friend on the back. "Annesley, what brings you here today? I would think your father would still be needing you counting livestock or some other such activity this time of year."

"Counting livestock, indeed. Must we discuss such things in front of the ladies?"

Chloe felt his gaze on her again, and she spared a quick glance and another smile. She dared asked the question most on her mind. "Oh, but I'm interested in such things. Do you really count your animals?" Her face immediately warmed, and she wished she hadn't spoken.

But Annesley reached forward and lifted her fingers with his own, placing them on his forearm. "I am pleased to find someone—anyone, really, but especially someone as lovely as you, Lady Chloe—who is interested in the mundane dealings of my estate."

Amanda chuckled. "Oh, but Lady Chloe and I are not typical ladies."

Halloway chuckled beside her, but Annesley's arm tensed and shifted beneath Chloe's fingers. "You two are diamonds among women, no doubt. The best the *ton* has to offer, I'd wager."

Chloe wondered if her neck and throat were as red as her cheeks felt. What could he mean by complimenting her thus? Though she enjoyed it, she didn't know how to respond.

Her friend tipped her head in acknowledgment. "You are too kind. Too kind to me, at least, but you give an accurate portrayal of our dear Lady Chloe. You may well remember that she and I have participated in many activities not necessarily experienced by the other, shall we say, more *refined* ladies of the *ton*."

"Have you?" He tipped his head to the side, leaning down a little to catch Chloe's eyes. "From the maker of three-stone stew, I would expect nothing less."

She giggled and shared his gaze for a moment before turning a questioning look to Amanda, who nodded in encouragement.

"We cannot divulge all our secrets," Chloe said. "Of course you understand, but let's simply say we are familiar with diversions like fishing, games like toss the stick, and, dare I add"—she raised one eyebrow—"the tops of several large trees as well."

"Ho-ho! A fellow tree-climber. I am all amazement." He leaned closer to Chloe, who stood as still as possible. "Do you recall that one large tree at the front of Lady Amanda's estate?"

"Oh dear, yes; it is the very one Amanda and I climbed!" She forgot her shyness.

"To the top?" His mouth opened in mock astonishment.

She stood taller. "To be sure, yes. Rather, as high as we could scramble before our governesses, the both of them, came out of the house, faces red and blustery."

All four joined her in laughter. How delicious to be among childhood friends. She wished social interactions could always be this enjoyable. Her eyes met Lord Annesley's, and he winked. Her cheeks warmed in response, and her smile widened.

Applause from the front of the garden area interrupted them, and they turned their attention to an open-minded friend and member of their suffrage committee, Lady Bleeker, who was speaking.

"We thank you for coming in support of our dear children in the orphanages. As you are aware, the Manchester location gains new children every week. They are having much success in educating these young ones and placing them in homes."

In response, the guests again filled the garden with applause.

With her hand still on Lord Annesley's arm, Chloe leaned over to Amanda and whispered, "My Becky went with Molly to visit the Manchester orphanage. I'd like to visit myself one day, if I may."

Amanda nodded immediately. "Of course you may. Shall we tour the one in London first on our return?"

Chloe felt Lord Annesley watching her but tried to ignore her new awareness of his attention. "I'd like that, yes."

Lady Amanda shifted her attention to include Lord Annesley. "I must make a bumble of myself in just a moment."

The roses formed such a lovely background for Lady Bleeker as she continued. "And now, for further details on what more we can do for these needy children, Lady Amanda has asked to share a few words."

"And here it is," Amanda said. She made her way to the front of the group, all smiles.

Some of the women shifted uncomfortably and tittered to one another behind their hands. Amanda's work for the orphanages was well received, if her suffrage efforts were not. But she outranked everyone present, so they showed her the respect her status merited as the daughter of a duke and soon-to-be duchess herself. At least, they did so outwardly.

"Has anyone seen the latest fliers?" Amanda asked.

Small bursts of conversation erupted, a few happy titters here and there. The men of the group especially seemed to appreciate this topic. Satirical drawing, a growing trend of the past decade, was something Chloe was just now beginning to appreciate. They had begun as lighthearted parodies of specific members of the *ton*, but now, with the addition of a cartoonist who called himself the Sparrow, the cartoons had turned to more political subjects.

Amanda continued. "The Sparrow got right to the point this time, didn't he?" She held up a recent flier. "The cartoon shows a man as a good political ally for women, standing beside a lady and leading her through the crowd to come forward to make her vote."

Chloe's admiration for her friend grew as she watched her step forward and bravely support both the orphanage and the suffrage movement. But not everyone would. Caring about such things wasn't *au mode*.

Murmuring followed Lady Amanda's description of the cartoon, and a few women frowned. The men with them shook their heads subtly and talked in low voices to each other. Some of the women brought their hands to their open mouths and glanced around to see the reactions of others. But some, a very few, nodded in agreement and some smiled openly, clapping and encouraging Lady Amanda, who paused.

She placed a finger on her chin. "I like the drawing, mind you, but I can't figure out what he hopes she will vote for. Will we have a say in the timing of the royal events at Vauxhall Gardens, perhaps?"

The nodding women continued and now smiled as well. A few clapped softly in support.

"Well, whatever the cause, women should have a say in it. I thought this piece to be quite entertaining. And now, for subject matter of my speech, the orphanages . . ." She looked around the garden and winked at Chloe.

Lady Amanda continued rallying for support of the orphanages. Chloe appreciated her strength and fire and respected and admired her efforts. She suspected Amanda felt much more strongly about the issues she spoke of than she revealed. Yet she always spoke without embarrassment, no matter how many people she addressed. She almost seemed to enjoy the attention. Chloe couldn't imagine a circumstance in which she would ever enjoy having so many people looking at her at once. If they ever did focus all attention on her, she surely wouldn't know what to say and the first thing to come out of her lips would most assuredly be something foolish.

Annesley whispered into her ear. "She certainly has a way with people, does she not?"

A thrill went up Chloe's spine at his nearness. She nodded. "A skill I envy."

He moved close to her ear again. "You also have a way with people, Lady Chloe. It's different but just as affecting."

She turned to him in suspicion but saw such earnestness in his face that she could only smile. "Thank you." She hoped he would continue his attentions but was unsure how to encourage him. "You are enjoyable too." She bit her lip and searched the ground for the toe of her shoe. Why did she *never* have clever words to say?

He placed his hand over her own on his arm.

As Lady Amanda encouraged giving aid to the orphans, Chloe's mind wandered. She wasn't sure she wanted the right to vote. Her parents, like many others, had focused her education on the more feminine subjects. She could quote poetry and excelled in her grasp of the romantic languages, but she knew very little of current happenings in the government or even any of the responsibilities the lords of estates took upon themselves or gave to their stewards.

If given the opportunity to vote, would she be able to do so responsibly? Her brow furrowed as she thought more on the matter.

"Why the troubled and ponderous expression, my lady?"

"Oh. I'm sorry. I was only thinking." She removed her hand from Annesley's arm and began wringing her hands together.

"I did not want to lose your attention. Forgive me for being so inquisitive." His eyes showed tender caring, the likes of which Chloe had never seen in them before.

She returned her hand to his forearm, and a warmth tingled in her fingers.

She decided to be brave and express to Annesley her thoughts. Perhaps he'd understand. "I am unsure if I know enough to be able to properly participate in suffrage myself. I would like for women to have the opportunity, especially if Lady Amanda desires it. But I'm afraid I'd make the wrong choice." She bit her lip, and her brow furrowed further. Her eyes sought his, turned away, and then returned to his, searching for his reaction.

Lord Annesley's head tilted to the side and he studied her for a moment, a hint of concern crossing his eyes, and then a small smile graced his lips before he responded. "Now, Lady Chloe, I'm wagering a guess, but I think you're an excellent judge of character. You are an attentive watcher of persons, are you not?"

Chloe pressed her fingertips into his arm. "I have been told that, yes. I enjoy listening more than speaking, you see."

"Right there, you are years ahead of many in the House of Lords and those voting in the House of Commons. The ability to listen is a gift to be prized. And because of that, I would value your vote in selecting those to make decisions in the government. Britain has been lacking your voice all these years, and therefore, we simply cannot trust those who are currently chosen to make laws for us."

Chloe couldn't help herself. She giggled.

Annesley continued. "I haven't always felt this way, mind you. But the more time I spend with Lord Halloway the more I agree with his confounded idealism." He searched the crowd and stopped when he saw his friend. "He and Lady Amanda both claim that the more people who have a voice the better our country will be because the people who are truly free turn back to bless the land they call home."

Chloe listened with rapt attention. She'd never heard suffrage expressed in such a way. Her heart beat in her chest, and her hands longed to be active, but she stilled them, keeping one on Annesley's arm.

He shifted his feet. "We are missing influence from half of our population. The gentler, more thoughtful half. And I feel we suffer for it." He used his finger to raise Chloe's chin so she could see into his eyes. "Trust your instincts; trust your ability to see things as no one else can, and rest assured in the knowledge that your voice is needed."

Searching Annesley's eyes, slowly breathing in so as not to break the spell, she wondered at his confidence in her. He spoke of qualities she'd recognized in herself as a young girl but had disbelieved since coming out in society. Did her voice matter to the course of events in her beautiful country? She tried to calm her breathing, but her feet fidgeted, dancing in place under her skirts. Unable to keep her expression mild, within acceptable constraints, she grinned a large, happy smile.

"Thank you, Lord Annesley."

Chuckling, he searched her face. "You are quite welcome, and further—"

Whatever he was about to say was interrupted by a footman appearing at Chloe's side, with an outstretched slip of paper.

Becky has gone missing. A search has been made, an attempt to find her, but as of yet, we have found no leads. Please advise our course of action. Thomas.

She clutched Annesley's arm, alarmed. Fear gripped her. The note was addressed to anyone in her household. "What should I do?"

She searched the crowd. She'd come to the garden party alone today, the other members of her family resting from the late-night ball of the previous evening.

"What has happened? Allow me?" Annesley reached for Chloe's note, which she handed to him without responding, unsure what to do next.

Amanda and Halloway rushed toward her, a similar paper in Amanda's hand. "Molly's missing." Pointing to the note in Annesley's hand, she asked, "Becky also?"

Chloe nodded, shaken. Her knees trembled beneath her skirts, and she leaned onto Lord Annesley's arm for support. "What is to be done?"

"You are amongst friends who know how to give assistance in situations such as this," Annesley assured her, and his confidence gave her strength.

She turned to the footman, immediately missing the support of Lord Annesley's arm. "See that this note is delivered to my father's bedchamber. Tell him Lords Halloway and Annesley are aware also."

Halloway's face lacked its usual sparkle; creases ran across his forehead, and his mouth flattened into a straight line. "Our note has little information. Thomas wrote that Molly and Becky had left for a short walk around the immediate streets near the orphanage. He blames himself for not following them."

"You know dear Thomas." Amanda's brow wrinkled in her worry. "He'll have no peace until they are found."

Halloway placed the paper into his coat pocket and looked at Annesley. "I could use your assistance."

"Of course. What do you need me to do?"

"Come with me to the orphanage. It is not far from here."

"When?"

"As soon as we can. On the hour."

"Of course." Annesley nodded. The two men began speaking quietly to themselves, seeming to forget everyone around them.

Amanda moved closer to Chloe. "I'm so worried about Molly. She often acts before she thinks. Manchester is not the safest place. She could have stumbled into all manner of trouble there."

"And I fear Becky would follow Molly wherever she led," Chloe added.

They both remained silent for a moment, though a tightness grew in Chloe's chest, larger by the second. She took a deep breath and slowly released it, hoping to loosen the knot. She turned to Amanda. "I'd like to help find them."

Her friend eyed her in pleasant surprise. "I was thinking the same thing—planning on it, actually, and hoping to situate myself in the carriage before Nathaniel realized what I was about." Her mouth lifted in a wry grin.

"I'll come with you. I cannot bear the thought of Becky being lost somewhere in the streets of Manchester without friends or assistance. I don't know what good I can do, but I want to be there and, well, I want to *notice* things, to help find them in some way."

"Happily the house party is much closer to Manchester than we would be if we were in London."

"I'll gather a few things and meet you." Chloe felt eyes on her, so she slowly turned around. Both men had paused their conversation and watched the women closely.

"You're not thinking of coming." Lord Halloway stiffened, watching his wife.

Annesley stepped close enough the air shimmered with expectation between them. "Lady Chloe, I fear for your safety." He reached for her hand again. "Besides, what could you hope to accomplish by going on such a risky venture? I would never support your coming, were I your father. We don't know what dangers we may encounter."

Tears filled Chloe's eyes. The effect of his conversation earlier that had been so enlightening and empowering was nearly washed from memory as new doubts entered her heart, plaguing her, freezing her into inactivity. Annesley was right.

"What *good* could she do?" Amanda's weight shifted as if she'd actually stomped her foot.

Halloway must have noticed because he reached for her elbow with a gentle touch.

But Amanda blazed on. "What could she *not* do, if given a chance? Her keen, sharp, listening ears and analytical mind would probably discern Becky's and Molly's whereabouts much sooner than anyone else's."

Chloe smiled in gratitude to Amanda but said, "Thank you, but he's right. I don't know myself what my purpose would be in coming along." At once, noticing things seemed such a weak addition to the endeavor.

"I do," Amanda retorted. "And our efforts will all benefit if you're present."

The men opened their mouths at the same time, ready to refute her, but Lady Amanda held up a hand to them. "Gentlemen, I hope you are prepared for *my* company. If Lady Chloe's father gives her permission to come, will you prevent her?"

Amanda's face must've been fearsome because both men swallowed, looked away from her, looked back at her, and even though Lord Annesley's expression still revealed hesitance, they both shook their heads.

Halloway pulled his wife closer to him. "Let us converse about this more inside while Edwards is packing my things. I feel we will not be returning to the party but will journey from the orphanage back to London."

Her mouth thinned into a line, but she nodded and said, "Of course."

Chloe knew that with Lord and Lady Halloway as chaperones, her father was sure to grant permission. He'd certainly send a footman to aid in the search also.

But the rising tension in her stomach and her racing thoughts all grew so uncomfortable that part of her wished her father wasn't quite so amiable, that he would instead forbid her assistance. An uneasiness took over that would not be quieted. What if the maids had found themselves in true danger?

CHAPTER SEVEN

THE WALLS OF THE ALLEY hemmed the maids in. Molly struggled to take
in a breath through the tightness in her chest. Surrounded by men she
didn't know, she tried to concentrate, to think of a way out. When Molly
caught Becky's eye, she would have laughed had their circumstances not
been so treacherous. Her friend had lowered her brows so much that
her brown eyes were almost invisible under them, and she scowled at
their new captor. Her fists had turned white from clenching them. No
cowering, scared miss, Becky proved to be a brave companion while
Molly's own knees shook underneath her skirts.

"Come now, these ladies are not our prisoners." The strange new
leader waved his gold-laden fingers at his men.

Molly cleared her throat. "Thank you, sir. If we are free to go, I
know our companions will be worried about us, so we'd best be on our
way." She took Becky's hand, and they both moved forward. Pretending
not to be intimidated, they sidestepped past the guards, making their
way back toward the street.

A deep, rumbling laugh chilled them and stopped them in their steps.

"Ho-ho. Now, now ladies. No one is in a hurry here. We hoped you
would stay for a bit as our guests. Perhaps we could give you a tour of
our neighborhood, show you about the place."

"No tour will be necessary," Molly said bravely. "We'll be on our way
now." Her answering chuckle sounded forced and nervous even to her
own ears.

A chill wind blew through the alley, rustling her skirts. She inched
forward, counting heartbeats; the alley met the street to her front—just

a few feet more—taunting. Molly and Becky moved faster, almost past the last guard until he reached out abruptly with a large and hairy arm, blocking their way.

Molly ran into it with her nose. "Oh! Ouch!" She backed away.

The leader's voice oiled its greasy response behind her. "Come now, back over here where I can see you better."

He spoke to his men. "We should introduce ourselves to our guests." The overweight man removed his top hat, revealing a balding hairline, and bowed in a gallant flourish. "I am Theodore. Most here call me Theo."

Surely he does not expect me to curtsy.

"Only Theo? You have no surname?" Molly turned to face him fully. Perhaps if she could just talk him out of this. Fighting a rising panic, she forced herself to look at him.

"Theo is all the name anyone needs to know." He smiled, but no light reached his eyes.

Becky stomped her foot and called out, "We are not without friends. We are in the employ of a duke and an earl, mind you. They won't take too kindly to our coming up missing, they won't."

Molly wished Becky would learn to control her tongue. Sometimes their association with nobility was best kept quiet.

"A duke and an earl, you say?" He ran a hand up and down his beard. His great laugh echoed in the alley and made the girls jump. "All the more reason for us to become acquainted, now, isn't it?"

The tight feeling in Molly's chest grew and spread to her stomach.

The sky had grown dark. Thomas would be out searching for them by now. That thought warmed her but with little hope. No one would expect them to be so far away or within the streets of the seedier slums of Manchester, in the very den of the worst crime bosses in England. Thinking of Jack Bender, the vilest man of Molly's acquaintance, she recognized his likeness in the evil that stood before her and was glad to be rid of him. She swallowed and commanded her voice to sound strong.

"We are on their errand, and as the hour grows late, I am certain they will be about, searching the streets for us."

"Then, let us move inside, where the fire can warm us, and we shall become better acquainted."

He lifted a finger in the guards' direction, and the two closest to Molly and Becky nudged them forward. When the women, of one mind, hesitated, a strong grip tightened on Molly's upper arm, and Becky gasped as the other guard surely did the same to her. Reaching for Becky's hand at her side, Molly squeezed it, offering as well as seeking reassurance, and stepped forward.

An awful, dark feeling started in her chest and threatened to consume her. Molly sensed such an icy, slippery air around Theo. She suspected he had no warmth or mercy in him. The guard tightened his hand on her arm even more, points of pressure from his fingers bruising her skin.

"Really, sir, must we be manhandled in this way? Surely we can walk without assistance."

Theo, who had been several steps ahead of them, turned his head and nodded. Promptly her arm was freed, and Becky turned to her with a relieved smile.

Within a few steps, much sooner than Molly was prepared, they reached a dark-gray door with a crest on the front. So small as to be almost unnoticeable, in the upper right corner looked to be a coat of arms similar to that of the royal family but not quite the same. On either side of the blue-and-orange shield were two animals holding it up with their paws, one a ridiculously spotted panther with fire coming out of its ears and the other a green dragon. Molly wasn't certain, but she felt like she'd seen the crest somewhere before.

The men ushered her and Becky into a musty room with a flickering candle illuminating the small space. The two girls sat closely on a small settee, which was worn but clean. They clasped their hands. Molly swallowed the panic rising in her throat, and she took several deep breaths, feeling some of the tightness leave her with each exhale. When Theo entered the room, however, he sat in the nearest possible chair to them, and the tightness returned full force. He leaned forward and patted Molly on the knee. Her body jerked involuntarily, and she scooted away, pressing into Becky's side.

He chuckled. "Now, now, no need to be alarmed or frightened. So skittish, like a new filly." His eyes gleamed as he looked her over, leaving Molly with a distinct urge to make use of a washbasin, a bar of strong lye, and several buckets of scalding-hot water.

"What do you want with us?" Becky's frown had returned, and she gripped Molly's hand so tightly she was liable to crush it. Molly marveled at Becky's courage.

Theo played with the top of his beard on his chin, running his hand down the front as if to comb it flat. The beard refused to be tamed. As soon as his finger passed, it bounced up and outward, a mass of gray and red curls below his mouth. He sat back in his chair, comfortable and calm. "We would like to offer you our hospitality for a time. Hopefully not for too long, but for a time—as long as it takes for your visit to be profitable, I suppose."

Molly's alarm grew. "And if we refuse?" Questions flew through her mind. "We are not at leisure to simply disappear for a time. Surely you understand that. Perhaps we can complete whatever it is you desire of us so that we may quickly return to our responsibilities." She stared him in the eyes and hid her fear as far beneath her other emotions as possible, sensing that this man capitalized on fear, fed off it. And through others' fear he ruled his kingdom, whatever it may be.

"Well now, the length of your stay with us depends entirely on how well you answer my questions and how eager your employers will be to encourage your return to them."

Becky leaned forward. "You leave them out of this. The House of Wessex is nothing but kindness and gentility."

Molly pressed her foot onto Becky's, but Becky ignored her.

"Ah, the House of Wessex, is it? Old Archibald, the Earl of Wessex himself?"

Becky gasped.

"Hush, Becky," Molly scolded.

Theo ran his hand along the hair at his chin one more time. "I'm sure the earl can be reasoned with. I have hope for an early departure—for you, at least." He said the last to Becky specifically and then turned to Molly. "Now, if your friend here works for the earl, you must work for the duke. Which duke might I contact about your whereabouts?"

Molly's eyes narrowed into slits. Nothing would make her drag Lady Amanda and Lord Halloway into this mess. She lifted her chin. "I don't know what you're talking about. I work in the dockyards doing odd jobs. No one would even know or care—"

"And yet, you were so concerned about your employers." He shook his head and tsked. "You will find this whole ordeal will be much easier if you simply cooperate. I am a better host, a better ally, and a better protector when my guests work with me."

Molly shrugged. "I have nothing to tell you. Earlier I was merely speaking in defense of my friend." She hoped that if Becky were to be released, others would be led to find her. She'd seen the reach of the duke's arms. His family and the earl's would communicate, and their combined influence would likely enable her release. At a suggestion men bowed before any duke. The law had no hold on him, and nothing stood in his way. Molly hid her smile at the flicker of hope she felt.

"Defiance will be peeled off you layer by layer until you acquiesce." Theo's voice jarred her. Where before his voice had dripped with honey in gentle, warm, encouraging tones it now rasped with anger. His eyes were darker, his face redder, his lips larger, spittle resting on them.

Molly's hands shook, but she refused to show any change in her expression. Another breath and she managed to return his gaze. She stared, unfeeling and cold, into his eyes.

He sat back in his chair. "And now for the other aspect of your cooperation. I have some questions for you."

Molly waited, wary.

"What were you doing on my street, making all that racket? Who were you running from?"

Becky tilted her head, eyebrows raised. "What do you mean *your* street? Do you own it?"

Theo proudly held his arms out wide. "These are my people, my children. They look to me as their provider, and I care for them as my offspring. I provide food, clothes, and entertainment, and they work for me. Each person has a job, a purpose, and each is rewarded for such." His eyes flitted to Molly's. "Or punished, as necessary." She felt a cold pit open in her stomach.

Becky leaned forward. "We came upon your street quite by accident. Those men were chasing us, and we hoped to evade them by running into the alley."

Dear Becky. If they ever had a moment alone in all this mess, Molly would counsel her to reveal less—as little as possible.

"Running from men. And who were these men?"

Molly shrugged. "We'd never seen them before."

"And we did not stop to discover why they were after us." Becky folded her arms across her chest and eyed him. "How did you come to our rescue with such impeccable timing? Our circumstances now are much more comfortable than they would have been had we been caught for whatever nefarious purpose they intended."

Theo laughed loudly, with his belly, such that Molly might have found the sound contagious had she not also suffered from gooseflesh breaking out all over her arms at the sound. No mirth, no joy emanated from it. She wondered why he made the effort at all.

"My dear, you *are* in much better circumstances now than you would have been. I imagine this sitting room is preferable to the bottom of the Irk River."

Becky gasped and brought a hand up to her throat. "They would not have—"

"Oh, they certainly would have. But I am still trying to ascertain their identities. So if you could indulge me, tell me what you know about your pursuers. Surely they had some reason for their interest in you."

Molly felt her suspicions heighten. Theo knew much more about them than he let on. "We are not so naïve as to not understand what men might hope to gain from two women cornered in a dark alley."

"I do not underestimate you, my dear." Theo eyed her. "But you must not assume the worst of me. You need my good will in order to return home."

Perhaps he sought to discover how much she and Becky knew about those men and their actions with the children, how much the two troublesome maids had seen. She suspected they'd stumbled upon Theo's own men. Molly thought to divulge something as a ruse at cooperation.

"A group of people were gathered around a carriage in the square several streets over—a family of sorts. A group of children and their fathers were all climbing into a carriage. They glanced in our direction, and then they gave a shout and burst into such a run toward us with such a look of venom on their faces that we turned about posthaste, and, not even choosing our direction, hurried down every street we came upon."

She paused and managed a small smile. "If not for your intervention, who knows what might have happened? We owe you great thanks."

Theo rubbed his forehead, studying her face. He did not appear completely satisfied, but he said, "You're welcome. Angel Meadow is mine. I try to keep my streets safe, protect the people who live within these blocks. They perform services for me in exchange for my protection. It is a splendid arrangement, a careful balance I cannot have interrupted by those men—or anyone."

He flicked a piece of lint off his pant leg and then stood, grunting. "But I delay. Your room is at the back of that hall. You will have food and water. You will not leave. You will not make undue noise." He eyed them both in turn and gestured, indicating his men who hovered about the room. "Or you will regret it. I will return when we have heard any news from your illustrious earl."

A great crash sounded at the front of the house. A moment later two more guards entered, restraining a kicking, writhing person. One guard pinned the man's arms together while the second immobilized his feet. When the prisoner stopped resisting, Molly gasped in recognition. This was the brute who'd chased them into the alley, who'd tried to usher the children into the carriage.

"Show the ladies how we treat intruders." Theo turned to Molly and Becky, who had stepped as far away from the struggle as they could. "Watch."

Molly shook her head but did not turn away.

At a flick of Theo's hand, the two guards held the victim upright, while another sent a fist deep and hard into his gut. Molly yelped at the first impact. A steady succession of hits followed, to his stomach, his side, and across his face. Shortly into the beating the new prisoner drooped, consciousness gone. Molly's heart calmed slightly, and she was glad that at least the man was unconscious. But the guard kept pummeling him. When one fist connected with his face again, she winced at the sound of crunching bones.

"Oh, stop. Please! Leave him be." Molly clung to Becky, who whimpered at her side.

Theo lifted two fingers. "Enough." Then he reached into his jacket pocket for a tin of snuff.

Becky shook with her tears. Molly swallowed again and again but could not rid her throat of the shard lodged there or of the rising panic in her breathing. Never had she seen such brutal force enacted on another human.

Rotating his shoulders and flexing his fingers, the guard turned from his victim and moved toward them. They shrank away. He walked past and grunted, "Follow me."

CHAPTER EIGHT

LORD ANNESLEY CHECKED HIS TIMEPIECE again as he returned from his short walk about the grounds and approached the front of the Waterfords' home. The footman had finished loading his trunks an hour previous. The hint of danger had brought forward all Annesley's spy instincts, and he had worked with the quick proficiency of a professional. And then, even though he was ready to move forward, his efforts were stalled at the incredible inefficiency of the civilian nobility. Friends though they were, he found it difficult to slow to their pace in matters of urgency.

Loud voices from inside the study gave him pause. The window was slightly ajar, and Lady Amanda's exasperation carried to him. "You know how I feel about this, Nathaniel."

"Of course I do, but the situation is different. We must be even more careful now that you are with child again."

"As if that changes my ability to walk around Manchester. Come now, Nathaniel. I have always been careful. All our children have been born healthy, and I am well."

Annesley entered the house so he was out of earshot. The conversation was clearly not meant for his hearing. He grinned to himself. They were expecting another child. Good news for his friends.

Lady Amanda was a wonderful, beautiful, engaging woman. And she was full of fire—an excellent quality in a friend, but it was not something Annesley would want to live with every day, especially during disagreements like the one they were all involved in. And Annesley was in complete agreement with Halloway.

No one knew how the maids had disappeared. Annesley remained unsure the orphanage itself was a safe place. If Lady Chloe and Lady

Amanda joined Lord Halloway and himself in a visit to the orphanage, he couldn't run a search of the surrounding area in Manchester *and* ensure their safety at the orphanage, and it concerned him. Even though Lady Amanda felt unhappy, the women's safety came first in his mind. He would prefer an unhappy friend to one in harm.

The door of the study swung outward, slamming into the wall of the entry hall behind it. Lady Amanda stormed out, cheeks flushed and fists clenched. She brushed past Annesley with a curt, "Hello, Lord Annesley," and continued down the hall, away from him.

Halloway exited the study and stood beside him, watching her go. Annesley rested a hand on his shoulder, studying his face. Annesley felt a chuckle brewing just below the surface. "You—you look as you did during your first meeting in the House of Lords, when they harassed you for your radical ideas."

Halloway rubbed a hand over his face and then mussed his hair. "She wishes to come look for the maids. She and Molly are close, but of course, according to her, when I try to dissuade her, it is evidence I don't appreciate how she would benefit the search."

A protective ire rose inside Annesley. He would not endanger Lady Chloe or Lady Amanda. "Joining the party can't be safe for them."

"I wholly agree and have expressed as much." He tipped his head toward the hallway where Lady Amanda retreated. "She has a history of running to assist in any way possible but with little thought of the consequences."

"From what I've heard, she's been rather successful at that." Annesley shook his head in wonder. No doubt he didn't know the half of it, but from what little he'd heard, Lady Amanda actively worked to help the working classes, which had involved her getting into more than a few dangerous scrapes.

"Her past successes give little credence to my efforts to protect her now. She brought down a gang trying to do harm to Lord Liverpool—with help, mind you, but even so."

"With *your* help, I'm sure." Grinning, Annesley faced him. "You're a brave man, Halloway."

His friend chuckled. "I wouldn't have it any other way. I hope you, too, will find a woman who fascinates you in every way." He lifted up the corner of his mouth. "And pushes and stretches you to your utmost limits."

Could he picture himself with someone like Lady Amanda? Perhaps, but Lady Chloe's gentle nature and sweet disposition entered his thoughts more strongly and warmed him down to his toes.

Lord Annesley's answering grin felt unnaturally tight. He checked his pocket watch again and asked, "Shall we be off, then?"

Halloway nodded. "I'm sure the carriages are loaded by now. I had Edwards pack up as if I were intending to go home. I don't know how long the search will take, and the house party will likely be over by then anyway."

The two accepted their top hats, cloaks, and canes from the butler. The air had a bit of crisp chill to it and smelled of winter.

At last we are departing, Annesley thought. *Would that we had done so two hours ago.* Walking down the front stairs, he turned to Lord Halloway.

"We can at least be thankful they became lost so close to the Waterford house party. This search would be dashedly more difficult from London." He stepped into the carriage, and his eyes had to adjust to the darker interior, where two outlines became two women seated inside. He stopped. How she had managed to situate herself so comfortably inside when only minutes ago she had been storming into the interior of the house he would love to discover. "Lady Amanda, Lady Chloe."

Halloway bumped into him from behind, reminding him to keep moving. Annesley hid the immediate spark of impatience and sat on the bench opposite the women. Having at last left the house, they might now be caught in the continued discussion and be stalled in the carriage.

Lady Amanda lifted her chin, back rigid and straight, her mouth in a flat line. Lady Chloe sat at her right, mimicking her posture.

In spite of himself, Annesley chuckled before he could bite the inside of his cheek.

Chloe's eyes snapped over to his, her expression filled with such a look of fire and determination that he sat back on his bench, struck by the emotion and drive he sensed rolling off her. A new wealth of admiration filled him, and he became immediately more intrigued and curious about the lovely Lady Chloe.

Halloway's face remained blank, but his eyes turned to steel.

Amanda returned his stare with strength in her own, but then her expression softened, her forehead relaxed, and one side of her mouth lifted. "We are so close to the orphanage. I need to inspect the school anyway, and it would be wonderful to take this opportunity to give Chloe a tour. She and her father would be a blessing as we look for more patrons."

Halloway moved closer, earnest. He said quietly, "Very well. You will stop at the home with us. But please, stay *inside* the orphanage. Grant me that *one* request. Do not go running about, trying to find Molly yourself."

Annesley looked away, feeling as though he were intruding.

"Yes, of course." Lady Amanda then leaned back on the bench, a tiny smile on her lips as she reached for Chloe's hand.

Halloway turned away, and Amanda studied her lap. A great awkward silence settled on them all.

Annesley sighed. No need to endure this uncomfortable heaviness that had descended on them all. "Well, if we are to have stowaways, these are two of the loveliest in my acquaintance. Shall we limit them to crackers and water? Throw them into the brig, I wonder?"

Lady Amanda and Halloway laughed, but not Chloe. She returned his gaze with a fierce one of her own.

Not forgiven, then. He had been overly blunt in his urging her to stay away from the orphanage.

Halloway moved to sit beside him on the otherwise empty bench. "Thank you for aiding us, Annesley. Molly is one of our best servants, but she is also a huge help to the campaign and a dear friend besides."

"And Becky too," Chloe said quietly.

He nodded in acknowledgment.

All this for their servants. Annesley's respect for his friends grew, and he leaned back on the carriage bench. "No one would ever confuse the lot of you with those who abuse and torment their staff." Pointing up at the front to where the driver was sitting, he said, "Let's be off now, shall we?"

The carriage lurched forward when Lord Halloway rapped on the ceiling, as if the horses shared Lord Annesley's eagerness to be off.

"I think dear Annesley will wither before us from the duress of waiting." Lady Amanda chuckled.

"Oh yes, I'm sure he has been ready to depart for hours already, impatient as we all know him to be." Halloway grinned, catching Chloe's eye.

She eyed Annesley skeptically, still refusing to be amused.

"I am nothing of the kind," Annesley said. "Naturally, I want to be in the carriage and moving if that is what we are about." He eyed them all. "If our purpose were to be sitting about on the lawn, I could do so most willingly, without the least complaint."

Halloway snorted.

"I could," Annesley protested. "This very afternoon, for example. I waited and sat and meandered for hours on end with you—"

The other three passengers began quietly chuckling.

"I did. If you recall, we discussed Lady Haverly's new bonnet and our costumes for the masquerade ball at great length."

Lady Amanda hid a smile behind her hand, but the others burst out laughing.

"What's the matter with all of you?" Annesley crossed his arms over his chest.

Lady Chloe joined the conversation. "I hope we didn't injure you with our bland conversation."

They laughed harder.

"Nothing's the matter," Lady Amanda said. "However, I don't remember you sitting placidly at the party." Lady Amanda leaned near Lady Chloe, and they giggled together.

"Or sitting placidly anywhere." Halloway pounded him on the back. "One of the things we most like about you, man. Your feet are always active, your hands occupied, and your brain turning with all manner of thoughts."

"And your mouth is always moving." Lady Chloe covered her own with her hands, her face reddening at once.

Charming. Her humor lit her face. He winked at her. "Do I talk too much, Lady Chloe?"

"Don't pester her so." Lady Amanda scowled at him.

Lady Chloe placed a hand on Lady Amanda's arm. "No, I am quite all right."

So pleased she responded, Annesley had tried to only casually take note of her comment so as not to frighten her into silence.

"You don't talk too much, no," Lady Chloe said. "I enjoy listening to you. I never have to think of what to say—ever, really—because you do go on." She quirked an eyebrow at him.

She was charming. And witty. She urged a great belly laugh from him without his realizing it. And her face glowed with pleasure watching him.

The carriage turned onto the main road, and the sound of the driver urging the horses forward brought a calming balm to the awkward atmosphere inside. The ladies were no doubt grateful to be present on the journey at all. Annesley felt relieved to finally be moving, and Halloway . . . well, though he didn't speak, Halloway did not seem calm at all. His brow wrinkled, and he stared out the window. A purposeful silence hung about him like the gray of a rain cloud.

♍

Chloe calmed her breathing, resting a hand at her stomach. The carriage pulled in front of the orphanage. Before it came to a full stop Lord Halloway jumped from his seat and out the door, with Lord Annesley not far behind him, although in their hurry they did stop to offer a hand to the ladies.

Lady Amanda waved them off. "We are quite well. Go inside. Thomas looks as though he's about to head the cavalry himself."

The Halloways' loyal footman Thomas waited just outside of the weathered orphanage home. His face was lined with worry. The house looked worn, which, from what Chloe understood, was part of the design and disguise. The Halloways hoped to hide the depth of their pockets from most others in the neighborhood to keep attention turned away from them as much as possible.

Thomas greeted the men with a bow, his face stern and tense, his eyes pinched together in a manner Chloe had never seen in them before. His concern for Molly was obvious to all, and Chloe hoped for the best for them both, if only Molly and Becky would be returned to them quickly.

She and Lady Amanda alighted from the carriage at a slower pace and directed the footmen to place their parcels and a trunk inside the house. The ladies caught up to the men, who preceded them into a library, and heard Thomas's next words. The men leaned over a map on the desk.

"We've circled the immediate premises the map shows here, again and again, I tell you. She's not here or anywhere close by."

"I understand, and we know our Molly. Thank you for what you've done already. Something must have distracted her and she went farther than usual. We will have to broaden our search. I am meeting a Bow Street Runner within the hour to get his opinion on the matter. Until then, I'd like to take a look myself, if I might. Do we have a map of the broader Manchester area that I might study to become familiar with our surroundings?"

He will go searching himself?

Lord Halloway always surprised Chloe with the efforts he was willing to make and the work he did—things most lords would never do.

Annesley stepped forward to grab a scroll, likely another map. "We should start looking inside a greater, outside loop. I feel the locations nearest will offer no useful information."

Lord Annesley will go with him? Warmth filled Chloe to think of his goodness, which was so unlike most of the lords of her acquaintance. How many did she know who would instead send other servants to search?

"Right here." Immediately Lord Halloway cleared the desk and unrolled a map, a grid of maze-like streets and alleys. The enormity of the ground that must be searched, the incredible spiderlike labyrinth that lay before them, drained Chloe's hopes to such a degree that tears came to her eyes. She tried to blink them back, but when Amanda sidled up next to her in comfort, she could not prevent their progress down her cheeks.

Suddenly at her side, Lord Annesley offered his handkerchief. She glanced up to thank him but stopped at the tenderness expressed in his eyes. Something in him saw past the tears to somewhere deeper inside her, acknowledging and understanding her pain. He smiled and then stepped back to the table, where Lord Halloway ran his finger along the many streets of Manchester, asking for clarification about their current location and discussing options on how to divide the search.

Thomas stood at his side and pointed out the orphanage. "And these are the streets we've already combed, up and down, all day; the owners and tenants are aware and willing to help. They're good neighbors to the orphanage, and for the most part, we trust them."

He moved his finger, pointing farther to the north. "But these outer streets we know little about. Farther out in all directions, the neighborhoods become less safe, less friendly. Somewhat seedy, even. Out here, starting here"—he pointed at a largely unmapped section labeled *Angel Meadow*—"the streets can be deadly. Don't let the name fool you. No law has sway or influence there but that of someone they call the Boss."

Annesley frowned. "Who is he?"

"We don't know his identity, but he seems to run every corner of the slum. Unless you look as if you belong there, you're swiftly sent on your way or roped into the service of the Boss. I would not recommend searching anywhere in that area without significant assistance from Bow Street or from a magistrate."

Chloe could not keep the wavering out of her voice when she asked, "Do you think they went . . . in there?"

Thomas turned in surprise. "Lady Chloe. I did not see you there. I wouldn't have spoken so frankly had I known."

He looked to Lord Halloway, who said, "Yes, dear Lady Amanda, Lady Chloe. Would you two like to get some tea? I am sure Cook is planning to accommodate us at all hours this day and night."

Chloe's indignation simmered. Why did Lord Halloway, and apparently Thomas, too, assume she could be of no use? What would she do to help while tucked away drinking tea and waiting for news of the others' planning?

Her dear Becky and Molly were likely in danger. She forgot her shyness, clenched her fists, and stepped closer to the map, the men moving aside to give her room. "I think we should go straight here," she said, pointing precisely at Angel Meadow. "Lady Amanda and I can go with a footman to the surrounding streets a little nearer, but you men could don some work clothes, perhaps smudge your faces with soot a bit, grab your Bow Street Runner, and head straight in." If they insisted on sending her away, would they rise to the challenge and go themselves? A small voice inside her suggested they would.

The men closed their mouths and stared at her with wide eyes. Amanda stepped abreast of Chloe and linked her arm. "Lady Chloe is right, of course. She and I will take some of the closer streets ourselves. However, I don't recommend your rushing off into Angel Meadow without preparation and a plan, lest Lady Chloe and I find ourselves with the formidable job of locating you three as well as Molly and Becky."

Lord Halloway cleared his throat. "My dear—"

"I know." She smiled and held up her free hand. "I was told to stay within the orphanage. And we will." She spared a glance for Chloe then leveled her gaze at her husband. "I can see there will be much we can accomplish here, within these walls, at least at first. I have a list of tasks I have been meaning to accomplish here with the children myself, and I would dearly love Lady Chloe's input on the matters."

Chloe felt her defiance rise. How could Amanda agree to sequestration indoors? She turned to her and spoke boldly. "And tomorrow, by the light of day, we will begin our own search in the safer neighborhoods. With a footman. We must visit some neighbors for other reasons—a goodwill sort of mission among them. You understand. We can probably discover much more than you men if we simply listen, gossip a little, and then listen some more." She raised her eyebrow in challenge.

Halloway eyed her with what looked like suspicion but then nodded. "With a footman."

"*Two* footmen," Lord Annesley added.

He met Lord Halloway's eyes, and the latter agreed. "Yes, two."

A knock sounded at the door, and Chloe startled, her eyes finding the floor. She felt her face heat as the surge of energy that had emboldened her began to drain away. She needed to master her emotions, learn to speak her mind.

Lady Amanda gestured for her to follow, and both ladies left the room as a short, stocky man with a tan cap pulled over his eyes stepped into the hall. Chloe turned, eyeing him with great curiosity as she followed Amanda away. The men shook hands and then huddled over the map, deep in conversation.

When they were out of earshot, Amanda smiled at her. "Looks like Bow Street to the rescue. I appreciate so much that Lord Halloway and Lord Annesley are the types of men willing to get involved. They are far more resourceful than most people realize, but it will be good for everyone when our other help arrives, and we have footmen and watchmen and others involved."

Though Chloe had suggested searching in Angel Meadow, the thought made her shiver. "I dearly hope Molly and Becky are not in that awful, lawless area. I'm so afraid they're in true danger. If we don't find them by tonight, where will they sleep?"

Amanda pulled her into a hug. "Don't you worry yet. Molly has lots of pluck. She's weathered more than any young lady should have to, and she's resourceful. Her strength will carry them."

Chloe felt great unspoken *if*s in the air. *If* they were still alive, *if* they were not in danger, *if* they were not already captured . . .

Lady Amanda stepped toward what looked to be a kitchen. "Let's see if any other women here have an idea of where they might have been headed, shall we?"

Chloe nodded.

As they toured the home and spoke with the women who taught or worked there, Chloe's angst grew. No one seemed to have any new information. Only what they already knew: Molly loved taking quick walks around the property and never wandered far. Thomas usually accompanied her, but that morning Molly had gone out with Becky instead. One woman recalled hearing her tell Becky they would be gone but a few moments.

More and more Chloe feared they were greatly injured, abducted, attacked.

At least the tour of the home cheered her somewhat. The children's rooms were brightly painted. Shelves of toys in organized groupings were mixed in with books stacked in precious piles. Evidence of the most popular stories showed in worn covers, thumbed pages, and looser bindings. Whenever she passed a roomful of children, their peaceful expressions gave her hope. Not all of them looked happy, but they all held expressions of at least contentment, and the sight warmed Chloe.

The longer she walked the halls of this place the more she wanted to become involved in the work here. She'd heard bits of some of the children's pasts and found herself wiping away tears more than once, grateful for the children's current environment: safety and security and health.

The schoolroom excited her most. "Lady Amanda, this is magnificent!" she said as she entered it. "Think of all that is open to the children if they can but learn to read."

Amanda turned to her with pride in her eyes. "My thoughts exactly. At some point they will all grow up, and what will become of them then? We do not wish to save the children when young only to throw them back onto the streets as adults into a situation in which they have little chance for a good future. We aim to provide the best opportunities for them we can."

Lord Halloway entered and waited for them to turn around. "We are going out and may be gone for most of the afternoon. The butler knows our planned route."

Lady Amanda stepped into his arms. "Do be careful."

He lifted her chin and tapped her nose. "Stay. Here."

Chloe stepped away, leaving their murmured conversation behind her. Moving closer to the window, she searched the expanse of streets below her second-story view. Rooftops stretched for miles, ending at her far right with a row of smokestacks. A thick black curtain lined the sky above them.

Lord Annesley stepped up beside her. "Textile factories, I believe."

She smiled up into his face. "You are going with Lord Halloway? The two of you, out scouring the streets of Manchester for a couple of lady's maids?"

His eyebrow rose. "Do you not think it a worthy cause?" His eyes twinkled at her.

"Why, yes, of course I do. I'm not accustomed . . . that is to say . . ."

His chuckle stopped her. "It's quite all right, Lady Chloe. I understand. We gentlemen spend an inordinate amount of time at Whites or imitating Brummell's masterpieces around our necks."

"No more time than we ladies spend with our gowns and kid gloves. Or on our hair. Don't ever encourage a woman to talk about her hair. You might be subjected to a lengthy and tedious discussion about pins and hot rolling and feathers."

He stepped closer, sideways so their arms brushed, and gazed out at the rooftops. "It is pleasing to look upon the ladies' efforts made on gowns and kid gloves. And on your hair, especially." He reached forward to curl a piece of it around his finger. Then he let it loose, watching it bounce lightly against her neck.

It tickled her neck, causing gooseflesh to rise up and down her arms. She opened her mouth in question.

He shrugged. "I have wanted to do that since you began styling it thus."

"For three years? I daresay your first thoughts were not so gently intended." She knew she blushed, but she still met his eyes, teasing him. "My guess is that, if given the chance during our younger days, you might have yanked my curls often."

"Ho-ho! Not so, I assure you. I might have been young, and you a mystery, but I would have been as gentle then as now." He turned toward her, searching her face. "Do be careful."

A delicious thrill ran up her legs at the thought that he could be worried for her safety. "I don't expect to be in any danger." Her words came out flat, disappointed. She did not mean to sound bitter or unhappy; she'd hoped to comfort him.

But he responded quickly. "Lady Chloe, I am sorry I spoke so strongly against your coming."

She opened her mouth to assuage his guilt.

"But I don't regret it."

Stepping away slightly, she moved to fold her arms across her chest, but he reached for her hand and secured it first.

"What I mean to say is you may have misunderstood the reasons behind my protestation."

She allowed him to keep her hand and raised her eyebrows, waiting.

"My motivations have little to do with how much you could contribute and more to do with your safety. I've seen the dangers of this world, and I know the risks involved in endeavors such as this one. I would wish you never to witness—or experience—any of it."

He looked so earnest. She searched his face and saw remnants of pain or perhaps worry. Something important, deeper than ever before, had passed between them. She nodded. "I understand."

He raised a hand to the side of her face and looked into her eyes for a moment longer. "Thank you." Then he stepped away.

She felt the air beside her cool, and with it a great loss, as he moved down the hall, and she realized they hadn't even said goodbye.

CHAPTER NINE

A FEW MINUTES AFTER BEING closed in their room, Molly pressed her ear against the door, straining to catch more than a word here and there of the men arguing at the front of the house. She tried the door handle, and to her surprise, it turned. Suspicious, she peeked through a small crack in the doorway.

Becky grabbed her arm. "What are you doing?"

"Shh." When Molly couldn't see anyone, she crept farther into the hallway, looking up and down the narrow corridor. Walking on the toes of her boots, she headed toward the voices, determined to discover more about this boss and his hold on the neighborhood. But within two steps a guard appeared from around the corner and she walked into his large chest. She bit back a yelp, her heart suddenly racing.

"Get back inside. No one said you could leave." His large frame bore down on her.

"Oh, um, may I have a drink of water or tea or a bite to eat or something?"

"A bite to eat? Tea? What do you think this is, an inn? Get back inside. You'll get fed when Therese is good and ready."

From the front of the house the men stopped shouting, and Theo's voice carried to Molly. "Men, have I ever disappointed you before? You've forgotten who is in charge. I have everything under control here. Your job is to bring in the children. Pluck them off any street. Their parents will be grateful for less drain on their resources."

His thick laugh sent chills up Molly's arms.

"You leave the rest to me."

As the guard grabbed at her upper arm, pulling her back toward their door, Molly heard a man toward the front of the house grumble, but he didn't argue with Theo. Shuffling sounds moved closer to the front door, and then it opened, one man calling out something about remembering to grab the whiskey.

The guard's fingers squeezed around her upper arm. "I said get back inside. Unless you're lonely and are looking for a bit of company." His gaze travelled up her body, and Molly shuddered and wished for a lock on her side of the door.

His eyes gleamed, and he moved closer. She inched away until her back pressed against the wall. Their breath mingled, his blowing wisps of her hair, his chest pressing against her.

"I could make you real happy while you're here." He reached up and toyed with a loose tendril of hair.

She clenched her fists, ready to shove him away, when Becky exited their room, shouting, "No you won't!" She swung a book at his head, the corner connecting with his temple.

He yowled and held his head, and in the quick moment of his inattention, they ran down the hall toward the rear of the house, passing through a small study, away from Theo's voice. Molly hoped for a back door or a place to hide.

Feet pounded behind them. The guard had not alerted the house; perhaps he thought he could deal with them himself. Molly's heart raced. She thought of Thomas. He would never have let anything like this happen to her. For the rest of her days Molly would be safe if at his side. She turned a corner into another room and stopped, finding herself in a small room with nowhere else to go.

"No!" Panic rose in her throat. She started to shake and rushed to the nearest door—it led to a bedroom, by the looks of it, which was clean and organized. It smelled of men's cologne—like Theo.

Becky slammed the door behind them and turned the lock. Rushing into the small space, they searched for a solution—a place to hide, anything.

"The window!" Becky pointed across the room.

They unfastened the latch. The window swung easily outward at street level into a dark alleyway. No stars were visible above them, and very few lights from windows lined the street, the darkness that much thicker. They didn't have time for their eyes to adjust. Molly leaped out the window and landed on a soft form beneath her.

"Oof." Someone grunted but remained still, his soft form warm beneath her slippers.

She looked closer and then gasped as she stumbled off the belly of a man, passed out beneath the window.

Before Molly could warn her to be careful, Becky had landed beside her. At the sound of pounding on the bedroom door above them, they turned and ran down the alley, trying to avoid the large shapes in front of them. As the back alley was not connected to the front street, they had to run in small alleyways for another two or three minutes. Molly was unsure which roads they were taking and certain they would be terribly lost in the morning. They continued to run, Molly's lungs aching and her heart pounding. Her throat and teeth hurt from the exertion.

Molly raised a handkerchief to her nose. The smells of human waste, vomit, and dead animals overpowered her. She forced a breath in as her lungs squeezed tight. Her feet pounded the cobblestone, but the sharp, pungent odor of death and decay continued to burn her nose.

When their feet slowed in exhaustion, Becky stopped completely and leaned against a wall, sinking to sit on her heels. "I cannot move anymore. Go! Go without me."

"Don't be ridiculous. Of course I won't leave you here. You have to stand. And move." She checked the street behind them.

"I can't." Becky grabbed at her heart. "My lungs are dying. Every breath. A knife."

"You must." Molly reached for Becky's arm to help pull her in the right direction.

The two stumbled forward, only the force of will and the desire to live pushing them on.

CHAPTER TEN

ANNESLEY'S BOOT SLIPPED, SMEARING SOMETHING into the stone ground until the boot caught traction again. He didn't even look down to see what had defiled the sole of his shoe. Maybe it would clean itself by the time he returned to the orphanage. It mattered not, since everything he currently wore was fit only to be burned. He wasn't sure where Halloway had found the worker's clothes, but they smelled of mildew and dust.

He approached a group of men, two of them leaning against a building. Smoke from a cigar circled their heads. He concentrated, focusing on a time he had had to go undercover as a longshoreman down by the docks. After joking with them for a minute, he asked, "So who runs things here in Angel Meadow?"

A wiry, tall man grabbed him by the front of his shirt and shoved him through the nearest door, shaking him and spitting venomously in his face. "We don't speak of 'im. Ask again and I'll kill you with me own hands." He stumbled out the door again and walked away, muttering.

Shaken, Annesley waited for a moment before walking back out the door to where the other men stood avoiding his eyes.

For the first time in the six hours Lord Annesley had been walking through the worst of Manchester, he reconsidered his motivations for doing so. Why was he so determined to risk himself like this? A warm chair with a cup of brandy waited for him at the Waterford home. A good ride through the beautiful country was on the schedule for tomorrow. And yet here he was, his face smudged with dirt from the flowerbeds outside the orphanage, wearing the work clothes of a servant as he sought out two actual servants. Lady Chloe's large and trusting eyes entered his mind, and he recognized his changing feelings for his dear friend.

He'd made a commitment to himself and to his mother that he'd leave "clandestine hero adventures," as she called them, behind him. After too many near-fatal incidents, he'd chosen to return to his land, his father, his duty, and his inheritance as the next Earl of Westchester. Yet here he was again.

But as the most skilled of their group, how could he refuse? If he remained in Angel Meadow long enough, he'd find clues about the two women and their whereabouts.

Or so he'd thought. Six hours hadn't been long enough to discover so much as a whisper of where they were. He had, however, learned enough about Angel Meadow to become greatly disturbed. Whoever ran things here did so with such an iron fist of terror that mouths clamped shut in a way he'd never seen.

Feeling disheartened, he limped along another side street, swaying with a deliberate drunken gait and singing to himself, all the while searching the shadows up and down the street with a precision hidden behind his inebriated façade. A small sound within a home to his right caught his attention, and he quieted his singing to a low hum.

A woman shouted a swift, "No you won't!"

Annesley knew immediately the woman did not belong. Her words were a bit too polished, and the force and confidence with which she spoke was too strong. That kind of confidence did not come from these streets.

He ducked into the next side alley and listened, but no other unusual sounds came to him. He made note of the location and waited, watching. He peered around the next corner, seeing no one, then backed up to the other wall. He slumped against it as if he'd collapsed in a drunken stupor, the side of his face pressed into the dirt. There, with one eye glued to the door, he waited, ears catching every scratch of the passing rats.

He passed the time analyzing his growing fascination with Lady Chloe. She offered so little of herself; he drank in the tiny bits she opened to him with eager curiosity and fascination. She was easily the most beautiful woman of his acquaintance, and he hungered to know her mind, her heart. The more he came to know the more beautiful she appeared to him.

The door of the home he was watching opened with a bang. From inside a voice said, "And don't be forgetting the whiskey either. Can't stand another minute of these two while sober, mind ye."

A man, overly large and brutish in appearance, with a square jaw and steely, small eyes, moved to kick Annesley's prostrate figure in passing. At the last second Annesley moved out of the way. The man tipped off balance and nearly toppled to the ground. Cursing, he stumbled forward, caught himself, and then continued plodding ahead, his thick boots marking the cobblestone street.

"Get off the street!" he called to Annesley. "It's past curfew. If you don't wanna go home to yer missus, find a pub, but get off the street." A sharp kick from a second man punctuated the words, and Annesley grunted in real pain. He made a show of picking himself up off the ground and limping slowly away from the house, heading toward the edge of town.

A door slammed open. A pair of burly hands shoved a woman onto the dirt in front of him.

"Hey, now." He bent to offer her a hand. Her wide eyes opened wider, and she shook her head, turning her attention behind him.

He moved aside and dodged a swinging arm aimed for his head.

The air smelled of rot and whiskey and sweat. The man shifted his weight, and his greasy hair fell into his eyes. He jerked his head to flip it away and scowled in such a look of rage even Annesley was surprised.

"Easy now." Annesley held up his hands. "Passing through."

The woman got to her feet and scampered back around to stand beside her assailant, apology in her face, and fear. She backed up, standing on the threshold of the house, the door still ajar.

Many sets of eyes peered out from inside. Hollow fearful, and dull, they filled the open space around the door. Annesley sought women, ladies' maids, but all he saw were children, unkempt and scared. As he had so often in his work as a spy, he felt overwhelmed by a situation he could not fix. Then he was distracted by a crest on the door.

Keeping his hands out in front of him, swaying still as if with drink, he asked, "What is that crest on your door?"

A short squeal from one of the children surprised him, and then the door slammed shut.

The man lowered his fists and stood taller. "That ain't none of your mind. Be off with you." He pointed toward the street corner.

Annesley nodded and backed away.

⸘

Chloe and Lady Amanda hurried down the street, carrying baskets of food from the kitchen. Amanda grinned. "There's a home of sorts up here a ways. It's a group of flats, really, and everyone pays rent, but the caretakers are a couple who have been married for many years and look on and treat the tenants like family."

Chloe smiled. "That's lovely. And remarkable. Are they really as good as that?"

Amanda nodded. "You will love them. The next establishment is not so warm, nor the tenants so lucky."

"Oh dear. Must we step inside that one?"

"They could use the visits." Lady Amanda cleared her throat. "The teachers at the orphanage say many there are confined to their beds because they are old and have no one to care for them."

"And you think they might know of Molly and Becky?"

"They might." She shrugged. "At least the owners might."

After a cheery visit with the caretakers in the first home, they left in high spirits, leaving word everywhere they went that they were searching for Molly and Becky. Only one thing dimmed an otherwise delightful visit, and as they walked to the next home, Chloe wrung her hands in her skirt as she recalled the disturbing detail. "He said children are disappearing."

Amanda sighed. "It's becoming a problem around these parts. As many children as we try to help, that many more disappear. People have taken to hiding their own children. We are extra watchful of our orphans."

"I think I might be ill." Chloe reached for Lady Amanda's hand. "What a dreadful place for our maids to go missing."

"They could be caught up in the middle of the children's disappearances. If Molly saw little ones in danger, she'd be right there, helping."

They stepped up to the next door and knocked.

It opened a crack. "What do you want?" a gruff voice said. One eyeball peered through the opening at them.

Lady Amanda leaned to the side to see him. "We have food from our kitchen at the orphanage . . . the one down the street here."

"And what do you want me to be doing with it? We don't run no charity here."

"I know." Lady Amanda tried to push the door open with her foot. "We were hoping we might make a few deliveries to your tenants."

The low voice grunted. He stepped away from the cracked door and opened it wider. "Don't be all day about it. Strict rules, we have. Tenants only."

"I thank you for allowing us in. I do believe they benefit from our gifts and visits."

Chloe surprised herself by adding, "Yes, they must. And thank you."

Four doors later great chains of hopelessness weighed down Chloe's optimism. Under her breath she finally expressed some of the darkness seeping into her mood. "Miserable. Every person here."

The last person they talked to had once been a governess. She said others in the building were also former governesses, cast aside by their employers. Renewed guilt tore at Chloe's conscience. A thought, small at first, began to fester and would not leave her be. This was the life her family had left Miss Gracely to endure.

Lady Amanda must have heard Chloe's comment, because she responded, "They do cheer up, don't they, once we start talking?"

"I suppose," Chloe said. They turned the corner to another hallway of flats. "Then they must darken again as soon as we leave." She lifted her head, surprised at her own negativity. "I apologize. I am feeling overwhelmed at the great sadness we've seen, and I feel helpless. We have helped four people, for a tiny amount of their day, and see how many more must live here! And what of other buildings full of loneliness?"

Amanda stopped in front of a door. "I forget how hopeless this all felt the first time I came. To me, it seemed a plight worse than death, and it changed me forever."

They stepped up to the last door—only one more person to visit. Chloe had long since dropped the handkerchief she'd used to carefully shield her nose from the smell. Her headache grew because of the sharpness of the odor. She raised her hand to the thin wood door and knocked.

A weak voice rasped from inside. "Come in. Oh, do come in."

Surprised at the welcoming, pleading tone, they shared a glance and then pushed open the door. They allowed their eyes a moment to adjust to the dark room.

"Leave the door open, please, for a bit of fresh air in here, and some light." A woman's voice from the corner room drew them in farther.

Lady Amanda's voice soothed their host. "We've brought a basket. With candles. Shall we light one?"

"Oh yes, please! And thank you."

It was such a genteel voice, with something familiar about it. Chloe stepped forward, squinting in the semidarkness.

"Yes, come forward. Let me see who are my angels, come to visit me."

Behind Chloe, Lady Amanda struck a match and lit a candle.

The room flickered with a warm yellow. Chloe moved closer to the woman, who lay in a low bed pushed against the wall. "Oh, you are an angel, truly. But what is a lovely lady like yourself doing in a place such as this? You could well encounter such sights and such dangers . . ."

Her tone resonated with such familiarity that Chloe's heart skipped, and she knelt at the side of the bed, squinting into the woman's old and wrinkled face. The smile lines brightened her soft skin. When Lady Amanda brought the candlelight closer, two familiar gray eyes lit in recognition.

Disbelief filled Chloe. It could not be. She reached for the woman's hands, unsure. "Miss Gracely?"

"Chloe! It's my Chloe. Oh, child, how I've missed you. I moved to this new place, and as you can see, I'm in the direst way and I've had no paper or pen to write with." One lone tear left her eye. "And ashamed I am for you to see me thus. Does your father know where you are?"

Lady Amanda knelt at Chloe's side.

"Oh, forgive me. I forget myself." The old woman lowered her eyes.

Chloe squeezed her hands. "No, Miss Gracely, you are just right. This is a dear family friend. I call her Lady Amanda still, but she is Lady

Amanda Halloway, future Duchess of Somerset." Chloe turned to her friend, tears blurring her vision. "And this is Miss Gracely, my dear, much-loved governess."

Miss Gracely coughed. "Forgive me. Is that dear little Lady Amanda I remember from many years ago? Falling out of trees, if I recall, weren't you? I'm pleased to renew our acquaintance but sad to be seen in such a state. Grateful too."

"So good to see you again, Miss Gracely."

Chloe choked on a sob. "We have come to take you home." She held a hand up to her mouth, striving to keep her voice steady, filled with sorrow at Miss Gracely's situation, knowing she might have prevented it. "Can you be moved? Are you . . . well?"

"Oh, my child. Can this be real? Perhaps I am in a dream. I drift off so often, remembering when you first learned your lessons. You were such a lovely child—never complained, always happy to see me." Miss Gracely was silent for a long moment, and Chloe worried she had drifted off. When she was about to ask her questions again, her dear governess responded. "I-I don't know. I am so weak. We eat very little." She wiped at her crusty, dried eyes. "Are you truly come to take me away from here?" Her eyes widened in such a look of hopeful desperation that Chloe wanted to fall on Lady Amanda's shoulders and cry.

"Absolutely." Lady Amanda spoke Chloe's own determination. "We will help you."

And Chloe knew she would. Now that Miss Gracely was back in her life, she didn't want to let her out of her sight.

CHAPTER ELEVEN

ANNESLEY HEADED IN THE DIRECTION of the orphanage, but he went the most roundabout way possible to shake anyone who could possibly be interested in a limping drunkard and his whereabouts. He found the edge of the river and walked along it. Small ripples created by the wind caught the moonlight and shined bright beams through the darkness.

Annesley's eyes sharpened as a figure dashed from the shadows between buildings across the street and to the river's edge. The figure seemed small; perhaps it was that of a woman. She held a bundle, something wrapped in what could have been brown linen. She carried it carefully, as if it were fragile, almost as one would a baby; only then she leaned over the water and placed the bundle onto the surface. As Annesley moved closer, caught up in the mystery of the unknown woman and her bundle, whimpering and the sharp cry of an infant broke through the silence around them.

He broke into a run. "You there! Stop!"

The woman jumped, her thin face white, her expression crazed. Once more she looked down into the water at the sinking child then raced up the alley from whence she'd come.

Annesley rushed to the water's edge, the smudged and dirty wrappings around the infant's form sunk just below the surface. The weight of the linens seemed to ensnare the babe, dropping like a stone into the depths. Annesley plunged his arm into the bitter-cold river, fingers grazing the edges of the fabric. He jumped into the water, reaching for the child at the same time. His hand found the linens. At last he succeeded in pulling the bundle into the blessed air with one arm while trying to remain afloat with his other arm and legs. He navigated back to the shore, a slight current pulling him downriver. Reaching for the stone-lined bank, he placed the now-silent child on the stone edge and heaved his own dripping, heavy body beside it, motivated by the eerily disheartening silence from the blankets.

He unwound the wrappings, pulling at the last of them to find a tiny infant, blue and unmoving.

"No." He gritted his teeth. Then he placed his ear at the baby's heart. The faintest flutter gave him hope.

He turned her upside down and tapped her back, gently at first and then with greater strength, whispering, "Please, please," with every pat. "Live. Live."

He lifted the infant upright again and hugged her to him, still patting her back. A moment later a cough—a tiny whisper of sound—was followed by the quick exit of water from her mouth. "There's a girl!" Hope spurred him on. Holding her on her side to allow more water to flow out, he continued the pressure on her back, encouraging any extra fluid to exit. Then the most blessed sound filled the night air as she began to cry, the sound weak and raspy but a cry, and she did not quit.

"Good girl. You keep crying." She would live, if he could get her warm.

He undid his shirt and pressed her body next to his naked chest, wishing for a bit of warm clothing, and took off at a run toward the orphanage. If he could make it there in time, maybe they could save the child. At once the purpose of his existence, all of his work as a spy, all the risks and training, combined in one night to help him save a life.

The babe was not the only person he'd saved, to be sure, but in this moment, she felt like the most important of them all. He ran as though he carried his own child.

Pounding on the back door of the orphanage, he startled many a servant when one opened it to him and he burst into the room, shouting, "Warm clothes, warm water, a fire! Something for an infant to eat! Quick, man! A child's life depends upon it."

After a moment of stunned silence, the servants began running. As they were accustomed to rescuing small ones, they'd soon met all of Annesley's demands and more that he hadn't considered.

Halloway appeared in the doorway. "Not the persons we were expecting to return to us, but important nonetheless." His face communicated concern.

Mrs. Featherstone came in just then. "Oh, blessed dear!" She gently took the babe from Annesley's arms.

"She was left to drown. I saw her sinking." Annesley leaned forward, head in his hands. "Angel Meadow, it's called. If ever a place were designed to suck the hope out of humanity, that is the place. I have only the tiniest lead to your maids and much to despair over. I pray they are nowhere near those streets and that we search there in error."

"Amanda and Lady Chloe have heard no news of them in any of the closer areas. It is as if the maids simply vanished, sinking into the very stones beneath our feet."

"I did hear something, a minor thing—three words—but it may be a place to start."

"Three words? What can you mean?"

"It's probably nothing. Please do not communicate false hope to Lady Amanda and Lady Chloe, but my instincts suggested something out of place is worth investigating."

"Good show, man! We should send men now to check it out."

"We must think of another way to investigate this particular location. Already I was seen passed out in front of the door. They have strict rules of curfew and kicked me out straightaway."

Halloway eyed him. "Should I question why you so easily take on the role of casual drunkard?"

Annesley allowed his mouth to turn up on one side. "Not unless you want to hear great tales of debauchery and ruin."

"And tall tales they would be." But Halloway eyed him with no small amount of curiosity.

A sharp cry, stronger than before, drew their attention. The housekeeper had the child changed, in warm clothing, and wrapped in warm blankets. A wet nurse had come to feed the child, and Mrs. Featherstone was leading her around the pantry door in the kitchen to be close but beyond the men's sight.

Chloe and Amanda entered the kitchen from the front stairs at a run. Lady Chloe searched the room. "I heard voices and crying." She

stopped when the infant made a cooing sound and peeked around the
pantry door. "Oh."

She stepped forward gently, a look of wonder on her face. Annesley
could not look away. Her hair, falling around her shoulders, looked
as though she'd brushed it out for the night. Her mouth turned up
in a small smile. She again stepped carefully forward, slowly, her hand
reaching out as if to touch the child behind the door, but she seemed
hesitant to do so. Another expression passed across her lovely features
and mesmerized Annesley. The emotion lay beneath her surprise and
awe. It was such an expression of intense longing, yet perhaps it was one
she was not yet aware of.

Halloway cleared his throat, startling Annesley. He raised an eyebrow
in question.

"Oh, hmm." Annesley grinned sheepishly, caught in his intent
fascination with the lovely Lady Chloe.

Halloway looked between him and Lady Chloe. "Lord Annesley
saved this child from the river."

Embarrassed, Annesly cleared his throat. "Yes, but she is doing well
now, it would seem. Mrs. Featherstone, what is your assessment?"

"I am greatly heartened she takes food with so much strength. That
energy could well save her life. She's a fighter, she is—not going out of
this life without taking a stand, she ain't."

Lady Chloe wiped a tear from her eye. "Oh, I hope she keeps
fighting." She leaned forward and said in a whisper, "Try, dear one. Try."
She stood at the door to the pantry, leaning forward over the child,
Annesley assumed. She turned back to the room but stopped, looking
from face to face at all those who studied her.

Annesley cleared his throat. "May I escort you back?"

"To my room?" Lady Chloe's face showed confusion and a bit of
something else, perhaps teasing.

Halloway cleared his throat and looked away, grinning.

"Um, well, no, I guess not." Annesley felt his face heat. He stepped
away, desiring nothing more than to spend a quiet evening at Lady
Chloe's side. But perhaps that moment could come another day.

She rescued him. "I do feel in need of a bit of air. If you would
not mind walking in the back garden with me, I would appreciate an

escort and some company there." She smoothed over his awkwardness. Welcome warmth and gratitude toward her filled him.

All grace and charm and kindness, Lady Chloe stepped toward him and placed her hand on his arm. "Oh! You are all wet! Did you jump in after the child?" Her eyes widened, filled with admiration and worry.

Recognizing for the first time since he'd arrived that he was indeed very wet, he felt a shiver go through his spine. "I do believe I am, aren't I? Shall we go outside for your bit of air? I am still available, but I won't offer you my rather soggy arm, for which I apologize."

"Oh, of course not. You must dry yourself, please, before you catch a chill." She turned to a maid who was tending the fire near Mrs. Featherstone. "Would you make sure Lord Annesley's room has a warm fire in it? And even"—she looked to Lord Halloway for approval—"water for a bath?"

Halloway eyed his friend in amusement but also with concern. "Yes, of course, if we have hands to spare to bring up some warm water for a bath, that would be most appreciated."

Annesley bit back a retort about coddling when he saw the earnest manner in which Lady Chloe watched him, and he nodded in gratitude.

The back door opened again, and loud boots in the hall announced Thomas. His face drooped, its lines pulling downward. He watched his boots as he moved into the room, likely unaware of their presence. The baby shifted and cooed. Thomas's eyes shot upward at the sound and moved through the room, taking in its occupants, resting briefly on the space behind the open pantry door.

"What's this?" His voice was raspy and weak.

Annesley felt for Thomas. He looked as though he'd been disappointed too many times in his search.

Halloway crossed to Thomas and gripped his shoulder. "Lord Annesley rescued a baby tonight."

"A baby." Thomas grunted. "What of Molly?" Something in his tone sounded sharper than Annesley had ever heard from him.

Thomas must have realized his misstep, because his gaze found Lord Halloway's. "Forgive me, m'lord."

"Of course." A moment passed between them. And it was obvious to Annesley yet again how much Halloway cared for his staff. "It is approaching midnight. Let us all find our beds this eve and arise early. The footman and magistrate will be here, and with any luck, our Bow Street runner will have returned to report something positive."

Thomas nodded, his head falling forward at the end of his nod, and he began to shuffle in the direction of his sleeping quarters.

Annesley nodded to Lady Chloe. "I must be off as well." He tipped his head to everyone in the room and then travelled down the hallway himself, anxious to lower himself into warm water and then fall between the covers on a bed. As he was about to turn the corner, he added, "Mrs. Featherstone, if anything changes during the night with our little one, would you please wake me?"

She nodded and said in a hushed voice, "That I will, milord."

CHAPTER TWELVE

MOLLY DRAGGED THEM BOTH DOWN another two streets, Becky's breathing labored and rasping until they rested again under an awning.

A shadow to their right shifted its position, making Molly jump. "Be quiet now," the figure whispered. "Come with me, or he'll find you for sure."

Molly couldn't make out a clear face and she questioned placing trust in anyone at this point, but the voice was female and sounded older than Molly, maybe belonging to someone her mother's age.

"Hurry. Never stay in the same place for long out here on the streets." The stranger moved away from them. They would lose her if they didn't follow.

Becky could barely stand and reached for Molly's hand. Together they followed the shadow until it seemed to have disappeared into a wall. Gooseflesh peppered Molly's arm. A great feeling of unease settled inside her, and she almost followed her first instinct, which was to run the other way.

The walls around them looked blank, empty. She and Becky turned in circles, searching the blackness around them for the woman who'd led them here. She dared a whisper. "Where are you?"

She heard a soft thump at their feet and felt a quiet movement. There was a shift in the air followed by a hand tapping her ankle.

She jumped, a tiny cry leaving her mouth before she bit her tongue. She and Becky crouched down where the hand had been and felt air blowing against their faces. A musty odor met their noses, but nothing pungent. They glanced at each other and then, in silent agreement, lifted the grate and shifted it to the side.

Becky went in first. Molly followed, her feet finding stairs. She turned around to replace the grate.

"Leave it be," a voice below and to her right said, making her startle. "I will go up and cover the entrance after you."

Molly nodded, though it was too dark to be seen. "Thank you," she whispered. Then she turned back around and moved down the set of stone stairs. As she descended, cooler air curled around her feet. She moved lower into the depths of the room, where the air cooled her arms.

"Becky?" she called.

"Yes."

"Are you well?" She bumped into a body and recognized Becky.

"Yes, I'm fine," she whispered. "Do you suppose we should keep walking?"

Molly cleared her throat. "Excuse me; do we keep walking?"

Only silence responded. So Molly began moving.

The stairs had levelled out, and now they walked down a corridor in the dark. The ground felt solid beneath their feet, the crunch of gravel and broken-up stone beneath their feet the only noise, but the darkness continued. She hoped they would fare better in their new situation than they had in their last. With any luck, they could leave these awful streets this very night and return to the orphanage long before morning.

"What next?" Becky pulled her to a stop. "Do we keep moving forward in the darkness, not knowing where this path leads?"

"I say we do. I'd like to get as far away from wherever we were as possible. Wherever this goes could not be worse."

A voice, throaty and low, laughed. "Oh, it's worse." The voice's owner struck a match, and light flared before their faces, blinding them and creating blocks of purple spots in Molly's vision.

Blinking, trying to make out the woman to their front, Molly backed up.

A pair of hands gripped her from behind, vice-like on her upper arms, twisting her arms and tying rope around her wrists before she could wriggle free. She kicked backward, but more strong hands shoved her to the ground and restrained her at the ankles. Becky fell to the ground beside her, wiggling against her own restraints. Molly pressed her cheek into the dirt floor, trying to leverage herself to rise.

"Stay right where you are," a feminine voice sounded behind her.

Molly squirmed on her belly, moving to her side so she could twist her head and see who spoke. A tall woman's shape loomed above her, with two other women at her side, their faces flickering in the shadows of candlelight.

Acting much braver than she felt, Molly whispered, "Look at who knocked us down."

Becky twisted and craned her head. "She's but a slip of a thing."

A thick boot covered in mud pressed into Becky's back. "No more talking."

Another pair of hands lifted Molly by the shoulders, forcing her to her feet. She almost stumbled taking her first step. She'd been tied at the ankles but loosely enough for her to take small steps.

The leader said, "Now, walk. Don't make any noise; just walk."

They continued down the same corridor, guided by the flickering candlelight, surrounded by new danger in the faces of these vicious strangers. Their movements were slow and awkward, their shuffling feet straining against the ropes that held them bound. Molly's skin became first sensitive and then raw where the rope rubbed her ankles.

"How far do we have to go?"

A hand slapped her across the back of her head. "I said no talking."

Molly turned to glare at the woman. "Why are you doing this?"

Something hard hit her, sending her forward to the ground. For a moment she saw nothing and felt blessed rest and quiet, and then the sound, smell, and pain came rushing back like a great tide. Her head pounded. Hands jerked her to her feet again.

"Walk."

Molly stepped forward, one shuffle at a time. She wriggled her wrists so the rope sat more comfortably on her arms and then clasped her hands together. Her stomach pinched tight with hunger, and her throat chafed with thirst. How would they ever leave this hole?

At length, when she felt her ankles were surely bleeding, they stopped at a brown wooden door. The lead woman knocked six times in quick succession. A hatch opened. Eyes peered out, and at some sort of signal from behind Molly, the person closed the hatch and opened the door. She did not want to cross that threshold. But hands shoved her again, and she nearly lost her footing as she tried to maintain her balance.

They entered another hallway, this one lit by candles in wall sconces. Doors with bars lined the hallway on both sides. A bit of fabric hung behind the bars on some. Noises, breathing, and whimpers sounded behind the scraps of material, and Molly's own breathing began to quicken.

She wished she could douse each one of the wall sconces and blacken the air again so she would no longer have to gaze upon the sight.

"No. Ooh no, no, no." Becky's voice behind her rose higher and louder with every word.

The sound of a slap made Molly jump.

"Quiet. You're disturbing the patrons."

Becky whimpered in response, just under her breath.

Patrons? Molly thought in horror. With her hands shaking, still tied behind her, Molly began to slow her mind; she tried to plan, to make sense of their situation, but nothing fell into place. Rising panic clouded her vision and her thoughts.

A lumbering, enormous figure stepped out of the shadows. She stopped with only inches between her and the man. His breath was strong with the scent of whiskey, and he swayed in front of her. Then he reached for her arm. "She'll do." He pulled her farther down the hallway.

"No! Let go of me." She twisted her arm and freed herself from his inebriated grip. But he turned, venomous, and gripped her tighter. She could feel bruises beginning to form. Her body jerked forward as he yanked her into the nearest empty room.

"Leave her alone!" Becky tried to run forward, but the ropes at her ankles made her fall onto her face, her cheek slamming against the dirt floor.

One of the women who'd tied them up stepped forward. "She just arrived. She hasn't yet been trained or conditioned. You may have a struggle with her."

He leered, smiling. "Just the way I like 'em."

He grunted and pushed Molly farther into a caged nightmare. Pure panic rose within her. Her throat was too tight for her to swallow, and her heart beat wildly. She stood as still as stone. She scanned her surroundings, but she could see no escape. The man sat on the bed and pulled off his boots. Then he struggled with overly long socks, pulling at them, stretching them high over his head. When they were finally free of his feet, Molly gagged at the smell of old cheese.

She inched as far away from him as she could and diverted her eyes. He swayed on the bed as he pulled off his suspenders and worked on the buttons, not once glancing in her direction, and Molly irrationally hoped he'd forgotten her.

Then he turned to her, the greed on his face making her ill. He held out his large and swollen hand toward her.

Molly shook her head.

Then he stood and grabbed her wrist, yanking her in one swift action tumbling into him. She dug in her feet and threw her weight back. She squirmed and twisted, but her feet were still tied.

In the hall Becky whimpered as they led her away. As the door swung shut, the fabric fell. Darkness, thick and eerie, blanketed Molly as the brute fell back onto the bed, pulling her rigid form with him.

She gritted her teeth, preparing to fight with everything in her.

But he did not move further. She waited, ready to strike. Even with her arms and legs shackled, she would resist. But he did not move again. Instead his breathing steadied. Within moments a snore escaped his nose.

Molly breathed out a choking sob. Could she be so blessed?

"Don't wake him," a voice said in the blackness.

Molly could see nothing. "Who's there?"

"I am." A young, delicate hand entered the bars through a break in the fabric. "Stay still for another moment, and then we will get you out of there. I slipped something into his whiskey."

Molly slowed her breathing, not daring to move. After she'd counted to one hundred several times, the cage door opened with a small creak, and a thin woman Molly had not yet seen helped lift her off the man.

Molly dared breathe only after they'd exited the hallway and the cages were out of view.

"Oh, thank you. How can I ever thank you?"

She grabbed Molly's arm, jerking her close with surprising strength. She whispered a breath of a sound in her ear. "No one must know." Then she continued walking, speaking louder. "It is nothing. I help all the women recover. Only my job." She held up a set of keys. "I must now take you to join your friend."

Wait. She was still to be held captive? "How can you do this? Treat women like this?"

"I could have left you there until he woke."

Chastened, Molly nodded. "And I thank you." After shuffling a few more steps, she asked, "Is this your employment?"

She scoffed. "I do not get paid. I'm forced into it, same as you."

"But they gave you keys. Could you not run?"

"I'd be captured again. Even so, I would flee if I could, but they have my Freddy. I can never leave Angel Meadow. Theo would send my baby to the most dangerous part of the factory. He wouldn't last a week."

Molly pondered for several more steps; the horror of this woman's life was difficult to comprehend. "You deserve better than this, and I'm sorry you must live your life in this way." Her face pinched, her mouth turning down. Her hands shook as the horror of her experiences started to catch up. Her breathing sped up, and her head felt light. She swallowed, trying to erase the smell of that brute from her memory.

The woman's keys jingled in the near darkness. "We are here." When the door opened, she indicated that Molly should enter.

Stumbling, Molly tripped on a bit of her skirts and fell forward. Becky caught her but tripped with her, the tightness of their ropes binding them, and they tumbled to the floor together.

Becky whispered, "Are you well? Was it . . . terrible?"

"Saved, I was." She sat up, but her savior had just closed the door, the lock clicking in the dark.

"Then he didn't . . . you're all right?" Becky hugged her and then fell back onto the stone floor. "So tired. Drugs, I think . . ."

They lay there, still and silent, until Becky's breath began to follow the regular patterns of sleep.

"You must not let your friend sleep."

Molly's body jerked in surprise. "Who said that?" She wiggled, inching forward, and pressed her hands against the floor to ease herself upright. She searched the dark room for the source of the voice.

"They call me Jewel. I just led you to your room. I'm in the room next door."

Molly inched toward the sound of Jewel's voice until she felt a wall. "Where are you?"

"Down, to your left. I'm speaking through the grate."

Molly turned so she could feel the wall then moved her hands along it until her fingers touched the metal grate. "Why shouldn't Becky sleep?"

"Because if you do not escape before morning, you may never leave."

Great relief filled her. And fear. "Do you know of a way out? Can you help us?" Molly leaned down so her face was closer to the grate, as if being closer could ensure a greater chance of help.

Jewel was silent for so long Molly feared she'd left, fallen asleep, or given up on them. At length, she spoke. "You are lady's maids, are you not?"

Molly hesitated, again fearful to divulge the identity of her employers.

But Jewel calmed her fears. "Do you know someone who could help us?"

"Yes, Jewel, we do! We work for noble houses, but they don't know where we are."

"But can they free us? I can help you escape, but I must ask that you come back for us or send someone who can. Will you do that?"

Of course she'd come for them. She'd do all she could to stop the horrors of this place. But what if she could not fulfill her promise? Molly thought for only a moment. "Jewel, I will do all I can to free you and every woman here."

"Swear it. Swear on your life you will come back for us."

Molly knew that after seeing this place, she could never feel happiness or peace again, knowing women suffered here the way they did. Come what may, death or imprisonment, she *would* return for these women. "I promise, Jewel. While I yet live, I will work for your freedom."

"Then wake up your friend."

"I'm awake." Becky's voice sounded strange, but she was conscious.

The grate by Molly's fingertips slid to the side, and then Jewel removed it altogether. A hand reached through the hole and touched her own.

"I'm here." Molly squeezed her fingertips. This woman. Molly had not even seen her face, and she had saved Molly from the greatest ruin, a life of unspeakable horrors. A life Jewel herself lived. Molly pulled her hand in between her own. Jewel withdrew, and her hand returned with the keys.

"The same you used on our door?"

"What?" Becky asked. "Is she giving you keys?"

"Shh." Jewel was already moving the grate back into position. "If you get caught on the way out, I don't know you and you don't know me. Don't let them see the keys. They will punish you most severely and put you at the base level of any of the women here. You will have no say in your partner or who can pay for your services. But you do have a chance. From your door, turn right two times, climb the stairs, and risk Theo's men up on the street."

"Thank you, Jewel. I will not forget you."

"I cannot be suspected of helping you. Leave the keys on the floor, and I will find them later. Remember your promise."

"I'll remember. You are an angel."

A whispery laugh answered. "I'm no more angel than this meadow. But for the sake of my son, I beg you to keep your promise."

"You have my word."

"Now, go."

After Jewel disappeared, Becky scooted closer to Molly. Molly couldn't see or feel her, but the smell of her lavender bath oils filled the air.

"How will we loosen our bands?" Becky asked. "We can't take a step until we do that."

Heart sinking, Molly said, "You're right. We can't run with our feet tied. And we're sure to draw attention on the streets if we appear thus."

Becky moved closer still. Reaching with her fingers, she leveraged herself until she sat at Molly's feet. Straining, grunting and crying out in frustration, Becky worked on the knot binding Molly's ankles until, with an exultant cry, they watched the ropes fall loose.

"You did it, Becky! Can you free my hands also?"

"Move over here by my hands."

After much wiggling and straining, Becky managed to loosen the ropes enough for Molly to slide her wrists through. Molly winced as each rope slid over the raw and tender skin of her hands. But she turned and worked on Becky's knots, freeing her much sooner, and then the pair were once again navigating a dark corridor in search of their freedom.

"If we die trying to get out of here," Becky said, "maybe others who search for us will discover their awful plight and help them in our behalf."

"With that cheerful understanding, I believe we have found a door. I do not know where it leads—it may stand between us and perhaps another dark corridor or evil men or women in cages or, quite possibly, freedom."

Becky stood beside Molly and placed her ear to the door. "I don't hear anything." She straightened and then gave the door a great push.

Cold air from the other side brought gooseflesh to Molly's arms. An empty alley stretched to the left and right. She wanted to jump in circles with Becky and cry out with joy as they had as little girls, but Becky wisely placed a finger to her lips. Then she stepped forward into the night. One star was visible above, through the rooftops. Molly followed close behind, turned, and threw the keys down the hallway. They shut the door behind them, with its coat of arms in the upper-right corner.

They pressed their backs against the building, watching a group of rowdy boys run by, the smell of liquor filling the air.

"We must be very quiet," Molly whispered.

Becky grunted. "Yes."

They moved along the street, keeping their backs pressed against a wall at all times, unsure in which direction they should travel but certain they had to keep moving. When they reached a crossroads, they paused.

"Let's go right," Becky suggested.

"Why? What is to the right?"

"I don't know—a feeling."

"A *feeling* is to the right . . ."

The group of boys came running back up the street at their back.

"Run! Now!" Molly moved to the right, once again pressing her back to a wall on the next street. "How will we ever escape? We need a place to hide where we can blend in a little better until morning."

"Blend in as we did yesterday? I don't think that's possible until we can get some different clothes."

"Psst."

Molly and Becky froze.

"Psst!" To their left, a pair of eyes stared at them from the crack in a doorway.

"Run!" Becky whispered.

"No." Molly grabbed her arm. "Now *I'm* getting a feeling."

With pursed lips, Becky approached the person in the doorway. "What do you want?"

"You must get off the street, or you'll be captured by any number of people. Get off the street. Now."

"We have nowhere to go," Molly pleaded.

"What? No home here?"

"No," Becky said. "Please. Do you know where we might hide?"

The door shut in their faces.

"It's probably for the best." Becky swayed a little on her feet and then moved to continue their walk along the wall.

"Psst."

"What?" Becky's voice held a hint of irritation as she turned back.

"Quick! Come inside."

"Oh no," Becky said. "We've done that before, and believe me, you don't want to—"

"Come, Becky. We have no other choice. We won't last out here on the streets."

The sound of revelers reached them from the next street over and moved closer.

"Hurry!" Molly pulled her friend's arm, and they pushed the door open. They rushed through the doorway into a kitchen, small and clean and smelling wonderfully of tea.

"Oh, heavenly. I knew we could trust you." Molly breathed in deeply.

"Follow me." A short man with dark hair led them away from the kitchen.

Becky glared at Molly. "If he goes down a staircase, I'm running."

"Agreed." Molly nodded.

If they'd been in any other situation, Molly would have quite liked the looks of the old man. He stood about the same height as she herself. He was thin, wore spectacles, and carried himself in a straight-backed walk through the tiny house. Upon reaching a closet of sorts, he turned around and held out his hand.

"I am Victor Bartholomew. You are welcome to stay in my home, in this room, until just before daybreak, when I need you to leave through the same door you came in. If you get caught, forget you ever saw me. Understood?"

Molly nodded. "Understood. And thank you." She nudged Becky.

"Yes, thank you. We haven't met many kind people today."

"I imagine that is the case," he said, his mouth drooping. "But don't worry. You have nothing to fear here. In my home, you are safe."

And Molly believed him. She sank to the floor in the room and rested her head on her hands, closing her eyes.

In the early predawn hours, Molly felt eyes watching her before she awoke fully and slit hers open to get a good look at whomever had come to spy on them.

Staring unblinking at Molly was a sweet girl with a heart-shaped face and plump, small lips.

Molly's lips turned up in a small smile. "Hello."

The girl jumped. "Oh! I shouldn't be in here."

"I would guess not, but don't worry. You've nothing to fear from us." Molly sat up, every part of her body aching in some way.

"I know." She tilted her head to the side with a small smile. "Your dress is pretty. You work for one of the houses of nobles, don't you?"

"Yes, we do. They are very kind. I am a lady's maid."

"Oh, I should like very much to learn to be a lady's maid. But Papa says I need to hide here for as long as I can 'cause of the bad people."

"He's right. There's hardly a street out there without a bad person on it. You should listen to your papa."

"He says you are about to leave."

"I suppose that's true. Is it nearly dawn?"

A woman entered, trying to hide her fear. "Sarah, return to your room."

"Yes, Mama." The bright warmth that had filled the room in the girl's presence left with her.

"She has nothing to fear from us."

The woman grunted. "But now you know she lives here, don't ya? Old Theo'd give a lot for a child as beautiful as she."

Sick dread filled Molly's heart at the thought of sweet Sarah in the room with the cages. "I would never reveal her. You have my word."

The woman eyed her for a long moment and then nodded.

"If you please, before we go, why is this place so awful? Is it Theo?"

"What isn't the cause? That's the better question to ask, isn't it?"

Molly shrugged. "I don't know."

"How about I share the plight of several of our neighbors? That sums it up." She put one hand on her hip, and with the other, pointed at the wall to their left. "Those folks next door? She works as a barmaid and takes opium to help her get through the night. Addicted, she is. And her man? He's lying about on the streets with a bottle in each hand. Their kids is what pays for it all, putting in time at the factories for the Boss."

She swung her arm to point in the other direction. "And there is what I most fear, the woman through there. Two of her daughters is working in a place like the one you just ran from." She indicated the rope burns on Molly's wrists. "Ain't nothing she can do to get them back. But she takes to the streets all day and night looking for them. Them that know just laugh at her. Their little ones work at the factory with the rest."

"I never knew people lived like this." Molly felt ashamed of every moment of frivolous complaint. And she vowed to remember.

CHAPTER THIRTEEN

Their kind and matter-of-fact hostess showed them out. She opened it but a crack as her husband had before.

Molly searched the street through the crack. "I don't see anyone." She put her ear to the door's opening. "And for now, I can't hear anyone either." They opened the door farther and stepped outside.

"Goodbye, and good luck to ya." The door shut behind them.

Above them the sky glowed with a warm pink, and Molly smiled at the sight. But when she trained her eyes on the street head of them, Molly almost wished for the earlier darkness. Bodies lay in heaps up and down the alleyway—some sleeping, others passed out or perhaps dead. Other piles of unmentionables dotted the ground around them.

"We should hurry, before the world wakes up," Becky whispered close to Molly's ear. Molly nodded.

They moved forward of one accord, stepping carefully around the figures at their feet. The kind couple had given them directions and a general path to follow to finally be rid of this place forever.

No, not forever, Molly corrected herself. She would speak of the horrors she'd seen and rescue Jewel and the others, even if she had to return herself with some burly footmen. A small voice inside warned that such a mission would require much more than a determined maid and a few footmen, but she set that thought aside. She moved more quickly with Becky through the morning darkness, hoping to leave Angel Meadow before the sun fully rose. So intent were they on avoiding the obstacles at their feet that they didn't notice a group of men leaning against the wall at the end of the block until they had almost come upon them.

As soon as Becky saw them she froze all save her arm, which reached for Molly's to pull her the opposite direction.

One man slumped against the wall in a dazed stupor while the others smoked, murmuring together. The ladies could have left with no one in that group the wiser, but Becky stumbled over the leg of a man sprawled in front of them. He grabbed her ankle, and she cried out. One of the men at the corner looked up and said something under his breath. The others turned at once to eye the maids.

The tall man holding up the wall pushed off against it and began a slow saunter in their direction, tottering and tipping as he strove to stay on his feet. The others followed him, not taking their eyes off Molly and Becky.

The women bolted in the opposite direction. With any luck, the men were too drunk or tired to catch up. But footsteps pounded behind them, far too close.

Soon arms encircled Molly and turned her about to face yellow eyes and saggy cheeks that reeked of liquor. Forcing her to turn about had been the first of this man's poor choices. With as much force as she could muster, she rammed her knee and connected with his more delicate parts.

Molly's father had made sure she could defend herself after an incident when he was a butler and oversaw a young maid who had been abused. He had taught her well. The half-drunk man doubled over, grabbing himself and cursing her. Becky took heart at Molly's success and shoved her pursuer, who, distracted with laughter at his friend's plight, fell over all too easily, and the girls took to running again.

Rounding the bend of another corner, they nearly barreled into another man. He stood about a head taller than all the others. His hair was a light-brown, sandy color, and even though they ran straight into him at a direct impact, he did not budge. He raised his hands to steady them. "Whoa now, girls. Be careful."

"Thomas?" Molly nearly choked on her relief.

"Molly! Becky!" He reached for them, crushing them to his chest, his body heaving in great gulps of air. "You are well."

Thomas.

The original pursuers caught up to them. "Ah, I see you found our early-morning company," one said. "Thank you for keeping the ladies warm for us."

Molly shivered, and Thomas stiffened, but when he spoke, he sounded carefree. "Ho-ho! Keeping them warm indeed. These are my ladies. Bought and paid for, fair as day. You can find your own company elsewhere." His pulse beat wildly on his neck, but he appeared as calm as the morning that was upon them—a bit stern even.

The other men moaned about the unfairness of it all, saying couldn't he share one of them, and why did he feel he needed two all to himself? Thomas moved Molly aside and rose to his full stature. He walked toward the men, pulled a small club out of his waist band and began swinging, letting it slap against the palm of his hand—two times, three times—as he approached the men.

When he stood close enough he surely could smell them, Molly held her breath.

"Go find your own company," he repeated. "Now."

The men, each a head shorter than Thomas, stepped back. Then the smallest of them, a thick beast of a man, reached up and shoved Thomas in his chest. Thomas took a step back but did not flinch. Molly hadn't realized how strong Thomas had become. He'd always towered above everyone, but in the past year his body had bulked up, and now he stood before these men as a force they could not overcome.

Laughing, he shoved the short man back, sending him tripping backward to the ground. The others, drunk as they were, surely knew they could not hope to overcome Thomas and backed away, shrugging and still grumbling about the unfairness of the situation.

Thomas watched them until they rounded the corner. Then he turned in great haste, wrapped his arms around Molly's and Becky's shoulders and walked with them, swaying as if drunk, in the general direction they'd been heading.

"You must laugh and be silly," he whispered to them. "Act as though we're returning from a night of revelry."

Molly leaned in to him, giggling, and swung her free arm through the air. A new security and trust filled her, making the show that much easier.

"That's it, Molly. Keep it up like that, and you too, Becky, until we can leave this awful place."

They passed another group finishing the night and heading for their homes, but most of those they saw were passed out on the ground or dazed, staring at their toes.

"Almost there."

Ahead, the main street that led to the orphanage came into view. Molly smiled with relief, recognizing at last the way back. She clung to Thomas, feeling sheltered, safe, even though the orphanage was still a good distance away.

"How did you find us?" she asked.

"You found me, remember? And praise God for it. We'd checked everywhere else, combed every street. This forsaken place was all that was left."

She pressed her fingers into his forearm. "Thank you, Thomas."

He had come, had endured the awful streets of Angel Meadow, for her.

Becky leaned on his other arm. "You'd not believe all we've come across. Thought we'd never find our way out, I did. What with being captured and the awful guards and women in—" Her voice cut off.

Molly leaned forward to see what had interrupted Becky. And then her mouth opened, her eyes bulging.

Ahead, Theo stood with his back to them. He'd stepped out a door with two of his guards. One caught sight of Thomas immediately. "You, there! Not morning yet, is it? Get off to bed with ya, or find a pub."

The Boss half turned, his attention caught by the conversation. Molly and Becky hid their faces in Thomas's chest. And Molly began to panic. Thomas immediately turned them about so they faced away from the men and led them into the first alley to their left. Molly breathed in deeply, a moment of relief calming her.

"Wait." The Boss's commanding voice reached them.

"No!" Molly half whimpered. Molly and Becky ran forward. A long, empty street lay ahead, with nowhere to hide, except for a pile of refuse five feet away. They dove into it, soiling their clothing and covering themselves entirely, then lay together in a heap of ripe aroma. Becky began a strange maniacal giggling just as a guard rounded the corner.

Molly clamped a hand over Becky's mouth and held as still as possible, her view of Thomas unobscured.

"What are you doing?" The guard bore down on Thomas, a man the same height.

Swaying, indignant, Thomas answered, "Just what you said. Try'na get these ladies and m'self off the street and back to bed, if you know what I mean." His mouth opened in great, loud laughter.

"Ladies? I see no ladies."

Becky echoed the laughter. "Act drunk," she whispered to Molly.

Though she questioned Becky's reasoning, Molly threw bits of trash into the air, keeping her face turned away from the opening of the alley and the guard who had turned his face toward them with Becky's noise.

"Ugh." Thomas wrinkled his nose. "Such as they are."

The guard pounded him on the back. "My condolences. Be off with you now. You don't want to be seeing anything that's about to happen on these streets. Take 'em over to the pub on Elm Street."

Thomas nodded and put a finger beside his nose. "I think you've got the best of it. A man'd have to drink a few more pints first."

The guard laughed then jumped at a shout from the street.

"Hurry up, man!"

The guard turned the corner back to the street from the alley without another glance in their direction. His voice carried to them as he walked away. "Nothing to worry about in them."

Thomas ran to the ladies' side. "Well done, you two. Probably saved our lives."

"What did he mean about something's about to happen?" Molly took Thomas's hand to help her up, shaking her body with the hope that much of the filth would fall off by itself.

"We're leaving, so we'll never know."

The cawing of a crow made Molly jump. Crows were never a good omen. She nodded in agreement and gave up on exploring what could possibly be valuable information about Theo. With obvious relief, Thomas let out a huge breath, and the three hurried down the alley in the opposite direction.

⁓

Molly refused to leave Thomas's side, so she was grateful when Becky opened the back entrance to the kitchen. Everyone in the room stood up in surprise. Mrs. Featherstone sent a footman off immediately to summon the lords. And then the room erupted in squeals of joy, followed by loud exclamations and some gagging sounds. Apparently the putrid smell of garbage had not left them. Molly could barely move her feet, so exhausted was she. Lady Amanda and Lady Chloe threw open the kitchen door and moved to embraced them but stopped several feet away.

Lady Chloe brought a handkerchief to her nose. "It must have been dreadful."

Tears welled up in Lady Amanda's face as she stepped nearer. "Are you well?"

"Y-yes, m'lady, thank you." Molly sniffled. "I'm so sorry to worry everyone so . . . again."

Lady Amanda waved the comment away. "We must hear all about it. But first—"

Everyone in the room finished the sentence for her. "A bath."

Grateful for that sweet mercy, Molly and Becky followed the ever-resourceful Mrs. Featherstone to a back room, where the wonderful housekeeper and one other maid proceeded to help peel their clothing from their bodies and begin a good, deep scrub with water that had no doubt been warming for cleaning dishes. But no one cared about that. They seemed as grateful as Molly herself was that the two maids had returned.

While Molly finished scrubbing away all the filth from her nightmare of a night, Mrs. Featherstone gathered her things and prepared, Molly hoped, to burn them. The dear woman wiped a tear from her cheek as she turned away with Molly's things. Molly led a blessed life, she did, surrounded by many caring people.

⌒

The next morning at breakfast Lord Halloway and Lord Annesley were not as keen to rush back into Angel Meadow as Molly would have liked.

"There are better ways to go about this. Research, gathering a team, determining who runs the place," Lord Halloway reasoned.

Annesley set his teacup down. "I agree. Running straight to the location would not be wise."

"We've got to go after them. I promised Jewel." Molly rose to her feet in immediate indignation.

Becky nodded. "I've never seen such miserable circumstances as those women are subjected to day after day." She blushed. "I cannot speak the particulars in front of such refined company."

Molly reached for her hand, and they stood side by side. "At this moment, were it not for Jewel, we would be trapped there still, of no use to you ever again, being so defiled."

The maid cleaning out the fireplace gasped at Molly's blunt and open speech.

Halloway turned. "Leave the fire for now," he told the maid. "If you could, tell Mrs. Featherstone we are not to be disturbed."

She nodded, curtsied, and hurried from the room.

The servants were trusted not to blurt their story to all and sundry outside the orphanage, but Molly knew everything the scullery maid had just heard would be shared with all those who worked under this roof. She felt at peace with that. They would understand far easier than those in the nobility what it was like to be almost ruined and blamed for it. And she liked the staff here and would likely need their help if Lord Halloway could not be swayed.

Lord Halloway waited until the door shut behind the scullery maid. "Molly, were you to ever be so defiled in such a vile manner . . ." He cleared his throat and looked away. "We would always be in need of your services here, and your friendship."

He shared a look with Lord Annesley, who nodded agreement. "Once you have shared the entirety of your dealings in that forsaken place, we will talk with our men to see what can be done about it. I, too, have seen the evil in Angel Meadow and want to run the whole place under."

When Molly's expression must have shown her impatience, Lord Halloway added, "We, too, feel a debt of gratitude toward Jewel. I will not allow your promise to be in vain. You have my word."

CHAPTER FOURTEEN

THE SUFFRAGE COMMITTEE OFTEN MET at Lady Amanda's home. Three weeks after her first suffrage meeting, Chloe sat in the middle of the room instead of her usual spot in the back, wringing her hands. She'd brought Becky, who had immediately joined the cause and hovered about Molly, the two of them ready to do half the work themselves. Many of the women would be looking right at Chloe soon, after the announcement. She would prefer they not even announce her name; she'd rather just get to work with the maids.

Thoughts of the lovely Miss Gracely filled her with peace. Her old governess was warm and comfortable and happy now. But her situation would not have ended so well if Chloe hadn't stumbled upon her. Now she was ready to defend women with a similar plight. Women needed a voice, a way to protect their interests, their needs.

Annesley had seen in her a strength she did not know she had. She wanted to prove she was just as brave as he believed her to be.

The woman conducting continued with the news of the day. "Lady Chloe has agreed to work on the awareness committee."

The announcement elicited supportive smiles and mild exclamations of surprise. Chloe felt grateful for Amanda at her side but unnerved by Lord Annesley at the back of the room.

What can he be thinking, attending our meetings?

He had said he wanted to become involved. Amanda had confided to Chloe her suspicion that Annesley had romantic intentions toward Chloe. And while her heart jumped a little bit at the thought, Chloe remained unsure. Something she could not define hovered in his changing eyes, and it unnerved her even more than his normally jovial constant presence would have.

"And now we will hear from her about our new exciting plans."

Chloe's thoughts screamed to a halt, and her mind went blank. Amanda nudged her, so she stood and stepped forward. She turned to face the room, and Lord Annesley's smile, overly large and proud of her, gifted her with a small smile of her own and a nervous giggle. She cleared her throat. "We are planning to hold our first rally in one month's time, here in London."

Molly stood. "Are you sure that's wise?" Her face was strangely pale, and her eyes bore into Amanda's.

Amanda moved to Molly's side, eyed the women behind them who were obviously shocked at the abrupt interruption, and indicated to Molly they should again be seated.

When Molly stiffened and remained standing, Amanda added, "We all agree it is time for us to do more, to be more visual, to make our mark. We feel the timing is right. It will be a peaceful rally, with women speakers. We've invited *The Manchester Guardian* and other papers to attend. Perhaps the Sparrow himself will make a flier for us."

Molly nodded, swallowed, and returned to her chair. Amanda stayed by her side and occupied the chair next to hers.

Curious, Chloe thought. Molly had seemed unusually alarmed about the rally. Why?

With her own fear forgotten in the wake of her curiosity about Molly's objection, Chloe went on. "Yes, we want to emphasize that, as always, we are a nonviolent group. We will peacefully gather and listen to speakers. Each suffrage group in attendance will carry a different banner, and all the main demands of women will be represented. Today we are looking for team leaders and volunteers to make the banners."

As she watched the women nodding, listening to her words, Chloe felt less conspicuous. They were much more interested in the cause than they were in her as a person. They seemed to hardly notice her at all—only the words she spoke. She found that strangely comforting. As more raised hands to volunteer, she took their names and knew the rally would be a great success. Even more importantly, she hoped the press would talk about it, that people would take notice, and that lawmakers would feel pressured to keep women in the bill that would offer greater suffrage to the people of England.

After the meeting, Annesley approached. "You have embraced the cause." He smiled, but the pinched lines in his face remained.

She felt her face heat, but she held his gaze. "Yes. In small part because of your encouraging words. Whether or not we as women are aware of and participating in the affairs of our country, we should be. And we should be given the opportunity to do so."

He searched her face, his eyes sparkling with appreciation.

She returned his expression with a hopeful one of her own. "What do you think of our plans for a rally?"

His expression turned pained. "That is the one part of all of this I cannot support. Women in the square, shouting for the vote? Surely you can find a more sophisticated, more elevated manner in which to spread the word."

She felt a great weight fall to her stomach. "I thought—"

"Did you not consider that with such a public display, you invite ridicule upon yourselves? What's more, you invite danger. Have you consulted your father?"

"Of course. As you must know, my father is in full support."

"Remember those ruffians who captured Molly and Becky?" He ran a hand through his hair, obviously agitated and worried for her. "Or Peterloo? Do you not remember Peterloo?"

"No, I am not aware of Peterloo."

"The debacle in Manchester?" Lord Annesley said.

Chloe shook her head and meant to say that no, she hadn't heard of it, but she heard someone gasp behind her and turned to find Molly staring at Lord Annesley with wide eyes. Her face was pale, and her hand clutched her throat.

Confused, Chloe turned back to Lord Annesley for an explanation, but he looked somewhere over her head. She turned and watched Molly exit the room with Amanda at her side, eyes showing great concern.

He sighed and finally looked at Chloe again. "Peterloo was a great tragedy. And it was a rally such as the one you are planning. The magistrate grew nervous about the crowds, about the incendiary nature of the working class, and brought out swords. People died. Hundreds were injured."

"Swords?" Her heart pounded. "Why would they do that?"

"Because a violent uprising was expected instead of the great, peaceful assembly it was always planned to be."

"And Molly? She is so opposed."

He still looked toward the door through which Molly had exited, and he shrugged. "I do not know why she grew upset at the mention of it."

Lord Halloway approached at his right. "She was at Peterloo. Witnessed the whole event. We all were there—Lady Amanda, myself . . . and Charlie."

Chloe considered this new information. "Have I met Charlie?"

"He died that day," Halloway said. "He was a dear friend, close to us all but perhaps closest to Molly."

"I see." Chloe brought a hand to her mouth. "I am terribly sorry."

Lord Halloway stepped closer. "Do not apologize. The topic of a rally is a fearful one for some of us and a dreaded one for others. We are grateful to you for heading it up because none of us who were at Peterloo feels up to the task."

She folded her shaking hands across her chest. "But do we expect it to turn violent? What can we do to prevent another Peterloo?"

Annesley brought a hand to her elbow and nodded to Lord Halloway. "Precisely my concern. Who's to protect these women from all manner of interference? From the sword or even rocks? From harsh words? I have many concerns about holding a rally and wonder at your wisdom in even considering it."

Halloway eyed him with a strange expression, part confusion and part suspicion. "I'm surprised at you, man. You are not usually one to be so negative about a great idea, and this one is Lady Chloe's first effort on the committee."

Stung by Lord Annesley's words, Chloe watched the two of them staring into each other's faces. She longed to follow Lady Amanda and Molly out the door to learn how they fared. She had specific concerns and questions about this Peterloo, and she worried for Molly.

"Excuse me for a moment." She nodded to the two of them and hurried out the door.

Amanda and Molly stood together in a corner alcove, obviously seeking privacy, but several others were nearby, attentive to their conversation.

"But again, I ask, a rally?" Molly said. "Why didn't you tell me, my lady? I should have been the first to know." Molly's tears flowed down her face.

A voice cleared near them, a soft female nudge from one of their neighbors, a staunch matron of Almack's.

Molly stepped back and curtsied. "My apologies, my lady. I am terribly sorry to speak to you that way. Might I be excused to return to my duties?"

Lady Amanda reached for Molly's face, using a handkerchief to dry her tears. "What duties? You are here at my request to help serve on the suffrage committee."

A group of four women were paying much closer attention to the conversation than Molly, Chloe, or Amanda would like. Some showed open disapproval. None of the others would have allowed any servant to speak in that way. They surely expected a sharp rebuke would be forthcoming.

Before any of them could speak, Chloe stepped forward. "Molly, perhaps a bit of fresh air? I would enjoy a walk in the gardens, and I was hoping you could help me understand some things about our new committee."

Molly paused for half a breath in surprise, curtsied, and said, "Of course, m'lady." She turned to Lady Amanda. "If my lady approves?"

When Lady Amanda nodded, Molly followed Chloe down the hall and out the side door.

The sweet smell of roses met them immediately. They entered a well-worn path lined with red and yellow blooms.

"How delightful! They have an arch up ahead." Chloe hurried her steps to walk beneath an arbor that supported hundreds of cascading roses. She reached forward and ran her fingers along the soft petals.

They continued down the path, and when they had moved to a bench in front of the pond and were situated comfortably, she said, "You know far more about working on these committees than I do. I was hoping you could help me, guide me along as I get started."

Molly's face was a careful mask, so Chloe could not discern her true reaction as Molly said only, "I would be happy to, Lady Chloe."

Chloe tilted her head, trying to catch Molly's eye. Is this how others felt when talking to her own downturned face? "I must admit a fair amount of trepidation about planning the rally."

"As would I." Molly's face paled again, and she clasped her hands. "It will not be an easy undertaking, but there are others who will help. I think you'll find the hands you need to get it done."

She did not offer her own hands. Whatever troubled her about the rally carried emotions she perhaps did not wish to address.

"I heard you have been involved in a rally before. Is that right?"

Molly nodded.

"I'd never heard about any other rally before today, but just now Lord Annesley said something about . . . Peterloo." Chloe took a deep breath. "It sounds like it was an awful time. He said people died."

Molly nodded and wiped away a tear.

"I am terribly sorry. I do not wish to bring you greater sorrow by discussing it now, but I do have one pressing question. Should we . . . do you think . . . should we cancel our rally? Will people get hurt no matter what we plan?"

Molly remained quiet for so long Chloe felt sure she wouldn't answer.

"We were so excited to get to go to St. Peter's Fields. Lady Amanda even disguised herself as a servant. Thomas and I went with her. The three of us were chumming it up like regular folks do. But the square grew more and more crowded. At one point, I couldn't breathe—thought I would be sick. No one had predicted the numbers that gathered in the square. Well-nigh sixty thousand."

"That's incredible." Chloe didn't know if she should hope for those numbers or against them.

"Aye, it was incredible, and it would have been a right productive meeting, with all the newspapers there, Henry Hunt ready to speak to us, and so many people out to hear him. But the magistrate got nervous, and the cavalry came . . . and other evil men."

"I'm sorry."

"They swung their swords around, drunk as dogs, not caring who they hit." Molly turned toward her. "And then people started to run, trampling everyone in front of 'em. They ran and ran. Children got knocked down right in front of me, and there was nothing I could do about it. Lady Amanda reached for a child, only to see her disappear underfoot . . ."

Chloe's hand went to her mouth. Poor Molly, to have experienced such a thing. "You must have felt so powerless."

"I saw too many people get hurt, too many who stopped caring about the lives of others, too much evil. The only good thing to come out of Peterloo was the death of Jack Bender." When she uttered that name, Molly's eyes flashed with a surprising amount of venom.

"I saw Bender kill Charlie. Watched dear, brave Charlie fall to the earth in a heap." Molly's breath shuddered as she filled her chest with a deep breath. "Lady Amanda's face turned white as milk, and Lord Halloway, bless him forever for this, ended Bender's pitiful life soon after."

Chloe's hands shook. What a terrible experience they had all lived through together. She began to doubt her own desire to hold this rally at all. "Why do they want to do another rally? I would think that after that, one would have been enough."

Molly wiped tears from her cheeks. "Many more have happened since. The people are uniting. A rally just for women could let people know how many of us there are. But an awful sort of thing happens to a good person like yourself when you see evil stare you in the face."

"Is that what happened to you?"

"Aye, it did, and I don't know that I'll ever feel myself again. I loved him, you know, Charlie. We talked of a life together as soon as he finished helping Red win the vote for the working classes. The Liberty Seekers were everything to him."

Chloe's mind spun. New words, new people. *Liberty Seekers.* She loved the sound of that—liberty. A thrill ran through her. But who or what was Red? She resisted more questions, not wanting to keep pestering Molly for answers today. Molly needed comfort, love, hope.

"You say you will never feel yourself again." She took Molly's hand in her own. "That's all right, because you are changed. And change can be good."

Molly snorted then wiped her eyes. "I'd like to one day think so."

"No, it can. We are all always changing. You are no longer the self you were back then, but you are still Molly, and perhaps a better version. You know things you didn't before. You have had experiences you'd never before imagined. And you are capable of more now because of all of it."

She envied Molly the growth, the strength the maid had. Having never really pushed herself before, Chloe didn't know what that kind of change felt like. She hoped working on this rally could allow such growth for her, but not in the same tragic way.

"I see what you mean. Perhaps I can embrace a bit of change. The old me never would have survived the other night in the streets of Manchester, I'll tell you that." Molly chuckled to herself.

Chloe rested a hand on her arm. "And maybe the person you are still becoming isn't exactly who you imagined you would be."

Molly's energy seemed to rise, hope filling her face. "But that's fine, too, because I like the new me." Molly's eyes shone with a new light. "I suppose I don't relish all I had to go through, but I wouldn't want to go back to being the old me." She leaned in to Chloe. "At Peterloo I almost passed out when the crowds started to fill the square. Squashed, we were, pressed against one another. I couldn't handle it."

"And now that part probably doesn't seem so bad."

Molly shook her head, mouth turning up in a wry grin. "No, not bad at all." She sat straighter in her seat on the bench. "I'll always miss Charlie." She wiped the remaining moisture from her face. "But his memory is with me, and it motivates me all the time. It is partly for him that I do any work for this movement at all. If it was important enough for him to die for, then it is important enough for me to live for."

Chloe's eyes filled with tears. "That's beautiful."

They sat for a moment longer, watching a group of birds that had come to drink and bathe in the shallow waters of the pond.

Chloe pointed. "Those birds. They remind me of Lady Amanda's sparrows she used to keep all caged up. So happy, they were, always singing and hopping around."

Molly turned her face up to the sky. "I'm more like a raven, myself."

"Excuse me?" Chloe's mouth lifted in a crooked grin. "Did you say you are like a raven?"

Molly nodded. "I feel a bit dark sometimes. I've seen the alleys and the black hearts of people without love." She sat back, staring again into the sky. "And that is also why I work on suffrage. The working classes need help, Lady Chloe. The things I saw in Angel Meadow . . ." She shuddered. "They aren't worth mentioning here, in polite society. But those people . . . they live in the worst possible situations. They're trapped."

Something startled the birds, and they burst up from the water into the sky, circling above them.

"You say you have seen the darkness," Chloe said, watching Molly for a moment. "Maybe you feel a bit of it inside, as though you are sullied by what you have witnessed?"

She nodded.

Chloe pointed at the sky. "Ravens may be dark, but they still fly."

Molly tilted her head farther back, following the birds' movements. Then she turned and grinned. The joy reflected in Molly's eyes stunned Chloe.

"Yes, Lady Chloe. Ravens can still fly." She stood from the bench, suddenly full of energy.

Unsure what had just happened inside Molly to bring her such light, Chloe stood as well, and they both walked back in the direction of the house.

"If I may," Molly said, "I would like to help you plan this rally."

Chloe's mouth opened, but she couldn't think how to respond.

Laughing, Molly continued. "Yes, I think that is a great idea."

"Well yes, all right then. Shall we meet tomorrow?"

"Tomorrow it is."

CHAPTER FIFTEEN

THE NEXT DAY MOLLY STRUGGLED down the crowded London street, people pressing her and coming at her from the opposite direction. The shuffling and the nudging made her lose her balance several times. Happy she remained upright, she continued on, wishing the Halloway townhome were closer to the print shop. Lady Amanda needed the next batch of fliers before Lady Chloe's ball on Saturday. So Molly, as usual, rushed home from *The Manchester Guardian* printing warehouse with a heavy stack. The newspaper printed them on leaflets and also distributed them. The Sparrow ran a weekly cartoon in the paper that Molly and her lady could leave around town and at locales their friends of the *ton* would visit. All the fliers had been quite popular, though very few people knew Lady Amanda herself drew them.

Molly had neglected to ask for money to ride in a hack, and Lady Amanda had forgotten to offer. Frustration brimmed near the surface of Molly's emotions more often than it ever had. Her arms were tired and aching from carrying the heavy parcel. She wasn't paying attention and stepped in a puddle filled with soft mud. She wouldn't have been walking at the edge of the street at all had the walkway not been filled with ladies of nobility doing their shopping and promenading about with one another. Molly had stepped down to allow more to pass, and that's when the muddy water had slogged over the top of her boots and seeped to her toes.

She squished and splashed through more mud; now that her shoes were already ruined and her hemline muddy, it did not seem to matter much how careful she made her steps. She tried to fight her general feeling of dissatisfaction and thought back to the first day she'd styled Lady Amanda's hair. That was also Molly's first day as her lady's maid, and she'd been so proud with the way the hairstyle had turned out. With ringlets sitting just right against her face, her lady had looked a wonder.

With each success serving Lady Amanda, Molly had felt an added satisfaction of her own. And when her lady had agreed to marry Lord Halloway, soon to be Duke of Somerset, Molly felt her joy might overflow, even though the disclosure had been amidst the tragedy of Peterloo and Charlie's death. She'd found their joy a help in dimming her own sorrow.

Lately happiness was a rarity, and too frequently Molly felt frustration, which showed in her voice and actions.

She tried to make sense of it all. What had changed in her? She could not pinpoint any one event or moment, but with a touch of sadness, she realized that her happiness was no longer connected to Lady Amanda. Somehow Molly had accumulated desires and goals of her own, and those of Lady Amanda now fell second.

That morning, instead of taking an extra moment to savor the hairstyle she had spent a good half hour creating, she had hurried through dressing her lady and the finishing touches, almost shooing Lady Amanda out of her own bedroom at the end.

Mulling over her malaise, Molly didn't notice the closeness of a moving carriage headed in her direction until someone yelled, "Watch out!"

Her eyes came into focus on the instant. She stared into the faces of two horses, their nostrils flaring as they barreled toward her. She tried to get out of the way, but her boots sank into a new patch of mud. Frantically she jerked to pull out her feet and boots. A pair of hands grabbed her about the waist and pulled her sideways, making her yelp as she tumbled onto the person—apparently a man—now lying on the sidewalk.

She blinked as, beneath her, he moaned.

"Thomas? Oh, Thomas, thank you! I couldn't move." She scrambled off him and looked at her foot, where her boot should have been, and she instead saw a newly darned, bright-red sock. "Oh no! My boot." She tucked her foot underneath her skirts.

Thomas tilted his head toward the sock as he sat up. "Festive sock though." His smirk made her grin.

"And lucky for me it's darned."

A crowd had continued walking around them, most with distasteful expressions as they hurried past.

"They look as though we planned this display with the sole purpose of bringing disgust to their afternoon."

Rising to his feet, Thomas said, "Well, now, maybe I did." He pulled her closer to him, out of the way of passersby. "Plan it, I mean. I care not for their disgust." He grinned down at her, eyebrow raised.

"I'm surprised at you. Think of the scandal." She enjoyed his arms still lingering about her. "Not that I mind."

"A little scandal is good for the soul, I always say." His grin widened.

"Ha!" She scoffed. "You have *never* said such a thing. But if you planned this, as you imply, you owe me a new boot. Or at least help in fetching the one I lost." She pointed back over her shoulder toward the street. The top of her boot was visible, sticking up from the thick mud at the side of the road.

"At your command." He pretended to tip a hat in her direction and lunged forward, dodging passing pedestrians. When he came to the puddle, he reached forward with his long arm, grabbed the boot, and brought it back to her in all its dripping, sludgy mess.

"Oh dear. And now I must carry such a thing with all my fliers." She looked around her, searching the ground anxiously. "The fliers!"

Thomas tucked the package of fliers under his arm and offered his other one to her. "Anything else I can retrieve for you?"

Breathing out in relief, she curtsied to him and placed her free hand—the one *not* holding the dripping boot—on his forearm. Whenever his muscles flexed and moved beneath her fingers, a thrill of expectation tingled up her arm. He stuck to the walkway, refusing to move to the mud-filled street regardless of the other pedestrians. He stepped aside respectfully when necessary, of course, and everyone gave them a wide allowance of space as soon as they saw the mess dripping from her fingers.

"How is your foot?" he asked.

"My lovely sock will be a holy mess by the end of this, but so far my foot remains unscathed. I credit all those hours of running about as a child without my shoes on."

The sweet attraction, the awareness of his touch, and his nearness all rushed to her heart and distracted her senses. The world walked by, and the weather could have suddenly changed with a cloudburst drenching them, but all she would have noticed was Thomas.

And then a woman screamed, pulling her from the pleasant train of her thoughts. A carriage raced down the street. Thomas grabbed Molly by the waist and led her into the next alley, shielding her body with his own as a huge wave of brown water and filth sprayed the walkway and everyone on it, dousing Thomas's back.

Visible under his arm, the carriage flew by. Its door was marked by a familiar crest—the orange and blue shield, the spotted panther. She shivered, remembering Theo.

"Thomas, did you see that crest?"

He turned his head, following her finger, but it was too late to make out anything on the door as it careened around the next corner.

Women and men all around them lashed out with their tongues at the unknown driver. Many headed straight back to the walkway, now wet through, seeking conveyance home.

"You are dripping!" Molly said, looking Thomas over.

"I was hit straight on. Felt it go down the back collar of my jacket." He shivered.

"Are you cold?" She placed her arm again on his sleeve, wet as it was.

He leaned toward her, eyes intent, moving closer until his lips almost reached her own. "I'm warm enough."

She blinked, caught in his stare. What did he see when he looked at her like that? Without thinking, she lifted her chin, still watching his face, staring into his eyes. They lit, a sparkle brightening their depths, and he closed the distance between them.

She closed her eyes, and his lips touched hers, softly pressing, and then he backed away, leaving a tingling yearning where his mouth had been. Her eyes found his again, and she grinned. "You're cold." She giggled. "Your lips are cold."

His mouth quirked up in a crooked grin. "Not yours. Mmm. Warm against my cold mouth. Maybe we should try that again." He pulled her back to him, pressing his lips to hers, and warmth filled her. She clung to his arms while the world spun, and she lost her footing.

He steadied her. "I've got you," he murmured against her mouth.

"I know." She opened her eyes and stared into his. His strength moved her. Not his girth or height or the bulk of his arms, but the strength that shone from his eyes. He tilted his head to kiss her again, but she laughed, looking around at the street, which was once again filling with people. With a gentle shove, she moved away from him and indicated they should start walking back toward home. "We are a spectacle enough as it is."

What was she thinking, kissing Thomas? She shook her head. But she couldn't regret it. Not with the feel of his mouth still imprinted on her own.

Nearly home, they now walked on a wider, quieter street lined with lovely homes bordering the park. Happy peace filled her. For years she had tried to overcome her fear that she would ever be disloyal to the memory of Charlie but had been unable to conquer the constant heckling worry that she might forget him. And the guilt at the thought of loving another had always stalled any romantic feelings for Thomas. But now, in this moment, none of that plagued her.

Thomas slowed their pace, probably because Molly began a limp to spare her foot. She appreciated his attentiveness more than ever. And she needed his help. She hated to change the comfortable silence between them, but she must.

She turned to him. "That crest—"

Thomas said something at the same time, but she didn't quite hear. "What did you say?"

He blushed, and she nearly forgot what she was about to say. He laughed. "No, what were you saying?" He looked away and then back again, the pink in his cheeks fading. Her curiosity piqued, she continued what she had to say anyway. "The crest on the carriage that doused you—it was Theo's, from the slums in Manchester. I'm sure of it. We saw it on the upper right corner of many of the doors, all the ones with . . . questionable activities, and it was on the first door where they kept us prisoner."

Thomas nodded. "I didn't notice it. Perhaps you could sketch the crest or describe it to Lady Amanda, and she could sketch it for you."

"I have. But to see it on a carriage here in London? Something about that worries me."

"We can assume a noble family is involved. That could be a good thing and make it easier for Lord Halloway to discover Theo's identity."

Molly nodded and squeezed Thomas's arm. Her heart filled with hope. "Then maybe we can finally free Jewel." She breathed out in frustration. "I worry for those people. It's wrong, Thomas, and I can't live knowing such things are happening and doing nothing about them. Besides, I made a promise to Jewel."

"And you kept your promise, telling Lord Halloway straightaway."

She did not respond. Confiding in Lord Halloway had been an important step, yes. But she couldn't help but feel unsettled until she knew Jewel was free and the brothel destroyed.

Thomas cleared his throat. He seemed distracted, and Molly remembered he had begun speaking earlier.

She stopped and looked up into his face. "Oh. I'm sorry. What did you want to say?"

He adjusted his uniform, wet though it was, out of habit, she supposed.

They were nearly at the Somerset townhome. Thomas looked away, down the street, his face turning pink again. Then he made a real effort to swallow before turning to her again. "I care for you, Molly. You know I do." He searched her face, intently, his own full of emotion.

She watched him. "I know you do. I care for you too."

A small light sparked in his eyes, and he nodded. "I've waited. I know you haven't been ready. And I have been happy to wait, but I have never stopped caring." He took her hand in his own. "And I thought you should know."

His large frame seemed vulnerable, his strength not enough to protect him from the hurt she might inflict.

Searching his eyes, she stepped closer, feeling his love lift her own worries, wanting to love him completely, hoping he could wipe away her burden, her fears.

But as soon as the hope fully materialized, the familiar sorrow and dread over losing Charlie and over her traumatic experiences at Peterloo crashed around her again. And what was more, she didn't know if she was strong enough to love someone again. "We have been through so much."

"Yes, we have, and we are stronger for it." He spoke truth. She and Thomas had weathered the worst and come out better. Her hope grew. Could she love again? Trust again?

Thomas had lifted her from the ground, sobbing and incoherent, when she'd tried to crawl through the maimed bodies surrounding her at Peterloo. She'd been too far away to do anything to help Charlie, Lord Halloway, or Lady Amanda in the fight against Jack Bender. She'd rushed toward them, picking her way through many in her path but had fallen to the earth with Charlie, finally succumbing to the awfulness around her, giving in to despair. Thomas's strong arms had lifted her in that moment, and in the years since, his friendship had continued to carry her. But now she hoped she could feel more, that she could leave behind her sorrow, heal, and fully embrace Thomas and all he offered.

Her emotions awhirl but hopeful, she stepped closer and tilted her head back.

Thomas looked up and down the street and then wrapped an arm around her back, pulling her into the shadows at the side of their building. He cocooned her with his arms and leaned down, meeting her lips with a hopeful urgency she returned. His lips pressing into her own, softly quivering and pressing again and again, he pulled her closer with his kisses and his arms.

She found a completion with him she had never known. Could she finally let go of her past, release the terror inside her, and accept a safe life with Thomas, a life filled with the strength he offered?

A sliver of doubt divided her peace, tore through the passion building inside her. If she gave herself to another and lost him, could she bear the pain? The fear of that possibility squelched her joy and destroyed the union. The emotional horror of the days surrounding Peterloo returned to her, and the protection she built around herself, the walls to keep Thomas away, returned.

Stepping back, she shook her head. "Thomas. I can't."

His breath still shaken and rasping from their kiss, he reached for her hand, tugging her closer again. "What?"

"What if something were to happen?"

"Then we'll still have each other."

He could not guarantee anything. "But what if we don't? What if I lose you or you lose me? I'm not strong enough to endure that again. The hurt is too great."

Confusion flashed through his eyes. Pain followed. "I'm not enough."

"You are." She shook her head, rattling her brain with her intensity. "More than enough. If I let myself, I could be quite lost in the joy of our love." A part of her hoped for it still, hoped he could convince her to risk all, to take that step and love again. She wanted him to say something, to bring back her earlier confidence in their love.

But he stepped away, the lines on his face deepening. "You say that to appease me. If it were true, you would welcome all I offer." He turned from her.

"Thomas, wait."

But he kept walking, rounding the corner toward the rear servants' entrance.

"Let's talk. Please!" Her voice followed him down the now-empty street.

She needed to love him, yearned for his strength in her life, for love. Oh, she longed for it. But she feared it more. She clenched her skirts until the knuckles on her fists turned white. Desperately looking all around for answers she would not find, Molly raised her hands to the heavens, silently crying out her frustration and once again learning that no solution could erase her torture. She crumbled to the ground, clutching her sides, and let the tears fall. When all her misery dropped to the stones and a sort of empty peace filled her, she moved to stand, brushing off her skirts.

A footman rounded the corner. "Excuse me, miss. But Lord Halloway is asking to see you in his office."

She wiped again under her eyes, smiled with quavering lips, and moved to follow him into the house, leaving her boots at the back entrance.

Knocking on the study door, she heard a firm "Enter," from inside.

Lord Halloway's office was one of her favorite rooms in the house—full of books he had collected, some rare. From the time she had first learned to read, his collection had inspired her to work hard, even when she felt frustrated, so she could learn to read them all.

"Come in, Molly. I have news of our heroine, Jewel."

She moved quickly to approach. "Do tell me. It is good news, I hope." Her heart picked up. The promise to help free Jewel had grown into a plan to close down the whole operation, to save all of the women, present and future, from that brothel. It was as important to her as suffrage, perhaps even more so; how could women even care about voting if their basic needs were not met? Then again, how could their basic needs be met if no one represented them amongst the lawmakers?

"Some of it is good news, yes. With Thomas's help, we have discovered the main entrances and exits to the place. We have been watching and understand their basic comings and goings." He cleared his throat. "Sad, I am, disgusted that such behavior exists. I am ashamed of my gender for behaving in such a manner toward women."

Molly felt her face heat. Helping the dregs of society from their plights called for uncomfortable conversations, and she wished Lady Amanda were present. She cleared her throat and moved past the embarrassment. "So what will be done? How soon until Jewel is free of that awful place?"

"That is the more difficult news." He shook his head slowly. "We have not been able to discover one central leader, though we know he exists. His identity eludes us. We have no idea how powerful their organization is or what kind of reinforcements their leader may employ. This Theo is a complete mystery." He ran a hand through his hair. "I don't feel comfortable moving in until we have more information. When we act, I want to ensure they won't simply reorganize in a new location."

She slumped in her chair. Each day was another Jewel spent locked in that horror while Molly herself was free. She used to live in freedom without care; she now lived with a measure of guilt that her blessings were not shared by others and that she owed the very peace and safety in her life to one woman who did not have any in her own. Molly's guilt festered like a wound in her every thought and stole her peace. "I must do something. Perhaps it would aid things if I returned there myself, see what I could discover?"

"Absolutely not." Lord Halloway's voice cut through her mental preparations. "I will not have you lost to us again." In his frown she saw the makings of the duke he would soon be and knew she'd get no further in convincing him. And what could she realistically do? Having escaped the first time with her reputation still intact, she daren't tempt the fates with another visit to the brothel from which she would surely not escape.

"What else is being done? It's been so long already, and I am just sick thinking of her and the other women suffering all manner of things while I am free."

"I understand this. I assure you we are doing all we can. I have come across some suspicious and concerning theories about who is in control, information that complicates the normal methods we might otherwise use to exert our influence. In some ways, Angel Meadow sits outside our reach. And it appears some very powerful people are involved."

She gasped, remembering. "I saw a carriage drive by today, with the same crest I saw on several doors in that place, including Jewel's."

Lord Halloway sifted through his papers and held up a drawing. "This one. We asked Amanda to sketch it according to your description if you recall. Does this look accurate?"

She reached for it and nodded immediately. "She got it just right." Her smile came naturally. "As usual. She's brilliant."

His eyes sparkled in pride. "Of course I agree." He reached for it back and studied it again, frowning. "Something is familiar about this crest and yet it's foreign. I feel as though I have gazed upon it many times, and yet I've never seen it."

"If it is also on carriages, driving about London, could it be from a noble family?"

He nodded, still studying the paper. "Yes, or if not noble, wealthy to some degree. The powers involved in Angel Meadow are far-reaching indeed."

A dark cloud of disappointment settled inside Molly. If even Lord Halloway's influence was stymied, how would she keep her promise to Jewel?

"I have not given up, Molly. We will not stop until we determine the best ways to free her and the other women. I would like to shut down the whole operation and establish some sort of order in the whole area." He smiled compassion up into her face. "Unfortunately these things take time."

She raised her head and tried to show her appreciation. "Thank you, my lord. I can't truly feel peace until I have kept my word and she is safe." Something inside her hardened with determination. A knife sharpened, and plans of her own began to clear the mist in her brain.

Perhaps Lord Halloway sensed her resolve, sensed the change in her. "I have been thinking about your employment here with us."

Molly clenched her hands together.

"Are you happy as a lady's maid?"

"I would do anything for Lady Amanda."

"Yes, I know. We love you like family. But I can't help wondering if there are other places to serve within our estate that may suit you better."

"You'd send me away?"

"No, not at all. Well, that would not be the purpose. Consider whether there might be a better place to use your growing talents—a rise in station as a servant, perhaps? A housekeeper at one of our other estates? I can't put my finger on it, but I would like to see you in a position appropriate for your increase in talents and education."

Molly nodded, sick with dread and feeling darkness cloud in around her. She did not want to lose her place.

"Don't misunderstand. You are the best lady's maid London has ever known. We all know it. But I can't help but wonder if you've grown past your position."

She was comforted somewhat, but wary. Perhaps she had indeed become too much of a burden on them both.

CHAPTER SIXTEEN

CHLOE STOOD IN LINE WITH her father and mother to welcome their guests to a ball, hosted in their home, with the intent to raise awareness for the orphanages and to make a surprise announcement in support of women's suffrage. Her first attempt at hosting such an event already appeared to be a huge success. She greeted each guest in turn with more ease than she'd ever had in speaking with others. Smiling, she knew that while she might never be as proficient in conversation as Lady Amanda, improvement sat well with her.

Chloe fingered the pendant at her neck. She and Amanda had had the design commissioned at a jeweler and had quietly given pendants to those on the suffrage committee, known supporters of their efforts. Already several women had commented on hers as they entered, and each time, she smiled. Soon the women would notice similar gems on other women and no doubt would want one of their own. A thrill of pride filled Chloe as she held the pendant between her fingers.

Someone she had never seen before entered and joined the line of guests to greet them. "Father, who is that man coming in just now?"

Her father finished talking to a couple who had passed Chloe by with a brief nod, and then he turned his attention to Chloe. "Which man, my dear?"

She nodded in the direction of the entrance. "He is in line to greet us. Large, bald head."

"Great heavens. I wouldn't believe it if I wasn't seeing him with my own eyes! That is Lord Oswald himself. Didn't think I'd ever see him again. He has been in India for years." Chloe's father nearly left his place to greet his old friend, but her mother placed a hand on his forearm.

"He will be here soon enough. We must stay and greet the guests in line before him."

"Yes, of course you are right."

Chloe appreciated this quirk in her father. For a highly ranked noble and member of the House of Lords, he had such a genuine and caring nature, completely independent of social norms and customs. He had been taught them, naturally, had been raised on them as were babes on milk, but the lessons had refused to internalize. He mostly did whatever he chose, to be corrected by his wife if he stepped too far out of bounds. The *ton* humored him because of his stature and great wealth. The family was from one of the largest and most ancient noble lines, their wealth maintained by generations of careful stewards. Or, at least, that is what she'd been told by her mother over and over again.

Chloe eyed the new Lord Oswald slowly moving toward them. Something about him sent a chill down her back. His eyes darted through the crowd gathering on the dance floor. He smiled and laughed with those nearby, but the spark never lit his eyes. Why was her father so excited to see him?

At length, he reached them, and her father leaned forward to embrace him, pounding him on the back. "Oswald, my old friend! How are you? Come back to us from India, have you?" Her mother didn't even try to dissuade the over-exuberance. Chloe met her eye, and instead of a cheerful resignation to her father's eccentricities, Chloe saw concern in her mother's face.

Lord Oswald laughed, the sound big and loud. Everyone in their vicinity turned in shock to see the cause of such an outburst. "I have returned, Archibald. Sure as elephant ivory, I'm here." He leaned closer and, in a mock whisper that all could hear, said, "Found a profit here closer, and I aim to continue to grow the holdings, if you know what I mean."

Chloe shivered.

"Are you cold, my dear?" Her mother stepped nearer, eyeing her closely, and placed a protective arm around her waist.

Lord Oswald laughed again and winked at Chloe, as if he knew that he, himself, was the cause of the eerie tingles running up her spine and raising gooseflesh on her arms.

Chloe turned away, lowering her eyes to study the hem of her skirts.

Her father stood taller. "I would like to present to you, my dear Lady Wetherton and Lady Chloe, a friend from our school days, Lord Theodore Oswald."

At the mention of his name, several of the women closest to them gasped, and one brought a hand to her mouth. She hurried away and began a conversation just inside the ballroom doors. Chloe could almost see the news travel through the room. This Lord Oswald's arrival would be the talk of the ball. She had hoped they could focus more on the orphanage and suffrage. Her curiosity about him grew, and she dared a look at him again, only to see cold, calculating eyes searching her face.

With a start she realized she had not yet greeted him. "Pleased to meet you, Lord Oswald." She curtsied and offered him her hand, which he held briefly, bowing over it in turn. His many gold rings flashed a reflection of the candlelight, and Chloe wondered at such an ostentatious display on one hand.

"Enchanted. Might I have a dance with your lovely daughter, Archibald?" His eyes never left her face.

She froze, forcing herself to swallow, cornered by his gaze. Blood pounded in her ears. She did not want to spend so much as a moment with this man. Everything about him called at her to run. But, of course, she could not. Through the pulsing in her ears, she heard her father agreeing to a set for her. They inquired of her which set she yet had free. She mumbled something about the third, and then the air cleared as Lord Oswald left them.

"Are you all right, my dear?" Her father reached for her hand and gave it a squeeze. "I know Theo is a bit old for you, but humor your father and help him enjoy his dance. We were fast friends during our days at Oxford, you know. I'm sure nothing more will come of it."

"Of course, Father. I will do my best. But something about him is not right."

"He does seem a bit formidable, doesn't he, with his bald head and wide girth?" Her father stared after Theo for a moment. Several of the older men in the room had already moved forward and surrounded him. "But I'm sure there is nothing of concern there, especially in a ballroom." He squeezed her hand once more and released it.

She was not so sure.

The line of guests seemed to have dwindled enough that the host and hostesses could move out onto the floor and begin dancing. Her parents opened the dance together, and Annesley approached, having secured the first dance with Chloe.

He bowed briskly and stood to her front, displaying full formality.

She eyed him with curiosity. "And how are you, Lord Annesley?"

He held out his arm for her to take. "The only thing disturbing my great peace of mind is my inability to come collect you sooner. I was a bit impeded by the arrival of your rather large, popular guest." He inclined his head toward Lord Oswald and raised an eyebrow at her in question.

She sighed and walked with him to the floor. "That is Lord Theodore Oswald. He knows my father from their school days. Apparently he is newly returned from India after being away for many years."

Lord Annesley stopped suddenly and turned to look at him again. "So *that's* the mysterious and scandalous Lord Oswald, is it?"

"Scandalous?" She turned again to study Lord Oswald, who was still surrounded by and talking in an animated voice to three gentlemen at once.

"Scandalous in what way?" Did her father know his old friend was associated with some sort of scandal?

"Many here question his reasons for disappearing so suddenly and for such a length of time to India."

She searched the room. Her mother was deep in conversation with several ladies who took turns looking in Lord Oswald's direction. Her father would soon know all there was to know about the man's history with the *ton*.

She tried to shake off the uneasy feeling and trepidation at the thought of dancing with Lord Oswald in the third set. Lord Annesley led her to the top of the line, and they stood next to her parents. The music began, and she smiled at Lord Annesley as she curtsied.

His mouth barely turned up in response.

What was wrong? He seemed so stiff and formal. He searched the room, and she knew his mind was elsewhere. She hid a sigh and swallowed a bit of hurt. Had he lost interest in her?

As their dance continued and she moved through the steps, switching partners, spinning, and returning to Lord Annesley, her heart lightened.

"You look lovely tonight, Lady Chloe."

Her eyes found his. A portion of his energy and interest had returned to focus on her. His eyes crinkled at her and waited for her response.

She dipped her head. "Thank you. I am happy so many came. We hope to purchase books for the orphanage and flowers for their gardens." She brought a hand up to the pendant at the base of her neck. "And we have a special announcement later."

"Is that new?" he asked, indicating the necklace. "It matches your skin to perfection. It's lovely."

She tilted her head, studying him. "Thank you." He said all the right things, but his heart didn't seem to be in them. In fact, when complimenting her pendant, his eyes had sharpened and he had watched her response carefully, as if he suspected—accurately—that it was more than a new trinket.

Completely unnerved, she felt relief to move away from him in the dance as she circled the others. Each time they came back together, his manners were impeccable, but his spark and fire and fun were all gone. She sighed inwardly. Perhaps he found her too dull and quiet, like all of the others had.

During the second set, he led her over to the drinks for a lemonade. They stopped in front of Lady Amanda and Lord Halloway and a group of men.

"Hello, my dear." Lady Amanda's welcome was a balm, as always.

She left Lord Annesley's side and moved to Lady Amanda's. Perhaps the two of them could slide a foot or two away to hold their own conversation.

Lord Annesley joined them, dashing that hope. "Lady Amanda, am I correct in noticing that you and Lady Chloe have matching necklaces?"

"You are. And you may notice others with the same jewel."

He nodded to her. "It is lovely. But I suspect it has some other purpose than simply adorning your exquisite skin."

Lady Amanda nodded. "It does. And we will make an announcement about it later. If you pay attention to who is wearing them, I am certain you will ascertain the elusive topic of our planned discussion."

Lord Annesley scanned the room. The sense that his interest held another purpose disturbed Chloe's peace once again.

A handsome young baron with thick ebony hair overheard them and chuckled. "A mystery to solve. I am intrigued. I must seek out all the ladies with a pendant such as yours and draw the information out of them."

The other men laughed. "How?" one asked.

He held up his hands. "Gentlemen, if you don't know how I plan to go about it, pay close attention, and perhaps you may learn something about the gentler sex."

Lord Halloway rested a hand on his shoulder. "Still not lacking in confidence, I see. Have you met my wife, Lady Amanda, or our dear friend Lady Chloe?"

"I had the pleasure of briefly greeting Lady Chloe upon entering. Our gracious hostess has agreed to my company for a set later this evening." He nodded at Chloe, the corner of his mouth lifted in a charming smile.

His cheerful nature put her at ease. Yes, she could see how many a lady might be willing to reveal anything to those eyes. "I'm looking forward to it."

She felt more than saw Lord Annesley bristle beside her.

Lord Halloway continued. "Lady Amanda, this is Lord Smythe. Until recently, he has been on the quiet of his estate."

He bowed over Lady Amanda's hand, kissing it. "A pleasure to meet any woman who managed to capture my good Lord Halloway. You, I am certain, are a queen among women."

Chloe knew he meant his words as a compliment, but she felt Lady Amanda shift beside her. Hoping to avoid an overly flippant joke with Lord Smythe as the target, Chloe tried to catch Lord Annesley's gaze.

Seeming to understand her wordless plea, he said, "So a mystery it is, gentlemen, to discover the secret behind these lovely gems. Perhaps a bit of subterfuge is in order, coupled with a contest."

The other men laughed their approval.

"Ho-ho!" Lord Smythe said. "The first to discover their true meaning? Shall we place a wager? It shall be much more interesting than any of the other wagers people have placed of late. The books at White's are dull—nothing of import there—though I am sure many a bet will be placed regarding the return of Lord Oswald."

The group turned to watch the newcomer himself exit the room. Chloe's heart warmed with the hope that he might have forgotten their set, which was to be next.

Lord Grey, who had been hovering at the edge of their group, interrupted. "Well, I, for one, hope this pendant isn't some childish grasp for attention by women begging for suffrage. Surely you are more dignified than that."

Lord Annesley coughed into his hands, and Lady Amanda stiffened beside her, clenching her fists. Her face a mask, she said, "And what if it's an ingenious ploy to raise awareness, Lord Grey? As prime minister, do you not support engaging women in the vote?"

He stood taller. "I do not. Enfranchising each woman would be a waste of everyone's time and energy. Do you not agree, Annesley?"

Chloe's mouth opened, and she turned to Lord Annesley, feeling equal parts hopeful and fearful.

He cleared his throat. "I most certainly disagree. Each individual, whether man or woman, should be given the opportunity to choose those who represent him or her in making laws. I am certain there are issues in which you and I might disagree, for example, and the wisdom of women would be most helpful."

"Rubbish."

Chloe brought a hand to her mouth in shock. She had never heard Lord Grey be so abrasive. In fact, he was known by many as a man heralding reform, bringing in the Whigs and all their new ideas.

Lord Halloway stepped forward, almost like a shield between his wife and the prime minister. "Now, Grey. Surely this discussion is better had somewhere else—"

"Why? The women wish to be involved in politics; why not have a discussion about it in their presence?" He nodded his head in Lady Amanda's direction. "I say let her hear it, plainly and simply stated." He turned to the men in their group and directed his next comments at them. "One vote per household is sufficient. The law governs property and its use, as well as goods produced by them for commerce." He turned with a meaningful look to wait for Annesley to speak up.

Annesely cleared his throat. "I would have to agree with our venerable Lord Grey on that point."

Chloe frowned. "You do?"

He did not look at her. "I see the logic, but my thoughts center on different lines. What purpose could women have in trying here, at a ball, to gain the right to vote? They put themselves up only for open ridicule and discussion amongst those who would most certainly disagree. It would be best to keep these conversations to smaller parties, dinners, and teas with one another, surely."

Lord Grey stepped forward an inch or two. "Exactly. You women discuss the matter amongst yourselves all you like and then express to your husbands how you hope the vote will go."

Chloe's indignation rose stronger inside than the fear she felt at speaking to so large a group of strangers. "And if we do not have husbands?" Several people nearby quieted, listening.

"Is that your worry?" Lord Grey laughed. "My dear, you need have no fear of never marrying. Given your family's great wealth and name, I daresay there isn't a single man in the room who doesn't hope for an alliance with your house."

Not daring to look at the men in their circle, she studied the floor, but indignation simmered ever warmer inside her.

"And you think marriage is the sum total of her hopes?" Lady Amanda's voice had a deceptive ring of humor in it. "To be married to one of the men in this room?"

Before anyone could respond, Lord Annesley stepped aside to allow Lord Oswald to approach. He bowed before Chloe and then to them all. "Lady Chloe, if you would be so kind, I have come to claim our dance."

Chloe looked to Lady Amanda for some comfort to sustain her, but her friend's attention was locked on Lord Halloway. An inner conversation of some sort was taking place between them. Lord Annesley's eyes found hers, and a definite apology shone in them. His behavior tonight was such a mystery to her.

One last glance over her shoulder warmed her. Lord Smythe tilted his head in her direction and saluted. She chuckled, and Lord Oswald turned to her.

"What is it? Have I already bumbled my way about something?" He wiped his head with a handkerchief. "I fear I've been away from polite English society for many years."

Her heart warmed to him a little. Perhaps his cool, calculating persona was merely his way of determining how to navigate their social world. She could understand a bit of awkwardness, to be sure, so she turned and gave him a small smile of encouragement. "You are doing very well, Lord Oswald. I was merely laughing at my companions. You seem to be quite an intrigue and a mystery to most people here."

They arrived at their place in line. "I suppose I am a mystery, but a mystery is useful, is it not? Like those pendants you ladies are wearing tonight. Mystery adds interest." His eyebrow raised, and as he waited for her response, she felt anew the cold sensation that had given her gooseflesh before.

"I see what you mean."

As the music began and they circled each other, he said, "You are lovely, Lady Chloe. A calm, quiet, and angelic creature. I would welcome someone like you at my side. I may not have much to recommend me as far as appearance goes, but I am the wealthiest man in this room by quite a large amount."

They separated, and she could feel her face flushing. Frantically, her thoughts flew about her brain as she tried to find something to say that would stop this line of conversation.

"Wealth probably means little to you, as your own family's wealth comes close to matching mine, but consider the power I wield. See that man over there?" His eyes guided her to Lord Annesley's father, Lord Westchester. "I own him."

What? How could he possibly?

"He does my bidding, all with the promise of wealth and success. And he will have it, for a price."

They separated again, and Chloe could hardly keep her feet moving with the music. What horrible person was this Lord Oswald? How could she ever look at him with anything like a pleasant effect again?

"Do you think the young Lord Annesley's suffrage thoughts are his own?" Lord Oswald asked and laughed. "Of course not! I put them there with my intricate web. He is but a puppet in my hands." He demonstrated leading marionettes in the air. "The puppet master holds the strings." They moved closer again. "Consider the benefit of being close to a puppet master."

For the briefest moment, he moved closer to Chloe than was strictly permitted during this dance—so close she smelled mint on his breath. Then he stepped away again, circling through the other couples, smiling graciously to all. When the music ended and they bowed and curtsied, he did not continue in the previous thread of conversation, but the shiver down her spine lasted through several other dance partners. She wondered at the ominous doom hovering about the man.

CHAPTER SEVENTEEN

As soon as Chloe was delivered to her mother, Lord Smythe arrived with a hand outstretched. Great relief filled her as she placed her hand in his and smiled up at him.

He bowed more elaborately than one usually would. "I am grateful for such a welcome. I am looking forward to spending some time with you."

When they returned from the ballroom floor, laughing and carrying on as if they were old friends, a frowning, disapproving Lord Annesley met them. "I believe we have the dinner set," he said to her, holding an arm out to escort her.

Lord Smythe turned to her and wiggled both eyebrows, causing her to giggle again before she released his arm and took Lord Annesley's.

The baron bowed and thanked her for their time together, with a couple of winks. Lord Annesley's frown only deepened.

Chloe nodded to the baron then turned to her new companion. "Lord Annesley, is something troubling you?"

He paused, watching the baron swagger off before turning his attention to her. "I have a confession to make." He leaned closer, and she could feel his soft breath on her neck. "I am a bit tired of dancing. Would you care for some lemonade and a turn about the gardens?"

Her face must have shown her surprise and perhaps disappointment. Did he not wish to dance with her?

He placed a hand on the small of her back. "I merely noticed you have not had a rest. You must be in as much need as I of a simple stroll or taking a seat or whatever our whims dictate."

His expression was so caring, so perceptive, that Chloe immediately felt at ease. "There is nothing I would like more at this moment than a respite in the gardens."

Appearing greatly pleased, he winked at her and led the way to the back verandah. She placed her hand on his arm, and he led her directly to one of her favorite places on the estate.

Flowers cascaded down the stone walls, and arbors overflowing with roses covered all four entrances to a quiet courtyard. "This is lovely. You've chosen my favorite spot."

"Have I? How fortuitous; it is my favorite as well." They strolled slowly around the fountain at the center. The sounds of gurgling water, the rich smells of flowers, and the gentle, warm evening encouraged a deep breath of satisfaction to fill Chloe.

Annesley searched her face until she blushed and looked away. She enjoyed his new attention, but she wasn't sure how to respond. "Thank you. This is lovely."

"I don't think I've seen this particular part of your gardens in bloom like it is now. Quite remarkable."

She dared a look into his face. "Thank you. I helped the gardener plan them."

"Did you? Then I am all the more impressed."

They continued in quiet for a few more steps, and then Annesley said, "So you survived your set with the infamous Lord Oswald."

"Oh, let us not speak of it. I did survive . . . just."

"This sounds grave. And judging by your expression it was the severest torture, although he seems a decent enough chap."

"There was nothing untoward, precisely, no. But he is rather forward." She hoped Annesley would move on to another topic—any other topic.

"Many a man was watching you with half an eye." His face contorted into a ridiculous expression, exaggerating watching her as he described. "Just so."

She laughed. "Really, come now. If you saw so much, then you were watching with your whole eyes."

He joined her in a quiet chuckle. "Too true. You've found me out. I was watching intently, noting every whisper and move of your lovely gown and your soft slippers."

"What? Surely you jest." Her face warmed, and she looked away.

He chuckled. "Of course you would think so. We always carry on as friends do. But that does not mean I cannot give a sincere compliment when merited."

She cherished this new side of Annesley and did not quite know what to do with him. The evening felt soft around her. The full moon lit their way. Lanterns lined pathways. Everything had a magical tint, and soon she was enchanted.

"Tell me, Lady Chloe." He paused and glanced around at the flowers and the hedges. "How do you pass the time in this lovely place?"

Grateful for a safer topic, she turned to him, smiling. "You'll think me silly, I am sure, but when I come here, it is to do nothing."

"Nothing? Surely it is not possible to do *nothing.*"

"Oh, but it is. I am not sure you could manage it. And please do not think me idle or dull when I tell you there are times when I long to do nothing, and this is the perfect place."

"Do you sit while doing nothing? Or is your nothing more of a walking activity?"

"You tease me." She squeezed his arm. "I often do both. I begin walking, as we are now, and then I sit." She indicated a bench with flowers on all sides, set back in an alcove.

"May we?" At her nod, he guided her to the bench, and they both sat. "And what further does nothing entail?"

She leaned back a little on one hand. "Oh, nothing." She raised her other hand to her mouth, laughing. "Truly. I sit, I watch the clouds, I wait for birds to join me. When I am here, a great quiet settles over me, and the pieces of my life fall into their proper places."

He watched her for a moment. "I think everyone could use a bit of nothing. Shall we try it?"

"I don't know if it's possible to do nothing with another by my side, especially you." She turned away, immediately afraid of the bravery of her last two words.

"*Especially* me? Am I distracting your nothing?" He raised an eyebrow, eyes sparkling with this new revelation.

She searched his face. "You are distracting, yes. You are humorous, witty, and perceptive. You see right inside me, straight to the things I don't often show." She held his gaze, and his eyes warmed. His intensity unnerved her, so she looked away. "You see? Without saying anything at all, you might summon a laugh from me, and there goes my nothing, away to the night sky."

Annesley straightened his coat. "Am I that entertaining? What a lovely thought." He reached for her hand. "May I?"

"Certainly."

He placed her hand on his arm while they sat. "But I shall strive, for just a few moments more, to be utterly dull, and we shall experience nothing together."

She shook her head, thoroughly amused by this new side of Annesley. His eyes were closed, and his head tilted upward. She brought her free hand to her mouth, stifling a giggle. But if he was taking her desire so seriously, she must be grateful. She joined him, taking in the sounds of the evening and focusing on the splashes of falling water in the fountain. Everything else faded, and her mind felt quiet.

When Lord Annesley rested his hand on her own, she blinked and returned from her lovely respite.

His voice quiet, almost a whisper, sent happy gooseflesh up her arms. "Your expression was so serene, so charming, I resisted disturbing your nothing as long as I could, but they will be calling us to dinner soon."

She squeezed his arm with her fingers and moved closer to him. "Did you enjoy your nothing, or were you distracted by my serene brow?"

"It was quite enjoyable, I assure you."

She noticed the avoidance of her question but stood with him. "I thank you for this respite. It may be the most enjoyable memory of the evening." Her eyes found his, and she tried to show her sincerity.

"For me as well. Perhaps the next time I call, we might repeat the experience?"

"I would like that very much. Please come calling whenever you are able."

He held out his arm for her to take. "Shall we return?" He leaned in closer to her. "I performed a bit of subterfuge on our behalf. At first we were to be seated with Lord Grey, but when no one was looking, I traded our cards with those of Lord Oswald and your father, placing the two of them with the prime minister instead. I hope you don't mind."

Relief filled her. "Mind? You have saved us from a very long and uncomfortable dinner conversation. But how did you do it? Perhaps you are a spy of sorts in your spare time?"

He coughed. "Luck, I suppose. I merely waited until no one was looking." His cheeks turned a light shade of pink, and he appeared unsettled and unsure.

She sidled up closer to him. "Well, I thank you for your subterfuge. I will have to keep in mind you have these unique skills."

She was pleased at the prospect of being seated beside him at the time of their suffrage announcement. After feeling equal parts unsettled, confident, scared, and happy all in one night, she craved a bit of the surety she always felt whenever Lord Annesley praised her efforts. She hoped he'd returned to his usual supportive mood.

He led her into the dining room and pulled out her chair at their end of the table, which she was relieved to confirm sat comfortably on the opposite end of a long table from Lord Oswald and the prime minister.

"What should I tell the servants you'd like to drink?"

He was so attentive. "I prefer lemonade."

He motioned for a footman, and as Lord Annesley turned back to face Chloe, Lord Smythe came to join them.

"What good fortune to find you are seated by my side," the baron said. "Dinner will be an enjoyable one indeed."

So she would not be forced to make conversation with a stranger on either side of her; for that, she was immensely grateful, though she wasn't certain their dinner would be entirely relaxing. Annesley's face had changed from soft caring to the more rugged lines of irritation. Chloe laughed, trying to cover her worry at the awkwardness. "Hello, Lord Smythe."

Annesley eyed the baron. "Uncanny luck, I'd call it. I would have thought you'd be situated closer to your mother."

Lord Smythe raised an eyebrow, recognizing a challenge, and retorted, "And I would have placed you closer to the prime minister. But there's no sense in squabbling as if we'd moved the place cards to improve our circumstances or some such."

Lord Annesley tipped his head and looked ready to say more, so Chloe placed a hand on his arm and spoke first. "You've found us out.

We had an uncomfortable few words with certain members of this table, and Lord Annesley was so kind as to move us farther from them."

"Yes, his cup overfloweth with kindness."

"I was happy to be of service."

"Yes, I'm sure you were."

Chloe turned her head from one man to the other. "Yes, good fortune for us all, as we will enjoy lovely dinner conversation." What was she to do with this surprising turn of conversation?

Neither man responded. Instead they sat, one on either side of Chloe. The awkwardness that brought on her natural shyness began to settle in. Chloe studied her hands in the folds of her gown. Several minutes passed, and at last the first course of the meal was brought out. She searched her brain for something to say to alleviate the silence.

"Oh my, Lady Chloe!" Amanda would save them all. Lord and Lady Halloway joined them, sitting directly across from them.

Relief flooded Chloe. "Lord and Lady Halloway, how wonderful to see you."

Amanda winked at her then looked from Lord Smythe to Lord Annesley. She looked at Chloe and mouthed, "What's wrong here?"

Chloe raised her eyebrows and shrugged.

Lord Halloway reached to shake Annesley's hand and then Lord Smythe's. "Lovely evening we are having, and your ball is one of the best of the Season thus far. You are to be congratulated, Lady Chloe."

"I quite agree," Lord Smyth said. "I have not enjoyed myself this immensely all Season." He brought his glass to his lips.

"Nor I." Lord Annesley took her hand in his own. "You have outdone yourself."

Lady Amanda's eyes danced with amusement. Chloe squeezed Lord Annesley's fingers then retrieved her hand from his and took a sip of her own drink.

Chloe gently cleared her throat. "Thank you. I have enjoyed myself. I hope the evening does much good for the orphanages and our other causes."

Lady Amanda leaned forward. "We are to have a brief speaker over dinner. I look forward to the remarks." She looked meaningfully at Halloway, who shrugged in humility.

"We will see what comes of it, won't we?"

"Are you giving the message tonight?" Lord Annesley's eyes held a light of hope.

"I am indeed. No need to appear so surprised, Annesley. My studies at Oxford lend themselves to times such as these."

"You know I am in complete support of your more intellectual side finally showing its face. I suspect marriage agrees with you."

"I wish I could take the credit," Amanda said. "But our dear Nathaniel has many hidden talents he keeps tucked away." She rested her hand on her husband's forearm and expressed such a look of intimate affection that Chloe had to look away.

Halloway raised his glass to Chloe and then to Annesley in turn. "Annesley, too, has hidden talents," he said.

Annesley's eyes sharpened, and Chloe felt a change in the air around them. Something important passed between the two men. Halloway nodded briefly, almost imperceptibly.

The baron leaned back in his seat. "All these hidden talents and strengths. I am afraid there is nothing hidden about me. Lord Smythe, at your service." He dipped his head gallantly to them all.

Chloe smiled, grateful for a lessening of the tension. "And that is what we most enjoy about you."

He sat up in his seat and puffed out his chest, winking at her.

The servants brought their food, and as they began their meal, Chloe relaxed, but Annesley remained more aloof than usual, an uncommon tension bristling off him.

CHAPTER EIGHTEEN

As THEY WERE FINISHING THEIR final bites of baked custard, Chloe's father stood at the front of the room. The master of ceremonies called for their attention.

Her father smiled to them all as he scanned the tables. He found Chloe and then addressed their guests. "We are so thankful you have come and are enjoying the food and dancing. Ladies, you look particularly lovely this evening." Women tittered behind their hands, and the men smiled. "This may seem somewhat out of the ordinary, but tonight we gather for a greater purpose than our own enjoyment."

Several in the group nodded. Others raised eyebrows in surprise.

"As expressed in our invitation, we are hoping that through our efforts tonight, we can lend support to the orphanages founded by the future Duke of Somerset, Lord Nathaniel Halloway."

The guests clapped politely, and as Halloway stood and moved to the front, the women turned with great interest. He took his place beside Chloe's father and addressed the other guests. "In an effort to save a few of the many children born into poverty and starvation, most without homes or parents to care for them, we have built two orphanages, where we provide safe, comfortable places for such children to live. We teach them the basics of reading and mathematics, with the hope that when they grow and reenter society, they will be empowered to contribute in some way. Many of you have donated clothing or care baskets, and I have seen firsthand how the children have benefitted from your generosity.

"At this time, we would like to announce, with great excitement, the opening of a third orphanage. We have seen a great need to help more children in Manchester, so our third home will join the second already located there."

Lord Oswald scoffed. "Manchester indeed."

Gasps followed his interruption.

His voice carried. "There is no need for such things there. The children can find work and build productive lives in Manchester. Build your orphanages where the children cannot work to provide for themselves."

Women murmured, some in agreement. Chloe couldn't fathom such uncaring. A chill moved up Chloe's back at Lord Oswald's uncouth lack of kindness.

The prime minister and Lord Westchester nodded in agreement, expressing what seemed to be quiet words of support to Lord Oswald.

"In this, Lord Oswald, I think you will find we disagree," Halloway said. "The preparations for the orphanage are underway as we speak. Tonight we ask for any funds or items you would care to donate to aid in its opening. We hope to house forty children there—a great deal below what is needed, but helping forty is better than helping none."

Chloe's father added, "I have committed to support this cause, and I have commissioned weekly milk delivery to their front doors."

The guests clapped politely.

"Anyone else who would like to step forward and support, please speak with me or Lord Halloway."

Loud muttering from a group that included Lord Grey and Lord Oswald attracted a few sideways glares. Others watched the prime minister, fear and indecision clearly crossing their features.

Chloe twisted her feet together under the table. Perhaps now was not the best time to make additional announcements.

But her father seemed unaware of the tension. Cheerful as ever, he continued with their next item. "And now, it is with great excitement that we announce a surprise purpose to the evening's events. After talking with my daughter and her friends"—he gestured toward their end of the table, and Chloe smiled at Amanda in gratitude—"I would like to announce my support of a new and long-overdue movement amongst the ladies in the *ton*: women's suffrage."

Silence filled the room. As it expanded and grew heavier, the ball of dread in Chloe's stomach increased. A few grumbling lords were preferable to the complete absence of response. Fear rose in Chloe's throat. She'd pictured a much friendlier audience, had hoped to feel as if she was among friends. She knew her friends were present but not applauding—perhaps just cowed by the earlier loud, interrupting complaints. Chloe let out a deep breath and stood at her place at the table, fingering her jewel pendant. Amanda stood with her. And then, one at a time, other women joined them.

"Ridiculous!" Lord Grey shouted to the group. His outburst broke the silence.

Gasps followed, and several women lowered back to their seats.

"Women are better suited as the pride and ornament of the domestic hearth than as a participant in the political arena." Several men nodded, some grunting in approval. Lord Grey continued. "What do women know of politics and the complex debate that happens in the House of Lords?"

"Lord Grey is correct," Lord Oswald said. "As lovely as our women are"—he nodded toward Lady Chloe—"each household has a vote already. Why clog the voting process by adding additional voices?"

Chloe felt the fire in her heart grow. The words she must say burned, and before she could hide in fear, her voice carried across the room. "Because my voice is my own."

Exclamations echoed through the hall, followed by whispers. Everyone had turned their attention to her. She swallowed. She dared not look at her friends. She could feel Lord Annesley's eyes on her as she continued.

"When I marry, I do not wish to lose my voice. I am a unique and valued person in my own right, and I deserve to have a say in the processes of our government and in who represents me."

Her knees began to shake. She'd need to find her seat soon.

Her father nodded. "Thank you, my dear. And it is for these reasons we stand in support of the orphanages, for children, and for our prettier members in search of suffrage. As I consider women's vote myself, I ask, what would their vote harm?"

"And think of the good it could do; think of the women who would be heard." Lady Amanda's eyes shone as she nodded to Chloe.

The women who had previously sat now stood again and clapped. And some of the men joined them.

Chloe's father continued. "So we ask you to consider, you lords among us and all of us, to broaden our thoughts on suffrage in all respects, among the working class as well as among women."

More clapping followed, and he and Halloway returned to their seats.

Chloe slowly lowered to hers. She played with the folds of her skirts, hands shaking, but a peace filled her heart. She lifted her chin and met Amanda's eyes. Understanding filled her friend's face, and Chloe smiled.

She turned to Lord Smythe, who watched her nervously. She looked at him, eyes questioning.

He cleared his throat, and his face held an apology. "I think I much prefer laughter, a good ball, or a fast game of cards." He reached for her hand and gave it a squeeze. "I leave law-making and serious talk to the men who enjoy it. There is so much more to life than such paltry, argumentative nonsense."

She tried to smile through her disappointment. Even the easy Lord Smythe could not be swayed.

Annesley joined their conversation. "Lady Chloe, forgive me." His voice was hushed. "You have positioned yourself for ridicule and to be shunned by the *ton*. Is that what you want?" His eyes held sadness. His words sank deeper than they would have if they'd been spoken by anyone else.

Would she be ridiculed? Chloe searched the room and found nearly all eyes upon her. Many guests whispered to one another. From their bland expressions, she could not tell what they said, but she suspected not all of their assessments were positive.

Lady Amanda returned her goblet to the table. "I think what she did was brave. Braver than I've ever been." She wore a strange expression, but it passed too quickly for Chloe to name it definitively.

More than a little surprised at her friends' uncharacteristic reactions, Chloe said, "Honestly, I didn't think about everyone's response. Speaking my mind seemed the right thing to do. I couldn't allow Lord Grey's ugly comments to stand." Chloe would not regret her words, even though she still trembled inside from the experience.

Annesley tried to catch her eye. "And what if they label you a bluestocking? Refuse to include you in their invitations? What if no one asks for your hand?"

She brought a hand to her mouth. "How can you say that?" Had she lost Lord Annesley's approval? Was he saying she no longer seemed a suitable marriage prospect? To him?

His face turned pink. "I don't mean offense. I'm speaking as a friend, in warning."

She sat taller in her chair. "If others no longer wish to associate with me, then I suppose I shall spend more time at home." When she could not stop her tears, she stood to escape before she embarrassed herself further.

Annesley stood and stayed her with a hand on her arm. She turned to him and found deep emotion filling his eyes. She couldn't identify his feelings, exactly—sorrow, guilt, admiration?

"I worry for you," he said. "Why can you not keep such conversations quiet, between you, your friends, and your committee? You would have a much greater impact if others are not aware of your efforts."

She choked back emotion and saw people taking note. "How can that be? How can we influence those in power if they don't know our opinion exists?"

"But they *do* know. By standing a moment ago, you alerted those who would oppose you and gave them clues on how to limit your influence. And you made yourself vulnerable for attack." He ran a hand through his hair, mussing each well-placed lock. "Why can you not leave these efforts to those more practiced at participating?"

She straightened her back in indignation. "Who are more practiced? The men? Do you have such little faith in women? Have we no place in these conversations?"

Lord Annesley looked to Halloway and Amanda for help. They returned his gaze with questioning ones of their own. Halloway's expression held a hint of challenge.

"You don't support women's suffrage, do you?" Chloe returned to her seat, ready to challenge him. "All your talk of supporting women and wanting my voice to be heard"—she choked on her words—"was just talk. When I finally actually do something about it, your true desire comes out. You don't want women to speak up or have a vote, do you?" She held his gaze, her eyes staring back into her own.

Finally he sighed. "I support you. You know I do." He looked out across the room. Many scrutinized their group. Those closest at the table took in every word. "I just think you must strategize better. I am aware of other forces at work who would do you harm. I see what a danger your work for reform could be to your reputation. I question your wisdom in standing in front of a group of the *ton* as the example. And I cannot fathom what your father is about, openly supporting suffrage before the present company." Annesley shook his head.

Confusion clouded her thoughts. Chloe had thought to move forward with Annesley's blessing, the strength of his support. And when he tore at her efforts, she recognized how much she had relied on him. The emptiness that filled her, the sense of betrayal was too much. All she wanted was the quiet of her room.

"I am sorry to have disappointed you." She stood, with no tears this time, and exited the room.

CHAPTER NINETEEN

MOLLY GATHERED HER THINGS IN a knapsack and hid it at the back of
Lady Amanda's closet. She wouldn't take much. She didn't have much
that truly belonged to her. And of a truth, she couldn't be appearing to
be anything more than dirt poor in the dregs of Angel Meadow. The
longer she waited the longer Jewel continued to live her horrific life.
And Molly couldn't stand it any longer. As soon as they finished the
suffrage rally, she was off to Manchester. At least she could stay in the
orphanage nearby.

Her heart hurt when she thought of leaving Lady Amanda. She
could be back soon, within ten days, but something inside whispered
she would never return. She wanted to be out in the world doing
something, anything, of import, anything that helped the plight of her
people in England. And it began with Jewel.

She rushed out of the closet and nearly ran into Thomas. "What?"
She caught her breath. "I'm sorry. I didn't see you."

"Slow down. What if I was the missus?"

She stood taller. "Well now, you weren't, were you? I know where
she is, and it wasn't likely to be her at any rate." She frowned. "Why are
you in here?"

"I came to talk to you."

She took a deep breath, preparing herself. Thomas had given her
nothing but frowns since they had last talked. Since their kiss. She felt
her face heat again and looked away, wishing to hide.

"Molly. I've come to say I'm sorry."

Her eyes whipped back to his. "You have?"

He stepped nearer and reached for her hand, his rough, large fingers toying with her small ones. "I can't be forcing a decision out of you. That's not fair. So I just wanted you to know I respect whatever time you need." He lifted one side of his mouth. "But, Molly, don't you think you could try and figure all this out soon? It's been ten years, lass, and I can keep waiting, but why should we? We could be really happy together." He brought her hand to his mouth like the nobility did and pressed his lips there, watching her face.

"I know, Thomas. I'm trying. I thought I had moved past it, and then Lady Amanda drew his likeness."

Thomas stiffened.

Molly held up her hand. "And the likeness of others, and it brought the whole nightmare back. I've been feeling funny and emotional ever since."

"I knew it was something." His frustrated scratching at his head brought a smile to Molly.

"Oh, Thomas. I love you; you know that." She blinked. Could she have just said that out loud?

Thomas stilled and pulled Molly into his arms in such a loving circle of comfort that she melted into him. "Do you, now?"

She nodded. "I do." She reveled in the admission. And she felt free. She loved Thomas. She had for a long time. And that was all right. "I love you so much I could shout."

His grin started small and grew. "Don't be doing that now." He ran a thumb across her bottom lip. "And I love you, too, Molly. I'm yours another ten years if it takes us, and forever, but please—"

She put a finger to his mouth. "Hush now. I'm almost there. I've just got a few things I need to accomplish. Then we can be together, here or somewhere else—it won't matter, as long as I'm with you."

His joy, apparent in the crinkling around his brown caring eyes nearly broke her heart. Then he pressed his lips to hers in a fierceness that made her forget everything else. She reached around him, pulling him as close as she could and returned his urgency with a desperation of her own. She hoped to see him again, hoped she could return, but first, Jewel and Angel Meadow.

CHAPTER TWENTY

FOR THREE DAYS CHLOE HAD refused to see him. The prime minister continued to make ridiculous demands on his time, and Annesley felt like a betrayer to those he most cared about. He gripped his hair with both hands and fell into a chair in his study. How could he continue this charade? Hurting Chloe was killing him slowly by degree. She'd refused to see him twice this afternoon when he had called. He didn't know how to mend things, didn't even know what he could offer, but he knew his words at the ball felt like a betrayal to her.

But what choice did he have? He knew the prime minister and those who controlled him were not above hurting any who stood in their way. Annesley's very livelihood and future estate sat precariously in their hands.

"You are doing well." Lord Grey's oily voice startled him and made him ill.

"Don't you knock?"

Lord Grey sauntered into Annesley's office as if he owned the place. "You've delayed so long in returning to the drawing room I thought you'd retired for the night. Tsk-tsk. Neglecting your guests? Your father, the venerable Earl of Westchester, will being asking after you."

The manner in which Lord Grey mocked Annesley's father in tone grated. "I'll be down shortly."

His father had insisted they host a dinner party and that his son be present. "Well, now that I've found you, there's no hurry." Lord Grey took a seat. "I'll take that report from you."

"I have nothing new to report."

"Oh, come now. You sat with Lady Chloe all evening in a rather heated conversation. I've never seen the girl string so many words together at once." His laugh frayed Annesley's every nerve.

Annesley wished he could forget that evening had ever happened. "What is there to say? You knew the substance of their announcement before a word of it was spoken."

"I must be sure my efforts to stop women's suffrage will be successful. Are you sure of the bill's authorship? William Lovett has no cosponsors?"

"Besides yourself."

Lord Grey had positioned himself as a firm supporter of greater reform for the working classes; adding his name to sponsor the bill had surprised no one but Annesley, who knew his true feelings on the matter.

When Lord Grey refused to respond, Annesley continued. "I am certain. Lovett is planning to leave the language nonspecific about gender, following the current pattern in our law. The women are of course hoping for more specific and inclusionary language about their rights to vote. There are no large groups of influence and no other authors of the bill. From what I can tell, Lovett is on his own, acting on goodwill, because he believes such a change is the right thing to do."

"Bah! Activating women is not the right thing for my goodwill or fortune." He stood and reached out his hand as a farewell gesture, but Annesley refused to acknowledge it.

Lord Grey's eyes hardened. "I want you to attend the rally they're planning. Give me a full report of the speakers, what they say amongst each other, their future plans, all of it." He turned to leave. "I'll ask your butler for my hat and cloak and be off. Give my regards to your father." His laugh sounded in the hallway until he'd turned a corner.

Annesley did not tell him, could not reveal, the one hope for these women, their one chance to succeed. And it rested in Chloe's father. As a strong supporter, he unknowingly swayed many of the opinions in the House of Lords, including that of William Lovett himself. Nothing about the bill's future success or failure would happen in drawing rooms or parties or even rallies. The outcome of women's suffrage in England would all be determined quietly in the heart of each man who would vote and in the chambers of the lords during their deliberations.

The lords were convinced England needed to franchise its working classes. Halloway had worked well with the various groups, and at last that broadening of suffrage was to happen. As long as women's suffrage was tagged on in the bill, or at least not denied women, Annesley did not foresee the lords declining the vote to so many of the country's landowners simply because women were included, unless the prime minister created such a stir that the inclusion of women halted the granting of general suffrage. Annesley thought the best strategy for women in this circumstance would be for their vote to be included without much ado—beneath notice. The more who became aware of its potential inclusion the more opportunity there would be to fight it in the House of Lords.

He stood to return to the drawing room. The sooner he returned the sooner he could bid them all goodnight.

Lord Oswald's voice carried from the drawing room out into the hallway. The man's mellow tones felt soothing until Annesley drew close enough to discern his words.

"The factories are a gold mine, gentlemen. Come our first quarter returns, all your financial worries will be at an end." Annesley did not trust Lord Oswald's methods of raising money.

"And what if we lose cheap labor?" someone asked.

Annesley entered the room, bracing himself for uncomfortable conversation.

Lord Oswald leaned back in his chair and rubbed the top of his head. "We won't lose it. I've got my families in such a state of poverty they can't afford rent unless they send their children to work for me. They should be thanking me. What would the children do otherwise if they remained at home? Alone? Their parents are working themselves or in the pub all day. I'm a regular nanny, I am." His frame shook with laughter while he brought a match up to light his pipe, sucking in and puffing out in earnest to get it started.

"And what of the women's vote?" This from a new acquaintance of Annesley's, one his father had insisted was necessary as one of the men who had influence. "What will stop these women from exerting their influence over child labor? We have no control over their womanly concerns and opinions."

"And how can we be sure our investments will remain a secret?" Lord Haversham pulled at his cravat with one finger. His face appeared flushed, and perspiration speckled his brow.

Lord Oswald paused in the puffing of his pipe, his face menacing. "Afraid you will tarnish your estate with funds from trade?"

Haversham coughed. "Come now, Lord Oswald. We know money from trade does not disturb your sensibilities, but we still have girls to marry off, wives to include on invitations, that sort of thing. Surely you understand."

"I see no lack of invitations addressed to me. Once your 'friends' feel the tightening nooses of debt and overspending, you will feel the power of great wealth. You will know what happens when those who used to snub and ridicule you, those who drove your wife to her bed in loneliness and despair, now come begging to you to save their estates. Look down on trade if you will, but all nobles must one day be sullied by money from trade, or your families will crumble around you and the dilapidated walls of your estates." Lord Oswald raised a glass of brandy in a mock toast and downed it in one gulp. He rose. "Now, if we are finished here, I think I shall be off."

Annesley's father stood with Lord Oswald. "So soon? Allow me to walk you out. I had so hoped to solidify my own part in this. I don't hold the same queasiness about association in trade." They left the room and continued down the hall.

Lord Grey turned and made eye contact with Annesley, watched Lord Westchester exit, and then returned his gaze to Annesley again, who nodded in return. Message understood. His father's participation was contingent upon Annesley's continued cooperation. Tied tighter than a noose, with no way out, Annesley measured his breathing.

When all the men had left, Annesley's father sat, leaning forward, with his head in his hands. Annesley watched him for a moment, some of his frustration ebbing. At length, he stepped forward and sat in the chair at his father's side. "Father, what has happened? Why are we in this situation?"

His father slumped lower in his seat. "Your mother doesn't know. Please don't ever tell her." The pleading, the desperate tone, brought bile to Annesley's throat. How had he not noticed the decline of his vibrant, strong father?

"Do you remember talk of Lord Oswald when you were younger? Many of the lords talked about him at the time. They called him Ossy."

Two or three connections fell into place. Lord Ossy, as they'd called him at Eton, had been great fuel for laughter in the *ton*. He'd courted a young daughter of the Earl of Gloucester, asked for her hand, and the word was that he went to her father to talk with the solicitors and draw up papers for a marriage agreement. Ossy had stayed for the greater part of three hours, shouting and carrying on. When the lady's father discovered that some of his amassed wealth had come from trade, the father had promptly refused to give his permission to marry.

After that Oswald had travelled to India to see to his plantations and hadn't been seen or heard from since.

Annesley's father looked up, his eyes tired, and the lines around his mouth and sagging jaw contrasted starkly with the young and energetic father Annesley had always known.

"Factories will be the big money-makers of the future," his father said. "Every noble will eventually need to invest in trade or be left behind, like Oswald said. He has a way to reduce expenses, and he promises a large piece of the profits if we can help him keep costs low." He held up a finger. "And the key, the clincher—he doesn't have to pay most of his workers."

"How can anyone have free labor? Who would work without pay? Do you mean slaves?"

"Of a sort, yes, though their parents agree to it, gratefully. No other choice, I'd bet."

"Child workers? That's his large money-saver?" Annesley knew of a bill being written that would restrict child labor. He wondered how that bill would factor into the bullying and manipulation. His gaze fell on the table in front of them, to a letter, sealed in blue wax, addressed to his father. "What's this? The seal is familiar to me."

The seal bore a coat of arms with an animal on one side. Immediately a door and the scarred and hungry faces of children filled his mind. A ball of dread settled low in Annesley's stomach.

"Who left this letter?" he demanded.

His father did not seem to notice Annesley's distress. "Lord Oswald. He detailed our financial arrangements. I hope to sign the agreement and be on my way to financial rescue as soon as possible."

Horror filled Annesley, and he didn't know how to respond. He wanted to throw the letter into the fire and watch the seal melt into the wood below.

Long after everyone else was in bed, Annesley paced the floors. Lord Oswald was the boss-lord of Angel Meadow. He was the one who had controlled Jewel and countless other women. Theo, as he called himself, used addictions to opium and alcohol to rule over families. He used children as his workers in his factories. He'd kidnapped Molly and Becky and blackmailed the prime minister.

Suddenly Annesley's mind returned to the woman he'd seen lowering her precious infant into the water. Considering what life that child would have had, he now understood her actions.

Theo was so evil and dripping with cruelty that Annesley doubted his ability to maintain composure the next time he saw the man.

This was the man who controlled even Annesley himself in his loathsome spying. Theo pulled strings, and the Annesley men kicked up their legs. The longer they left him master the tighter his grip became.

CHAPTER TWENTY-ONE

THE SCENT OF ROSES LIFTED and flirted with the breeze. The lovely sort of gentle movement stirred up Chloe's curls to tickle her neck. A servant approached with a calling card. She took it and sent him away. She turned Lord Annesley's calling card in her hand, studying again his signature. He'd been calling for days. She would not see him. Confusion warred with hurt. For the second time that morning he'd left a card. Her mother raised her eyebrows in surprise at Chloe's second refusal to see her old friend.

Chloe answered her mother's unspoken question. "I can't. He just doesn't understand me anymore."

Her mother didn't respond, but her small smile surprised Chloe.

Motivated to defend her choices, she continued. "He openly discouraged my efforts last night; our whole end of the table heard him."

"So you've said." Her mother trailed her fingers on the petals of their roses. "It seems to me he is trying to protect you."

"Whatever his motives, I no longer wish for that kind of discouragement."

"He's a good man, Chloe. That much we know. You'll figure things out." Her mother kissed her head and then left her to finish her walk alone.

Chloe didn't think she could bear hearing disapproving remarks from him. She had heard too many already. Her confidence was shaken.

At the dinner, anger had fueled her departure, but only for about ten steps. Then insecurities and sadness had crashed down upon her, and the tears had started to flow. Lady Amanda had found her in her bedroom. She had hugged her, pulling her close. And then she'd said, "I am so proud of you, Chloe. You have done more tonight than I have ever dared to do. I will stand by you in this."

But the worst part of the whole evening was a lingering hurt caused by Lord Annesley's disapproving frown, which stuck in her mind and heart and felt worse as she relived it today. She would do anything to avoid seeing that frown again.

She thought of his brilliant eyes, of his lovely, thick hair, his sharp jawline. And her heart raced. More than a family friend, more than a man she'd known her whole life, he was a man who mattered to her. How had she never realized just how much he mattered? She could spend many an afternoon simply staring into his eyes. She blushed at the thought. But now, what to do about her newfound feelings? To regain his approval, would she have to withdraw her efforts on the suffrage committee? Or was it too late and she had lost his good opinion?

Sighing, she walked toward the house. She tried to tell herself to give up her work for suffrage. Others would step in to fill her place. Molly, so much more than a lady's maid, could plan the rally alone. In fact, Chloe suspected she would not be merely a lady's maid for much longer.

Chloe could step away and quietly resume her watchful participation of the worthy efforts of her friends.

She shook her head. But she couldn't feel at peace if she kept her opinions to herself. She would be nagged with unsettling dissatisfaction. Strange. Not so long ago, she would have done everything she could to remain unnoticed.

And whom did she credit for her sudden bravery? Lord Annesley. Thoughts of him had given her the courage she'd needed to speak out. Then, to find he disapproved . . . Another tear trailed down her cheek.

She couldn't give up suffrage. Yet that would mean giving up Lord Annesley. But she couldn't do that either. Several more tears followed. Losing Annesley would feel like giving up a hand or a foot . . . or her heart.

◡

Lord Annesley paced the park across from Lady Chloe's house. She refused to see him. He had called two times yesterday, the day before, and again this morning. She couldn't know the impossible position he was in. In desperate middle-of-the-night moments, he'd planned to tell her all—of his forced hand, of Theo's hold on his father—but when morning had dawned, he couldn't bring himself to do it. What kind of husband would he be to her if the estate he brought with him was near to ruin? What kind of husband would he be if the family he represented was controlled by a crime boss and factory owner? What lady would willingly sully her name and reputation by joining such a family? No, he could never tell her.

He had to get out from under Theo's thumb. Somehow he had to free himself from the man and his influence. Annesley had checked the books with his father. Even a healthy dowry would only partly restore his holdings. And he couldn't stomach the prospect of using Chloe's money to pay his father's debts.

Fists clenched, Annesley turned to walk in the other direction, back across the park before her house. Twice he'd considered that all in the house might have noticed him, but he no longer cared. So great was the blackness in his heart and the feeling in his soul that he no longer cared about anything except being free to be his own man so he could prove himself to Chloe.

And not just for Chloe. He detested being controlled by Theo. Everything the man stood for was in opposition to Annesley's work in the House of Lords. Annesley supported a widening base of voters and agreed with Lord Halloway—the more who could vote the better England would be. He also supported widespread education for all classes. And he detested the idea of child labor. His work on the latest bill, which prohibited children under nine from full-day employment, was one of the best uses of his time in the House of Lords. It had at last been introduced as a viable bill. After years of work on his part, the Cotton Mills and Factory Act had passed. The language they had all agreed upon lacked key elements of accountability, but it was a step in the right direction.

An image entered his mind of Chloe, her delicate expression as she'd studied the face of the tiny infant he'd rescued. And he smiled. She would be a loving, kind, and dear mother.

The look on her face when he had discouraged her efforts at the ball, the hurt that had crossed her eyes, hurt him anew. Pain shot through him. Was she lost to him forever? How could he ever redeem himself? She wanted to hear his full support of her role in women's suffrage. She wanted his praise. She wanted him to work at her side for the cause. He stopped walking. Nothing. He could do nothing. He couldn't offer any of those things until he was free to act for himself, and therefore join her. Chloe shouldn't be burdened with his negativity and entrapment until he stopped spying on and reporting her efforts to the very man who would oppose them.

His thoughts turned to his family's holdings. What good were they to him or his family now? Trying to rescue his estate held him bound. He placed his hat on his head and adjusted his gloves. Even if he could not benefit from his own holdings during his lifetime, he wanted a healthy estate to pass along for future generations. The Annesley family might never again have wealth, and he might never marry, but the debts could be gone if he took drastic steps. A new idea began small but grew quickly.

Cinnamon, his stallion, snorted in surprise as he approached. "Whoa, boy. We've got work to do."

He swung his leg up over his horse and headed toward town and his solicitor.

❧

Chloe and her mother watched Annesley ride away from an upstairs window again instead of approaching the door to call.

"I was certain he would call on you again." Her mother turned to search Chloe's face.

"I'm grateful he didn't," Chloe said, but she secretly wished he had. Though she could not be with him, though she would have to give him up, she craved the sweet torture of sitting with him, laughing at his humor, and feeling the strength she always did when he was near.

Her mother turned to face the park again. "He is one of the best lords of the past three Seasons, his influence in parliament rising, and he is from an excellent family. Every mother has her eye on that one."

"Hmm." Chloe knew him to be everything her mother said and more. Admitting it out loud seemed the cruelest torture.

Why was life so unjust that she only realized how much she treasured Annesley's presence in her life after she knew she would have to give him up?

CHAPTER TWENTY-TWO

READY AT LAST FOR THE rally, anticipating the culmination of much work, Molly entered the square with Chloe, all thoughts of Angel Meadow and her rescue of Jewel put aside temporarily as she carried out plans for this historic rally. Even though she could never feel at peace until Jewel was safe, she felt comforted that Lord Halloway had promised his men were still working tirelessly for a solution.

It was a beautiful location lined with trees, and the weather cooperated. The sun shone behind clouds and a light breeze cooled the women. Other ladies milled all around them, their gowns brightly swirling as the women moved from group to group in happy chatter.

Even though this rally bore little resemblance to Molly's first, immediate memories from Peterloo stopped her feet. Her breath started coming faster, and moisture beaded on her forehead.

"Are you well?" Lady Chloe placed a small hand on Molly's arm. A group of women pushed past, holding a banner. Molly looked away, images of the beautiful white dresses trampled underfoot flashing through her memory.

She nodded, closed her eyes, and tried to control her breathing. Then she shook her head. She was not well. The memories were more powerful than she'd predicted, and she felt as if she'd stepped back in time. She half-expected Thomas to help push their way through the crowd as he had at Peterloo. The bayonets, the men on horseback, all seemed present though they weren't. A large group of women had closed around them, and Molly's head spun from the awful, trapped feeling.

She and Lady Chloe were jostled right and left with people trying to enter the square. "I just don't like the crush, Lady Chloe. I think we should find a place along the outskirts somewhere, away, with a little air around us."

"Yes, let's. I had no idea the crowds would be like this."

"You never can tell who will show up to a rally, my lady."

"Shh. Molly, I am not 'my lady' here. Call me Chloe, please."

Another parallel from her first rally. Lady Amanda had thought it quite an adventure to dress as a commoner.

Molly and Lady Chloe pushed through the group and stood against a wall at the side of the square. They were farther from the front now but would probably still see and hear just fine.

Molly needed to get control of her racing thoughts. Chloe watched her. The less Molly said the wider Chloe's eyes grew.

"I'll be all right. This will be nothing like the other rally." At least no jumpy magistrate waited at the back of the group. No yeoman scowled, with their hands on their swords. And Jack Bender would no longer terrorize them. No cavalry had arrived as backup, and what was more, the crowd was mostly women.

Chloe squinted her eyes in suspicion but seemed to relax a bit more. "A beautiful sight, aren't they? Look at what we accomplished!" Chloe clasped her hands together in front of her, and her eyes lit with hopeful anticipation. "The House of Lords cannot ignore these numbers."

They had worked hard to discover all of the different groups forming to work for suffrage and to then invite them to the rally. The main problem Molly had found with the whole movement was that they lacked a sense of congruity. No two groups were the same, and each approached the cause in their own unique ways. She sighed.

"Is something wrong?" Chloe searched her face.

Molly smiled as big as she could. "Nothing at all." She paused. "Well, nothing that can be solved today. Do you see all these women? They need to unite. We need one group, one banner. But it will come. I hope." As her gaze travelled over the great crowd to their front, a great peace filled her. "The rally is going to be perfect. And I am so proud of you, Lady—uh, Chloe." Molly waved her hand to indicate everything around them. "The speakers have arrived. The newspapers are here, and all the different suffrage groups are represented. I'd call this a wonderful success already."

As the first two speakers, Abiah Higginbotham and Harriot Taylor Mill, stepped forward to address the throng, a great cheer arose. They stood together, hand in hand.

Abiah, a tall woman, her head in a blue bonnet, began. "Great thinkers, indeed, at different times, from Plato to Condorcet, besides some of the most eminent names of the present age, have made emphatic protests in favor of the equality of women."[1]

The crowd cheered again.

Harriot raised a hand in the air. "We deny the right of any portion of the species to decide for another portion, or any individual for another individual, what is and what is not their 'proper sphere.' The proper sphere for all human beings is the largest and highest which they are able to attain to. What this is, cannot be ascertained without complete liberty of choice."[2]

Abiah held up one finger. "*Resolved*—That every human being, of full age, and resident for a proper length of time on the soil of the nation, who is required to obey the law, is entitled to a voice in its enactment."[3]

Harriot held up two fingers. "*Resolved*—That women are entitled to the right of suffrage and to be considered eligible to office, . . . and that every party which claims to represent the humanity, the civilization, and the progress of the age, is bound to inscribe on its banners, equality before the law, without distinction of sex or color."[4]

The women cheered. Molly searched the crowd, her smile growing wider as she noted rapt faces, listening. Among them were members of the working class, the nobility, and women of different races and colors. Suffrage was the great unifying topic. Her desire that these women unite under one banner grew and filled her.

Abiah held up three fingers. "*Resolved*—That civil and political rights acknowledge no sex, and therefore the word 'male' should be struck from every State Constitution."[5]

---

1 From Mrs. Stuart Mill, *Enfranchisement of Women*, London: Trubner and Co., 1868, 7 (spelling has been adapted for this novel). See also Author's Notes.

2 Mrs. Stuart Mill, *Enfranchisement of Women*, 8. See also Author's Notes.

3 Mrs. Stuart Mill, *Enfranchisement of Women*, 4. See also Author's Notes.

4 Mrs. Stuart Mill, *Enfranchisement of Women*, 4 (spelling has been adapted for this novel). See also Author's Notes.

5 Mrs. Stuart Mill, *Enfranchisement of Women*, 4. See also Author's Notes.

With that, the crowd shouted, their combined voices a clarion anthem of support. Harriot waited for the noise to quiet and then held up four fingers. "*Resolved*—That the laws of property as affecting married persons demand a thorough revisal, so that all rights be equal . . . control over the property gained by their mutual toil and sacrifices, and be heir to her husband precisely to that extent that he is heir to her, and entitled at her death to dispose by will of the same share of the joint property as he is."[6]

Excellent! Molly's heart cheered. Looking around her at all the hopeful faces of the women lightened her heart. Happy, strong women were finally united in the cause of suffrage. If they could continue in this manner, they would have the vote much sooner than imagined.

An itch tingled at the back of her neck, and she raised her hand to rub at it while searching for the source of eyes on her. She felt them but could not discover from where. Trying to shrug off the feeling, and blaming her nerves, she clapped when more speakers and some newspaper representatives walked onto the platform.

Then Theo stepped out from behind a banner and approached at her front, not twenty feet away. She clutched Lady Chloe's arm, ready to drag her and run down the nearest alley. His bald head shone in the sunlight. His immaculate clothes were of the finest cloth. His eyes flicked between her and Lady Chloe, calculating.

Before Molly could move, Chloe said, "Why, Lord Oswald! What a pleasure to see you. Do we share a fondness for the cause of women's suffrage?"

Molly turned to Chloe, mouth open but unable to speak, trying to piece together how her kidnapper and the crime boss of Angel Meadow could be on good terms with Chloe.

"Yes, your father never mentioned your interest in attending today's event." He smiled, but no happiness lit his face.

Lady Chloe shivered beside Molly.

"It is a good cause, as I have said." Lady Chloe lifted her chin and added, "One we naturally support, and I'm glad you are here."

"I can't help but wonder at *your* presence here," Theo said. His eyes wandered over her dress. "Perhaps your father is unaware of your activities. As his close friend, I would, of course, support his wishes."

6 Mrs. Stuart Mill, *Enfranchisement of Women*, 4. See also Author's Notes.

She stood taller. "Lord Oswald, I can assure you I am here not only with my father's knowledge but with his support, financial and otherwise. But I thank you for your concern."

Theo stepped in front of Molly, blocking her view. She leaned to the side to open a view to the stage, but he stepped in front of her once more.

"And who, may I ask, is this?" he asked, indicating Molly. "Might I have an introduction? Perhaps another lady parading as a commoner?" His eyebrow rose, and his eyes bore into Molly's. An icy chill travelled down her back. She shifted and squeezed Chloe's arm, hoping that somehow her friend would understand and not disclose her identity.

Chloe paused, searching Molly's face, and then turned to him. "This is a new acquaintance of mine. I'm afraid I am not in a position to offer an introduction." Her eyes stared coldly back at him.

Molly's mouth opened in amazement at Chloe's bold tone, but then she quickly wiped her face of any expression. Chloe's bravery grew every moment Molly spent with her.

Theo nodded to her, bowed over Chloe's hand, and then turned to join some of the few men in the audience to their right.

As soon as Theo was out of earshot, Molly made to pull Chloe away. "We are in danger here."

"What? From Lord Oswald?" Chloe watched him for a moment, and Molly followed suit.

His interest in them seemed to have ended, and he rocked on his heels, talking with the small group of men around him.

"I admit to feeling my skin crawl in his presence, but he is quite reliant on my father's good will," Chloe said. "We needn't worry about any trouble from him."

"Forgive me, my lady, but I disagree so strongly I believe it would be wise for you and me to leave." Molly had had no idea Theo was a member of the *ton*, had no clue he'd been ingratiating himself into Chloe's father's good graces. She couldn't wait to tell Lady Amanda. This information could save Jewel and help them track down all the people involved.

Chloe frowned. "Leave? I couldn't. After all we've worked for?" She shook her head then turned to Molly. "How do you know him?"

Molly gripped Chloe's hands. "Listen to me. Lord Oswald—"

Before she could say more, a group of women from their suffrage committee approached, laughing, and surrounded them, talking all at once.

Theo had conferred with his men, and they were now separating and moving through the women at the rally, positioning themselves.

Molly swallowed. "I don't like this."

Chloe rested a hand on her arm. "Remember, this is nothing like Peterloo." She turned to one of their fellow committee members at her side, answering the woman's questions.

Molly had never seen her so animated or participatory in a social gathering. The cause had certainly brought out a side of Chloe that Molly hoped to see more of.

Perhaps Chloe, a lady, would be safe surrounded by friends. Molly couldn't feel the same about her own safety. Unless she found a way to protect herself, she was in grave danger from Theo. The only thing protecting her was Lord Oswald's confusion about her true identity and his lack of understanding of her relationship with Lady Chloe.

A great crowd of women entered the park, making more noise than any others had dared. Molly squinted at their banners. *No Child Labor.* She started to piece ideas together, her mind spinning. The next banner read, *Votes for women gives votes to children.*

A new speaker stepped to the platform, and the crowd erupted in cheers. Energy from the women filled Molly, and for a moment she forgot the danger and breathed deeply the satisfaction of a united group of women combining their efforts, working together. The sight was beautiful to her. She allowed the strength of their numbers to fill her and give her peace.

The speaker was a leader in one of the suffrage groups. After welcoming everyone, she said, "I have excellent news. The child labor bill has passed." A great cheer rose from all of the women. "I received news just now that children under the age of nine are forbidden to work full time."

A great cheer sounded from the women entering with the banners, and clapping came from many others. Molly's own heart lit with happiness, and a small ache for her twins at the orphanage in Manchester urged her to visit again soon. Many of the children in their orphanages were now saved from dangerous work inside the factories, doing jobs no grown man would, risking their very lives and surviving on little sustenance. Maybe a united group of women could do more good than simply enfranchise themselves. Maybe if they were motivated toward common goals, much more good could be accomplished through them.

Molly felt dark eyes watching her again. Her skin crawled from the awareness. She turned her head to find Theo's gaze boring into hers. His skin was purple with anger, his fists clenched. She swallowed, grateful half a square and a hundred women stood between them. But there was no mistaking his fury or that it was targeted toward her.

While his hatred terrified her, a great thrill also filled her. Finally she'd discovered the identity of the man behind the evil in Angel Meadow. Two of Theo's men stood close enough to her that she'd be able to overhear their conversation if she could just get nearer from behind. It was time to do some investigative work on her own to see what else she could discover about Theo and what he planned to do at the rally.

She was soon close enough for their voices to carry to her. "—child labor. He lost a big battle this week."

The other man grunted. "Lost his temper, he did. Right near killed me."

"As would you if you'd lost a good piece of your workforce, now, wouldn't you?"

"It's not as though he's lost *all* the children, and I don't think I deserved Theo's swing at my face. It's not as though I'm in the House of Lords, am I?"

"He's coming." They stopped talking.

Sure enough, Theo made his way toward them. Molly adjusted her position so she crouched behind a tree. Women surrounded her, and their voices drowned out what the men were saying. She moved around the tree, inching as near to them as she dared.

"—the orphanages," Theo said.

Oh no!

"We will defy this new law." Theo's voice barely masked his anger. "No one will enforce it. How will they know the ages of working children? Many are unusually small for their ages. What of those with no parents to vouch for them? Orphanages, men. We go to the orphanages next. We must grab them early next week, before the Halloways return for another visit."

Molly's hands started to shake, and her breathing came in short pants. He planned to kidnap the orphanage children. *Her* children. The twins and all the others she'd grown to love.

She moved without considering the consequences. She stood too quickly, tripped over a root, cried out, and fell to the ground.

"Get her!" Theo yelled.

But she jumped to her feet, ignoring the sharp stabbing and pulsing pain through her ankle. She raced toward the edge of the tight crowd. If they caught her now, no one would know to warn the orphanages. She tore through the throng of women, who squealed and shouted. Some fell to the ground as she shoved past. Not caring where she went so long as she escaped, she ran. Hearing the men behind her, she pushed deeper into the crowd then dove to the ground, crawling at people's feet. If she could reach the front, she'd be close to Lord Halloway and the reporters, and she'd be safe. Theo could not hurt her there, with so many looking on.

But crawling was near impossible in a skirt. She pushed on, knowing that at least she was invisible to Theo and his men. At first the women pulled away, shocked at her presence and giving her space to move, but as she pushed forward into the ever-thicker crowds, there simply wasn't enough room. She pressed through legs and knees and long skirts. She had more room down by their feet than she would have pressed against them and working past their shoulders and hips.

Her heart pounded and sweat dripped off her face to the ground, yet she remained grateful for the hemmed-in crowd, grateful for the legs and feet and skirts that hid her.

Up ahead, space opened in the crowd. Bits of platform became visible. She brought herself up to a low crouch and began to move on her feet again—oh, the relief to her knees. But as soon as she did, a man grabbed her arm.

"You'll be coming with me. Don't make a sound."

A sharp point through the side of her dress made her yelp.

A tall man dug the blade in farther. "I said no sound."

The blade hadn't broken her skin, but she felt the point through her dress. He stood close and forced her to rise, standing among the women all around them. Then he placed his arm around her as if in an embrace.

He whispered in her ear, "Act like we are together, love. We're gonna walk through all these people and get some air."

Molly shook her head, and the man dug his nails into her arm, pressing the blade closer to her skin at her side.

Women around her wrinkled their noses with looks of distaste and tried to pretend she and this ugly, large man hadn't just appeared in their midst. Black mud marks on the front of her dress, however, were plenty evidence that she'd been crawling about on the ground. She knew she looked a sight, but she still tried to make eye contact with any of the women. They each avoided her gaze.

The man pushed through them all, pulling Molly away from the square. What could she do about it? Shout, fight, push away? But part of her mind froze. She blinked, trying to clear the fog, but terror paralyzed her. She didn't want anyone else around her to get hurt, didn't want the mad stampede of Peterloo, didn't want to be stabbed. She forced herself to think. He didn't give her any respite, instead continuing to move to the right of the platform in front. Her breath came faster, and she forced herself to move. Jerking away, she tried to create space between them.

"Easy now, love. We're almost there."

"I'm not your love." She strained against the vise grip on her arm and the knife pressed deeper, jabbing at her through her clothing.

When she was almost to the edge of the crowd, a welcome voice shouted above the melee. "Here she is, folks, trying to get up front! Give her some space."

She and her captor turned.

Thomas smiled, but his eyes were determined. Her knees almost buckled in relief.

Thomas waved and winked at her and beckoned for her and the man to come forward. Her captor stopped, frozen in place, looking all around him. Every eye turned to them. Molly used the moment to shake off her captor and move through an opening in the crowd toward Thomas. Never had she seen a more welcome sight. When she reached him, Thomas pulled her to his side, with one arm around her waist. He called out, "I've got her now, everyone. Let's hear it for one of the women pivotal in our movement, Miss Molly O'Malley."

Those in the back who couldn't see her mud-stained skirt or the strange manner in which she clung to Thomas responded quicker than those who could. But soon all were cheering and calling out as they had for the speakers. The man who had just moments ago held a knife at her side now backed away, scowling.

"Thomas, what do I do now?"

"Talk to them. Say something inspiring. Then we'll leave." He winked at her again. "Say what's in your heart. They need to hear it."

She gulped. When she stepped forward, everyone went quiet. Those closest to her opened their mouths in surprise, clearly eyeing the mud stains at her knees, which made her even more nervous. What should she say to all these people? Thomas had moved away, honing in on her captor.

She found Lady Amanda, standing to the right on the front row. Her friend's face had deep lines of concern, but her eyes shone with pride. Dear Lady Amanda. The woman who'd first lit the fire in Molly for rights and independence. The woman who had risked everything to help those who needed a nudge to help themselves.

Then Molly's gaze travelled over the crowd, over all of the beautiful women. They'd found something inside them worth fighting for. They'd finally discovered that their voices mattered, unique and independent. Pride filled Molly, along with a sense of her own great worth. She belonged with these women.

And she'd helped the Sparrow, dear Lady Amanda, wage a full campaign in support of suffrage for all classes, including women. She'd helped run the suffrage committee that was spreading awareness. She'd organized and planned ways to help women in separate and unique efforts to gain the right to vote. She helped, among the ladies of the *ton*, to run the aid for orphanages. And even if she hadn't had the opportunity to work on any of these causes, she, Molly, was still worth a great deal. She stood taller.

Her eyes found Thomas again. He had followed her captor and grappled with him, securing his arms behind his back. Others stood at the perimeter, watching. They danced a fine line, all of them—Theo not wanting to draw attention to himself, Thomas hoping to stop their efforts, and Molly just wanting to stay alive and well.

She would have to hurry with her remarks so she and Thomas could find their way to Lord Halloway and safety.

"Sisters!"

The crowd erupted in cheers, which surprised Molly but brought a huge smile to her face. "My dear sisters! We are here, united!" More cheers stalled her speech. "Look at us, united from all classes, all situations, and all different suffrage groups, united with one cause." They cheered again.

The various groups each came with their colors and banners, but the prevailing unifying theme among them was the color white. Many women wore white—scarves, bonnets, aprons, skirts, or dresses.

"We are united in the greatest cause of our day, the cause that will benefit not just us but our families—our children, our daughters!" She thought of Charlie. She hadn't missed him in a long time; the sharp pain and fear that had accompanied memories of him were gone now. His smile warmed her face. And then she felt him drift away in her thoughts. He wasn't her only *why* anymore.

Her captor walked away between the arms of two strong men. And Thomas stood in front of her, arms across his chest, smiling at her, right in the middle of the women.

And she smiled back and finished. "The greatest cause for all of the families in England. For men, women, and children. Suffrage, not just for some but for all! Votes for women!"

And the women jumped in place, cheering and clapping and calling her name. Thaddeus, a reporter from *The Manchester Guardian*, stepped forward.

Her speech complete, women all through the crowd still cheering her on, Molly stepped off the platform. Blood coursed through her, and hands shaking, she forced herself to move. Aware of eyes still on her, she stepped into Thomas's arms. He held her. He rocked her, resting his chin on her head.

And she knew this was home. Danger would come. Life would bring any number of hardships their way. She didn't want to face any of it without Thomas.

He pulled away, keeping her close, and searched her face. The tenderness in his eyes brought tears to her own.

"Oh, Thomas." She brought a hand to the side of his face. "I love you."

"Do you, now?" His face lit up, and a great smile filled his face with warm crinkles. Then he looked out over the crowd. Most were watching John speak on the platform, but some attention still lingered on the two of them. "Hold on to that thought, Molly. Come with me." He grabbed her hand, and they ran for the trees along the park's edges. Once in the shade of their great branches, he pulled her close, wrapping his great arms around her. "There."

Molly giggled. And then Thomas leaned down and pressed his lips to hers. Their softness warmed her. Gentle, pressing into her own, his lips moved over hers. Shivers ran up her legs and into her core. Trembling with happiness, she smiled beneath his mouth, and he smiled in return.

"I love you too," he said.

She reached up to pull him closer, when his face rammed into hers. Pain shot through her face and into the top of her head. Her hand went to her nose, blood dripping through her fingers. In a daze she watched Thomas fall to the ground. A man with a club stood over him with a menacing scowl. She tried to scream, but the sound came out of her throat like a scratchy whisper. Then a sharp pain at the back of her head made the world start to turn black. A small cry left her lips as she slumped to the ground.

CHAPTER TWENTY-THREE

ANNESLEY STEPPED OUT OF HIS solicitor's office, grim but determined. Money would be tight for many years, likely for the duration of his life, but he'd saved his estate from ruin. Years ago his father had given Annesley full legal authority to run the estate, no doubt assuming the need to exercise such a power wouldn't come until after the earl's death.

Annesley then sent a sealed letter to be delivered to his father, explaining how Annesley would sell off two of their holdings, lease out the others, and take steps to save and consolidate their estates.

Writing the letter had been a painful experience. In it he'd explained that there would be no extra funds of any sort for gambling, cards, horses, or investments in Manchester factories. All funds would be used to fix the estate; they had nothing extra.

He breathed deeply. Now, if he could keep the prime minister happy for a short time more, Annesley would soon be rid of his lingering extortion as well.

Annesley's timepiece burned a hole in his coat pocket, reminding him that the suffrage rally was already well underway. He closed his carriage door and told the driver to hurry toward the square. Then he sat back in happy expectation of seeing Chloe again, knowing he could pursue her in earnest and honestly knowing his name and holdings were not tarnished or beholden to any unsavory person or endeavor. As soon as all the changes he'd set up took place, Annesley would be a free man.

As the carriage pulled closer to the park, his smile grew. The rally had a tremendous crowd. Chloe would most definitely be beaming with happiness.

He walked up to the group just as Molly stepped off the stage, full of confidence, the crowd still cheering at what must have been a speech. And yet, something seemed amiss with her. Disheveled, her dress was covered in black streaks of dirt. When she reached Thomas, she fell into his arms as though seeking comfort there. Annesley's sharp eye scanned the group. Men, strategically placed, lined the gathering. Theo, as Annesley had suspected, stood at the back, conferring with two others.

Molly and Thomas appeared to be having some sort of romantic interchange at the front. Annesley grinned. Thomas then led Molly toward the side of the crowd and the edge of the woods.

Well, happiness for the two of them. If only Annesley would be so fortunate.

He moved forward, seeking the one person he most cared to see, while keeping an eye on the men in the crowd.

Banners supporting the lowered child labor age caught his eye. He grunted. This would not be good. The more Theo connected women with his children workers, the worse chance women had of being included in the bill and the worse chance the law had of passing in their favor.

He skirted the crowd, moving behind Theo all the way to the other side where Chloe, Lady Amanda, and Lord Halloway all stood together watching the platform.

"Annesley." The prime minister, dressed in his blackest attire, approached.

"Lord Grey. I'm surprised to see you here."

"I had to come to see what sort of crowd would turn up. For the most part, it appears to be the dregs of society complaining of their lot, as usual, though I see a few ill-advised nobles and their families as well." With a tip of his head, he indicated Lord Halloway's group, including Chloe.

Annesley gritted his teeth. "I would hesitate to hold the future Duke of Somerset in disdain. If you'll excuse me." He moved to step around him, but Lord Grey blocked his path. "We have matters to discuss."

"I have nothing more to report right now. I have told you everything I know."

"This event is much larger than you led me to believe it would be. And the presence of child labor protestors surprises me." He stepped closer. "I don't like being surprised. I engaged your services to prevent these sorts of surprises. Our benefactor will be less than amused at the report of this rally, I assure you."

Annesley must keep Lord Grey happy for a short time longer. "I had no way of knowing the numbers of who would attend. I am certain the women who planned it are equally surprised. As for the child labor protests, the group I am monitoring was not involved, which is why I heard nothing about them either." He moved to step away, but the prime minister held up his hand.

"A moment. Are you certain your emotional alliance and friendships are not impeding your ability to provide all the information I require?"

"I have done everything you have asked. Anything I learned about their plans was in your hands nearly the moment they spoke it." Annesley raised his voice. "I gave you whatever knowledge you required of me. If *you* failed in your efforts to dismantle the suffrage committee, that is no concern of mine."

The prime minister's face flushed. "It is very much your concern. Or have you forgotten how closely your future is linked to the results of this upcoming election?"

"Of course not. But again, I've done all you've asked of me. Every time Lady Chloe made new plans, you became aware of them immediately." He vowed that after next week, he'd never again talk with this man. "Now, if you'll excuse me."

Annesley desired nothing more than to shake the conversation from him forever. He turned from a blustering Lord Grey, who stuck close, following him, and Annesley nearly stumbled over Lady Chloe. She stood before him, her face pale and tears welling. His heart felt as though it had lodged in his throat.

"Chloe." He moved toward her, but she turned and ran from him, shouting, "Stay away from me. How could you?"

Farther ahead, watching them, Lady Amanda's eyes widened in concern. When he shook his head helplessly, she moved quickly to follow Chloe.

Lord Grey backed away.

With slow feet, Annesley approached Lord Halloway, at a loss as to how to mend all that had just been broken.

The crowd erupted in another great cheer, and Annesley could tell the rally was winding down and soon would be over. Already women on the outer edges of the park were stepping away and leaving the area.

As soon as he arrived at his friend's side, Halloway pounded him on the back. "Would you look at these crowds?"

Annesley grimaced.

"Oh, come now, whatever it is, it can't be as bad as all that."

"Worse. It is undoubtedly worse than what you are imagining."

"That sounds grave." Halloway eyed the women. Annesley turned. They'd found a bench and now sat together, deep in conversation, Chloe wiping her eyes.

Annesley shook his head. "I only hope you and I can yet be friends after Amanda hears the lot of it." He scanned the crowd, as he was accustomed to doing, and his attention sharpened on the far edge of the woods. "What's over there?"

Halloway chuckled. "What do you see? If it is a pair of my servants having a romantic dalliance, I can only say it's about time." His eyes followed and frowned.

They both took steps in that direction, where Theo's men had gathered outside the wooded area. They were talking animatedly together.

Theo's men took off running, leaving together, with no sign of Molly or Thomas. Annesley and Halloway began to run as well. By the time they reached the woods, Theo's men had departed in a carriage marked with Theo's crest.

Halloway called to Annesley and ran deeper into the woods, noting an area of pressed earth and many footprints. He turned around in circles, looking in all directions, while Annesley searched the ground then pulled a lavender ribbon from the ground, where it had been crushed under some earth.

"Is this Molly's?"

Halloway shook his head. "I can't be sure, but she did have that color on today. Amanda would know." He turned in a circle and raked a hand through his hair. "They are nowhere to be seen in here. Let's have a look about the park."

Annesley grunted. "There are simply too many people to do a proper sweep of the area."

They burst from the trees and nearly ran into Lady Amanda and Lady Chloe.

Amanda grabbed at Halloway's arm. "What? What is it?"

Chloe added, "We saw you run." She would not meet Annesley's eyes.

"Molly and Thomas. We don't know where they are," Halloway said.

The men searched the crowd, their gazes sharpening on smaller groups, huddled together.

Running forward to get a better view, Halloway said, "Theo and his men were over here. We haven't seen Molly since."

Chloe spun to face them. "She told me we were in danger."

Annesley's heartrate picked up. He connected all the details and knew he must go after them. "Did Oswald see Molly?"

"Yes, they talked. Right after that, she said she wanted to leave. But I don't understand. How could they know each other?"

Annesley paused, managing a gentle tone. "It was he who abducted her and Becky in Manchester. He is Theo, the boss of Angel Meadow."

"No!" Chloe grabbed his arm, gripping it. Her face went white, and Annesley feared she might fall to his feet.

Becky ran up to them, curtsying as quickly as she could, nearly tripping over her feet. "Forgive me, my lords, my ladies. Th-The-Theo's here."

Chloe put her arm around Becky. "We just discovered that. Thank you, Becky, my dear. Is this the first you have seen of him since Manchester?" She shook her head in amazement that such a snake could be hiding so openly among them.

"It is, my lady. I nearly fainted when I saw him."

"Molly saw him, too, but I dismissed her fear as nothing, a shadow of her worries about Peterloo." Fresh tears welled in her eyes, and it was all Annesley could do not to pull her into his arms, but he knew his embrace would be unwelcome. He reached forward and caught a single tear on his finger.

She stepped away, shaking her head. "How can you stand here and pretend you care?"

Before he could answer, Amanda demanded, "Is it true you work for Lord Grey? That you are helping him sabotage the women's vote?" She had such fear in her eyes that his heart broke a little. About to lose the respect of his dearest friends and having already lost the confidence of the woman he loved, he filled with a hopeless desperation.

"It is not at all what you think."

Halloway cleared his throat and brought the focus back to the matter at hand. "I do not see Thomas or Molly anywhere in the departing crowd. They are not waiting by our carriage. They aren't with the presenters or other women in our group either. I fear they have vanished."

Annesley began to make plans to help in the only way he knew. "Theo knows where they are." Annesley fisted his hands together. "I'm sure of it."

"I'll summon the magistrate. And we must commence a search of the park and surrounding areas." Halloway stepped toward his carriage and waved to the footman, who came running.

Annesley could not stand around waiting. He turned and ran for his own carriage, his mind already switching into his professional habits, planning his next move, all the while searching his surroundings. He'd depart immediately for Manchester. He always had a packed satchel under the bench of his carriage for such a need. His first stop: Angel Meadow.

CHAPTER TWENTY-FOUR

MOLLY OPENED ONE EYE, BUT her mind wouldn't work. The cold seeped into her bones, and she shivered. Trying to see her surroundings brought shooting pain through the top of her head. She lay on a wood floor in a room with no windows. A desk and two chairs sat in the corner. Closing her eyes again, she listened.

Loud machinery. The floor vibrating. Oil, grease, sweat, and other unusual smells blended with the dust from the floor. She tried to sit up, but she had no use of her hands, which were tied together behind her, and she tipped over onto her other side. Jerking and pulling on the rope, she felt panic rise to her throat, so she breathed slowly, forcing her brain to focus, and tried to understand where she was and what she was doing lying hands tied in this unknown place. Her head ached.

Memories flooded her mind. Thomas. She gasped and both eyes flew open. She squirmed, moving in a large circle on the floor. She was alone. Where were they keeping Thomas? And what was this place? She bent her knees, and with her ankles tied together, she placed both feet carefully down on the floor. Then she tried to stand. Weak muscles and unsteady balance made her topple—twice—before she managed to remain upright. The rope was tied too tightly for any movement beyond standing, so she sat back down and used scooting motions to move.

She pulled herself along the floor toward the door. She worked her way to standing then backed up to the knob and used her tied hands to try to turn it. The knob jiggled but would not turn. Sighing, she leaned back against the door, tilted her head back, and tried to swallow tears. She was so all-consumingly tired. She couldn't seem to get control of her thoughts or emotions. All she wanted to do was lie down again and sleep, but she forced herself to keep moving. The memory of Theo's plan to abduct her orphanage children in the front of her mind, she knew they must act somehow, knew she must tell Thomas.

But Thomas was gone.

And where was Theo? He walked among the nobles. Was he a noble? He was friends with Chloe, or at least Chloe's father. *Serpent.* He was the evil behind Jewel's situation, behind all the horrors in Angel Meadow. His iron hand, with all its gold rings and ridiculous signet, fought against women's suffrage, forced children into slave labor, and entrapped working-class families into doing his bidding.

Until now, Molly hadn't thought it possible to hate anyone as much as she hated Jack Bender, but thoughts of Theo boiled her blood with a hot fire.

The door swung back behind her, away from her body. With a yelp, she toppled backward, landing in the arms of the man who was the focus of all of her anger.

"Well, now. I wasn't expecting such a warm welcome." He pulled her even closer against his large frame and caressed the softness of her neck. "But I'm not one to complain."

"Unhand me, you disgusting pig!" She twisted away but lost her balance and fell to the floor, slamming her shoulder on impact.

"No need to be uncivil. But then again, you are common, aren't you?"

He walked past her and into the office that was her prison cell. One of his guards grabbed her by the arms, jerked her back into the room, and placed her none too gently on a chair.

Across from her, Theo ran a hand over his bald head. "Now, let's have a conversation, shall we?" He leaned his abundant frame back into his comparatively tiny chair and laced his fingers together.

Molly scowled. "What right have you to keep me here? You must know I'm not without friends. You will regret this."

Theo's laugh rumbled in his belly. "Ho, ho! Your friends are but pawns to me. You sit in my kingdom now, Molly. It is Molly, isn't it?"

She scowled. "Where's Thomas?"

"The large brute who almost kissed you in the woods? I'm sorry to have interrupted such a moment, by the way."

"Where is he? What do you want with us?"

"Don't worry about him. He'll soon join us. He gave us a bit of trouble at first, but I'm certain that after a few more hours, he'll be as congenial as you or I. You *are* planning to be congenial, I presume?"

Oh, how she hated this man. His mocking, polite tone grated, and every one of Molly's hairs stood on end. If she hadn't been tied hand and foot, he might have felt her hand strike him across his abundant face.

"So why am I here?"

"I could ask the same of you. You seem to be becoming a regular guest of mine. The trouble is, you know of my plans for more children. I'll be wanting to know who else heard about them."

She scoffed.

"And you paid visits to many of my homes in the Meadow while you were there. Once a person becomes close to us, once they partake of our hospitality, such as you have, they are invited to a more *permanent* residence."

"My friends will know you are responsible for my disappearance. They *will* come calling; of that you can be certain." She stared into his face, hoping she showed only courage and none of the terror that shook her knees.

"Let them come." He shrugged. "I fear no man. Most answer to me, and those who don't soon will. Money brings power, my dear Molly. You should know that by now, employed, as you are, in a duke's household."

She gritted her teeth. He knew her connection to Lady Amanda. Molly's worry for Thomas grew. What did Theo mean, that Thomas would soon join them? Would Theo torture him? Such images toyed at the edges of her awareness. Whatever they did to Thomas, and wherever he was, she needed to find him. They had to escape, run to the orphanage, and warn the children. Protect them. Unless they were too late.

Maybe she could learn something from the overconfident Theo. "You don't control everyone," she said defiantly. "The child labor bill has passed. You had no control over that vote or those nobles." She felt an increase of peace at the thought.

"An oversight." His face turned a darker pink, and he squinted at her. "One that should never have happened. The law won't last." He picked a piece of lint off his arm sleeve. "We have more control than you know."

She drew a breath. *Keep him talking.* "Your power is not as strong as you think it is. And you're about to lose half your labor force." She guessed on the numbers, hoping to keep him talking.

"It is a ridiculous law. I own the inspectors who will verify workers' ages. The young ones are all small and undernourished. Any one of them could be at least nine years of age. And the Irish . . . well, they are all shorter than the English, aren't they?"

"But their parents—"

He pointed his gold-bedecked finger at her. "The ones without parents will aid us the most as we legalize the others. Never fear, Molly. We will continue without a single hiccup."

Her mind swam in a panicked desperation about how to get him to talk about the orphanage or whether her children had been captured. She couldn't think of a way, and she cringed inside in frustration.

At that moment two of his men came barreling in. "He's done beat the others to a pulp, he has. No one can keep him caged, and now he's out, running through the place."

Theo's face turned purple. "Follow him, you half-wits!"

"We are, m'lord!"

"*Don't* call me that."

"I forgot, sir. I mean, we are, Theo. What I mean to say is they are, all of them, looking for him, but he's plum disappeared, he has, and no one knows where else to look. All the doors coming in and out of the mill are locked, and I have men standing at them so he canna' leave, but there are plenty of places he could hide and children underfoot. We could be looking for days and never spot him."

"Offer rewards to the children for turning him in. Threaten them if necessary."

"Oh, good show, sir—I mean, Theo. We will do that right away sir—I mean, Theo."

When the guard closed the door, Molly couldn't help the smile that overtook her face. "You've lost Thomas."

But Theo wasn't in the mood to toy with conversation any longer. With great panting effort, he rose from his chair. Then he stepped purposefully toward her and slapped her face.

"See these walls? Take a good long look. You will never leave them. You will never have another view for the rest of your short life." He left the room, and his evil, overbearing atmosphere left with him. The lock clicked.

Alone again, Molly felt absurdly at peace, despite her hands and feet being tied, despite sitting on a chair, prisoner of an evil mill boss. Thomas was somewhere in this building. And they couldn't find him. Her mind started turning over possibilities for escape, for if Thomas could break free, she could too. And she was determined to do it.

Hours later her shoulders felt bruised from slamming into the door, and her fingers were raw from trying to rip at her ropes. All creative thought was exhausted, with no viable ideas as to how she would ever escape.

That's when Theo returned with two men at his sides.

He didn't speak to her. One man cut the rope at her ankles, and she moved her stiff legs, bending them carefully and stepping from side to side in the small space between the men.

Theo waved his hand. "Follow me."

They opened the door into a long, empty hallway. The sounds of machinery amplified once they exited the room, and she felt the hum and vibrations in her feet.

"Where are we going?" Molly tried to keep her voice steady.

No one answered.

At the end of the hallway, they exited onto a platform with a railing that looked over a great factory floor. Part of Molly didn't want to admit she was impressed. Huge weaving machines ran in rows, creating aisles between the looms. Children stood along each row. Their small arms reached forward, guiding the thread. Others walked up and down the rows, checking the gathering thread above as it filled a cone-shaped cylinder. Every so often the children reached forward and ran their small fingers along the thread, twisting and spinning the white filament. As she watched the process in fascination, Molly almost forgot she was a prisoner. In all her years as a lady's maid, she'd never known how a spool of thread was made.

A great buzzer sounded, and the machines stopped. A different group of children rushed forward, pulling the full bobbins off the top of each machine, racing them to the shelves, where they traded them for empty bobbins. Once all the full bobbins were replaced, the machines started up again.

"Children are the best workers." Theo's voice made her jump. "Small hands and fingers make them adept at this job. When adults try it, threads tear. Adults' fingers are too large to isolate a single thread. The children take great pride in their work, as you can see. Most hope to be spinners someday."

Theo surveyed the factory floor with a light in his face she had never seen there. Interesting. Perhaps his passion for the mills did not rest solely in their money-making opportunity.

At an unspoken command, the guards guided her to the right and down a steep metal staircase to the factory floor. The room was loud and smelled of a hundred things, predominantly of oil. A young girl ran by with a small metal can and spout. She darted in and out and around the machines, touching the tip of the can to the gears and moving parts as if they weren't about to squash her small frame.

Movement to her left caught Molly's eye while she walked down the stairs. Amongst all the singing machinery and color and loud noise all around, a specific motion and presence drew her attention.

Thomas. He peeked out from behind a nearby machine. He saw her watching and pulled his head back. She looked elsewhere, trying to hide her great breath of relief.

Doors at the back of the floor opened, and four men entered. They walked up and down the rows, examining the children and machines. They each made their way along a different row. Thomas ducked behind the fifth.

Oh no, oh no!

Molly finished the staircase with Theo and his guards. At ground level, she was not able to see over the machines. When she stalled, the men jerked her forward. With Theo leading the way, they walked along the edge of the room. The noise was almost deafening, the rhythm overpowering. She could feel her breathing keeping time with the folding and shifting of the great weaving arms.

The sight of Thomas's head surprised her again, this time closer than before, a few rows to her front. She tried to think of a way to help him. The guards stopped her in front of a smaller open area and another set of stairs.

A worker ran up. "We need to shut down for cleaning. At your request, we skipped it last hour and the gears are clogging."

The man at Molly's right shook his head. "They'll have to clean the machines without shutting down. Boss's orders."

The worker glanced at Molly and then to Theo, who pretended as though he didn't hear the conversation, and then back at the person to Molly's right, who must be some sort of manager. "But last time—"

"I know. They've got to learn how to do this quickly. The only way is for them to practice. We can't shut down for a whole hour."

"But when one of 'em gets caught, it takes some time to clean up the mess"—at that, Molly gasped—"I merely thought—"

"Do as I say."

The worker's brow furrowed, deep lines etched across his forehead. He chewed his lips but didn't say anything further.

A bell dinged, and a new group of children rushed in. Molly watched more children run from the sides of the room. They had quick fingers and even faster feet, dashing in and out of the machines, grabbing tufts of dusty cotton and cleaning out mule spinners, the manager called them as he called out orders. Fibers floated through the air above the machines and collected near the top and bottom of the spinners. While the arms moved, the children reached in, quick as a rat in the cellar, and grabbed at loose fibers before the machine swung back again and closed off the space. More than once, children very nearly lost fingers. Molly winced every time.

She could not believe the risk Theo exposed them to. "They could die."

The manager next to her grunted.

Theo's mellow voice brought bile to her throat. "Watch them; they are quite accomplished. Only the quickest become cleaners."

Molly couldn't watch any longer. At once, she felt gratitude for the lawmakers who'd banned these children from workplaces such as this. *Let the young ones be home.*

Thomas peeked out from behind another machine, and he stared at her as if he hoped she could read his mind, which she could not. But she was done with Theo and his factory. The younger children should know they couldn't be here any longer. Perhaps if enough left, Theo would be forced to shut down operations for a couple of days, at least.

She thought of her dear orphanage children, and great indignation rose inside her.

Then a great alarm pealed over the group. The workers gave a shout, and the machines ground to a screeching halt. A scurry of activity a few rows down drew everyone's attention. Shortly, a man appeared, running. He carried a boy in his arms whose hand was wrapped with a bit of ripped shirt and saturated with blood.

The room felt as still as death with the great roar of the now-still machines, a haunting echo in Molly's brain, the machines' silence almost sucking sound from her ears.

The boy's head fell limply against the worker's shoulder, his life dripping away with the blood down his arm. Horrified, hoping to put a stop to at least today's risk, Molly called out over the group, "Children! You are free. The law requires you not work here or in any factory if you are under nine years old. Go home to your parents."

"Be quiet." Theo lifted his hand, and the manager clamped a hand over Molly's mouth.

"They don't want us!" A young lad who couldn't be older than eight stepped forward, his mouth lifted in a crooked grimace. "Pa told me himself not to come back until I'd put in a full day's work."

She struggled and twisted her head, freeing her mouth. "But you are free from needing to work! The House of Lords—" And then she forgot everything, because Sally, one of her twins from the orphanage, stepped into an aisle. Molly gasped, and Theo eyed her with a huge, satisfied smile.

CHAPTER TWENTY-FIVE

THEO RAN A HAND DOWN his beard. "Did I tell you that you might recognize some of our workers? They came so willingly, begging to work for me. And since they have no parents to speak for them, I gladly took them in."

She shook, her words choking in her throat. "They're not yours to take. They have a home."

"So you say. But I say they have no one to vouch for them, no papers of birth or right of adoption. They may as well be mine as anyone's."

"You have no right."

"Oh, but I do. I have every right."

She lunged at him. "Those are *my* children." She kicked his large girth with her booted foot.

He grunted and doubled over, hands on his knees, wheezing.

She swung at the men nearest her, who approached to help Theo recover, and then ran from the group toward Sally. "Where are the others?"

"Stop her," Theo wheezed and waved the men away from him.

Sally held on to her. "Everywhere. We all got different jobs. I don't want to be here, Miss Molly."

"You don't have to be. We will get you out." She pulled Sally to a run beside her along the rows. Feet behind Molly pounded in pursuit. "I need something sharp."

"Oh, that's easy. It's all sharp." Sally pointed to the gears near the bottom of the weavers, revealing multiple cuts on her hands.

"Brilliant!" Molly held her ropes against the still gears behind her and rubbed them back and forth. The strands began to fray but not fast enough. The men would surely have already grabbed her by the time she got free. She looked back and, seeing Thomas, forgot her ropes.

Thomas had engaged a group of them and swung his fists with a power she'd never seen in him before. Opponents crumbled to the ground around him, but more stepped up, reaching for his arms to twist them behind his back. She hoped he could continue to resist them at least until her wrists were freed. The machines started up again. The gears severed the ropes, scraping her wrists. She pulled away fast enough that she didn't lose a hand. Heart pounding, breath coming quickly, she backed away from the machine.

She felt a tugging on her skirt—Sally. "Maybe you can talk to them all at once from up there," she said, pointing at the platform.

Now that the whirring of the looms had started again, she'd never be able to yell loudly enough for her orphanage children to hear. She turned to Thomas, who was beginning to tire.

"I have to help Thomas," she told Sally. "You go up top. See if you can get the children's attention. We need everyone from the orphanage and any others who want to, to leave with us."

Sally hurried up the metal stairs. Molly watched her, mostly relieved the child was out of danger and would not be an up-close witness to any more of the fighting.

Molly grabbed an empty bobbin from the shelves and ran toward Thomas. Hefting it above her head, she swung the large metal bobbin forward and slammed it into neck of the first man she came upon. At the same moment, Thomas struck him in the jaw.

They smiled at each other over the man's slumped frame.

Two more came for Thomas, and Molly shouted, "Watch out!" over the deafening, rhythmic pounding of the machinery.

Heeding her warning, Thomas stepped aside, and the two men reaching for him fell.

She didn't know how she and Thomas would ever escape with so many fighting against them. They were outnumbered, and the place was a maze.

Thomas directed her. "Get back up the stairs. The outer doors are up there."

"I saw Sally. Jonathon must be here as well."

His eyes widened. "And the others?"

"I think they're here too. We must get them out."

"Try to get their attention."

Another man swung at Thomas; Molly ran the other way, toward the stairs. Theo had disappeared. His absence made her nervous. She took the steps two at a time, trying not to stumble over her skirts. Once at the top, she ran to Sally, who stood with a group of around eight children.

"Where is everyone else? How do we find them?" Molly asked urgently.

"I don't know. We're all here somewhere. Everyone who could walk was made to leave and put to work straightaway, but I don't know where."

A loud alarm rang through the place, and the machines stopped. And the silence echoed around them again. Molly looked out over the factory and the children throughout. *There must be hundreds of children here.* Children who could help them.

"Children!" Molly yelled, cupping her mouth. "Quickly! Come with us! Let us leave this place, and be free!"

"Molly!" Jonathon's voice from at the far end of the room brought such a surge of warmth.

"My children! All of you. Come home with us. You do not belong here. Unite, dear ones! Run for the exit. They can't stop all of us at once!"

Thomas stood, his hand on the emergency button, towering over everyone, almost as tall as the machines around him. Four men lay on the ground around him. Smiling at Molly, he shouted, "Follow me, children! Let's go home!"

Molly waved her hands in the air, cheering as a good number of children—Jonathon and the others rallied around him—rushed to Thomas. The adult workers were outnumbered and surrounded. With no guidance from Theo, they looked unsure what they should do.

Where was Theo?

A sharp pain at the back of Molly's skull shoved her head forward, smacking her forehead against the railing. Crying out in pain, she twisted to see her assailant.

Theo held up a metal rod. "I could kill you for this."

"For what?" Molly blinked back darkness clouding her eyes. "For telling the children the truth? For taking back my own children? For protecting young ones from a lifetime of slavery? For—"

"You have no idea what you are disturbing here." He approached, the rod rising in his grip. "These children have nowhere else to go. Their families are starving. Their parents lie about all day in a drugged stupor."

"Because of *you*! You created their problems, and you benefit from them. That's going to stop."

He growled. "You are so misguided. You and your idealistic, uneducated attempts at reform. No magistrate will ever storm these walls or check the worker's ages. Their parents will continue to send them here, hoping to stay in their homes, which I provide."

She wanted to be ill at the pure evil in Theo and shook her head in absolute disgust. "Have you no care that Angel Meadow is the greatest hell England has ever known?"

He waved his large hands as if the idea was of no consequence. He reached for Sally. Molly grabbed the girl's shoulders and tried to pull her close, but Theo already had her tightly by the arm. "Take this child, for example. She was mine before you claimed her. The orphanage stole them from me first, and I deserve them back."

Again Molly tried to free Sally, but Theo's grip was like iron. Holding tightly to Sally, moving close to Theo so as not to hurt the child, love for all of the children nearly overpowered Molly. "That's where you are wrong. *I* care very much about what happens to every one of them. Many people do—powerful people you should have considered before involving these particular children. They will never again work in any factory of yours."

Shouts distracted them both. The children had begun a full revolt, running from the men, toppling bobbins, unravelling thread. The place would soon be destroyed.

At the sight, Theo's face turned the deepest shade of purple yet. "What is going on here?"

No one paid him any mind. Men continued to grab children, hitting and beating some when given the chance, until the stronger, older children pounded on the men's arms, yanking and pulling until the suffering child was freed.

"You!" Theo's fierce gaze turned all its ugliness on Molly. He stepped nearer, letting go of Sally at last, bearing down on Molly. "You are ruining my mill." His hands enclosed around her neck.

Molly pulled at his fleshy fingers one at a time to try to loosen their grip, but to no avail; he was too determined.

"You have destroyed six months of income today and scattered my workers." He forced her backward, pushing against the railing while his meaty fingers tightened their grip. She kicked at his knee and swung her arms at his face, but the length of his arms kept him out of her reach. She blinked as stars flashed in her vision and the edges went gray, darkening. She gasped for air.

Then something crashed over Theo's head, and his grip loosened enough for Molly to suck in a huge breath. With renewed strength, she wriggled free.

Sally smashed another empty bobbin against his face, and his rage turned to the child. He rushed at her, his large frame faster than Molly would have expected. He picked Sally up around the middle, lifted her over his head, and stepped toward the railing. "I've had enough of you," he said to Sally. "Enough of all of them!" He widened his stance as if preparing to hurtle her over the edge to the floor below.

Molly's heart raced, sending shots of energy through her veins as she rushed at him. She grabbed on to any part of Sally she could reach—hands, arms. Molly tried to stand tall enough to reach around Sally's shoulders. Theo kicked Molly and pulled Sally away again. Molly would have lost the child over the side in one swift motion of Theo's, but Thomas reached the top of the stairs at that moment. He hugged Sally to him, whisking her from Theo and rolling her to the ground, away from the railing, away from Theo.

Theo's eyes bulged. He pulled a knife from his belt and swung it at Thomas, catching the inside of his arm. It was only a scratch because Thomas moved quickly. Theo lunged again, and Thomas leaped backward.

Molly rushed forward to do something, anything at all, to help, but a firm grip jerked her backward. One of Theo's men. She twisted and wrenched, trying to free herself from the worker, but as she turned to face him, she knew she was outmatched. He towered over her. She kicked him and backed away, refusing to surrender.

Out of the corner of her eye she could make out Sally, who pressed against the wall.

"Go!" Molly cried to her. "Get the others and go! Run to the orphanage!" She didn't know if Sally could find the way, but if nothing else, Molly *would* free her children from this place.

Sally took off down the stairs. Relief lessened some of her tension.

Molly concentrated on the worker in front of her. He moved closer, his eyes dark, angry, and something else, which scared her most—hungry.

She clenched her fists and prepared to swing as soon as he was close enough. But before that happened, Theo toppled backward right in between them. Thomas appeared then, placing a foot atop Theo's large belly. Theo grunted and rolled to the side, his knife loose in his palm. Molly reached for the knife at the same time as her attacker, and their heads rammed together. She fell back, clutching her forehead at the pain shooting through her head from front to back.

Thomas stepped on Theo's hand, pinning the knife to his palm against the floor. Molly's pursuer backed away, wary, watching Thomas.

Theo grimaced from pain as his hand ground into the stone floor and kicked, hitting Thomas's lower back. He fell toward Theo, but Molly reached out and gripped Thomas's arm, steadying him. Her original pursuer used that moment to yank her away.

Theo rolled to his side and kicked again, knocking Thomas off balance and freeing Theo's hand that still held the knife. He thrust it and just missed Thomas's calf by a hair.

With Molly's arms pinned behind her back, she twisted and kicked. "Let. Me. Go!"

But her captor ignored her, grunting from the effort of keeping her restrained as he pulled her toward the stairs. She yanked, squirmed, and kicked again, but she was trapped by his strength. Planting her feet, she made him fight for every inch. He grunted again, his eyebrows furrowed, but moved steadily forward.

Sounds of Thomas fighting chilled her. One slip of that knife, one too-slow dodge, and she would lose him forever. If only she'd recognized what he meant to her sooner. She wished she'd told him of her love again and again every day, every moment they were together, that it was obvious in her every address to him.

The stairs loomed below her. At the top step, she fought harder. She couldn't leave Thomas. Somehow she must help him.

A great flurry of movement made her captor jerk her sideways. A mass of small hands pushed him, shoving him away from Molly and down the stairs. He fell, back first, and hit his head on a step, rolling down the steep metal staircase. His large frame stilled on the bottom four steps, sprawled awkwardly. And did not move.

The children turned to her, Sally and Jonathon rushing into her arms.

"Are you well?" Sally asked, voice full of concern.

"I'm fine." Molly squeezed them tight then pushed everyone back, away from the railing until they stood against the wall.

Watching Thomas and Theo fight from the corner of her eye, she said, "Thank you all for saving me. Now you must hide. All of you. Is there a place?"

"The-the storage rooms?"

"Perfect. Get out of sight; stay together. Be very quiet. If something happens to me or Thomas, you mustn't be seen. Do you understand?"

Sally swallowed and nodded.

Theo and Thomas crashed together against the wall and startled them all. Thomas held Theo's hand, squeezing until the knife fell from his grip. Exhausted, Theo turned to the children and gasped out, "We will find you again. We will track you down, every one of you. I *own* you."

The children cowered behind Molly.

"You don't own them," she said.

A high-pitched teeth-whistle echoed through the large factory. Doors banged opened, and the sounds of booted feet reached them on the platform.

"You will desist in this fighting at once," a man called into the room.

Those on the factory floor, children and adults alike, went still. Molly felt great pride in the children, standing together.

Thomas must have loosened his grip, for Theo kicked again and wriggled away. He scrambled for his blade on the floor and secured it in hand. Then he pointed it in Thomas's direction, swinging it wildly.

"Back away and leave me alone." Theo ran down the hall, heaving with each deep step, toward the other exit and stairs at the back of the factory.

A little girl tried to move out of his path, but he reached for her hair and yanked her to the side, holding a handful of her hair in his fist. The sweet girl's cry of pain sent Molly bolting that way without thinking.

"No, Molly!" Thomas ran after her.

As soon as the two reached Theo, he shoved the girl against the wall. She fell with a thump and was probably hurt but, gratefully, not by the knife.

Theo spun to face Molly and Thomas. He jabbed the knife forward; Thomas knocked it with his hand, but the blade sliced Molly's upper arm. Blood dripped from her wound; she squeezed her hand around it, looking away.

The injury sent Thomas rushing forward in a rage. "Back down, man. You don't have long to live on this earth."

Someone touched her skin, and Molly jumped. Sally's angel-soft hands pulled a piece of fabric tight and tied it around the wound. The pressure eased the pain and stopped the bleeding.

Theo's massive form barreled down on her, scooping up Sally and rushing for the stairs.

Two of the magistrate's watchmen were making their way up as Theo rushed down. Stopping, he shouted, "Leave me alone, or she dies!"

Molly sucked in her breath.

Just feet away, Thomas staggered to a stop, fear twisting his face.

The first of the watchmen held his hand out. "Leave the child and come with us."

"Do you know who I am? Do you know who you are talking to? I am Lord Oswald. Lord Theodore Oswald. I answer to no one. Certainly not to you." He shook Sally, who squealed in fright. The noise of her voice cut through Molly's heart. Theo's hands tightened around her young angel, his knuckles going white.

Thomas moved closer. "Let her go, Theo. Now."

Theo leaned back in a maniacal laugh. "I will not. You must be mad. Now, everyone let me pass, or she dies."

When the watchmen made no sign of movement, he shouted, "Move! Do you think I care one whit for this slip of a thing?" He grabbed Sally's arm and held her over the stair railing, two stories above the factory floor.

Someone turned on the machines. Chaos ensued. Children who'd been hiding underneath the machines now scrambled to avoid being squashed by the weaving arms. Men jumped aside. Thread tangled with fallen pieces of bobbins. Extra fiber and debris tangled with thread on the arms.

Theo shook her. "Move away, I tell you! Move or I drop her."

Directly below Sally, a monster of a loom ground to a start; its great arms bent and folded and weaved.

Sally screamed.

In the new confusion, Molly and Thomas rushed together toward Theo.

"It's all right, sweetheart! Be strong!" Molly reached for Theo's head from behind, pulling him backward, away from the edge. His grip loosened on Sally just as Thomas lunged for her, wrapping her into his arms and then urging her to safety behind them.

Batons in hand, the watchmen continued their climb. Theo righted himself and flailed his fists about, desperately trying to connect with anyone near him. He grabbed one of the batons and with it, smacked an officer on the side of the head, sending him backward into his partner.

Theo swung again, this time for Thomas, who ducked in time to avoid a hit in the face. He received more than one blow to the shoulders, chest, and arms as Theo wacked at him with all his strength. Thomas did the best he could to keep his head out of the way while trying to at last over-power Theo.

Each swing at Thomas, each connection with his midriff, shuddered inside of Molly, and she could take it no longer. Theo and all of the pain he had caused her loved ones had to be stopped.

She reached for the baton, but it connected with her hands. A great crushing pain filled her fingers, and tears blurred her vision.

At the same time, the officers had righted themselves and entered the fray. One seized Theo's arm and shoulder, and Thomas secured the other. The baton, pinned to Theo's side, was pressed between their bodies. They moved together, forcing Theo down the stairs. But they hadn't gone two steps before he was once more resisting, trying to kick and trip them. The officer in front stumbled and was pushed almost over the railing.

Theo slammed his weight against Thomas, who was stunned enough to release his hold for just a moment. Theo took the opportunity; he pushed his way through, down the stairs, clambering over the officers crumpled at his front. He tripped, his legs caught in the officers' limbs. Jerking free, he stepped onto the back of the first officer, who was trying to rise. The movement made Theo lose his footing. With one large swaying motion, he tilted to the side and fell over the railing, shouting.

Two stories down, he crashed through the threads and into the loom, where his arm was pulled into the gears. The loom's movement stalled as his leg jammed the machine. The engine started to smoke, filling the air with a putrid smell of burning oil. The alarm sounded, which turned off all the machines.

An eerie silence filled the factory floor once again. Theo lay unmoving across his machine, his limbs unnaturally captured, his face white and unresponsive. The children stood still, everyone waiting for a watchman to speak. A man ran to him, placing a hand on his chest. "He's dead." The stillness after a storm filled the room.

The magistrate stepped forward. Two men stood beside him in shackles. "You are all under arrest for evading capture and not cooperating with an inspection of underage workers."

A young boy in torn coveralls broke out into tears.

The stern man's face softened. "No, my dear boy. Not you. You have done nothing wrong. You—and all of the children here—must go home for the day. If you are under the age of nine, you cannot work in the factories anymore. If you are older, you may choose whether to stay. But I would urge you to work somewhere that pays you."

A pause filled with expectation hung in the air, a few of the children looking to each other. And then, as if permission had been granted, the children cheered, even the older ones, and made a rush for the doors.

Molly smiled at the thought that they might have at least a few days of leisure and play before they were captured back into labor elsewhere. She searched the area for her children. Sally stepped forward with fifteen of them, and she pointed to the factory floor. A group of around ten more stood together near the staircase.

Molly breathed out in relief and then felt her strength seep away. Her next tear wet her arm as she reached for Thomas. He caught her and cradled her until her sobs subsided.

An officer approached up the stairs, to where Molly and Thomas hadn't moved. "Molly? Thomas?"

They looked at him and nodded.

"We were told we might find you here. Could we get a statement about what happened?"

CHAPTER TWENTY-SIX

THE CHILDREN PUSHED THROUGH THE front door of the orphanage, shouting for Mrs. Featherstone. At last home, the children safe, Molly swallowed more tears, reaching for Thomas's hand.

They found the dear housekeeper tied to a chair, struggling in the kitchen, a great swelling goose egg on her forehead.

Molly rushed to her. "You poor dear."

"Check on Peter," Mrs. Featherstone whispered.

Molly rushed from the room and ran down the hallway. What she saw filled her with both pride and horror. Little Peter was asleep near the door, his bedsheets all around him on the floor, an unlit candlestick gripped tightly in his fist. Molly's tears fell freely at the terror he must have experienced when the other children were kidnapped.

She rested a hand on his shoulder as gently as a feather's touch. He jerked awake, swinging his candlestick. Molly avoided getting hit— having expected something of the like already, she was not keen on repeating the experience—and said, "Peter, the other children are back. You are safe."

His eyes—wide, crazed, and then calmed—searched the room, and then his gaze fell back on her. "I know you."

She nodded. "Can I help you get back into your bed?"

"The others. Are they well? I heard such noises, heard their cries."

"They're all back. We brought them back."

He wanted to see them for himself; Molly could tell. He deserved the reassurance along with some food, a good bath, and few other things. She picked him up and struggled against his height. The boy was not heavy but just skinny, tall, and unable to move his lower limbs. They moved down the hallway.

Molly called, "Children! Come, children. Thomas! Mrs. Featherstone!"

Thomas appeared first, fear evident in his features as he ran toward them. He stopped and took in the pair of them. After a moment his forehead relaxed, and he moved closer to take Peter from Molly's arms.

"Hello, champ."

"Thank you." Molly knew Thomas would always come when she needed him.

Mrs. Featherstone, stepping nimbly, holding the baby from the river in her arms, arrived next with the other children. "My dear, what has happened?"

Molly cleared her throat as she gestured to the young boy in Thomas's arms. "Everyone, Peter wanted to ensure you returned safely. He defended the orphanage while we were gone. I believe he deserves to look into the eyes of each person here."

So they all came forward and greeted the boy, Thomas kneeling so they were at eye level. Mrs. Featherstone hugged Peter as if he might slip away, and when the last had greeted him, they all drifted off to their beds, except for Mrs. Featherstone, the baby, Molly, Thomas, and Peter.

Then Thomas headed for the kitchen. "Let's get you washed up now," he said to the lad. Before the housekeeper or Molly could say another word, he disappeared around the corner with Peter in his arms.

A knock at the front door startled them. Molly squeezed Mrs. Featherstone's hand. After they made their way down to the door, they peeked out the front window.

An express rider stood waiting outside. Relieved, Molly threw the door open, and Mrs. Featherstone handed the rider some coins, but he refused them, saying, "It's already paid for."

Molly closed the door and ripped open the seal. "It's from Lord Annesley. *He* sent the magistrate to the cotton mill. Let's take this to the kitchen so Thomas can hear the whole of it."

When they entered, Peter was deep in the small wash barrel, and Thomas was finishing scrubbing him.

"An express has come." Molly held up the parchment.

Mrs. Featherstone laid the baby in a makeshift cradle, set up in the kitchen, and took over where Thomas stood. "I'll dry him."

Molly took a seat, rocking the infant while she reported on the contents of the letter. "Lord Annesley says the vote on the suffrage bill has been moved up. The House of Lords will discuss and vote on it in three days' time instead of in a week Thursday. He is riding through the night to get there in time." As she read more, Molly brought a hand to her chest. "And he cleaned up that awful place in Angel Meadow. Jewel—he has saved her." Molly fell forward to her knees, one hand holding her head. "She is free at last." She continued to scan his words. "The place is by no means perfect, but Jewel and all of the ladies in that pit of death are safe and in good hands, at least." She gripped the page in her hands, overcome. "Annesley is quite remarkable. He writes, 'We assembled a group of yeomen, and some old accomplices of mine joined us. Where the law was not on our side, good men were. Many miscreants were taken unawares in their activities, and others were discouraged from beginning. The inhabitants were sent away and the entrances boarded up. But most importantly, any woman there against her will was permitted to go free. You have done a good work here, Molly, and if they never have the means to thank you, I do now.'"

She choked on her tears and continued his letter. "'For I have seen with my own eyes the very moment when hope has replaced despair. Thank you, Molly.'"

A soft knock at the outer kitchen door startled her. Then the door creaked open, slowly at first, and just a crack. Thomas must have noted the visitor, because he rushed forward to swing the door fully open. A woman, holding the hand of a small boy, stood, watching them, her expression fearful. She searched the faces in the kitchen: those of Peter, Mrs. Featherstone, and Thomas, until she found Molly, still kneeling on the floor.

"Molly?" Her voice was small, hesitant.

Molly jolted her to her feet. "Jewel!" She ran to her, wrapping her arms around her friend in a tight squeeze. "Oh, Jewel, you are safe." She stepped back and looked her over, wiping at her own tears. "And this is your son?"

Jewel nodded, her face pinched with emotion. When she could at last speak, she choked out, "Yes. Freddy." Then she pulled Molly to her in another hug. "You kept your word. I prayed you would. Thank you." The two hugged for a moment more.

Molly's throat tight with emotion, she choked out, "I have had no peace until this moment. Grateful I am that you are out of that place."

"No more grateful than I am. My son and I owe you our lives. We are free at last from Theo and his ilk."

"You are. Forever. He's dead, Jewel. He'll never bother you again." She whipped around to Thomas at the realization. "Theo's dead. Annesley doesn't know."

Thomas's eyes filled with concern.

"And the vote." Molly's heartrate picked up. "No one in the House of Lords knows Theo is dead. They must be informed so they can vote their conscience, knowing that whatever hold he once had over them is gone. That knowledge could change everything."

"It might already be too late for that," Thomas said.

She read the last few lines of Annesley's letter. "He's leaving a carriage for us to return home when we are able." She took a deep, strengthening breath. "I must go, try to reach him, before the vote."

"Impossible," Thomas said. "He's on his horse, likely, and you'll be in a carriage."

"But perhaps I could make it to town before the vote. Someone must tell them Theo is dead."

Molly hugged Jewel again then hurriedly grabbed a bonnet as she called for the footmen to ready the carriage.

"Thomas, we must go posthaste. We have no time to lose."

"We can't succeed, Molly."

"But if I don't try, they will surely defeat the bill. The movement will be set back for years, generations even. Thomas, I must *try*."

His eyes showed compassion, love, appreciation, and pain. He understood, and she knew he wanted women's suffrage success as much as she did. "Go," he said. "As fast as you can. Overtake Annesley on his way. Take two footmen with you. Paul and John." After a moment, he added, "And one of the maids."

Fear rose inside her. "Aren't *you* coming?"

"I don't dare leave the children until the magistrate and Bow Street have arrived. Even then I worry they will get drawn back into the trap of Theo's work. We must arrange new measures of safety." He pulled her into his arms. "I can't leave our children, Molly." Pain reflected in his eyes.

And hers filled with tears. "I didn't even think of all of that." She squeezed him. "Thank you, Thomas. And I love you."

He held her, and they rocked together, with his chin on the top of her head. At last she reluctantly broke away and ran for the door.

"Molly."

She turned to Thomas and found his face reflecting pride. She rushed back to him, standing on her toes to reach him. He swung her around and pressed his lips to hers. Then, resting his forehead against hers, he said, "I love you too."

She smiled and turned to run from the room.

The last thing she heard as she moved toward the front door was his shout: "Be careful!"

With one last look over her shoulder, she rushed out the door.

CHAPTER TWENTY-SEVEN

As Chloe watched Annesley run from her after the rally, he dragged threads of her happiness with him, pulling out the very fiber of her faith in him. Such a hole remained inside her heart, an empty, dark crevice that might never be filled. And her anger still simmered over his betrayal.

His involvement in a sabotage of the women's suffrage committee did not make sense—it could not be. Yet how could it be otherwise, when she'd overheard him admit to his meddling himself? His own words condemned him: he was a spy. How could he take her words, her actions, and plans, and report them to the prime minister, knowing Lord Grey would use them against the cause?

Everything she thought she knew about Annesley had crumbled around her, and with it splinters of her own confidence tumbled too. If Annesley wasn't the moral man she'd judged him to be, how would she ever be able to assess the worthiness of another?

She watched him as he made his way to the carriages, as he called his footman and jumped in. The ease with which he quickly escaped seemed a practiced art for him. She had best become practiced in not including Annesley in the close, inner workings of her heart or those of her suffrage committee.

Amanda stepped up beside her. "Maybe it's not as it seems."

"I admit to having that hope." Chloe sighed. "But how can it be otherwise?"

Lord Halloway joined them. "I have dispatched footmen, and Annesley summoned the magistrate and Bow Street. I feel we have required their services all too often of late. I admit I feel more at ease now, assuming Thomas is with Molly."

"What can I do?" Chloe felt keenly responsible for Molly's absence, having ignored her warnings. At the time, she hadn't even looked at Molly fully, dismissing her concerns immediately. Ashamed, Chloe determined to do all she could to help.

She asked her most burning question. "What kind of hold does Lord Oswald have over these nobles?"

Lord Halloway indicated they begin walking toward his carriage. "Let us finish this conversation on the way home."

Upon entering the carriage, Lord Halloway laced his fingers with Lady Amanda's and then explained to Chloe, "From what I can tell, Lord Oswald is one of the wealthiest nobles in the *ton*, second only to your father. He has promised specific lords a portion of his business profits and an opportunity to gain some ownership in his mills if they form a political alliance with him and use their influence in the House of Lords as he dictates." He shook his head. "What I didn't know was that he was also Theo, crime boss of Angel Meadow."

"He's buying their votes," Chloe said, outrage boiling inside her. She met Amanda's eyes and knew the information was not new to her friend.

"Precisely." Amanda shuddered.

A vote was a precious gift, and throwing it away to highest bidder was at the very least disgraceful.

"He has offered this opportunity to those with insurmountable gambling debt, estates near ruin, faltering social standing—anyone desperate for a significant increase in income. Some feel they have no choice but to work with him."

Chloe's mind began to sift through ideas. "Do you have a list of those he might have approached with this offer?"

"We're working on one. It may not be complete, but it is a good start. We calculate he may have some sort of hold over one third of the House of Lords. That's a significant group of voters."

The more she thought about it the more determined Chloe felt. She suspected there was a way she could help. "So, many of these nobles would likely vote otherwise if they had means available to them another way?"

Amanda nodded. "I would think so. It stands with our previous reasoning. Chances are high women would be included if not for Theo's interference."

They stopped in front of Chloe's house.

As she prepared to step down out of the carriage, Chloe said, "I'm so sorry about Molly. I hope and pray we find her soon. And Thomas too."

"As do we. Thank you." Lord Halloway looked more strained than she had ever seen him.

Chloe's heart felt heavy, her steps slow, her mouth reluctant to smile, when she entered her home. Grateful her father's cheery light flickered in his study, she made her way to him immediately.

⌒

The Wetherton carriage wheels dipped into a rut, and Chloe braced herself, pleased with her success thus far. She and her father had convinced several lords to change their allegiances. In a way, she felt as though she was offering a rescue to these lords and their families. Her father had offered loans, with interest but from an honest endower, to these men so they had both a respectable and confidential manner in which to overcome their financial ruin. In the end, her father and his estate would greatly benefit from the interest as well.

She wasn't a part of those dealings, which occurred behind closed study doors. She took tea with the wives or daughters and enjoyed talk of fashion and circumstance. But upon exiting, the men's countenances warmed her. New hope, respectability—happiness, even—shone from their faces, and she felt gratified to be involved in improving their situations.

But now, she and her father were headed to a particular home that made her decidedly uncomfortable: that of Lord Westchester— Annesley's father, Earl of Westchester. She worried and stewed in her seat on the bumpy, dirty roads about what it meant that Annesley's father was beholden to Lord Oswald.

"Father, why do you suppose Lord Westchester is on this list?"

He took her hand in his. "I can't say for certain, but I would venture to guess he must be under some form of financial duress, like the others.

If that is the case, I am sad to hear it, as he has been a good friend all these years. And dear young Annesley is such a good lad, the best of men." Chloe's father eyed her. "I had quite hoped the two of you would make a match of it."

She felt her cheeks warm, and she looked away.

"My dear, no need to discuss such things, especially as we journey to their home in these uncomfortable circumstances. But if Annesley holds your heart, I daresay he'd make as fine a husband as any, regardless of his father's trappings."

She dared a peek at her father. His eyes twinkled, and his smile broadened. She leaned in to him. "Thank you, Father. I once thought he would be the best match for me, but I must admit, the situation of late gives me pause."

"Men do desperate things to please a parent. Perhaps there is more to the story than we understand, eh?" He patted her hand.

"Perhaps." She would love that to be the case. She'd love to have a reason to doubt what she thought she knew of Lord Annesley.

When they arrived at the door to Annesley's London townhome, the butler met them. Chloe's father had sent a card ahead, so they were expected. They were both ushered into the parlor. The men lingered for a moment and then moved their business to the study. Chloe remained with Annesley's mother, Lady Westchester.

Before she could feel nervous about trying to make conversation, the dear woman moved to sit beside her and took Chloe's hand in her own. "Oh, Lady Chloe! I am so glad you have come. I do hope you will help us."

Totally unprepared for such an intimate gesture, Chloe forgot to be timid.

"I hope so too."

"Lord Westchester thinks I have no idea, but of course I know what a mess he has made of things. I received a card from Lady Pillton early this morning, detailing what your father offered her family. A godsend you are, and your father."

Chloe found the toes of her shoes peeking out the bottom of her dress. "I am happy Father could be of help. I didn't know things were difficult for your family."

Lady Westchester squeezed her hand. "We had such hopes for you and dear Annesley. He is a good man and would never have made the same choices as his father. But we know nothing will come of a match now."

Chloe jerked her head up.

"No, no. It's quite all right, my dear. I understand that no family such as yours would want to align themselves with our difficulties. It is enough that your father will allow us a way to work through it. Perhaps Annesley's children will benefit."

His mother seemed at peace with their financial difficulties. Chloe detected not even a drop of bitterness. She spoke honestly and without anger.

Chloe wanted to comfort her. "I, too, am glad we could be of assistance. Annesley is a good man. I've always known him to be a step above the rest."

"The prime minister relies on him," Lady Westchester said. "He's been seeking Annesley's advice much more frequently of late. But my dear son does not seem pleased with the responsibility; it is almost as if Annesley aids him out of coercion rather than choice." She stared into Chloe's eyes with deep intent.

Chloe nodded, her mind spinning with hope and the possibility that Annesley had not willingly betrayed her.

"He used to work for the government, you know. Travelled, served missions across the channel, that sort of thing."

Chloe raised her eyebrows. She had *not* known that.

"I'm not supposed to know that either. But where do you suppose dear Annesley acquired his excellent skills at observation?" She winked, eyes twinkling, and sipped her tea.

And Chloe decided she loved this woman. "I am certain he got those skills from you, dear lady. Tell me, what else have your keen eyes observed that others might have missed?"

Lady Westchester returned her cup to its saucer and leaned closer.

By the time the men exited the study, they were laughing and carrying on as much as the women in the front parlor. All stood and said their goodbyes.

In the carriage her father wrapped an arm around her shoulder. "Your Annesley is the best of men," he said again.

She was beginning to agree with this sentiment all over again, and it filled her with a new kind of giddy happiness. "Why? What has happened?"

"We arrived moments after a letter from their solicitor. It seems our good Annesley took it upon himself to save the estate—sold off holdings, combined some ventures, and reduced the spending." Her father laughed. "I do admire that boy. He left an express note stating that all gambling and any thought of investing in the mills in Manchester were forbidden from now on. The estate doesn't have the funds, he says." He wiped his eyes, shaking his head. "Tied up all the moneys into rescuing from ruin the remaining holdings still in their possession."

"Did the Westchesters need a loan, then?"

He shook his head. "If they follow the plans Annesley has laid out, they can weather through their weak financial times on their own. If only the other members of the *ton* could think through things so intellectually, so prudently."

Analyzing all she'd learned from Annesley's mother, she asked, "Do you think they were being threatened by Lord Oswald?"

"I do, certainly. It is Annesley's story to tell, but I suspect the prime minister to be involved. Annesley's father suspects he has some sort of hold on the lad."

Chloe let all of this new information settle inside her, and as it did, drops of truth, like rain, cooled the fire of her heart's disappointment.

Perhaps.

CHAPTER TWENTY-EIGHT

Molly had pushed the horses all night for two nights then three, stopping at an inn to change them out but not to rest. The whole way to London, the footman searched for Annesley, asking for him at inns. They never caught him. But she had hoped.

On the streets of London they slowed to safer speeds, having arrived on the very day of the vote. The afternoon grew late. Molly bounced in her seat with the energy moving through her.

The closer they moved to the Palace of Westminster the more the crowds of London hemmed them in. Molly had never been inside before but had passed at its feet many a time. Carriages to their front, people walking, the shops, and venders selling their wares all delayed their journey. The maddening slow pace might do her in.

The carriage slowed to a stop in the middle of the road. She opened the door and leaned out. At times like these, it was freeing to be a servant. She had no one to raise disapproving eyebrows at her for sensibly trying to discover the reason for the delay. A carriage had lost a wheel and turned sharply, blocking the road in both directions.

Gritting her teeth, she slipped back inside, grabbed her bonnet, and then stepped out into the muddy street. "I can't wait for this. I'm off. Please go around to the palace. When I'm through, I'll be waiting along the river."

"I'll go with you." Paul stood and puffed out his chest a bit.

Gratitude warmed Molly. It would be nice to have a bit of company. "Very well, but you have to move your feet. We aren't taking a stroll, now, are we?"

"Yes, of course. I'm at your service." He mock-bowed and then leaped from the vehicle.

Impressed at his agility and willingness to help, she smiled and took off running down the street.

The others stayed with the carriage as Molly and Paul pushed through crowds, taking side alleys and rushing as fast as they could to arrive before the vote. Deliberations carried on for hours, sometimes weeks, but the suffrage vote would happen today. Annesley had given her the impression the House of Lords had finished deliberating, someone had pushed the vote forward, and all would be decided in a manner of minutes.

She thought of all of the men voting under Theo's thumb. They had to be told of his death. They needed to know they could freely vote their conscience. The responsibility weighed on her in a way no one else knew.

She ran as though her whole life's happiness depended on it.

⤳

Lord Annesley arrived moments before the guards shut the palace doors at Westminster, barring any other entrance. Lord Halloway came to stand at his side, and the two surveyed the room.

"How did it go at Angel Meadow?" Halloway asked.

"We took it down. Jewel is safe, as are the other women."

Halloway clapped Annesley on the shoulder. "Good show, man. Excellent."

Annesley grinned. Dismantling the whole operation had felt particularly gratifying, as had pounding into any man who resisted. He flexed his knuckles. "I sent the magistrate in after Theo, straight to his mills."

Halloway breathed out in relief. "Are Molly and Thomas safe, then?"

"Likely, yes. The magistrate knew the whole of it. I told him to tread with caution, but he brought a veritable army with him, searching every mill. Your two uniquely adventurous servants should be back in the orphanage as we speak."

Halloway continued to look at those seated in the room. "And here we are." He leaned in, speaking so low Annesley had to pay close attention. "Who do you think we need to influence?"

"Anyone Theo could have had a noose around. We can tell them the mills are in jeopardy, the children set free, and the mills will no longer be as profitable."

A loud voice from the front interrupted. "We will move to speeches and the vote. No more individual deliberations will be necessary."

Halloway called out, "May it please the chamber, I request twenty minutes' more time of deliberation in groups. We have news that may influence the vote."

"News, you say. Wait for the time for speeches, and then do enlighten us as a whole."

A rumble passed through the group. Lord Pillington called out, "About time. Let's just move to vote. We've almost killed the bill with talk."

The gavel quieted the room. All eyes turned to the front, and the first of the speeches began. While Lord Chancellor stood to speak, a group of men to his right took up coughing. Over and over they coughed. And Lord Chancellor tried to speak over them, but to no avail. All his words were drowned out. This did not bode well. Lord Grey wished to streamline the voting—cut the conversation and push it through.

Halloway and Annesley moved through the room, leaning over chairs to speak with some of the lords, spreading the word that Lord Oswald had suffered a serious blow to his industry, hoping to encourage them to pass this reform. Annesley watched Lord Lovett, seeking a moment with him, but Lovett was always pulled away, distracted, or surrounded by others.

A voice at the front announced, "There have been amendments."

Halloway and Annesley had suspected amendments would be written. Annesley waited to hear what they might be, but no one explained further. Only loud grumbling followed that announcement.

Then a proposal was made that a new bill be printed so they all might read it.

Relief filled him. At least the lords would move forward sensibly.

But others argued against that, saying it was an effort to delay the passing of the bill, which must go in effect tomorrow.

Halloway added his voice. "Surely we should know what changes have been made." His brow wrinkled in concern.

Molly rushed to the front door of Westminster Palace. She pulled the handle—locked. She knocked. Waited. Knocked louder. She commenced banging on the thick wood until sharp pain in her fists demanded she stop. She kicked. She shouted.

"Open the door! This is an emergency! Please! Open the door. I have a message."

A watchman of some kind behind her stepped forward. "Oh, now, what is this? The House of Lords is meeting now. You'd best step away from the door."

"I must get inside."

He laughed. "No one enters when they're in session." He turned as if to leave, still chuckling.

She grabbed his arm, and he pulled away, watching her.

"I must get inside. I have a message for Lord Halloway and his father, the Duke of Somerset."

"You? Have a message for the Duke of bloomin' Somerset?" He laughed a bit too long. "I think it's time you went back home."

"Please! You must let me in." She stared into his eyes, pleading.

"Oh, let's see what they say."

"Thank you." She stood as close to him as she could when he knocked on the door.

A guard answered, and the watchman explained her plight to him.

The man inside took in her clothing—rumpled but well-made. She stood taller, and he searched her face. Something in his eyes changed. "I can send a message to the secretary. If he sees fit to let you in or to deliver your message, then so be it."

"Thank you! Tell him the message is for Lord Halloway, and it contains vital information that many of the lords need before today's vote." She pulled out a piece of paper. "It is written here." She'd scribbled it, spilling ink everywhere on their too-fast ride from Manchester.

He took the paper, eying her warily, and shrugged. "As I said, we will see what the secretary says."

"Thank you."

She waited. As soon as someone stepped away from the cracked the door, he tossed her note aside as if it weren't important. Outrage and desperation filled her. Before the door closed, Molly pushed through the crack, slamming the door wide into the face of the guard on the other side.

"Hey, whoa now. What do you think you are doing, miss?"

"I must get inside. I have a message for the Duke of Somerset and his son. He will want this information, I assure you. That note is of the greatest urgency."

The guards burst into laughter. "What could you possibly have to tell him? That his cakes and tea are ready?"

The men laughed some more, so she tried to push past them and into the building. But they each grabbed an arm at the shoulder and shoved her into the street.

The watchman crossed his arms over his chest, his frown lines almost hiding his eyes.

"Now, off with you."

⌒

Annesley wanted to pummel Lord Grey and force him to swallow every duplicitous word he uttered. The prime minister stood before the House of Lords, delivering a speech, and he would not stop talking. He called for immediate voting on the Great Reform Act, without a careful reading of the amendments. He touted that the amendments were small, simple wording changes, nothing universally altering in intent. He encouraged every member of the House of Lords to support the bill. "And the king and I, in response to the great dissatisfaction of the people of England, are determined that such a broadening of suffrage occur."

Annesley and Halloway looked at each other with a good amount of skepticism.

"There is no one more decided against annual parliaments, universal suffrage, and the ballot than I am. My object is not to favor but to put an end to such hopes."[7]

Annesley had heard him say such things before, knew he opposed universal suffrage. Lord Grey then announced that although he did not support this new proposed law, did not feel that any of the working classes needed a vote, he also knew the house must vote in favor of the bill anyway, forced into a better form of representation for the "mindless whelps."

7 "Reform Riots" in *1832 Reform Act*, http://spartacus-educational.com/PR1832.htm.

"They are rioting in the streets. They demand change. And we are about the task of giving it to them, lest we each be ousted from our seats." As Whigs, they must work for reform—reasonable reform. The man went on. Annesley couldn't stomach a minute more of his words. At great length, the prime minister sat. Strange he was pushing for immediate passage of a bill he obviously didn't support. Annesley's suspicions rose.

Then Annesley took the stand. "I bring helpful information to note that Lord Theodore Oswald's cotton mills are struggling as we speak. A good portion of his laborers were younger than nine years of age and have been sent home to their families. Two days ago a magistrate was present in Lord Oswald's largest mill and cleared out the younger children and shut down the mills for several days hence."

Lord Wilmington stood. "What does that have to do with the law at hand? Stick to the topic. We've had deliberations enough."

"Yes! Let's vote already."

"Fair enough. The city of Manchester will have representation and a seat in the House of Commons. I know Lord Oswald has been vocal about his opinions on the matter. As we move forward to vote, I encourage us all to study carefully the wording. The next amendments must at least be read aloud, if not printed."

Enough of the men agreed that Annesley sighed in relief. Perhaps they would do so. "I do think we are all in support of such an important and inclusive bill. Reform is needed. The working classes have suffered long enough. And William Lovett has drafted a fair and important change to the law that will become a great first step toward universal suffrage."

The group grumbled at that, drowning out his words. Very few desired universal suffrage. Quality instead of quantity was often touted. Annesley waited until they stopped making noise.

"Yes, universal suffrage. Every man in England must be heard." He stopped, recognizing his own words as unfair. Then he continued. "*And* women must be included." He searched the white-haired wigs for Lovett and finally found him staring at his boots. *Not a good sign.* Where the man had once been his loudest, staunchest supporter, he now sat quietly.

A rumble followed Annesley's remarks, and he moved to stand down, walking as quickly as his feet would allow, to William Lovett himself. He must speak with him about these amendments. The last Annesley had heard, the law hadn't yet included women but also did not exclude them, and in that regard it was similar to previous bills' language about suffrage.

As he pushed through the lords, Annesley caught sight of Halloway. He stood, a pillar of strength. His face lit with hope in the face of all the dissension, a smile of satisfaction curling his mouth.

Halloway had sacrificed and risked much so the House of Lords could be where they were today. It was due to his efforts in the Liberty Seekers that the crowds in England gathered, that Manchester would receive representation, that these stiff lords were moved to action in such a way that they were on the cusp of voting in significant change. Come what may, the bill must pass, and they owed its success amongst the populous in large degree to Halloway. And few in the room knew his role. Annesley would have bowed to the man right then and there were it appropriate.

Annesley swallowed, determination rising inside him. Women's suffrage or no, the passage of this bill was a vital move in the right direction.

Another stood to read the amendments.

But the coughing began again. And a raucous calling throughout the hall: "Just pass the bill. Let's call the vote."

The speaker droned on, but no one heard what he said.

Annesley pushed forward again, seeking a word with Lovett. Before he could reach him, the amendments were finished, and a vote was called.

So soon.

There was nothing Annesley could do to further delay the vote or understand the wording. Each lord was called by name to announce his aye or nay.

"Lord Nathaniel Halloway."

He straightened his back, his voice filling the room, "Aye!"

"Lord Wutherford Annesley."

"Aye," he shouted. At last, England would broaden its decision-making power.

In overwhelming amounts, the lords voted aye. As expected, the law passed. By a staggering margin. Annesley fell back against the wall behind him. One great step in the right direction. A great sense of exhilaration filled him.

But he couldn't rest for long. A splinter nagged at his peace. He saw Chloe in his mind, her wide, hopeful eyes, and he knew how much this vote would mean to her. He needed a copy of the law, wanted to read it for himself, to see what it meant for women's suffrage.

A crowd gathered around the author of the bill. "William Lovett. William Lovett."

Annesley turned instead to the prime minister.

⌒

Molly stepped back one step then two and then turned and ran. Not away but along the building, around the corner, and to the back, where there had to be another door.

Then the double doors opened, and the lords began to exit onto the street. Carriages began pulling in front of Westminster Palace. Men in long robes with white wigs jostled her on the left and right. And not one paid her any mind.

She approached a man, the back of his white wig moving through a sea of the same. "Excuse me."

He turned away.

She tried to see Lord Halloway or Lord Annesley, but the men moved too quickly, and all looked the same in their white wigs.

Frustrated beyond the ability to remain polite, she grabbed the jacket of an aide with both hands in a crazed, maniacal manner. "And what of women?"

He backed away, searching the street. "What of women? This wasn't a vote about women." He pried her fingers from his front.

But hope still remained. Chances were strong that this lad did not know the language of the bill. And if it didn't mention women, if the language remained consistent with previous bills, women still had a chance to gain suffrage.

"This vote was about the working class," the aide said. "Working-class *men*. Lord Grey made sure of it."

"But what does it say?"

He grunted but then pulled out a notecard and read from the bill. "'An Act to Amend the Representation of the People in England and Wales.'" He went on, reading the law's wording directly. Then he stopped. "If you didn't catch that, it grants voting rights to 'male persons' who occupied premises of an annual value of ten pounds." He placed the card back into his pocket. "Which means my father can cast a vote." He stood taller, eyes shining. "And right proud I am to be a part of it all."

As soon as Molly heard "male persons," she turned from him, ignoring the rest, and moved toward a bench along the river to wait. At first she didn't quite know what to feel because, in that lad, she'd seen Charlie. His excitement, his goals reached, or at minimum a huge move in the right direction. Charlie's father would be able to vote—Charlie himself, she imagined. She forced herself to face her next thought. *Were he alive.* So, in many ways, today was a moment of celebration for thousands in England. But the success was not complete.

A gray mist fogged in her brain, and sharp despair settled heavily, like the colder air swirling at her ankles at the docks. As she watched the happy crowds learn the news and break out in cheers and celebrations all around her, she recognized the power of perspective. In the midst of all their raucous noise-making, did they stop to consider, even one of them, that an act meant to broaden suffrage had eliminated the vote for half the population of England? Once that realization hit her head-on, she could no longer endure the city she lived in and all its happiness. She collapsed onto the bench with her head in her hands and cried out her frustration.

⌒

Later, in the dark of night, the Somerset carriage pulled up to the palace along the riverfront. Lady Amanda and Lord Halloway climbed out together. "Oh, my dear!" Lady Amanda called out, and they rushed to Molly's slumped figure on the stone. Halloway lifted her carefully, and they climbed back into the carriage together.

"Are you well?" Halloway asked as he placed Molly on the seat, and Amanda wrapped her in a blanket.

Molly shivered. "They wouldn't let me in. I could have stopped the vote. I tried to tell you, Lord Halloway." Her legs and arms shook from the cold and exhaustion and the devastation of her failure.

"Oh, you are ice cold." Lady Amanda put an arm around her. "I'm so sorry, my dear. There was a bit of trouble with Annesley's carriage in town. The footmen just got back and waited too long to tell us where you would be."

She hugged Lady Amanda. "Thank you for coming for me."

Lord Halloway cleared his throat. "It may seem useless now, but what would you have told me?"

She widened her eyes. "I wrote it in a note. I came to tell you Theo had died, that the lords needn't be controlled by him any longer."

He nodded. "Thank you, Molly. Your courage and continued efforts for suffrage are unmatched. You did everything you could have." His eyes were filled with compassion. She tried to feel comforted.

"They had already changed the language of the bill," Molly said quietly.

He nodded. "They had, with last-minute amendments Lord Grey pushed through with great haste."

Lady Amanda sniffed. "I feel as though I should be happy; this is what we have worked for. But instead a great sense of betrayal fills me, as though something were taken that I almost had, right here." She held out her hand and fluttered her fingers. "And it slipped away."

She pulled Molly closer in an embrace, and the two held each other. Then Lady Amanda's grip on her tightened, and she shook in Molly's arms. They rocked together. All they had worked for had been tossed aside as if it had been nothing. Molly clung to the only other person who understood the depth of her sorrow. Lord Halloway reached his strong arms to encircle them both. Then, remembering always her place, Molly said, "I'm sorry. I'm likely the worst lady's maid in the *ton* right now."

Lord Halloway's chuckle reverberated through her. "Or the best, depending on your perspective."

CHAPTER TWENTY-NINE

THE WHIG LORDS EXULTED OVER the passing of the first broadening of suffrage in England. And they had good reason to rejoice. Annesley, too, was pleased such a thing had finally come to fruition. But if they had only stopped to listen. Impatient to at last pass the bill, they had brushed Annesley's attempts and all of Halloway's efforts to talk to the lords one by one, aside. He sat in his chair as the chamber emptied. A copy of the amendments still fisted in his hands, he gritted his teeth.

Male persons. William Lovett and his amendments had betrayed the people's trust. When he thought of the rallies, the Whig reformists, the Liberty Seekers all over the country, Annesley was sick at the betrayal. The man had gone against his own principles out of fear.

Annesley released his fisted hands and flexed his fingers. He sat alone now in the chambers of the House of Lords, alone with his dejection. Even Lord Halloway had left him there. The room settled into darkness, and he couldn't stop his frustration from seeping inside and dampening his heart.

Restless, he refused to sit still any longer. Exiting the room and pushing his way out the main door, his gaze flitted over a strange woman, curled up on a bench. She reminded him of Molly.

He was relieved Molly and Thomas had made it out of the factory. That, at least, had been a bit of good news.

After freeing Jewel and her fellow workers and arresting the men running the operation of that vile place, he had felt hope the situation in Manchester could improve. And now that the district had been given representation and a vote, the chances for a better life as a worker in the mills improved greatly.

With all the good that had happened, he suspected the reason for his continued malaise rested solely in a pair of blue eyes.

Chloe, whose wide, calm eyes were always a balm to his troubled memories, now unwittingly tormented him with guilt and the despair of having disappointed her. The thought of losing their approving sparkle sent his peace into great upheaval. His heart twisted in a new form of agony that no partial success in the House of Lords could alleviate.

What could he offer such a woman? With his estate stripped of wealth and many years, perhaps decades, of effort to bring it back to what it once was facing him, he was unworthy of her. Even with all the losses to his eligibility, he had still hoped to maintain her approval and kindness. But how could she or *would* she ever look at him with anything but suspicion after she had discovered his many acts of spying on her? Her wide-eyed hurt after hearing from his very lips her name and connection to the suffrage committee as he'd relayed them to Lord Grey, her shock and sense of betrayal so obvious on her stricken expression, had stabbed him with a new kind of grief, and the wound festered still, raw and open.

With a great sigh, he worked his way down the street to his hired hack. The others would be meeting at the Halloways', so he gave that address to his driver, but he would have preferred to sink into the earth and sleep for the next ten years or more.

A surprisingly cheery group awaited him. Thomas had already arrived, and the others were laughing with him and planning his manner of proposal to Molly. Annesley's mouth turned up at the corner. They deserved every happiness. A truer maid and footman he had yet to find.

He stepped into the room. "Thomas, my congratulations." He reached for Thomas's hand and pumped it with great enthusiasm. This happy news was just what he needed to lighten his spirits. "And where is Molly?"

"Here." Lady Amanda entered, smiling, her arm draped around Molly's waist. Becky followed close behind. Lady Amanda held out her other hand. "Please, everyone, sit down. I'll call for some tea."

Molly stopped, and Thomas opened his mouth, concerned lines marring his forehead. "Lady Amanda, thank you, but we'll be getting down to the servants' quarters." He bowed his head to her.

"You will do no such thing," Lady Amanda said. "We have much to discuss. How did this all come about? A great puzzle has come together, with a few important pieces missing, and I would like to hear the whole of it. Now, sit, Molly, Thomas. Please." She indicated the couch, and the two servants obeyed, with a considerable amount of discomfort obvious on their faces.

Lord Annesley chuckled. "Demanding employers, aren't they?"

At that, Lady Amanda turned to him. "And you. You will need to enlighten us also."

"As will I." Chloe smiled in the doorway, taking in the room until her gaze found Annesley, and then her lips turned down and she looked away.

Annesley's lighter mood dampened somewhat again. He found a chair at the edge of the room.

Thomas arose and stepped forward to get everyone's attention.

They cheered, Lady Amanda clapping her hands together.

Molly tilted her head. "What's this all about?"

Then Thomas knelt at her feet.

And she placed a hand on her heart, a brilliant blush filling her face. "Oh." Confusion and happiness warred together on her features.

"I love you, Molly. You know I do."

The smile on her face could have lit a whole ballroom. And Annesley couldn't help but smile with her.

Thomas reached for her hand. "I figure no two people have weathered more difficult storms than the two of us. If we survived all we have until now, imagine what we could do together."

Everyone chuckled. Molly's hand went to her mouth.

"So I'm asking, Molly. Will you be my wife?"

She pulled him up from his knees. "Yes, Thomas! Oh yes. I love you too, and I-I'm ready. I can't imagine my life any other way."

Thomas pulled her close. Then he slid a ring on her finger, his eyes full of love. The two seemed to then become aware of their audience, for both turned a deeper shade of red.

The room burst into loud clapping and cheers of congratulations, the loudest cheers coming from Becky, who bounced on her feet.

Thomas cleared his throat.

"Now that you two have finally come together"—Halloway grinned—"with our great blessing, my dear wife will burst from the curiosity of not knowing what has come to pass this past week. Let's put together all of the pieces now. First, Thomas and Molly."

Thomas's grin suggested he enjoyed the attention. He called out to the room, "Molly, according to her former habit, was abducted and brought to one of Theo's cotton mills."

Molly swatted his shoulder. "You were abducted, too, don't forget."

He winked. "True. They separated us."

"'Cause Thomas gave them a bit of trouble."

Her proud grin made Annesley laugh. He leaned forward in his seat, interested in how this part of the recent events had carried out.

"Yes, I broke free and hid amongst the machinery, looking for Molly."

"Thanks to Annesley, who sent in the magistrate, we are all here and the children are safe." Her voice caught, and she waved her hand in the air. "And all you really need to know is that Theo's plans backfired, and he will not bother anyone further."

Thomas nodded. "Just so. And the children were so brave. I'm right proud of our little ones."

Lord Halloway and Lady Amanda shared a look and a small smile.

Annesley warmed inside, happy for his dearest friends. He dared a glance at Chloe, who was watching them also, a wistful expression on her face.

After a moment of silent communication between the Halloways, Lady Amanda said, "Molly, you were the best of lady's maids, until you weren't."

Molly looked down, and Annesley wished he could wipe the worry from her mind, because he saw what she did not. Her employers' eyes twinkled, and she moved across the room, taking Molly's hand in her own. "You have become so much more. Your abilities have surpassed those required for the duties of a lady's maid."

Molly's smile began small then stretched across her face. "Thank you, my lady."

"And you will be far more valuable in another capacity—other than helping me dazzle the room with my presentation."

"I quite agree." Halloway looked to his footman. "And I feel the same about you, Thomas. You are hereby dismissed from my service."

Annesley's heart hammered in his chest. What was Halloway getting at?

Thomas's face had gone ashen. He cleared his throat. "Thank you, my lord, but if it's all the same to you, I'm not seeking other employment. I would much prefer—"

"No, it's decided, Thomas. I no longer have need for your services."

"Oh, stop, Nathaniel. What we do need," Lady Amanda hurriedly added, "are positions to be filled in our orphanage: parents, if you will. A head gentleman and lady of the home, positions that can be filled by"—she looked at each in turn—"a husband and wife."

Color rushed back to Thomas's face, and then he nodded and went back down on one knee in front of Molly.

The room responded with laughter, Becky's loudest of all.

"Oh." Her hand went to her mouth, and her eyes glistened and welled with moisture.

Thomas brought her hand to his lips and kissed the ring on her finger. "Would you not *only* marry me, Molly?" He glanced behind him at Lord Halloway. "But *also* help me run the orphanage?"

She pulled him to his feet once more and threw herself into his arms. "Yes! Oh yes again, to all of it!" They both turned to smile at their employers, and Molly added, "Thank you, for everything."

Annesley couldn't help but feel pangs of loneliness. He once thought he'd have a moment as good and sweet as this one, but now he wasn't so certain. The woman with whom he'd hoped to share such a moment refused to look at him, even now.

"It is time we hear from dear Lord Annesley," their hostess said, her face full of light. Even with the crushing defeat they had suffered only hours ago, she found room for hope and joy. He admired her for it.

"What is it you want to hear?" he asked.

"Your part in our great puzzle, if you will."

His gaze travelled over the faces in the room, all so dear to him. "After an unfortunate conversation at the rally . . ." His eyes found Chloe, and he tried to apologize for all he'd done, for all she'd overheard him say to Lord Grey, with the most penitent look he could muster.

She did not turn away but returned his gaze with an intensity that sent energy coursing through him.

He looked away, reluctantly. "I travelled by carriage straightaway to Manchester, where I put into play some of the plans Lord Halloway and I have been working on for a month now."

Everyone seemed to lean forward with interest, and Lord Annesley felt an unfamiliar thrill at being the point of interest for a good story.

"Upon arriving, with the yeomen we hired, it was simple enough to dispatch the men into the establishment and accompany the women who desired to leave, particularly Molly's dear friend Jewel. Then we moved to other homes and informed as many as we could of the new law for child workers." Annesley shook his head. "Some did not appear coherent enough to understand. I wish I'd shut down the bars and opium trade also while we were there."

"I cannot thank you or Lord Halloway enough." Molly looked from one man to the other.

Annesley's heart warmed at her sincerity. Never had this sort of work felt as worthwhile as it did under the glow of her gratitude.

"Upon settling Jewel safely in a home and sending a force of yeomen and the magistrate to the cotton mill to aid Thomas and Molly, I rushed to Westminster Palace, trying to delay the vote."

The memory of the defeat darkened his mood. "If we'd been able to reach William Lovett sooner, perhaps we could have had a different outcome."

Molly piped up. "Hope is not lost. I will begin renewing our efforts immediately, using my original, more . . . um . . . visual tactics."

Thomas turned her gently to him. "With rocks?"

She reached a hand up to his face. "Let us discuss this later."

Everyone laughed.

"My condolences." Halloway smirked at Thomas.

"And now," Chloe said, standing and clasping her hands, "I wish to add my puzzle pieces to all of this."

All eyes turned to her, and she returned their open curiosity with a new confidence Annesley had not seen before. The change in her was remarkable. She now at last stood before him as the Chloe he had always known, the strong woman inside, who was so apparent in her as a young child. As her gaze travelled over everyone and then fell on him, he couldn't have felt prouder.

"As soon as Lord Halloway brought me home from the rally, I hurried to my father for assistance. You see, once we learned that Theo's success at bending others to his will was largely due to the financial distress of many in the House of Lords, we rushed to their homes, offering solutions—loans—to aid in their financial emergencies. We'd hoped they would then choose to vote their consciences." Her face fell. "I sincerely hoped women would not be excluded."

Annesley wanted to rush to her, pull her into his arms, and kiss away her sadness. He surprised himself with the intensity of his feelings.

But Amanda put an arm around her friend instead. "The lords were offered only one choice: help the working classes or not. Of course, they all chose to pass the suffrage bill, and doing so was long overdue." She paused, her face tightening. She swallowed twice before continuing. "This is but the beginning. Now, because of the passage of this law, those who rallied and those who were injured and died at Peterloo did not do so in vain."

Molly rose and stood beside her, and the three women clasped hands. Annesley couldn't help but admire their strength, especially standing together as they were. He shook his head in wonder, pondering the mark they made on the world and the potential that was theirs.

Then Chloe turned shy eyes to Annesley.

His heart skipped.

"We wish all were as noble as Lord Annesley, who had made his own changes financially to his estate and did not need a loan from my father as a result." Her eyes shone with pride.

He started. *How could she know that?*

The two searched each other's eyes for so long, Annesley full of questions, that Halloway clapped his hands. "I'll ask cook for some of her delicious tarts, and we shall celebrate together. I want to thank each one of you. Because of all those involved, an evil empire has toppled, a brilliant vote has passed, and our orphanages are in good hands."

Everyone stood to clap and cheer while he pulled the bell rope.

Annesley couldn't wait another moment. He approached Chloe. "Might I have a word?" He gestured toward hallway.

"Of course." Chloe's cheeks turned a faint pink, and Annesley's heart lit with a flicker of hope.

She was so beautiful—her cheeks a warm rose, her eyes flashing and brave. He'd nearly stammered when he spoke.

They walked to the front entry, and when they stood at the base of the stairs, Annesley turned to Lady Chloe. Her beautiful heart-shaped face stared up into his, full of hope.

"Lady Chloe, I apologize for my behavior to you and to your suffrage committee. I have not given the support I felt in my heart I should provide." She had every right to distrust him forever. He breathed in deeply, filling his lungs with the courage air sometimes brings. "I did, in fact, report your actions to the prime minister, which he, in turn, tried to use against you." He hated to say it. Fear rose up in his throat.

Chloe's eyes darkened and waves of trouble crossed her features. "But . . . why would you do that? You encouraged me. You are the reason I dared take the actions I have taken." She paused, looking at her twisting fingers. "Dared to even try."

"I am?" Hope emboldened him. Perhaps he could mend this. He reached for her hands, stopping their nervous twitching.

She searched the base of her gown. He wondered which slipper would poke out for her to stare at.

But she surprised him and returned his gaze. "You did not answer my question." The fierceness in her voice both surprised and warmed him.

He bit back a smile. "Why indeed. I was coerced, forced by the prime minister himself. He threatened my father's estate, my family's name and fortune. But I assure you, I did no damage to you or the other ladies. I gave him just enough information for him to believe I was telling him all, but I withheld anything I felt might harm you or your cause."

The corner of her mouth turned up, and she stepped closer. "I hoped that was the case."

Annesley studied her face. Did he dare feel any sliver of hope that she might welcome his love?

Her eyes widened. "My father said you did not need a loan as the others did, that you'd arranged matters so everything would be well with your estate." Her eyes held sparks of admiration, and he thrilled at the thought. "He thinks very highly of you."

His heart overflowing, he asked, "And does his lovely daughter share this high opinion?"

"I may. Especially knowing you did not sabotage our work."

"You have my word. I did only what I had to, and I hated every moment. I withheld so much I was no true help to him at all." Just the thought of his behavior made him cringe. He hoped to impress upon her the depth of his sincerity.

Her lovely lips frowned, and he was fascinated with their shape, though he wished to never be the cause of such an expression on her face.

"But if you had reached out for help, confided in someone . . . in me . . ." The pink on her face darkened.

"And admit how undeserving I am of you?"

Her smile started small and then grew. "In what way would you be undeserving?"

"If I ever wanted you to consider me as someone, shall we say, *important* in your life, I wouldn't have much to offer: a shattered estate wrapped in the claws of an evil man and a crime boss in Manchester."

She giggled. "Indeed, that is not much to recommend you."

He sighed. "I still do not have much to offer. My estate will not recover for many years, perhaps not for a whole generation." He rubbed his thumb across the back of her hand.

"And what if the things that recommend you the most have nothing to do with your estate?" Her face turned a furious shade of red, and she looked away, studying the wall to their left.

His heart thrilled at her kindness and her interest, but did he dare open this opportunity? Did she not deserve so much more than he could give her?

After a moment she looked up at him once more, her eyes alight with a fire and passion that stopped his breath. She stood before him as a pillar of strength and bravery, confidence shining from her features. She stepped nearer, searching his face.

He waited for her to speak, wondered if she would. She lifted up on her toes, her lips close enough to kiss.

His heart pounded in his chest. He forced his eyes away from her mouth. Who was this new creature? He was as much terrified as he was fascinated.

As close as she could get to him without pressing her mouth to his, she said, "Perhaps you'd like to come call on me tomorrow?" Her breath brushed over his mouth in a soft whisper.

He swallowed. "Yes, I'd like that."

"Wonderful." Her eyes sparkled into his, and she stepped back a half step. "The group will be pleased to have you."

"Pardon . . . ?" He faltered. "The . . . group?"

"Yes." She grinned and then giggled into her hands. "Our suffrage committee meeting is tomorrow, and you will be our first male member." She turned from him with a saucy lift of her hip as if to rejoin the others.

The corner of Annesely's mouth lifted. "Ah, Chloe?"

She turned her head.

"If I may?" He stepped toward her.

She swallowed, rocking back and forth on her feet.

He approached, his courage growing, and reached for her hand, linking their fingers. He reached forward and rested the back of his knuckles on the soft skin of her face.

She leaned in to him until he opened his hand and cupped her cheek. He placed her other hand around his back and then wrapped her in his arms. "I wasn't finished yet."

"You weren't?"

He tipped his head, returning his lips to the space just above hers, her breath again tickling his mouth. "No, see, here we were."

"Oh yes." She lifted her chin. "I remember."

He paused as she closed her eyes, just a moment more, thrilling in the beautiful woman before him, in her gentle strength, her constant goodness, her forgiveness. Then he pressed his mouth to hers. Her soft lips responded to his gentle touch. He pulled her closer and pressed his mouth again and again until he thought he would never get enough.

At length he paused.

Her small sigh made him smile. "I love you, Chloe."

"I love you too."

CHAPTER THIRTY

IN THE DARK OF NIGHT, Molly's cheeks were still wet from her tears, but her pen continued to scratch across the parchment, stalled only by her need to dip the nib into her inkwell. Thoughts flew through her mind faster than she could get them down, but she scratched on and on, capturing them the best she could.

> *Dear future daughters, sisters, mothers, wives, and all women,*
>
> *Do not tread lightly, dear sisters. Wipe gentle, careful words from your vocabulary. Words like* diplomacy, peace, consideration, cooperation, *and* compromise. *You have no use for these. Not any longer.*
> *You matter . . .*

The candle burned on, late into the night, as Molly's pen scratched words across her page.

CHAPTER THIRTY-ONE

Eighty years later
Liverpool, England, 1910

FOG SWIRLED AROUND WOMEN'S ANKLES, rolling over their skirt hems. They waited until after their shifts at the factories, after serving dinner to their families, after putting their dear children to bed. They'd come to hear Miss Pankhurst tell tales in the dark of night of suffrage for women. The way she described it, a fairy tale was in the works, in which women were listened to, respected even. These late-night women loved Miss Pankhurst because she promised a dream.

The heroine herself stepped up onto the platform, waving an old brown book in her hands, and began to speak. "I've found it, ladies! I have it in my very hands. Hush! Quiet now, so I can read it!"

"Let her read it, you lot. Quiet," an older woman, wrinkles lining her weathered skin, called out.

"Oy now, I want to hear it, don't I?" Another called from the opposite side of the crowd.

Miss Pankhurst cleared her throat. "I found this journal." She held it against her heart. "Found it amongst my family's possessions. It was written by a fellow suffragist, from a time long past. And believe me, ladies, I think her words will change everything."

Her voice carried over the hushed group of women as she read,

> *"Dear future daughters, sisters, mothers, wives, and all women,*

Do not tread lightly, dear sisters. Wipe gentle, careful words from your vocabulary. Words like diplomacy, consideration, cooperation, *and* compromise. *You have no use for these. Not any longer.*

You matter . . . You matter so much that I write you this letter, here in my journal, with hopes that you will always know. You matter not just because you are someone's wife or mother or daughter. Those relationships are important. But you matter because you are a woman. Not just any woman, but you, *the only woman like you anywhere. And your voice matters. Your individual, specific voice. It counts and should be counted. Your voice must be heard.*

Do not tread lightly, dear women.

If the day has not yet arrived that each human voice is counted by vote, then let it be known that you are past waiting. That you are done being silent or diplomatic or careful. You are beyond attempting the careful route.

Here I am in 1830, with proof that the careful way does not work. How far into the future are you from 1830? That's how many years we have as proof that all our attempts to encourage with words failed. Words do not always disturb peace. Well, let us disturb peace.

Until they are uncomfortable, until their tea is cold, their dinners uncooked, their women marching in the streets, they will not move one inch away from their warm fires, pipes in hand and slippers on their feet. Now is the time for action, women, for doing, for getting attention. Make it the very goal of your breath to never let humanity forget a thing called women's suffrage. Don't let them comfortably find their pillows at night without first worrying over what you did or might do tomorrow.

We are past words, women. If you never say another thing, silently go about doing and acting and demonstrating that you will not go away, that women are ready to stand, ready to discard all careful conversation until there is change, not until government says they will change but until the actual change is before your eyes and you are standing up and taking your vote and electing your choices into office in the House of Commons. Do not tread lightly, dear women. With great stomping strides, make your footsteps known. Do not tread lightly.

Molly O'Malley

AUTHOR'S NOTES

As with all historical fiction, some of the elements of this story are true accounts of history and well-researched fact. I used original sources and journals wherever possible, and the setting and characters are accurate to the Regency and the beginnings of the Victorian time period in England. In addition, the following people and events deserve mention as nonfictional parts of the story:

This story takes place roughly ten years after the Peterloo Massacre, a central event in my first book, *The Nobleman's Daughter*. All historical fact and the liberties I took to tell an accurate story in that book apply also to this one. The characters described in that story are the same as told in this.

In the Epilogue of *The Nobleman's Daughter*, which takes place five years after the story's end, the Halloways have two boys, and Lady Amanda is expecting her first daughter. The pregnancy mentioned in this current story would be her second daughter and fourth child.

Mary Fildes is mentioned. She was a woman involved in Peterloo, leading a women's group and speaking out. The account spoken by Lady Amanda is true. Mary Fildes continued to be a valiant and strong supporter of women's suffrage.

There were many rallies like the one described, with different women's groups carrying their respective banners. The people uniting as they did was the main reason the lords started to attempt reform. At first it was simply an effort to appease the populace, and then sincere efforts at change made a real difference.

The women giving speeches were real women in that day, and the words they speak in this book are words they wrote or spoke a little later in their lives. *The Enfranchisement of Women* was written by Harriet Taylor Mill and was inspired in part by the words of Abiah Higginbotham. It was not published until 1850, but the ideas were being generated and discussed during the time during which my book is set. I wanted to include the direct quotes, even though they were published at a later date, because they became timeless and have been quoted and used in multiple places since, including in the United States in its own fight for women's suffrage.

The Great Reform Act was a real law. Up until that point, no law had defined what gender could vote. The irony that the first broadening of suffrage to many more working-class men was also the first law to prohibit women is portrayed accurately. During the passage of the bill, however, there were no last-minute amendments that I know of. It took the passage of three reform acts through the House of Commons before one finally passed through the House of Lords. I combine this political process a huge degree for reader enjoyment.

William Lovett did not draft the bill, but he was a real person who played a huge role in reform a few years later. Ironically, he was so dissatisfied with the Great Reform Act of 1832 that he worked to make additional changes to the law. I created a fictional situation in which he drafted the bill, was controlled by Theo, and therefore would have spent his life trying to fix it.

I read the minutes of the bill being passed and the one before it and several after. The general raucous, the coughing to drown out noise, and the calling out were all part of the process. Even Lord Grey's speech, encouraging the passage of the bill that he wasn't overly excited about is accurate, though I created the words. Hardly any of the lords desired universal suffrage; the impression I get—and it's a loose one and I don't speak for others—was that they wished to offer something with hopes to appease the great crowds who were fighting for suffrage.

Lord Grey did play a significant role in gathering a Whig force large enough so reform was possible. He worked tirelessly for this, and he did admit he didn't even support universal suffrage but was motivated to make the changes because of frequent and significant rallies of the working-class people who asked for change. Every time parliament did not pass a reform bill, rioting took place around the country. It was a real concern and proves that the voice of the people will be heard. I take liberties in my story with his personality, and I have no evidence at all that he ever used extortion to force anyone's hand, nor do I suspect that he did so.

The child labor law did pass, years before my book begins and was called the 1819 Cotton Mills and Factory Act. It forbade the employment of children under the age of nine, but it provided no means of enforcement. It did give parliament a precedent to use when writing other acts to protect children working in factories. I used it as the bill in this story to point out the first step in a good direction. Better laws were created and, eventually, children were protected.

Angel Meadow was a real place, often called "The Medda." It was worse than I portray. There was a woman who left her baby in the river as described and a man who saved the child. Opium and alcohol addiction were common. Waste littered the streets and the homes. Disease was frequent and deadly. Until the Reform Act, Manchester had no representation in the House of Commons and had been left to squalor in such a devastating way, with no one creating laws of protection or governing the area, that areas like Angel Meadow came to be.

Lord Theodore Oswald is a completely fictional character, though I imagine there were some like him who took advantage of the lawless and unrepresented situation for the poor in England. And there were factory owners who benefitted greatly from child labor and abused it. It was a common practice to buy votes in those days. In fact, they created a law preventing it not long after the Reform Act was passed.

A note about Molly's letter. Her rousing words are meant as a foreshadowing and a lead-in to the suffrage movement that finally brought about the vote for women. I personally have a passionate belief that words do matter and are the best motivators for change. Words have power. But I do not believe Molly would have thought they worked very well for her, and I know Emmeline Pankhurst and the other more militant suffragettes were dedicated to making a lot of noise and ruckus.

So what happened? Why did the quest for women's suffrage fail, leaving women without a vote for almost a hundred more years? I have not been able to determine one reason alone. There were many suffrage groups during this time period. One of the reasons women did not see earlier success could have been due, in part, to the fact that they did not unite under one front early enough. It helps to understand the thinking of the people during the time. Lawmakers were so desperate to pass the Reform Act that if they thought women's suffrage would hold them back, they would have eliminated any wording that supported women. It was not socially acceptable for a woman to vote. It was not even morally acceptable for a woman to vote. Some said it took away from her God-given responsibilities in the home. Also, since votes were tied into property, many thought it ridiculous to have two votes per household. If the married couple voted the same, one vote would have been sufficient; if they voted opposite, they cancelled each other out. I'm sure there are many more reasons—as many as there were lawmakers at the time. I, for one, am grateful for the early activists who kept pushing, kept asking, kept defiantly acting and working for suffrage, even though they were declined time and again. Because of their sacrifices and efforts, I reap the benefits today.

ABOUT THE AUTHOR

JEN GEIGLE JOHNSON DISCOVERED HER passion for England while kayaking on the Thames near London as a young teenager. Unrelated but fun, she also once greeted an ancient turtle under the water by grabbing her fin. Now an award-winning author and mother of six, she loves to share bits of history that might otherwise be forgotten. Her first book, *The Nobleman's Daughter*, was published November 2017. Whether in Regency England, the French Revolution, or Colonial America, her romance novels are much like life is supposed to be: full of adventure. She is a member of the RWA, the SCBWI, and LDStorymakers. She is also the chair of the Lonestar.Ink writing conference. https://www.jengeiglejohnson.com

Enjoy this sneak peek of Jen Geigle Johnson's 2020 release,

LADY ELIZABETH'S DECEPTION

London, England, 1817

THE COZINESS OF THE STUDY, usually comforting, closed tighter around Elizabeth in a suffocating narrowness. "Father." Liz tried to reason with him. "His teeth protrude so far forward that he cannot even close his lips around them." It was not the largest of her concerns about the vile man's suitability, but it was one that surely her father would recognize.

Chuckling while his gaze travelled over the ledger on his desk, he responded, "Lizzy, Lizzy. Come now. What is a little awkward teeth placement when you consider his station in life, his holdings, his family. You could live in any of his lovely estates, have every opportunity, every frivolity."

He glanced up at her. In his eye a glint of apprehension hinted that he might be set on the match. She tried harder. "All of that without love or affection would feel like prison. You ask too much."

Turning to the next page, he ran a finger down a column of numbers. "I hope you will change your mind. Get to know him. You have hardly spoken three words to each other."

"Which is why I cannot fathom your acceptance of his suit without consulting me, without even knowing him properly." She had been able to talk her father out of every other suitor; she would succeed with Lord Nigel Pinweather as well. She leaned forward, palms down on her father's desk, hoping he would look into her eyes. "He might be cruel, prone to fits of temper."

At this the earl leaned back and laughed. "My dear, he is as thin as a rail and short besides. You could squash him like a bug, temper or no."

"You are not thinking, Father. He could command the household to lock me up. You might never see me again. 'Oh, she is unwell today,' they would say. 'Oh, she couldn't make it this trip.' Years could go by, *years*, and you would never speak to me, not knowing if I lived or died."

For a flash of a second, sympathy crossed his eyes and a touch of something else. Guilt? He shook his head. "If it weren't such a frowned upon profession, I would have encouraged you to be an actress." He dipped his pen into ink. "I have no time for your theatrics."

Liz rested her elbows on her knees and held her face in the palms of her hands. Thinking on the last ball, she breathed out in exasperation. The room had been full of handsome gentlemen; kind gentlemen; smart, engaging men; and who did her father accept? Lord Nigel Pinweather. Pinweather. Was she really to be Lady Pinweather? Although, if she were to be completely honest, she was not impressed with any of the available lords this Season—stuffed, pompous do-nothings. There must be more to life than what she had so far experienced.

Her father pulled his timepiece from his pocket. "Did I mention he is coming to walk in the park this morning? Should be arriving any moment."

"Ugh! Father, you did not mention it, no. I would have been completely indisposed had you brought it to my attention." She stood. "As it is, I feel a headache beginning to pinch between my eyes." She held the bridge of her nose with two fingers and walked to the door.

Lemming, their butler, stepped in front of the doorway just as she moved to exit.

"Oh, do excuse me, my lady."

Her father waved him into the room. "It's all right, Lemming."

"Lord Nigel Pinweather here to see you, my lady."

She reached out a hand to steady herself on the wall.

Lord Davenport chuckled. "Early riser. As he should be. Lemming, please show him into the morning room."

"Very good, my lord."

Liz paced in front of her father. "Must I entertain him? Alone? Where is Mother?"

"Of course your mother will join you; don't be silly. Now, give him just a moment to get settled in, and then pour the man some tea."

"And we're to go for a walk?" She craned her neck to see outside, but alas, the birds chirped prettily on a bright and sunny day.

"Come now. Give him a chance, my dear. Who knows but that he has a charming personality with a bit of wit to recommend him?"

⌒

A full thirty minutes after her first sip of tea, she longed for their promised walk to relieve the tedium.

Lord Pinweather pointed at her with his cup, slopping some over the edge.

Her mother winced.

"And then the swine all ran to the far corner of the yard, chasing the young lad while he yelped and hollered. He sounded like the hounds were after him." He laughed with deep heaving breaths. "You understand. As if he were on the hunt . . ." He looked from Liz to her mother with his eyebrows raised.

Her mother forced a smile.

Liz did not. During his first such account, she had waited for more, for the purpose, but it had never come. Just his laughter. And his was a cruel sense of humor. Watching him rock, celebrating his own abysmal lack of wit, she wondered if he noticed no one else cared. Or did he think they were all as enthralled as he?

And his teeth. She did not consider herself so utterly frivolous that his teeth should matter, but his lips could not close properly. Would she ever have to kiss those lips? She brought a handkerchief to her nose, hiding her disgust as she felt a slight burning at the back of her throat.

Food passed across the front of his mouth, and his tongue couldn't quite reach to dislodge it. Tea didn't fully wash it away. She found herself distracted, cringing at a piece of cucumber marring the yellow surface of a front tooth. And then a bit of sandwich flung outward and landed on her knee. Watching that piece of soggy bread soak into her lovely pink taffeta, she knew Lord Pinweather could not be her future. How was she to dislodge breadcrumb spittle from her person? And *how* was she to dislodge such a suitor?

Perhaps if she made herself ridiculous, he would turn away and seek a suit elsewhere. Interrupting his next inane account, she rose. "It is time for our walk, is it not?"

Her mother's eyebrows rose.

If she had to endure a walk in the park with this man before he would leave, then they had best get started. "Do you not agree, Lord Pinweather?" She giggled and snorted, wiping her glove below her nose. She offered the same gloved hand to him.

His smile widened as he clasped her hand in his own. Then he raised his eyebrows twice before bowing. She cringed when the weight of his lips pressed into her fingers—those same appendages which had just now been wiping her nose in such an uncouth manner.

Subtlety would not turn him away.

She pulled her hand from his grasp. "Oh, come now, we have no need of this romantic gallantry. Let us be off, shall we?" She pulled at his arm, dragging him toward the door and ignoring the raised eyebrows of the footman, who scrambled to open it soon enough that they could pass.

"*Lady* Elizabeth, really." Her mother's soft tones of disapproval did nothing to dissuade Liz from her course. She turned to eye her mother with a look of defiance.

Unsympathetic eyes searched her face for a moment, and then her mother sighed and nodded her head in acceptance.

With that, Liz snorted and burst out in real laughter while she used more force to yank Lord Pinweather down the hallway.

"Lady Elizabeth. Such strength. Excellent for bearing sons." He patted her hand where it gripped his sleeve.

She released him. *Bearing sons indeed.* "You are too bold."

"Am I? I feel it is almost decided between us, is it not? Your father seemed most pleased."

"I cannot speak for him, but as for myself, I am not decided."

They waited at the front door for the butler to open it. Her maid fell in behind them. Lord Pinweather stepped closer. The garlic on his breath was so strong Liz tasted it on her tongue.

He placed a hand at her elbow. "A proper courtship would be dull, would it not, if I could not spend my efforts convincing you? Turning your heart to mine?" He squeezed her arm and gave it a little shake.

She returned her eyes to his face, pulling her arm from his grip. "Hmm. I am unprepared for such an effort in my behalf. I do believe you might be better served focusing elsewhere." There, she'd said it. Perhaps he would desist without her father knowing she'd been the cause.

"Naturally you are unprepared. But I am happy to step in to help, as they say, prepare you." He raised his eyebrows a couple of times and leaned forward, teeth first, toward her own mouth.

She yelped and stepped back, bumping against the wall behind her. "Lemming!"

"Yes, my lady." He entered the hallway from their drawing room.

"We are ready to be off to the park."

"Very good." His eyes held sympathy. Then he straightened his jacket, stepped forward, and opened the door.

⌒

After a full hour in the park, Liz stomped into the house, threw her bonnet at Lemming, and would have shouted to the walls if she hadn't first heard laughter from her father's study. And her name. She stepped closer.

"But she must go through with it. How can you be sure she will marry the idiot?" A man's voice Liz didn't recognize sounded rough to her ears, poor even. Why was he a guest in her father's study and discussing her in this manner?

"Yes, quite a bit hangs on your daughter's amiability." Liz shuddered. They were discussing Lord Pinweather's suit? That voice sounded like possibly one of her father's friends. Why would he care whom she married?

"She will. Has no choice, really." Her father's voice sounded strange—giddy, desperate, even.

Liz's heart sank in cold dread.

More laughter carried out into the hallway and hid her loud gasp. Glasses clinked together.

"Lord Pinweather will make up for any grief you hear from her. Padding your pockets, he is." The first man acted as though he were on equal footing with her father but sounded so crass. Could he be a servant?

"Couldn't get anyone else to marry his son!" The other man's voice cleared. "Been through three Seasons and no one will take him."

Liz fisted her hands.

"Lord Pinweather's father made the whole arrangement quite lucrative. I'll be making a dowry instead of spending it."

"'Cause you already spent her dowry, now, didn't you?" The rough-sounding voice had a rasp to it, and she hoped never to meet its owner in the dark of night.

A pause followed. "I'd never force her like this, you know, if we weren't in such a bind." Her father choked a little, and the regret in his voice might have comforted Liz if her panic was not rising, blocking all other emotion.

"Ole Horace." The man's tone sent gooseflesh up and down Liz's arms. "He wants his money, that's all. And now we're gonna give it to him."

"Then back to the tables." Liz tried to place this man's voice. She'd heard it before.

"Or the races. I've got my eye on a bit of horseflesh—a sure thing, and no one knows it but me." Liz wanted to shake a fist at her father's irresponsibility. Wasn't that behavior what had brought her to this horror in the first place?

"Ain't that always the way?"

More tinkling of glasses followed. "To freedom!" Her father's jubilant voice twisted her stomach in knots.

The sound followed her as she ran down the hall and up the stairs, straight for her mother's sitting room. She burst in unannounced. "Mother, you cannot let Father go through with this."

Her mother frowned. "Leave, and come back in with more decorum. We have not raised you to be the harridan you appear at the moment."

Sighing, Liz turned and waited at the entrance to the room.

"Hello, Liz, won't you come in?"

Stomping, she came forward in a flurry. "Father is being compensated for my marriage to Lord Pinweather. I am part of some sort of *business deal*."

She waited for the shock, the denial, the worry—any expression—to cross her mother's smooth features.

"Every marriage is a business deal of some sort."

Liz's mouth opened. "How can you say that? Was yours?"

Her mother waved the idea away. "Of a sort, yes. His father met with mine, and they arranged the financial details."

"But this is worse. They were laughing and patting each other on the back about it, calling Lord Pinweather an idiot even. Father wants me to marry an idiot?"

Her mother's lips pursed, and her brow wrinkled. "You were eavesdropping on your father?"

"Mother, this is my life! Surely you can reason with him. I don't want to be tied in marriage to a man my own father does not respect."

For a moment her mother's eyes showed compassion, and she said, "Come here, dear."

Leaning in, she hugged her mother. "You will speak to him, won't you?"

"I will not."

"What?" She pulled away, sucking in a breath.

"Lord Pinweather is a decent enough person. He thinks very highly of you and will make you a safe and comfortable life. That is all I have ever wanted for you. I am quite pleased and relieved you will be so happily situated."

"Happily situated? No. That's just it. I won't be happy."

"Please, Liz, I have nothing more to say on it." She leaned closer to Liz, quieting her voice. "I will let you in on a little secret though. He plans to propose tonight after dinner at our dinner party. Wear your lavender dress."

Liz froze. "Tonight?" She brought a hand to her face. "But, Mother, I cannot accept him."

Her mother rose from her chair. "You will accept him. We have given him every reason to believe you will accept him. Do not embarrass us or cause scandal tonight, Liz." She brought a hand up to Liz's chin. "This *is* your life now. Learn to accept it, welcome it even. Many young debutantes are not so lucky." She stared into Liz's eyes with an unyielding look of stone. "There is more going on than I hope you ever know. I promise this marriage is the best possible thing for you right now."

From that moment Liz knew she was finished with her childhood home. Shaken, she blinked back tears. How could she have been deceived into thinking her parents actually cared for her?

CHAPTER TWO

SHE RUSHED TO HER ROOM, grabbed her bonnet and reticule, and then walked down the hallway calling her maid.

Soon they were in the carriage. Heidi, her maid since childhood, looked curiously on.

"I just needed some air." She couldn't explain, but she felt like talking. "I told the coachman to drive around London in no particular direction."

Heidi nodded. "Yes, my lady."

As a result, they traveled roads Liz had never seen before until they approached a loud, energy-filled square. "Stop here, please."

"Oh, my lady, you shouldn't be getting out here." Heidi's face pinched in worry.

"I'm not thinking of exiting the carriage. I just want to see."

They pulled closer, and the shouting and calling-out became clearer. A group of people, servants by the look of them, stood in a line. Others walked by, looking them up and down, asking questions, sometimes poking and prodding.

"What's going on here, do you think?"

Heidi answered, "Those are them what need work, and the housekeepers are out choosing new hires."

"What are those papers they're holding?"

"Those would be their letters of recommendation, now, wouldn't they?"

Liz's mind spun, a wild sort of excitement rushing through her. "What happens if they don't have a letter?"

"Well, now, it's right difficult to get hired that way, but there's always positions open if you're willing to leave London. The best positions require papers."

Liz swallowed the lump in her throat and straightened her skirt with shaking hands. "Tell the driver we wish to stop at that bookseller up ahead." She tried to summon courage. She would just go look, walk amongst the employers, and see what she thought.

When the carriage arrived in front of the bookseller, Liz and Heidi exited, and Liz told the driver to return in several hours. A footman stayed behind, and soon he and Heidi were deep in conversation. Heidi's giggles told Liz she had a few moments before she would be missed.

She rushed back into the carriage and borrowed Heidi's overcoat from the bench, slipped around the back of the shop, and made her way to the group of people hoping to be hired.

As soon as she arrived, a woman approached. "Papers?"

"No, I don't have any."

The woman eyed her, taking in the overcoat, obviously noticing the finery beneath. "Do you read?"

"Yes."

She raised her eyebrows in appreciation. "Any experience managing a house?"

"Yes, quite a bit, actually." She had helped her mother host any number of guests. "And planning menus, purchasing . . ." She paused. What else would apply? Her trips to the modiste must count for something.

The woman took some notes. "Without papers, I don't have much to offer here in London." She shuffled through her notes.

"I could leave." Her voice shook. "Really, I could go anywhere."

The woman's eyebrows rose. "Willing to go to America?"

Shaken, Liz tried to slow her breathing. Swallowing, clenching her tremoring fists, she conjured Lord Pinweather's face into her mind and said, "Yes."

"All right then, sign here. You're hired. Come around to the docks, slip forty-seven, noon, Tuesday."

And it was done.

⌒

Liz threw things into a small bag. One nice gown, her hairbrush, several sheets of paper. Thoughts, pushed as far away as her emotions could send them, tried to reason with her. She didn't know the first thing about running a household. She had never cared one wit to know what went on below- or abovestairs.

But what choice did she have? If she stayed here, she would be stuck with that goat of a man. Perhaps she could reason further with her parents. She would prepare to leave and give them one final chance to change their minds.

Heidi walked in at that moment. "What are you doing, my lady?" The alarm on her face almost shook Liz from her purpose.

"I'm going away, just for a time. It isn't safe for me here."

Heidi eyed her for a moment. "We've been talking about it. And we all agree. We'd do the same. It isn't right what they are doing to you."

"I am shocked . . . and proud . . . to hear you say that. Relieved, too, because I'm going to be needing your clothes and salary. You did get paid yesterday, did you not?"

Heidi's face went white. "I did, my lady, but that money is for my mum. She needs it at home."

"I'm sure my father will get you some more. Hurry now."

Heidi swallowed and went into the closet, where her bed and things were kept.

Liz called in to her. "Come out with two of your dresses and skirts to work in, and an outfit for Sundays."

"Yes, my lady."

Heidi's voice sounded quiet; maybe her maid would miss her. What a sobering thought. Was Heidi the only person in the household who would? Perhaps she should take care of her, leave her some way to buy new things.

A knock at the door made Liz squeal.

"Really, Liz, must you always be so dramatic?" Her mother's voice sounded strange. "Might I come in?"

Liz ran to the closet and tossed the bag inside, just missing Heidi by a hair.

"Yes, open the door."

Her mother's eyes were red as though she had been crying.

"Are you well, Mother?"

She waved her hand. "Yes, yes, I am fine. I am just having some emotion at the thought of you, my darling angel, receiving a proposal of marriage this very night."

"He isn't my first suitor." She narrowed her eyes at her mother.

"Oh, all right. I have had a bit of bad news about your father's financial dealings, and I am only in here to make sure you understand you are to say yes to Lord Pinweather."

"Mother, you have made that abundantly clear, as clear as my gloves are white. I am certain you want me miserable."

She rested a hand at the side of Liz's face. "I just want you safe. This might be the last chance for you to be secure and happy."

"Again, you fool yourself. Lord Pinweather is not my fount of happiness. Would he be yours?" Liz scoffed.

"Please, have a modicum of trust in your mother. This doesn't seem like it now, but it is the best I could do for you in the time allowed."

Her mother was not making any sense to Liz, at all, and she felt such a large sense of betrayal from her that she could hardly complete the conversation.

"Please, promise me you will accept him."

She searched her mother's eyes, and something there made her nervous—a sort of desperate crease lined her mother's forehead. And she knew if she didn't promise, her mother would not let up.

"I promise."

Her mother let out a huge breath, as though the weight of the house rested on her agreement.

As soon as Liz's mother left, Heidi came back out with the bag Liz had tossed into the closet. "All packed. I added the necessities as well as a few of my own things." She swallowed. "I don't have much by way of clothes. Do you think your father will provide more for me?"

"Of course he will. You have to have clothes, do you not?" She thought for a moment, concerned that her father would not replace Heidi's clothes. She knew nothing by way of servants or their interactions with her parents. "Take any of mine you like. It'll be a trade." She rummaged through her jewelry and found a pendant. "And this." She pulled parchment out of her drawer, and her ink and pen. "I shall write a note. All of my clothes I give to Heidi as a gift. And the blue pendant." She read it out as she wrote it then handed it to Heidi.

Heidi nodded nervously. Then she stood taller. "Let's get you ready for dinner and your proposal." She raised her eyebrows a couple of times and giggled. "Do you think he will get on his knee?"

"Or have a ring?" Liz thought about it for a moment. "I hope so. I could sell it."

"That is very smart of you, my lady." Heidi paused in her preparations. "But are you sure you can do this? Take care of yourself like this?"

"Absolutely. My new employer will take care of my passage and, once I'm there, I'm sure will explain what is expected as well."

"Your new employer?" Heidi's eyes went wide in disbelief. She didn't even try to hide her shock.

Liz frowned. "I've accepted a position as a housekeeper. I know a bit about managing a house, menus, shopping, and the like."

"But it isn't just that. Life is . . . different for a servant. People aren't as nice. Sometimes things even cost more for us."

Liz waved her hand in dismissal. "I'm not concerned, though I am a bit nervous. Terrified, to be exact. But all I need do is remember my company only a few hours earlier and I have plenty of courage to carry this through."

Heidi nodded in sympathy. "I can well believe it."

Liz looked lovely wearing lavender as her mother had requested and showing off a new hairstyle from Paris Heidi had insisted on, saying it might be the last time she would get to try it out on Liz's hair.

Lord Pinweather's hungry expression when Liz walked into the dining room made her ill. What about this situation gave her mother hope for the future? Liz couldn't understand it. She turned to her mother with a question in her brows and witnessed a similar upheaval in her mother's stomach upon seeing Lord Pinweather. Why in the name of the sheep in their borough did her mother want Liz to marry someone who made her own stomach churn?

None of this made any sense and built up her courage that much more. She was going to need it. Her hands still shook at the thought of what she was about to do.

After an arduous dinner filled with stories from Lord Pinweather, all without purpose or entertainment except to prove him ridiculous, he cleared his throat as though to make an announcement.

"As you know, I am here with a clear purpose tonight. I hope to be greatly blessed this very evening with some wonderful news." He turned to Liz, and she had a full view of his teeth. "I have watched you, Lady Elizabeth, for months—all your comings and goings, your trips to the ladies' parlor during balls, your meals at suppertime, those times you sought solitude in dark hallways. I know how many times you have worn the color lavender—my personal favorite—and how often you sip your water during mealtimes. I have paid close attention and determined long ago that you must be mine; I would prove myself worthy and, come what may, have you for a bride."

Liz and her mother shared a glance, and for the first time, she saw a hint of nervous fluttering in her mother's demeanor.

"And the day has finally come to make that a reality." He stood, pulled back his chair, and kneeled at her side. "Lady Elizabeth, will you be my wife?"

She looked from father to mother, giving them every opportunity, pleading with her eyes, but both nodded to continue. Her father even pointed, indicating she turn her attention back to Lord Pinweather.

She shrugged. What other choice did she have? She would now be a stranger to her home, her family, even her country.

"Yes." With that one word, she bid her parents farewell and determined to board a ship to America.

As soon as the horrors of dinner with her new intended were over, Liz rushed back to her room. Heidi waited, wringing her hands. "I don't know. I don't know. My lady, are you certain life with His Lordship would be as awful as giving up what you have?" A small pile of Liz's new belongings sat at her feet. As she realized that small pile would be all she owned in the world, the enormity of what she was about to do began to settle on her shoulders. But she summoned Lord Pinweather's parting words from just moments before. He'd said, "We shall have a wonderful time of it, you and I. I don't imagine the door between our rooms to be closed often, do you?"

Liz shuddered. "I'm certain. But perhaps I shall bring all the rest of my jewelry, no?" Lord Pinweather hadn't even given her a ring, unfortunately, but she had a few trinkets that might be of worth.

Heidi nodded. "To be sure. You won't be having anything else to your name, my lady. Or anyone to be helping you. Steerage on a passenger ship—"

"Say no more, Heidi. My mind is quite made up, as I'm sure yours would be were you to stand in my place."

Heidi's face wrinkled in indecision, but at length she nodded and reiterated what she had said earlier. "I do believe I would run, same as you."

Liz was grateful for her agreement. It gave her strength to move forward, and she was going to need Heidi's help. "I leave before first light. Who on the staff might be agreeable to assisting me?"

"I asked two footmen. If you can leave early enough, they will accompany you to the docks and return before their work begins. With any luck you can board the ship before sunrise."

A cloud of fear that hovered about, waiting to douse Liz's courage, began to shroud her heart. "Heidi, we don't know the first thing about this ship. What if they don't let me board? I cannot be standing about the docks by myself." The pounding in her chest picked up and she clutched her fists together, desperately trying to slow her breathing.

Heidi was at her side immediately. "Breathe. Breathe."

Her soothing words and soft hands removing the pins from Liz's hair brought back a semblance of calm. Her eyes found Heidi's. The uncertainty in her maid's face did little to comfort, but her gentle calming had eased the panic and made way for determination to return.

"I shall find a way because I must."

⌒

After two days on the ship and unable to spend another moment in steerage, Liz grabbed the ropes piled at her feet inside the jolly boat that hung in its place at the stern of the ship, and wrapped them tightly around herself, the soft white skin of her palms scratching and scraping as the rough fibers left their mark. The boat swung violently in this new storm and she second-guessed what she had originally thought a clever hiding place. The ship pitched again to the left, throwing her up against the side of the small boat.

When she heard the pelting noise of water droplets hitting the fabric above her, she was grateful at least for protection from the elements. She did have a pallet of her own on a top bunk down in the general passenger hold, the steerage—the shame of it still rankled. And she would have to make use of it again, she was sure, but the privacy and quiet of her new accommodations brought a small smile to her face.

She was doing all she could to avoid the man with the wandering hands. He had become all the more persistent, and she did not feel safe this night, sleeping in such an unprotected and public place.

When she had left the protection of her father and her position in the nobility, she had not considered what that would mean for her safety. She hadn't considered a lot of things, truth be told.

The boat pitched drastically to the left. If not for the ropes holding her inside, she would have toppled out onto the deck. Each end of her lifeboat attached to the rigging like a hammock, and her small jolly boat swung freely back to the right. She worked to secure the fabric more tightly above her. Then, curling up into the tightest ball she could, she lay on her blanket.

Despite the noise, sleep almost brought its solace until a burst of wind ripped at the ropes, detaching the boat from its secured anchors, tearing the rigging free. One side of the craft fell to the deck. She fumbled with the canvas tied tightly above her, in an effort to exit and retie the ropes. But then the other corner came untied, and the boat fell free of the rigging. Her boat started to slide, picking up speed across the tilted deck. She fell against the side, her hands scratching at the ropes, too weak to loosen the knots she herself had secured.

The ship tilted low in the front and sent her tearing down the deck in the opposite direction. A great crashing and splintering sound had her grabbing for anything secure and was followed by an unfamiliar weightlessness. Her stomach jumped to her throat and stalled her scream.

Her boat crashed to the waves, jarring her jaw so her teeth clenched together. Water dripped through the canvas above, and the boat tipped forward, down a steep wave.

She was adrift at sea.

CHAPTER THREE

NIGHT ROARED AROUND LORD ANTHONY Barton, second son of the Earl of Sussex, in the cramped cabin aboard his ship to freedom. Out his porthole window in the darkness, water splashed up against the glass. So much water battered the small circular frame that it looked to be more under than above the waves. Anthony gripped the door handle in his small accommodations on the ship. At least he had been able to acquire a cabin alone. In his hurry to leave the estate, he had taken the first available ship to Philadelphia. His trunk slid across his cabin, knocking him in the shins. "Blast and maggots!" His body followed the trunk, sliding down the dipping floor, but his hand held tightly to the door, so he pulled himself upright and opened it. The ship tipped back, and the hallway to his front became a steep decline. Thanking the builders who had included handrails, he inched forward, bracing himself when the boat tipped backward again and his path ascended.

He'd spent the last two days attempting to empty his already barren gut, and with the crackers that now resided inside had just earned his sea stomach, as the captain called it. But this storm tested his new anatomy, and all he wanted was a bit of air, to drink in great gulps of the cool freshness that was bound to be on deck.

With that motivation, his knuckles turned white in their grip, and he pulled himself to the door at the end of the hallway. Once unlatched, it slammed open with a force of the gale, and Anthonoy questioned his wisdom. Wind whipped his face and rain soaked him through from his vantage point still in the hallway.

He faced the stern of the ship. A man, a deckhand, finished tying down a sail and shouted, gesturing that Anthony should return to his bunk. The man tied a rope around his middle and ran for the other end of the deck. Anthony admired his courage, as he no doubt kept their ship intact through this unforeseen weather. The ship dipped backward, sending a wave of rolling water across the stern of the ship.

A burst of lightning lit the night sky. The jolly boat swung on its ends violently in the wind. Everything else seemed motionless, tied, secured. Just the ship itself dipped and swelled with the waves. Anthony's stomach a bit better but certainly not calm, he yanked at the door to secure it again against the elements and return to his bunk. But a great cracking of wood drew his attention back to the night sky. The jolly boat had broken free of its rigging and lay, unsecured, on the deck. One more swell and the thing would start sliding. Sure enough, the ship tilted sideways, and the small boat went with it. A scream carried on the wind—a woman. Surely he imagined it. But as he watched the small conveyance, a white hand, thin, feminine, broke through the fabric in the top corner. He ran toward the boat, determined to rescue the woman. And then the whole thing slid the opposite direction, barreling toward him, missing the mast by a hair. He leapt for the boat, grabbing at the side, but the power of its momentum won against his own strength. He fell backward to the deck and watched as the boat broke through the railing and dropped off the side of the ship.

Anthony's heart pounded. "No!" He ran toward the opening at the rail and almost barreled over the deckhand he had seen moments ago.

"Your boat went over!" Anthony's shout was almost lost in the wind.

Irritated, the deckhand shouted back. "I see that. Get back to your bunk."

"But someone was inside! A woman!"

The man's eyes widened. He looked out to the broken rail and back at Anthony. Then he shrugged. "At least she is in the boat."

"Someone must go after her, save her, something! She will be lost."

"There is nothing we can do right now." The man gestured all around him, and lightning cracked above them. They ducked when the thunder followed immediately after. "If she lives, we will search for her in the calm."

Anthony ripped off his jacket, his waistcoat, pulled off his boots, and tossed them back down the hallway. "Give me your rope."

The man's eyes widened again. "You are not serious. You cannot do this. You will drown."

Anthony pulled at the knot around the man's waist to loosen it himself.

The deckhand shook his head, knocking Anthony's hands aside. "Don't be an imbecile."

The more he delayed the farther the jolly boat drifted and the less chance Anthony had to live. He gripped the man's shoulders, shaking them. "I must go after her."

With another swell of the sea, the man stumbled back, held up his hands, and said, "Take the rope. Take it. And may you not drown with those as your last words."

Anthony ripped the rope from him and tied it securely around his middle. Then he ran for the broken railing. Almost there, the boat tipped again and he stumbled backward, slipping in the ankle-deep water that flowed across the wood. He reached for the mast and held on until the ship righted itself. Then he skidded to the rail and looked out across the water for the boat. Surprised, he saw it crest a wave directly to their front.

A voice in his ear startled him. "Your rope is not long enough. I brought extra."

He smiled and fumbled with the rope at his waist. The man retied the line. "Now, don't lose hold of this. You lose this, you lose the ship."

Anthony nodded. "Thank you." He gripped the man's shoulder.

He turned and ran for the opening in the deck railing. Pushing off the edge with his feet, he dove out into the rolling and dark waters. The icy water engulfed him, but he kicked to the surface. Gulping in air, he spun around, searching for the ship. The deckhand waved to him. Anthony put the ship at his back and swam to where he had last seen the jolly boat. If he could tie it to the ship, he and the woman could wait out the storm together, he hoped.

But swimming through the rise and pull of the great waves of the ocean was nothing like he'd expected. Every effort forward was countered by a great pull backward. The boat crested a wave to his front. It was farther than he'd thought, but he kicked toward it, rising and falling with each roll of the sea. He tried to ignore the icy feeling spreading through his limbs as they slowed their movement. Saltwater on his lips, blinking the same from his eyes, he kicked and pulled himself through the water, with the sporadic views of the lifeboat as motivation. Sometimes it would dip low, behind a wave, and other times rise above him as if preparing to crash on his head. Reaching the end of his rope, he had but five feet to his front. Five small feet from his tired body to the jolly boat. Maybe he could shout. "Hello! Hello! Can you hear me?"

No answer. "Hello! Miss! Are you still there?"

Movement in the fabric on top filled him with hope. A head popped up through the hole—dark curls whipping wildly in the air, a tiny nose, and wide, fiery eyes looking about the water.

"Here! I am here!"

She spotted him and waved. "Oh, help me!"

"Do you have any rope?"

"Oh! Oh my! Just a minute."

She disappeared inside the boat and brought out something in her hands. "I have this!"

"Tie it to something."

"What?"

"Tie it to something, and throw it to me."

"Throw it? Yes! Here it is!" She reached behind her and threw the whole coil out toward him, but the wind caught it and blew it the other direction. She yelped and reached for it, grabbing a piece before it all blew away. She turned to him. "I'll tie it first!"

He nodded vigorously. His limbs were stiff and his legs tired from the effort to keep himself as close to her as possible. "Hurry!" What was this woman doing inside the lifeboat to begin with? A splinter of irritation lodged itself inside him, and he gritted his teeth.

With the rope tied about her waist, she threw the other end to him. It sailed out over the water, hovering in the wind for a bit, and then fell in a coil in front of him. Thankfully, a good amount of rigging had come over the edge with the boat. Anthony stretched forward. Inches. He needed just a few inches. He looked over his shoulder. The deckhand had stepped away from the edge. Looking back at the woman's rope, it was now a foot away and floating. He untied the rope about his waist, lunged for the piece connected to the lifeboat, and then swam back to his own, still floating just below the surface. Hands stretched out, each holding a rope, he pulled at the jolly boat, grunting in his effort until the ropes united. Then he tied a good strong knot, connecting the ship to the small boat.

Pulling himself along the rope, he reached the boat at last.

The woman disappeared inside again.

Weak, worn, he lifted one arm and clung to the wood on the top. For a moment, he allowed himself to hang there.

The woman leaned over the edge, tipping the boat dangerously close to the water. "What are you doing? Pull yourself up."

He again gritted his teeth. "Back away."

She squealed and disappeared again under the fabric.

He took another minute to garner some strength and then gripped the side of the boat with both hands and pulled his weight up, his shoulders quivering with the strain, and onto the top of the boat.

Their small boat rode the swells of two waves before he moved from his spot draped across the top. He jerked at the opening, making it wider then pulled his legs up, out of the water, stuffing his feet through the hole and inside the boat.

A pair of wide eyes watched him from the other side of the boat. He reached toward the woman. "Give me the rope."

"What?"

"The rope." He indicated the line tied about her waist.

"Oh!" she fumbled with it. "I am better at tying than untying, I'm afraid."

He crouched over to her along the middle of the wobbly vessel. He worked at loosening the remarkably tight knot around her middle. Returning to the opening in the fabric, he stood up in the storm again, leaning out over the front, feeling a wave of stomach unease as the craft dipped low. He reached for the ring below him and tied the rope to it. Then he pulled his head back inside the shelter of the boat.

The woman sat as far from him as possible in the darkness on the opposite side of the boat, a small blanket curled around her. Her eyes wide, she asked, "Are you all right, sir?"

He grunted, turned himself around, and sat. Then he leaned back against the wooden side and breathed out. "I am now, I believe."

The wind shook the canvas above them, and a great splash of water poured down on Anthony's head through the opening.

"Oh look! You've let more water in. Please close that hole straight-away." She looked down at her feet and began to mumble, "I would think you'd have done that already. What kind of person leaves the thing open in the middle of a rainstorm? I don't even know . . ."

"Pardon me? Are you mumbling about me over there under your breath? I can hear you, you know." Becoming frustrated, he reached up and pulled the canvas material as tight as he could back across the opening and tried to secure it with the ropes available, but many were tied from the outside.

"I tied it earlier. Allow me." She crawled over to him and stretched across his body, nearly pressing against him while she pulled and yanked at the ropes. A hint of lemon and something else, maybe rose, filled the small space around them. "There." She pushed away and sat back down in her spot at the other end.

He looked up in the darkness, trying to see the result of her handiwork. Too dim to make it out entirely, he did notice it seemed secure. "Well done. It must be a handy knot you did there. Some sort of maritime expert, are you?"

"No, horses." She shuffled, seeming to adjust her position on the blanket. "Maritime expert. When would I ever learn to be a maritime expert?" She continued to mumble, and he found himself equal parts amused and exasperated.

He could no longer see her features, but her smell lingered about him. Grateful he was for it; it was the only pleasant thing about his situation. Dripping wet, his stomach would not settle. The boat rolled to the side, throwing them both against the wall of the boat. He shifted quickly back to the middle and stretched himself across the width, hoping to stabilize the wobbling somewhat. And then, without warning, his stomach lurched violently and he lunged for the opening. Only just reaching the night air in time, he vomited all the contents of his stomach into the night wind.

Dropping again along the bottom of the boat, he grunted, "I apologize." A shiver coursed through him. "Since we cannot see one another, you wouldn't mind too much, I suppose, were I to strip myself of this wet shirt?"

Her voice, purposefully nonchalant, answered, "No, of course not. We have many hours yet until light, I'd imagine."

A great pause followed in the darkness while he undid his buttons and tried to hang the shirt above him, tucked into some of the rope. This woman was a different sort of person, he assumed. Still hadn't voiced a word of thanks. He scooted down a bit, along the side of the boat, tipping it lower, thought better of it, and crouched more in the center, right in the puddle of water gathering at the lowest point.

He shook his head. He had wanted adventure, anything different from the everyday life of doldrum and boredom and agony that was his. But this . . . "Ha!" he laughed. This was adventure of a different sort. His brother would seethe in envy and his father ne'er believe it.

"What?"

"I was just thinking of home. They would be surprised to find me in such a situation."

She snorted then covered her mouth, giggling. "Oh, I'm terribly sorry." Then she snorted again. "How unladylike of me. I just . . . well . . . my family would be surprised as well." She mumbled, "To say the least. Horrified, more like. Ruined . . . now that I'm here with you." She gasped and mumbled more, incoherently.

He chuckled. "Do you often mumble?"

"Oh! I'm terribly sorry. Again. I just said that, didn't I? Well, at any rate, I do mumble. Not so much in recent years—thought I was cured of my habit. My governess—oh, that is to say, my friend's governess—would be dreadfully appalled to hear me now. Horrified about all of this, I suppose, really. But at any rate, no, I do not often mumble. Anymore."

He chuckled again, low in his belly, and felt a bit braver than he would in any other situation. "You're terrible at it, you know."

A tiny gasp from the corner where she sat made him smile.

"How so? How does one become terrible at mumbling?" Under her breath she continued. "Mumbling isn't some sort of art . . ."

"Ho ho! See? Isn't the point to remain unheard? I hear you plain as day every time."

Silence followed. "Well, I see what you mean. But I feel it very ungallant of you to correct me. What if I took great pride in my mumbling?"

His laughter bubbled up. "Pride? In your mumbling? Well, if that be the case, then my advice is much more needed. No sense taking pride in something you do so abysmally."

She laughed, and it was a musical sound.

"You sing."

She drew in her breath.

"I can tell by your laugh that you sing."

"I do enjoy it, yes." She cleared her throat. "While we are correcting one another so honestly, I hope you don't mind that I make a few suggestions on your rescuing effort?"

He couldn't respond. What to say to that? Did she not know she would, at this moment, be floating adrift were it not for him?

"May I take your silence as agreement?"

His exhaustion was setting in, and he had not stopped shivering yet, sitting as he was in a puddle of water in the middle of the boat. He shifted his weight. "By all means."

"Very sensible of you. To begin with, I am astonished you had not thought to bring a longer rope. Why swim all the way out here in this awful storm with a rope that is too short? And furthermore, had you not thought about how to get me back to the ship? Arriving here is lovely, please understand, but now what? How shall we return?"

He gritted his teeth. Of all the ungrateful . . . He pulled in a long, slow breath. "We are tied to the ship. When the water calms, we shall simply pull ourselves closer, and they will throw down a ladder, I'd imagine."

"The sea might not calm for hours yet. Had you thought of that?"

"No, I was most concerned with first attaching your conveyance so you did not drift out to the open sea and be lost forever."

"Forever? My, that sounds rather dire, does it not? Surely I could be found."

"Does anyone know you were inside this boat?"

Silence replied.

"Would anyone have known to seek you out, discover you were missing?"

Surely she had family aboard, likely a chaperone at least. She sounded as well-bred as the best of them, as impractical and spoiled as any lady he'd danced with.

"No, no one." The quiet response stunned him.

"Have you no one here to see you safely across?"

"No."

Silence filled their small boat, as thick and heavy as silence could be. The sea had calmed as well, the vessel still rolling with each wave but not nearly as forcefully.

Her voice full of forced cheerfulness, she said, "Let's check on the ship, shall we? Make sure we are good and truly attached?" She climbed toward him again, crouching low, stepped over his legs to what was the opening just minutes before. She untied his hastily secured knot and pulled the canvas back. Moonlight poured in. Their boat dipped in another swell, rolling Anthony over to his side. Her head disappeared out the hole. "The ship! It's on fire!"

Anthony leaped forward. "Please, allow me?"

She dipped back inside, allowing him a view. The top mast was indeed in flames. It must have been struck by lightning. But many a deckhand were hard at work with buckets and great sheets of fabric, working to douse the fire.

The sky had cleared in spots, and the moon shone directly above them, through a patch of clouds.

A dinging bell rang out across the water. "All hands on deck!"

The woman pulled at the canvas, creating a larger space, and stood beside him, eyes trained on the ship.

Her arm brushed against his chest and she jumped, turning to him, eyes wide. "I apologize." Her cheeks turned a deep shade of red, and she refused to meet his eyes. He pulled back as far as he could away from her, and she did the same. They both turned again to watch the activity on deck. But he couldn't ignore his awareness of her, and for some reason it added to his irritation.

He forced his attention back to the ship, fear setting in. Flames rose high up the mast, and the efforts of the men on deck seemed small and futile in comparison to the power of fire to consume.

The woman raised a hand up to her mouth. "Oh no."

He nodded. The jolly boat rose and fell with each swell in the water, and the woman lost her balance, falling against him. "Easy." He rested his hands on her arms to steady her.

"Thank you." Her voice, small, warmed him.

"You're welcome." He squeezed her arms, trying to comfort her, but she stiffened.

"You can unhand me now. I am quite able to stand on my own."

Irritation burned inside him anew.

Another great swell toppled him up against her in his surprise and pressed her up against the material at her back. "Really! Get off me at once. I see no need for this brutish behavior."

Brutish?

"Perhaps if you went back inside." He again gritted his teeth. "I see no need for us both to watch."

She sniffed. "Well, no one needs to watch at all, do they? What good can we possibly do? It's just a matter of curiosity at this point, and I am dreadfully curious as to our fate, and I assume you are as well."

She made no move to duck away, so he turned again to watch the ship. No changes, no improvement. But clouds again began to roll in, and just as he was about to suggest they both return under the canvas, the sky opened again and rain dumped down on them.

She yelped and dipped back underneath. He followed, yanking on the covering to pull it securely over the top once again.

The noise of water hitting the canvas blocked out all other sound, and a thick wetness in the air hung over them. He was relieved, to say the least. Surely the deluge would douse the fire.

The woman pulled her blanket up around her. Anthony gave up feeling dry anytime soon and leaned back against one side of the boat, his feet elevated against the other side, sitting squarely once again in the middle of the water pooled at the center of their boat.

He felt wide eyes on him, but he ignored them. Closing his own, he drowned out the noise and thought of home, or he tried to. But the shifting sounds and the breathing of the woman in the dark corner distracted him.

She was attractive, curiously so, and so gentle in her speech, but she dressed like a servant. He had never seen her before, at least he didn't think so. There was something familiar about her, but didn't all young girls start to look the same? He chided himself. At any rate, she was likely an educated servant. One with fiery, challenging brown eyes and flowing dark hair, who smelled of lemons. A small smile caught the corner of his mouth, and he shifted his shoulder. With any luck, the storm would pass quickly.